NIGHTMARES

AND

OTHER VICES

The SF-Horror Collection

Print Edition

NIGHTMARES AND OTHER VICES

The SF-Horror Collection

Print Edition

by

Bruce S. Larson

NIGHTMARES AND OTHER VICES
The SF-Horror Collection
by
Bruce S. Larson

Published by

TM

World Line One Press

For all whose greatest vice is reading, and who wink at shadows that grin in the night.

TABLE OF CONTENTS

ACKNOWLEDGEMENTS

Special acknowledgement must go to Erik England for his vision and indispensable assistance on all the _Nightmares_ covers. Through Erik's weaving, the spiders crept from strands of thought to stands of trees and city streets, and your nightmares.

Eternal gratitude is due to Bonnie Hammond for her swift and superb work on this cover design and others. These _Nightmares_ needed a solid back and sound spine. Bonnie built those with strength and artistry.

A salute must go to fellow writer Cristopher DeRose. His first reads and reactions to the works in this book helped shape and improve their content. This has been true for many projects over the years. For that, the Author is truly grateful. May Cris always cast Shadows in prose.

Thanks are due to author Michael McCarty for his virtual cheerleading. Many people are glad for the numerous written horrors he's created. A book walks into a bar....

A nod and _cheers!_ goes to all Second Thursday friends and compatriots. Keep the wax hot.

Lyrics are words set to music. They in turn inspire prose. The story "Darker Than Shadows or the Night" arose from listening to the song "Why Good Men Go Bad" performed by the band and Indie Rock legends The Green Pajamas. The song appears on their album "Green Pajama Country." Listening to all this band's music in darkness or daylight is time well spent.

Thank you one and all.

PREFACE

Yes. The Preface. You're tempted to skip this part, aren't you? I understand. The thrills are just pages away. However, what if there is something important written, here? What if I reveal a spell that will spare you from falling into the nightmares ahead? If you enjoy running from mysterious beasts and worse forms of darkness, then never mind. Turn the page. Still, best wear running shoes as you read. For all of you still with me, I'll be brief. I have to face something that's making odd noises outside. It's likely another idea I didn't capture for this collection. I'll have to ensnare it in other pages. They are dangerous when loose. The dark things here live on the page until released in your mind. This book collects the two *Nightmares and Other Vices* e-books into one, printed copy. All the terrors are here. Nothing escaped.

One character who repeatedly faces dark terrors is Joshua Grail, a.k.a 'Mr. Ice.' His adventures appeared in the since departed magazines *Dark Matter* ("Harlots"), and *Millennium SF&F* ("Public Service"). I'm still grateful to their editors for publishing the stories. (I won't mention the pieces of drinking silver, but they were nice, too.)

These few sentences are worth reprinting from the first *Nightmares* Preface: "This writer is fortunate to know so many fellow artists and friends whose support has never waned through set-ups, setbacks, and settings suns. A sincere note of thanks to all of you, and members of my family. In one way or another, you all cheered this collection into existence. I've included the very short piece "The Little Girl and the Shadow(s)". The story also appears on my website. I placed it here as bonus track for fans from the past. Join me as I raise a vice within a glass to the future."

So, *Cheers!* You need not thank me for causing you to bolt awake from sleep. The act will be gratitude enough. It's what nightmares are for. These here are ready to serve that purpose. Oh, about that spell. You will be released on the final word on the final page, at least until the next collection is published. Good luck and good reading.

Bruce S. Larson
Somewhere wrestling another nightmare
2014

EXPOSURE

Gushie was modern perfection. At least in her own mind. She needed a shower. For that, she needed a place with running water, clean running water. She practiced naked handstands in her dank room. The mat she put on the floor to protect her skin seemed to be breaking down. Lutch opened the door and entered without knocking. Gushie stood and glared at the man. It bothered her that he was so thin he almost folded inward.

"Keeping limber." Lutch said. "Good."

"Internet crash and you need a thrill?" Gushie snarled and sat on her tattered couch.

"Just keeping tabs." Lutch smiled. He held the door as if threatening to open it wider. "The fridge is empty. Today we do it again. When it comes time—"

"I always do." Gushie stopped him. "I'm the star for a reason. Don't annoy me."

"Okay, sunshine. But I run this place, so—"

"You want to power play me?" Gushie stood defiantly. "Don't."

"Or, what?" Lutch pushed the door open and thrust his hands to his hips.

"I'm a nice piece." Gushie stroked herself. "I look good naked. Who do you think our gang of hornos will whack if it came down between you or me? Take your clothes off and dance. They might just kill you right then."

"Well, I suppose that's a good point." Lutch bobbled his narrow head slowly.

"The best." Gushie said. She took the door and pushed it to force Lutch into the hall. Gushie blew a kiss, but then snatched it from mid-air. She brought her clenched hand to her mouth and acted to rip apart the captured kiss with her teeth.

"Remember, Lutch, dinner doesn't always have to be our customers."

Dread. It was Roth's favorite emotion. At least it was the one he experienced the most. The sensation was growing more prevalent across the city. He wasn't sure if that made it easier or harder to be a cop. In his career, he managed to rise through the

1

dread and dreck of city life, bureaucracy, and department politics and become a detective. He wasn't sure if that made life easier or harder for the city.

He approached his precinct's entrance for all municipal employees. It was a reinforced cylindrical hatch that looked more appropriate on some spacecraft design the government approved and then canceled. The hatch looked as though that spacecraft had crashed into the aging concrete wall. It slid open before he wanted his workday to begin. He entered anyway. With dread.

A display flashed across the curved metal wall. Roth considered it odd that technology grew like mold inside buildings and throughout daily life while their exteriors and living occupants fell apart. Roth sneered. He did that often enough that it had become part of his facial biometric.

"Scanning commenced." The automated voice announced. "Ambient emanations chemical analysis. Individual number: eight-five-nine-dash—"

Roth hit the onscreen 'mute' bar. He smiled remembering how originally the voice carried perfect inflection, but now sounded muffled with an off-key buzzing. This effect came after a fist hit the speaker. Roth paid the fine and the company installed a mute feature. They figured there was no point in fixing the speaker. The typical results flashed across the screen: 'Ambient analysis inconsistent with individual's internal biochemical composition. Pass.' The machine confirmed Roth didn't snort, shoot, or smoke any of the drugs and chemicals his clothes absorbed just walking through the city or doing his job. The computer's metrics verified his honesty. The inner door opened.

The pro-tech lens over his left eye became active as the dense, loud sounds of the precinct hit his ears. Roth retrieved his service pistol from a unit that looked nearly identical to a sandwich vending machine. It smelled about the same. Roth wondered about how far companies went in repurposing older tech. He holstered his weapon. He could choose the caliber. He couldn't choose the tech fused into it. Another lens peered from the .45's front sight. When drawn, the gun saw everything in front of its muzzle. Both eye and gun units beamed all images to department computers. Roth walked to his desk. His street informant dubbed Seep filled the chair beside it. Seep was a small, probably male ball of sweat. He looked up at Roth with a plaintive gaze. Roth sneered.

Lutch smiled. He wasn't just glad to see a paying customer, he was glad to see food. They were one in the same.

"So nice for you to dispose of your income in our fine theater, Mr. Holmes." Lutch said from behind the front counter.

Seep froze. He stared at Lutch. Lutch smiled even wider. The width of his lips almost wrapped around his narrow head.

"How, how do you know me?" Seep asked. Few people alive had even noticed him. Fewer ever knew his actual name.

"You think you're a blank? No records?" Lutch asked. "Close. Even the best blanks pop in front of a camera at some point. Then the company that owns the camera has another machine do face recognition. If it links your image to all your personal data, then that data and your face get sold and sold again. It can end up in the most obscure little shops. Like naughty ones that sell time to peep at girls."

Seep stood stunned. His lower lip flexed and threatened to detach and roll down his chin.

"But no worries!" Lutch slid from behind the booth and coiled an arm around Seep's shoulders. "We just watch who enters. There are no eyes in our booths other than your own. What you do is up to you. Judgment free, but for a fee. So pay up, buddy."

Seep lifted up a small wad of bills. Lutch snatched away the entire wad in a single, swift blur.

"You remember cookies on your PC?" Lutch asked. "Well, now your face is your cookie. It links to a file that tells and sells your life. Even one as sparse on data as yours, Mr. Holmes. And your data is very, very thin. Like me."

Lutch smiled at Seep as if he was a hungry man seeing his favorite sandwich. Seep slowly smiled back as Lutch pulled him down a dank, narrow hall with several mildewed, narrow doors.

"Thank you for supporting us in this hard, hard economy. Now you get that way, yourself." Lutch opened a door and shoved Seep into the booth. "The performer is Gushie. She's new, but hot. Hot, hot, hot. You'll eat her up. Enjoy!" Lutch slammed the door shut.

No one ever shoved Seep into a viewing booth, before. Usually people who ran adult entertainment venues didn't want to touch anyone that paid them. They pointed with gloved fingers and barked directions behind clear, but scratched plastic. Still, live revues were a rarity. Seep tried to support them as much as he could. He didn't mind the condescending or harsh tones from the people who worked at them. He cared about these places more than the workers did. Live performance was a dying art. Each naked girl was alive and unique. Seep read life stories in the lines of their faces, or lines on their arms or other places.

Seep was able to tell some stories he learned in places like this, and other locations that most people never saw. Roth paid him cash for some stories. Roth also let him come inside the precinct, steal coffee, and even use the restroom. This place and the man who took his cash were strange. Seep thought it might give him another story to tell Roth. His show began.

A wall of thick plastic faced Seep. It was tinted black. The black faded to clear. Seep could see into the small performance area surrounded by sections of the same, adjustable-tint plastic. The quiet assured Seep he was the sole patron. Gushie stood in the center. She wore a pink robe. It wasn't even a silky, sexy robe. It was an old and worn bathrobe. And she wore combat boots. Still, her shape under the robe was somewhat alluring. Seep sat in his booth's filthy chair. He expected to be aroused. Instead, he became unsettled. He doubted the view was one-way, only. Gushie didn't move. She just stood and stared, and she was staring straight at him.

"What, honey? C'mon!" Lutch's voice echoed through an old speaker. "You're not even going to dance for the man?"

"I don't dance for a steak." Gushie said while still staring at Seep who could hear her voice muffled through the plastic. "If I take a pass, I'll dance to keep our cover. If I think he looks good enough--yeah. He's good enough. Take him."

Seep's heart rate rose several times in booths like this one. Now it spiked for far different reasons. He stood as Gushie stepped closer. The door opened behind Seep. Gushie parted her robe and flashed him. It was a distraction. It worked. Two sets of powerful arms grabbed Seep from behind and slammed him back into the chair. He felt a sting in his neck. The glass seemed to darken. But it was the world going black, all except for Gushie's staring eyes. They didn't look at him to please. They looked at him with hunger.

"Hey, there!" Lutch repeatedly tapped Seep's face. "Wakies!"

4

Seep groaned. He laid stretched out on a gurney. It had no pad on its bed, but the cold metal somehow managed to stink.

"You're finally going to be a true blank." Lutch smiled down at Seep. "We're about to delete you. All of you. Even that little, sweaty face."

"Why don't we just do him?" Gushie sighed. "I'm getting crabby."

"Getting?" Lutch said drolly. "Look, I've got good, paying customers out there. And, darling, you're name is Gushie. Now make us all scream. Do the black widow."

"Fine." Gushie droned.

Gushie flipped off her robe. Seep twisted his neck to the side and saw in full what he paid for in the booth. Gushie slid off her boots.

"Roll him." Gushie pointed to the dark curtains.

The two thugs that grabbed Seep in the booth shoved the gurney forward. A sudden, bright light hit Seep's eyes as his strapped-down feet parted the curtains. Seep heard a small crowd murmur. He strained and lifted his head. Beyond the glare of aging spotlights, he could see people sitting in the raised seats of a small amphitheater. Seep squinted. They all looked naked. The murmur returned as the curtains parted again. Seep caught a glimpse of the naked Gushie doing cartwheels around the gurney. She vanished behind him. He jerked with fright as she spun the gurney and vaulted on top of him. Gushie straddled Seep. She looked at him and smiled. This time her face nearly held an expression of genuine kindness. It vanished in a predator's grin. Gushie thrust her head downward and bit into his neck.

Seep screamed from terror and pain. Gushie teeth were dull but her jaws were strong. Gushie popped up from her grisly work with a face of wet, dark reds and purple. She wiped her cheeks and drew an hourglass on her abdomen with his blood. Seep could feel the pain increasing as his consciousness was ebbing. Still, he fought against his bonds. Gushie thrust her mouth back to Seep's neck. Seep tried to scream but Gushie's teeth had crushed his larynx. The world went black one final time.

Roth glared. A cascade of names and numbers poured down his monitor as if the data was water. An algorithm cross referenced and categorized potential victims within his precinct. Too many,

Roth thought. One falling name caught his eye. He stabbed his index finger into the stream. It stopped. The name beneath his fingertip expanded. The individual's police file opened onscreen. Roth moved his hand as Seep's picture appeared and information scrolled. 'Peter Holmes. AKA Wet Rat. AKA Seep.'

"Okay," Roth sighed. "Crap."

"Catch one?" Detective Velkyrk asked from his adjacent desk.

"Some dumped clothes contained DNA of a CI. Since when do we get possible crime data from garbage trucks?" Roth asked.

"The trash company has its data-scan contracts with NalCo. NalCo is—"

"Our department's information system contractor." Roth finished.

"Hey, nice use of jargon. Welcome to the modern world, Detective Roth."

"Okay, leet boy." Roth turned to Velkyrk. "Tell me where Seep was last flashed."

"I might need a permission protocol if it's—"

"Just tell me." Roth cut in.

Velkyrk tapped. A second ticked. He read from his screen.

"Some off the grid nudie joint. A live nudie joint." Velkyrk paused in surprise.

"Compare prices, later." Roth said.

"Yeah, right." Velkyrk frowned. "That's what other informants have tagged it. It has no name. Just an address in the foreclosed commercial properties listing. Now on your mobile."

"Velkyrk," Roth paused. "There are times when I want to pat you on the back. Other times, throw dirt on your corpse. Today--"

Roth stood. He withdrew his weapon from his desk drawer. Velkyrk raised his eyebrows. Roth slid his gun into his shoulder holster. He reached over and patted Velkyrk on the back.

"If he was a CI, his disposition is considered an exigent situ." Velkyrk said. "You won't need a warrant."

"What do we need a warrant for, today?" Roth sneered.

"You need back-up?" Velkyrk asked.

Roth pointed to his pro-tech capped left eye and walked away.

Lutch bolted to the front counter. Security systems tipped him to an entrant. He cursed himself for not locking the doors. He soon realized he had. The punk he hired to watch them bolted across the street. The man that he let enter glared at the fleeing punk, then turned and flashed his badge in Lutch's face. A photo of Seep instantly replaced its image.

"Seen him?" Roth demanded.

"Um, well. We get a lot of—"

Lutch felt the hardness of the counter before the pain of fingers digging into his scalp as Roth slammed down Lutch's head.

"Stress levels indicate a lie. Bad move. Now tell me what happened, pencil neck." Roth demanded. "While I'm still in a good mood."

"Wuh-okay, okay!" Lutch uttered with half of his mouth pressed to the counter. "Luh-look, you obviously have a lot on us. You want more?"

"I want answers."

"Think big, big cop." Lutch said as Roth eased his grip. "I can serve up a whole lot of fish to fry. Big naked fish. You like fish?"

Lutch stumbled down the booth hallway. The muzzle of Roth's gun felt like a slow bullet pushing into his back.

"Where are we heading?" Roth asked.

"A very special venue. You'll love it. It's going to make you mayor. Congress. The President!"

"Shut up."

Lutch shut up.

"Just tell me what this place really is."

"We're a nudie revue. Honest! People come here to see things you can't see anywhere else. That's not a cliché. It's the truth. The very expensive truth."

"That why you killed Seep? He see your truth?"

"No. The beasts who force me to work here are cannibals. They eat people. They ate your boy. Say, why do you care? He was such a sweaty thing!"

"You freaks ate him?"

"Look, it's practical. The economy has gone south. Again. But the performers need to eat. The customers—the peepers—pay us. Just not enough. So why not eat the peepers?"

"Sick. How do you stay in business if you eat the clients?"

"We only pluck a few. Our biggest fans pay to see it. They're paying for such a show right now. Want to—"

Lutch's face hit the wall.

"Where?" Roth shouted.

"I'll show you. I promised!"

Roth held Lutch's left shoulder as Lutch stumbled forward through a changing room filled with folded piles of clothes, wallets, purses and a few briefcases.

"What is all this?" Roth halted their course. "Stolen property?"

"No. It belongs to the big fish I promised." Lutch said. "It's how we keep our shows from going viral. The only way to keep it secret, hack free, and a cash cow is—is, well, keep it really real. Live! So all the peepers strip and get scanned for tech. No wireless up your wire or elsewhere."

"Sick." Roth snarled.

"Life is what you—"

Roth's gun muzzle struck Lutch's right eye.

"Okay, okay!" Lutch yelled and threw up his hands. "They're in there!"

Roth pushed Lutch through the curtains. The fact his gun reported every time Roth fired it held back his desire to simply open fire right away.

Gushie was bound to the gurney propped at an angle to the audience. A large, hooded creep next to a cart with a tray full of scalpels and power tools pulled ropes tied to Gushie's limbs from behind her. Gushie had freed her right arm and torn off a section of railing. She swung it at the muscular thug in front of her. He stared at her and held up a saw ready to swing into Gushie's naked body. Gushie noticed Lutch and Roth.

"Lutch! You freak!" Gushie screamed. "You told them to chop me! Me!"

"Tell him you're the star, Sunshine!" Lutch said as Roth pushed him to his knees.

Gushie answered with a scream of hatred through bared teeth.

"Tweaker! Put it down!" Roth barked at the brawny man with the saw.

The man's eyes were pink and his face a slackened skin mask. Both were effects from a cocktail of personality erasing drugs. Still, reality seeped through his brain's erosions. Muscle memory took over. He dropped the saw and laid himself on the floor face-first with arms folded to the small of his back, ready for handcuffs.

"No one move! No one!" Roth ordered the crowd. "You're all in police custody!"

A murmur rippled through the audience as the small mass of people realized this was not part of the show. A few higher notes of fear rose over the low droning.

"Code seven. Seal this area." Roth said aloud to police observers at the first link in the data chain.

"You don't have back-up outside?" Lutch asked from the floor.

Roth stayed silent.

"No one worry! We're shielded." Lutch strained to lift his head. "Sorry, cop. Signal shield is our selling point. Mickey! Waste this pig!"

Roth slammed Lutch fully to the floor with his right leg as the hooded Mickey obeyed Lutch. Mickey tore a small, battered machine gun taped beneath the tray. The scalpels and power tools crashed to the floor as he spun it toward Roth. Roth fired a single, eardrum splitting shot. The bullet ripped through Mickey's chest. His body crashed onto the scattered tools.

Gushie shrieked. It wasn't a scream of horror but a battle cry. Roth was stunned that she had freed herself from her bonds with the broken rail and then grabbed the saw with incredible speed. That same speed brought the saw down at himself and Lutch. The gun blast blew Gushie's hair back as the bullet shattered what she always considered modern perfection. The bullet held no such aesthetic appreciation as it cut through her and exploded from her back. Her body fell and slapped against the floor. The saw clattered next to her. Roth looked for more assailants.

The audience bolted from the seats. Roth, his gun's camera, and his pro-tech lens witnessed the naked stampeded. Roth noted the wide variety of human forms. All pretense, status, and discrimination lay stripped off with their expensive suits or custom tailored dresses. The variations of shapes spanned age groups. Roth appreciated why nude modeling was a job typically reserved for the young and fit.

"They aren't listening to you. Why aren't you shooting them?" A stream of Gushie's blood rolled toward Lutch.

"I only shoot people trying to kill me." Roth answered. "And one way or another, all these people are going to be dead to someone. From politicians to beauticians, and all creeps in between. My gun and eye may watch me, but they also record everything I see. Everything."

"But your signal—"

"Is received and verified." Roth smiled, and actually enjoyed doing it. "Your shielding isn't working, scum bag."

"How can your signal get through? I've got crypt-nets. Lead sheets!"

"New day, new tech. Welcome to my world." Roth continued grinning while the audience jammed at the exits above the seats. "All these faces and naked butts and everything else have been broadcast to my precinct's tier-frame and copied to the central mainframe. This signal's data might be getting copied. Maybe cracked. All these fine people might be stars of their own unwanted nudie shows. Even if they don't get arrested, no one gets away with anything. They can't escape being exposed."

"Well, power to the police." Lutch said.

"Yeah. Power." Roth watched the last naked backsides squirm through the exits. "So long as the city pays the electric bill and the fees to the companies that own the computers."

"I can dig it." Lutch said while arching his head back from Gushie's blood. "I used to be a software designer for social media."

Roth looked down at Lutch and sneered.

"Can I get up now?" Lutch asked.

The distant howl of emergency sirens grew louder.

Roth adjusted his foot on Lutch's back. "No."

UNDERFOOT

The dirt was hard and icy. The cold reached straight to the bone even through thick calluses. Most people gathered around the communal bonfire to warm feet, bones, and hearts. There was a sense of peace in the moment and of strength from the tribe. The gathering carried a sense of human persistence in a hostile world. However, there was unspoken fear that reached deeper than the cold. Unlike the towering trees they lived among, the tribe was always ready to uproot and run in seconds. This was typical life in America, 2027 AD.

Humans survive, but their enemy has greater numbers and rarely rests. The enemy; the smucks. Mostly they're called gumbies. The name 'smuck' came from the annoying sound made from gnawing the stuff that destroyed civilization. 'Gumbie' came from the rubbery gunk itself: chewing gum. The world killer evolved in the discarded globs stuck to the sidewalks of every city on every street on the world. Some dubbed it the Soul Stealer Bacterium. A more direct name was the *Sole* Sticking Germ. It was the unseen horror on the bottom of your shoe. The pathology was simple. Stick to the sole, contact human skin, get in the system and take over the mind. It jumped several steps of punctuated evolution right underfoot. Its survival strategy was perfect. Control the species that controls the world. Now, something a thousand times smaller than a sidewalk stain dominated the planet. Its gumbie hordes always moved. Chewing. Smucking. Spitting. Chewing again. A generation had been born on the run from gumbies. There seemed no end to their supply of gum, or the horror brought by its constant, slow gnaw.

A murmur rose around the bonfire. People turned to the stump called the "soap box" even though now a single bar was a rare and precious commodity. A white-haired man looking like a sage from the past stepped on the stump. People exchanged nods and knowing comments in anticipation of the speech that was to come. It was well known, but tolerated. Besides, no one else wanted to speak and voice was the only form of broadcast entertainment available.

"People!" the white-haired man called Charles began. "My great, barefoot masses! It's time to unite! It's not too late to save our once-great, technical civilization! We can have the internet back. Space travel. We can once again live in cities! We can go back to wearing shoes!"

The crowd murmur grew louder.

"All we need, is this!" Charles reached into a pouch and thrust up a tool as if wielding a weapon of tremendous power. The murmur grew into laughter as Charles brandished a scrub brush.

"He's insane." Toshiro said with little pity.

Kaplan looked at her with surprise. "I'd expect a tone of sympathy from our tribal doctor."

"Well, trust me, he is." Toshiro shrugged.

"He's just old." Kaplan offered.

He glanced back at Charles and then back at Toshiro. She looked him over as if he lay out for an exam. Kaplan looked down across his passed middle-aged body. He sighed.

"Yeah. Okay. So am I. But I also remember life before the end of our cities. Before the fear of just stepping on pavement. And shoes."

"You saw it happen." Toshiro mused.

"I did." Kaplan nodded in reflection. "I tried to fight it."

"But there were too many." Toshiro offered.

"Oh, we might have beaten the parasites before the gumbies became so vast." Kaplan glanced over at several large, wooden vats on carts. "Now, we wait."

"For what?" Toshiro asked with interest.

"It's only a matter of time before their hosts die off completely. The smucks. Gumbies."

"Yeah? Really?"

"Yep. If we survive long enough."

"Will we?" Toshiro asked.

"Hell, I'm still here." Kaplan shrugged. "I didn't know a tree from a utility pole when this crap started. Now?"

Kaplan looked up at the expanse of interlocking evergreen limbs above them. The tree limbs were colored red by the fire light and blocked out the stars. He darted his eyes back to Toshiro who stared at the fire. She was half his age. Young. Attractive. That was no small feat now that make-up was a thing of the past, just as Wi-Fi and mobile phones. Still, there was little chance for romantic success, Kaplan thought. They were both scientists. Yet, Kaplan doubted his memorization of Benfey's and the ADOMAH

12

versions of the periodic table would wow her. She had no doubt memorized at least one alternate table, herself.

Kaplan was born before handheld machines could recall whatever data you needed and wherever you stood. Toshiro was born in the time when all those devices were omnipresent and then suddenly useless. Good memory techniques were important again. Kaplan was glad he could teach them to future Toshiros. However, on most days he wished he had studied podiatry instead of biophysics, just to take care of his own feet in a world without shoes and endless pine needles, rocks, and cones.

"You know, there's no damn reason we can't wear shoes." Kaplan grated. "It's purely a cultural thing. An irrational fear. Some nights I give a million bucks for a pair of socks."

"You work on that. I'll worry about the disease becoming airborne." Toshiro said. "It evolved so fast, before. I wonder if we would recognize such an infection in time."

"Well," Kaplan looked off as his mind scrolled back through history. "The first case was misdiagnosed as a psychotic breakdown. But, soon there were others. Soon the staff treating the first patient became zombie chewing machines. Just chew, spit, chew, spit. All the while seeding the environment with more brain-enslaving bacteria. Lovely."

"No drugs could kill the bacteria? None at all?" Toshiro asked.

"Nothing. It was a super bug. Both a microbe and a complex colonial organism. Mutated from other types of cephalic bacteria." Kaplan shook his head from long-lingered amazement.

"There was no way to stop it once it evolved." Toshiro said.

"Oh, maybe through quarantines and behavioral changes." Kaplan sighed. "But the gum lobby kept filing suits and hired the best ex-congress people and other ace lobbyists. It was a political quagmire. Of gum. Big and sticky. The people demanded action. The gum companies gave them new flavors. The problem grew. And our world got chewed—"

"Yeah, I got it." Toshiro shook her head. "Do you think its rate of mutation has changed?"

"I'm sure it has." Kaplan crossed his arms for warmth. "But so will people. I hope. For the better. In biology and otherwise."

"According to Charles over there, all we need is an ocean of bleach and a billion or so scrub brushes." Toshiro said.

"And gloves." Kaplan added. "But even today there's a black market premium for gum."

Toshiro gave a guilty nod.

"Just be sure to swallow it." Kaplan smiled at her.

The gentle murmur of conversations suddenly ebbed as several people heard shouting from out in the night. The words were indistinct but the urgency was clear. A watch runner from the East entered the far edge of the camp. Most people understood the warning and ran to their jobs before the runner's words were clearly heard.

"They're coming!" The runner drew a breath and nearly collapsed. He exhaled a scream. "Gumbies! They're coming here!"

Kaplan saw Toshiro bolt to her triage tent. He flexed his feet against the cold ground.

The tribe kept moving through the night. Their escape was so successful that they had to take a small group to double back for the nearly mindless horde to catch their trail again. The risk was necessary to enact their plan. Contrary to culture and the successful strategy of flight, the tribe's warriors would take a fixed position and attempt to stop the horde. The action would be similar to a castle stand of millennia ago, but with a huge backdoor to bolt through if it failed. Kaplan wished they had an actual castle. He also wished he could finally quit running.

"How did they find us?" the young Bayner asked.

It was easy for Bayner to run and speak. However, Kaplan wished he'd quit cigarettes while they were still being made.

"Well," Kaplan panted. "Just walk in one direction long enough—"

"This time we want them to follow us!" Marris said as he came up next to both men. "This time we fight and kill them!"

"This wave, anyhow." Kaplan panted on.

Kaplan glanced at Marris, the tribe's de facto military leader. A belly lurched from side to side as he ran. Kaplan wondered how a man whose discipline did not extend to his diet got the job of leading them into zombie combat. Still, he could jog faster than Kaplan could sprint.

Their destination was in sight. A bulwark ascended a hillside formed by a river delta. The dry river channel made a narrow canyon that would funnel the zombie horde in pursuit. The counter assault would come from the high ground ahead. Kaplan vaulted the ditch at the bottom and started to climb. Pride made him ignore Bayner's efforts to help him. He used his hands to help climb the slope in a style similar to a drunken chimpanzee.

"You know--!" Kaplan puffed. He looked across the bulwark while climbing. "Once we built sky scrapers. Out of steal, glass, synthetic compounds. Hell, ancient man built giant temples. Out of granite!" He puffed. "Now, we use plant fiber ropes. And sticks. Sticks!" He stood for a second and inhaled. "If the soul stealer bacterium was a man—" Kaplan puffed. "I would kick the crap out if it. In a pair of shoes—no, boots! With thick wool socks!"

They reached the summit. Marris offered Kaplan a battered plastic bottle filled with water.

"Got anything stronger?" Kaplan wheezed.

Marris smiled and pointed a thumb over his shoulder to the wooden vats. Their contents originated in Kaplan's strong desire for a very strong drink. The result of one experiment proved too potent for cocktails. It did become the tribe's best hope against gumbie hordes.

"Damn. I didn't bring marshmallows." Kaplan smiled and then drew a long pull from the bottle.

"What's a marshmallow?" Bayner asked.

"Worse than gum." Kaplan answered. He enjoyed Bayner's shocked expression. Bayner was child when the outbreak occurred. He had survived carried from civilization, and then made to run to survive. Now he entered adulthood in this weird, new world. Kaplan hoped society could soon enjoy aging in one place.

"You think anyone has tried this?" Marris asked Kaplan. "I mean other than the radiation weapons and flame throwers the military used."

"Yeah, hard to fight a war when the society you're trying to protect has disintegrated."

"I thought you would've stayed with them. Gone to a bunker, or something. Orbit?"

"Nobody sent a helicopter or humvee." Kaplan shrugged.

"Taxi?" Marris asked with a smile.

"Too expensive." Kaplan said.

Marris laughed.

Bayner knew he would get too annoying if he constantly asked about all the things Marris & Kaplan mentioned. He decided it was just a foreign language spoken by the old. And that maybe he shouldn't have skipped so much school.

"Others might've done something similar." Kaplan mused. "Maybe that's why after the global outbreak I heard Houston called the city of flames. Maybe the perpetual fire was from roasting gumbies." Kaplan shrugged.

"Where's Houston?" Bayner risked asking.

Kaplan glanced at the sun and jabbed a finger South.

"If it's still there." Marris said. He looked out across the landscape in the direction of his enemy's inevitable assault.

Sheckly watched for that assault while hidden atop a ridge along the river channel. He became worried. His precious binoculars failed to magnify a distant torch or glimpse someone running towards him. Somehow, the system failed. His friends in the messenger corps were either dead and eaten, or dead and marching with the horde. Now, Sheckly was the last in the line of messengers, but the first chance to warn Marris the gumbies were close. He heard the shuffling mass. He could smell the horde before they came through the dry river bend. The stench rolled into his sinuses as if thick ooze poured into his nose. The odors were a swirl of rotted meat and sickly sweet like flower blossoms and mint. It all wafted from the decomposition and artificial flavors of death. Sicker still was the sounds.

Smuckt! Pop! Smuckt! Skwirsh-skwirsh. Smukt!

The gumbie horde rounded the bend. The sight was worse than the sound. The ones towards the front looked almost alive. The subsequent waves were animate rot. All they needed was teeth and enough muscle to work the gum. Most outer skin, even checks, was optional. For a second, Sheckly wondered how the gum stayed in. Sometimes it didn't. He focused on a corpse in a tattered sundress. The gumbie lost her wad from a check-free face. She stooped to reach for it. The smucks behind knocked her over and trampled her into a flattened stain. There was no mercy even among the horde.

Sheckly recalled Kaplan's sickening briefings. When whatever biology remained needed a recharge, the faster ones would turn and eat the slower ones. All the while, they oddly had the presence of mind to save their gum. The eaten gumbie would attempt to scratch itself onward if so much as a finger with some attached muscle still linked to the brain on a thread of nerve. Sheckly became nauseous. He grew angry as all the stories of loss from the elders raced through his mind. He lost his sense of discipline and stood in defiance. It was a mistake. They saw him. Immediately the entire horde moved to ascend the ridge slope and reach him.

The distinct sound and smell also shambled at him from behind. A smaller group had climbed up from the opposite side of the ridge. Sheckly picked up his club. The family heirloom .40-caliber Sig Sauer P226 rested in his belt. It had five shells left in the magazine. He drew and fired. Five gumbie heads exploded in fast succession. The bullet impacts only triggered the spectacular head bursts. Most of the skull explosion came from the internal pressure built up by the bacteria. The bloody eruptions projected spores when a gumbie was finally immobile or head trauma came knocking.

The club never needed a reload, but it was a close-range weapon. Sheckly swung and shattered a gumbie skull. The gory mist of smashed gumbie brains and spores splashed his face. He swung again. He hit another skull with a loud crack and more gore hit his face. Another swing; another crack. He raised the dripping club again before the true enemy did its work inside his own skull. He collapsed against a wall of gumbies. They looked down on his body. In a moment, he would join them. But now he was still. Fresh. And they needed sustenance to carry on. The smucks removed their gum.

"They must've gotten the watch runners. Damn!" Marris shouted as the gumbie horde appeared in the distance.

"Here they come." Bayner said, and suppressed a shudder.

"You still want to be here, doc?" Marris asked Kaplan.

"Yep." Kaplan answered. "It's the only show in town. If there was a town."

"There's a prepared defense. Thanks to you." Marris said. "I'm glad our tribe has your genius."

"The real genius was simplified stills on wheels." Kaplan said. "But the stroke of luck was finding that valley covered in huckleberries."

"I love huckleberries." Bayner added.

Marris turned to his troops of all genders and ages to yell orders. "Get ready, people!"

Those stationed at the vats' valves and levers tensed. Fire crews stood ready to light their torches. A chorus of metal bolts and heavy springs rippled from the rifle teams chambering rounds into well-maintained but aging assault and hunting rifles.

"At least the predicted rate of shuffle is still the same." Kaplan said.

"What's that mean?" Bayner asked.

"The bacteria aren't modifying the hosts to be faster." Kaplan answered. "Good news. Sort of."

"Hey, old man." Toshiro crouched next to Kaplan. She slung a large satchel onto the ground. "You ready?"

"Are you?" Kaplan smiled.

"Yep." Toshiro patted her satchel. "For bruises, burns and most other wounds. Anything short of a plague."

"We got one of those, too." Kaplan pointed towards to advancing horde. "We're about to use one of the most effective antibiotics to treat a very big infection. Fire."

"Hmm. All that meat and no barbeque sauce." Toshiro said

"Ooh, Dr. Toshiro, you're turning me on." Kaplan replied.

"They're over the covered troughs!" Marris bellowed. "Let it pour!"

Kaplan drew a deep breath as the crews up ended the wooden vats. His distilled hope began to flow down channels and into the covered troughs. Within them awaited several cisterns containing a napalm-like goo created from evergreen sap. The months of circuits through the forests and back to the dried river would be either a great victory or nothing more than a waste of time. People on the edge of doom needed hope and a project to focus it. The desire to fight back was a potent fuel for motivating people to scrape channels in hard earth and haul heavy sacks of berries. Kaplan was certain of success. However, he was also willing to take the brunt of the emotional backlash if it failed. He worried such despair would kill the tribe better than a bizarre disease spread by animate corpses.

The fire crews hurled their torches. Flames erupted in the exposed channels. The first eruption of flames didn't look intense enough to stop the gumbies who walked through the fires. Then an inferno exploded beneath the horde. The tribe's warriors cheered. Kaplan held back a smile. He stared intently at the inferno. He nearly jumped back at what stumbled out of the intense blaze. They were still advancing. Flaming gumbies shambled out of the fire holding their heads.

18

"Ah geez, the heads!" Kaplan shouted.

"Are they in pain?" Toshiro said looking at the gumbies.

"No! They're trying to shield the bacteria. Crap! Spores!" Kaplan bolted up and shouted at Marris. "Shoot! Blow 'em away before they get close."

The rifle teams charged to the edge of the bulwark and opened fire. Gumbie parts blasted off as bursts of automatic fire cut through the advancing, flaming gumbies like invisible chain saws. Gumbie heads began to explode from more precise rifle fire.

"The legs!" Toshiro screamed. "Shoot 'em in the legs!"

The tide of gumbies walking out of the inferno ran into a copper jacketed and lead wave. The tide stop. Flames rolled over the fallen corpses. A few eager rounds still flew into the blaze. The shooting stopped. The only sound was the wind rushing to feed the inferno curling into a searing, orange twister.

"What about the smoke?" Toshiro asked.

"We're safe." Kaplan answered. "The inferno is too wide for the spores to make it out even if they escape the heat." Kaplan bent and placed his hands on his knees.

A renewed cheer drowned the inferno's roar.

The tribe moved again. They would repeat the effort of distillation and excavation at another place. Yet all hoped never to see a gumbie horde ever again. Toshiro, Marris and Bayner accompanied Kaplan to scout the edge of the waning inferno.

"Don't touch that!" Toshiro yelled at Bayner.

Bayner froze, but he kept his eyes locked on the brightly colored box. Across the box's top, a dancing, bright purple hippo held a huge bunch of bright purple grapes across its top. The words 'Delicious! Delightful! Chewlicious!' swirled across all of its visible sides in bulbous lettering.

"Is it a peace offering?" Bayner asked.

"Are you nuts?" Marris barked. "They want us to become like them! Torch it."

"But it's grape chewlicious." Bayner said. He rolled his tongue in his mouth anticipating a sweet, fragrant, artificial flavor.

"It's suicide!" Marris barked.

"Can you test it to see if it's parasite free?" Bayner asked Kaplan.

"Nope." Kaplan said. He stood next to the box, and then kicked it into the remaining flames.

"Hey!" Bayner nearly bolted after the box.

Marris glared at Bayner. He jerked him thumb in the direction of the bulwark. Bayner obeyed and walked up the slope. The hippo burned away.

"Ow!" Kaplan shouted and began stomping his foot burning from a dab of evergreen napalm. He limped up the hill and sat on a flat edge of bulwark.

"You may have just saved us all." Toshiro retrieved her satchel.

"Yep. That's me." Kaplan rubbed cool dirt over his foot. "PhDs and a life of science, and I save humanity with a barefoot kick with my ass covered in dirt. I feel fulfilled. Really."

"Oh, shut up and take the praise." Toshiro said. She gently brushed some of Kaplan's tousled hair from his face.

"All right, I will." Kaplan looked up at her and smiled.

"So, to bring that gum." Marris said. "It took planning."

"Well, only maybe." Kaplan shrugged. "I guess it explains their constant supply. It's probably the one, sure thought of what's left of their brains. Back when this began, we figured the infected brain could still manifest rudimentary intelligence. But—"

"Has it evolved a smarter gumbie?" Toshiro asked.

"I don't think so. These smucks looked like any other horde. Some of them carry junk with them. In photos of the first hordes, I saw gumbies with purses, pack packs, dolls. One even carried a dead cat and a spatula."

"Yeah," Marris added and looked back over the field of ashes and bones. "Some of these smucks held chunks of wood or rocks."

"I think it's a rudimentary impulse to pick up something and carry it." Kaplan said. "This wave probably passed through some abandoned town and some did what comes natural. From our perspective, that case of gum made sense as part of a sinister plan. But it could just be just impulse. P-O-P."

"Pop?" Toshiro asked.

"Point of purchase." Kaplan answered. "In ye olde stores there would be stuff set up at the cash registers to lure you into an impulse buy. Stuff like gum."

Marris shook his head and walked towards his troops loading equipment.

"Impulse. Hmm." Toshiro said as she examined Kaplan's foot. "Well, why don't you come over to my place?"

"Oh, really?" Kaplan suggestively and raised his eyebrows.

"Yes." Toshiro said. "I'm the tribe doctor, and you have an injured foot."

"Well," Kaplan stood. "At least I didn't put it in my mouth."

Toshiro groaned. "Any more of that, and I'm kicking you into the fire trenches."

"Ooh! Hot!" Kaplan laughed.

Toshiro shook her head. She helped Kaplan limp towards the line of the living descending the opposite side of the hill.

REMNANTS

A belch of acrid black smoke burned the eyes and noses as the moving truck drove away. It was the smallest of the irritations Janice endured this frigid evening. The cold crept through the heavy layers of clothing as she stared bewildered at what now littered her driveway. The heavy, old aquariums looked more like reinforced glass crates. Twisting tubes and rusted equipment hung from all sides. The largest was almost the size of a sofa. A thick layer of mud coated its bottom. That wouldn't make it any lighter. Old, mildewed notebooks and a rough wooden box completed the mess. Janice looked with contempt at her husband Frank surveying his worthless inheritance.

"Well, let's get started." Frank said with mock glee and a taunting smile.

Janice threw a hard scowl over the top of her woolen scarf. It glanced off Frank as he opened the garage door of their cluttered suburban palace. The sight of several sedimentary layers of other salvaged debris stabbed at her more sharply than any spoken barb. Frank knew this, and turned to her with his smile even wider.

This time Janice had agreed to accept the heavy junk with some remnant of sympathy for Frank's loss. Of course, that sympathy was turned against her on Frank's widening smile.

"This is what the government paid for?" Janice asked through wool.

"For a while. It was for the war on terror, I think. But Dad said the military was too squeamish to use the results. Can you imagine that?" Frank's chuckle puffed mist in front of his reddened nose.

"Squeamish, or practical?" Janice sniffed, and fingered cold tubing.

"Hey, you met Dad. Once." Frank's glee froze over. "You know he was brilliant."

A brilliant con man, maybe, Janice thought. Or just delusional. That seemed a family trait. She knew Frank's scientist father had long lost government funding for whatever arcane research he did. Emphasis on arcane, since it all seemed nothing more than watery sleight of hand. Refusing to teach biology, or whatever it was he did, her father-in-law became a financial drain whose only bequest was the backache from heaving his discarded equipment.

"Don't worry," Frank said squatting at the end of a tank. He searched with his gloved hands at the edges for a solid grip. "Some fish loving sap will buy this stuff. It's perfect merchandise for somebody."

"That's what you said about the rest of your garbage." Janice strained at the opposite end.

"These assets are mint!" Frank protested as the tank jerked and rose slowly into the air between them. Frank and Janice shuffled and stumbled with their load into the narrow pathway inside the garage.

"You're looking at treasure!" he grunted. "Have some foresight."

"Sure. Treasure," Janice groaned. A treasure for an archeologist a thousand years from now, she thought. Some future nut interested in lost causes of 21st century losers will love it all. But not anyone today. Her elbow hit a box. Stabbing pain burst through the joint, yet even worse to her was the congealed smell of all the columns and drifts of foolish enterprise and compounded futility stacked around them. She hated that most of all.

Janice waited interminably for Frank to sell his amassed relics in some garage sale or on-line auction that never happened. The collection of useless artifacts and unwanted collectibles just grew, collected dust and moldered. Tonight had brought even more. And that would bring more complaints in a marriage that had spawned thousands. Yet they stayed together, perhaps out of compounding spite like volcanic heat and pressure fusing rock before the eruption.

Inside the warm house, Janice's Rottweiler, Bone Snapper, pressed against the front window. More nasal graffiti smudged over the existing layers from his canine snout. His reliable growling at Frank earned Bone Snapper the right to cover the plush furniture with fine, brown dog hair. He watched Janice and Frank work in surprising unity to move the heavy aquariums among the walls of clutter.

The last aquarium scraped across the cement floor next to the dented freezer. Veins, muscles, and bones throbbed. The job was finished. It had all gone smoothly. Quietly. Neither Janice nor Frank wanted the silence mistook for gratitude or conciliation. Something must be wrong. Each needed a flash-point. It sat to the side of the ice-covered driveway. The rough, wooden box stabbed splinters through fraying gloves and into sweaty, fatigued fingers. There was no room in the garage, finally. It would have to come inside, bringing with it the smell and spite.

Bone Snapper committed his usual barking attack once Frank entered the house. Something heavy inside the box kept shifting, making it hard to manage. Bone Snapper's assault intensified Frank's blue retorts. The box hit the carpet with a thud. Bone Snapper kept up his barking barrage, but at the box, not Frank. The dog stopped to emit a low squeal and growl of concern. He looked pensively at Janice, and then continued his loud, slobber spattering racket. Frank looked bewildered at the dog, but was pleased for once not to be the object of Bone Snapper's malice.

"It's too close to the heater, Frank!" Janice howled over her pet, breaking Frank's momentary pleasure.

"Look, it's fine!"

"Frank! I don't want the smell of whatever is inside to be blowing through the house. It's like dead--rotted eggs!"

The dog continued to bark and howl.

"Once you start cooking, who'll notice? Might even help cover the smell from the kitchen."

"Then you can eat what's in the damn box!"

"You know, I might. It couldn't be any worse than--"

"Frank! You lousy--!"

The dog's barks grew indistinguishable from the broken phrases of human raving threatening to drown it out.

Quiet returned, eventually. Full night hung black outside the windows. Bone Snapper still guarded the odorous wooden box from a distance. Janice fled the kitchen carrying moist paper packages under her arm. Bone Snapper followed her to the garage. Janice needed to freeze the steaks once intended for dinner. She and Bone Snapper would enjoy them later. Frank could make do with the canned chili laced with extra cayenne she eventually shoved in front of him. That was still more appetizing than the bowl of stale corn flakes he had poured for himself.

On the freezer shelves, other former meals sat packed beside jugs of frozen water. Janice had put the jugs inside the freezer to save money by filling empty space. Now they were in the way of preserving her future dinner, and there was no room on the floor.

Frost banged off two jugs as she placed them inside the odd aquarium with the muddy bottom. She hoped to God it was mud.

It stank like sewage, or those little agar dishes that kids and scientists use to culture germs and other repulsions. She looked more closely at the dark layer. The jugs wiggled atop the brownish-green mass as if on a foam mattress. She watched a drip of condensation roll off one jug and onto the questionable layer.

Were those shapes within the muck? Janice wondered. She couldn't quite make out their pattern through the glass in the low light. It seemed like an obscured cross-section she saw in a biology textbook many years ago. Whatever, it had all better scrub out easily—as if she would do that job herself! She closed the freezer door.

Heartburn. An hour later and Janice's chili worked its revenge on Frank. He should have eaten the corn flakes. He was still hungry and determined to eat one of those steaks. He would cook it right in front of her. He slipped on the garage floor. Something wet? He opened the freezer and grabbed both of the frosting meat packets.

"One for me and one for me," Frank whispered.

Light from the freezer's bulb lit the aquarium. Frank's eyelids widened in the dim light. The mud layer was now moist and missing big chunks. Slime slid slowly down the side opposite Frank. Two water jugs were inside the glass. One still dripped heavy condensation. The other jug laid ripped open by something jagged.

"Janice, what--!" Frank started, but Bone Snapper growled.

Frank looked down at the dog. Its eyes were fixed on him and the steaks. Frank closed the freezer and turned. He slipped again. One steak fell from his arm and slapped against the floor. Bone Snapper attacked. He tore away the butcher paper and ripped the thick, red meat in half.

Suddenly the dog's eyes shot up at Frank creeping to the house door, and then toward a pile of Frank's treasure that suddenly quivered. Bone Snapper gulped down his prize and thrust his nose into a stack of comic books and ancient pornography. A long, wet cord snapped tightly around his neck. Another whipped over his right, front leg and ended in a glistening black triangle that grabbed his shoulder. Bone Snapper's wide eyes locked on Frank in canine surprise and panic.

Frank saw the pile of clutter lurch. Then something-an eye?-reared up behind the dog. Eight shorter tentacles seemed to materialize across Bone Snapper's sides. Each muscular ribbon flexed and pulled. Bone Snapper's claws scratched against the cement floor as he attempted a choked-off bark.

Frank ran up the steps to the house and turned to grab the door. The clutter pile lurched again. Falling comic books and shattering china covered the dog and its bizarre attacker. Bone Snapper managed a low, almost human howl before the noise submerged in wet crunches. The dog's heavy collar flew out and hit Frank. He slammed the door shut.

Frank's fingers dug deep into the surviving steak. Frank dropped it. He was no longer hungry. His mind raced with other ideas of greater avarice. Divorce was expensive, but life insurance paid out money. Large sums of money. Perhaps his father had finally given him something useful. His advice on women had been lousy.

A minute of verbal sparring later, and Frank finally goaded Janice to cook the steaks for herself in spite. She stormed into the garage. Frank heard the screams immediately. First, she would see Bone Snapper's blood. Then, hopefully, her own. He crept to the doorway. Flailing shadows broke the cone of light from the opened freezer. Frank closed and locked the door.

Chunks of frost, frozen broccoli, and TV dinners battered the monster as it tugged at Janice. Her left arm held fast to the freezer shelves as her right hand grabbed for anything to throw. The impact of a frozen turkey drove the beast back. Janice drew a deep breath. A second creature attacked to her left. Janice glimpsed flailing tentacles around beak-like jaws through a cascade of broken china. Above the writhing mass, a great, menacing eye hungrily focused on her. It pulled her in, securing its penetrating grip. Her arm struck something heavy. She grabbed it with both hands and pulled out a rusted fire extinguisher. Janice heard the wet flops of the other monster circling. She swallowed the pain gripping her legs and fired a gush of chilling white foam at the noise.

The thing screamed, choked, and scuttled back into the dark. Janice spewed the froth at the beast now atop her thighs. It leapt over her. She covered its spiny, arched back with white lather as it fled. Janice scrambled from the junk pile. She shakily held the flexible spout of her weapon towards the shadows and reached the light switch. The old, incandescent bulb flash on as one of the things flexed to leap at her. It flinched for a moment in the sudden brightness. Janice buried it in foam. It leapt to the side and spasmed to shake off the chilling froth. The second beast darted from the junk. She aimed her nozzle. All that shot at the creature was a defiant hiss. The tentacles wrapped around her legs. She lifted the metal cylinder high and let out an ear-shattering shriek.

Frank covered his ears from the last scream. He felt the violent thumps subside through the floor. Timidly, but with anticipation, he opened the door. The body lay quivering. Its body! Fleshy chunks and spines lay scattered around the creature trailed by oily, purplish blood. Frank's eyes met Janice's own with shock. She took rapid, sharp breaths and didn't seem to notice her own blood seeping through rips in her once-blue jeans.

Janice leaned against the darkly spattered fire extinguisher. Her hands were white from her quivering grip. Wrapped around her right fist was Bone Snapper's collar. She thrust it at Frank.

"You knew!" Janice shrieked. "They ate him, and you knew!"

"Janice--!"

She swung the fire extinguisher overhead again. A fragment of spiny flesh slipped off the metal bludgeon. Frank thought to back away. Too late. Dull pain and flashes of light danced inside his head. Janice was yelling. Again. All Frank could hear was the *Thungk!* of the fire extinguisher across his skull. *Thungk!* again, then black.

The other beast exploded through from the center pile. Janice ruptured the fire extinguisher against her leaping attacker and slammed it into the freezer. She kicked the door closed, then bolted into the house. She heard the other beasts moving among the walls of Frank's worthless "treasure." Janice screamed and hurled the extinguisher into the garage. It hit a stack of boxes that reached to the ceiling. The stack toppled and struck another. Giant dominoes of magazines, china, toys, vinyl records, defunct electronics, and auto parts collided in succession and finally crushed the glass aquariums. A pall of dust drifted over the immense mound of aggregate garbage and compounded loathing.

The freezer door violently flew back open. The thing escaped, but Janice was already slamming the house door shut. She leaned against it and tried to control her breathing.

"What was--?"

Triangular jaws burst through the door by her ankles like chain saw blades. It stopped. Low moaning sounded on the other side.

The thing pulled its teeth from the door. For three seconds all Janice heard was her own gasps. Then Frank screamed her name. He screamed unintelligibly. He stopped screaming. Janice wondered where those old notebooks were. She might need them to prove what ate her husband. And to collect his life insurance. If the policy covered freak-monsters from now-dead scientist's crap.

Janice enjoyed the new quiet, interrupted only by the occasional sharp ripping of Frank's shirt and slacks, and the gentle crunch of his bones. For a moment her mind went blank. Then a thought jumped forward: Time to call 911. Quickly. She pulled out her mobile phone. It was shattered. She heard the things begin to move.

Janice made a limping sprint into the kitchen. Thinking of Frank, she knocked the emptied can of chili into the trash before grabbing the landline phone. She was slower to notice the increased pungent odor like sulfur and vinegar. Her foamy and bloody hands fumbled to grip the slick, plastic receiver.

Janice's finger made contact with the nine key. She then pressed 'one.' Something moved in the other room. Janice glanced around. Her eyes found the rough-hewn wooded box. She knew it had been too close to the heater. Broken planks littered her floor. Something had burst out of it.

"Frank, you lousy--!"

The clatter of chitinous legs against the kitchen linoleum cut short her final rebuke. She saw and at last admired her father-in-law's handiwork, even if the military never did. The swift beast from the crate gave Janice no time to hit the final key.

Bone Snapper shook himself and whimpered. He stopped to lick his wounds. He preferred the taste to his own blood to the slivers of his opponent's flesh still in his mouth. Once he had freed his head from the creatures constricting grasp, it was teeth versus beak. Teeth won. Bone Snapper vomited out the chunks of its flesh. It stopped fighting once he bit through its bony, internal shell near its center. The crunching sound echoed in his memory as he lapped air to rid the taste from his tongue. It took longer to push out of the collapsed, moldering mass than rip through his attacker. The second thing was an even faster kill. He caught it out in the open eating Frank.

Paws pushed the door to the garage open. Bone Snapper made his way through the house. He didn't want to stay here anymore. It was time for a new home. In the kitchen, the woman that typically screamed but also fed him had been partially eaten, herself. The same tearing jaws had also bitten through the front door. The hole was large enough for Bone Snapper to squeeze through. He yelped when his slashed shoulder and then haunches touched the jagged edge. Outside, the world was dark, icy and cold, but quiet. Bone Snapper peed on a bush. He sniffed odd tracks in the snow. The thing had gone down the street. His snout pulled in stress hormones wafting from its increasingly labored tracks. It had turned back to the house before a truck had run over it. It lay still. Smashed. Dead. Bone Snapper moved on. His heavy paws on the snow and ice were the only sound that broke the Winter calm.

TRANSLUCENCE AND SHADOWS

At night, someone heard screaming. By morning, the place was a crime scene. Mort Phal was there for the car.

"Careful!" The cop yelled.

Mort stopped and looked down. His left, patent leather shoe touched the edge of a deep, fresh puddle. It lay outside the driver's side door of the luxury rental car he was there to inspect. It wasn't the water or the cop that made him step back, but sudden revulsion. A thick, yellowish film slowly curled under the water. Mort thought he saw a face stripped free of bone roll to the surface.

"That's all we've found." The cop continued. "It's rotting skin. Maybe human."

Mort felt queasy. He always did, as if something was not quite right inside him. Something was not right in this vacant lot, rotting skin notwithstanding.

"There's no other evidence. Nothing inside the car." The cop said. "Why are you here?"

"I cleared with the detective." Mort answered with a smile, because they probably didn't have antacids in jail. "I'm the securities investigator. I find misappropriated assets. I'll—"

"A repo man!" The cop suddenly looked queasy, too.

"Not quite." Mort continued to smile. He wondered if the cop's pained expression was due to late payments on his own car. "I collect information."

"You've got one minute." The cop growled. "Get what you need. Then get out. And-!"

"Yeah, I got it." Mort no longer smiled. "Watch where I step."

Mort got nothing of what he needed. There was no record of identity verification of the car's renter, yet there must have been to hand over the keys. Even the data from the car's GPS was corrupted. But sophisticated thieves wouldn't abandon their prize. The only clues might come from the dead skin. Mort knew he wouldn't get that report. He did get a headache, and not just from the cop's lousy attitude.

Mort thought his headaches could be caused by his diet. Each night he bought various foods in various bags from various drive thrus. Yet he always ate it all at the same local park. Mort dropped uneaten bits along the bushes for the raccoons, or the crows if anything remained by morning. That way no smell of greasy leftovers hung in his cramped hovel overnight. Lately, Mort had taken to sitting in his car along the street and only gazed into the wooded park. He thought its weak lighting was a liability for the city. More than raccoons could hide in the darkness.

Mort thought the taste of his food was a liability. It probably gave him the headache. And nausea. He rolled down his car window and tossed it all into the quiet street. What was he eating? He couldn't remember what he just swallowed. Was it tacos, a burger, fried fish? Mort opened his car door to look. He instinctively turned to step out and retrieve the paper bag and Chinese noodles splattered on the asphalt. Then Mort stopped. His face went slack. He shuddered. For a moment, all his thoughts seemed to disappear and be replaced by impulse. Again. It was as if something was trying to occupy or erase his mind. What? There was nothing causing stress. All factors of his life were well organized and tidy. Impossibly so, really. But his head hurt. Swollen sinuses were the likely reason. Although he couldn't recall ever being sick.

Mort lit a cigarette. He strained to focus on the burning end where smoke rose like a fuzzy, inverted waterfall inches from his mouth. He wondered if he had ever smoked before tonight. It was the likely cause of his headache. Mort threw the burning cigarette into the street. He stared at its glowing end and scattered cinders lying near the noodles. Mort left his car in a sudden urge to collect the glowing embers. His thoughts shifted again. He looked over his litter and considered the wasted money. At least he still had a whole pack. Minus one. Minus, what? A form missing from a file? A missing thought. Information lost. Maybe he was trying to recall a distant memory with no context. Was this missing information the same thing as what was trying to assert itself? It felt as if something was trying to catch up to him. Or just catch him. But how can you run from something inside your mind?

A truck drove over the tossed-out food and obliterated the cigarette. Mort snapped back from his anxious musings. The street was quiet again. And then a noise rattled out from the park. It was an odd racket to come from a stretch of trees and dirt trails. It sounded as though several pickaxes where dropping on cement in rhythmic succession. The source was coming closer. Pickaxes. Sharp ends. Like crab legs. Or a spider's legs. A large, man-sized spider. It was blue, almost translucent, like azure pigment added to blown glass. He could see a smile of conic teeth from far away, but moving closer. The smile rode the spider's legs walking straight to him. Mort got in his car and shut door. The pulsing safety belt alarm sounded as he sped off. Mort never looked into the rearview mirror. A hard shudder caused him to swerve. Mort focused on driving. No sense in trying to rationalize a nightmare, he thought. Even one experienced while wide awake and with eyes open. He wanted to avoid madness. His medical insurance didn't cover that. And he had work to do. The alarm continued until he got home, almost keeping time with his rapid heartbeat.

The surges of blood slowed to normal. The flow of information spiked. Mort loved to absorb information. At home he watched TV, listened to the radio, and subsumed himself in the internet. At times, all at once. Somehow, his brain tracked and made sense of it all. That seemed impossible, really. When he stared at a point on the screen, Mort felt as though his vision could focus passed the graphics and down to the programming code, down to the ones and zeroes, down to the regions between electrons. Mort wondered if eyestrain was the reason for his headache. That pain was an anchor. It held back another sensation when Mort felt as though his all his experiences, weird and routine, surged from his mind to somewhere beyond himself. Maybe that was why something felt missing, or that something was trying to catch him. It was the rebound of a wave. Maybe it carried something back with it. Something translucent blue? Mort shuddered. He focused back on the screen. Sharp knocks on his door made him jump.

Mort opened the door and found the cop from the crime scene and the detective. They glowered. Each looked as though they had their own headache, or was a programmer's representation of that pain.

"You live in a motel?" the detective asked with disdain.

"Hotel," Mort answered. "We have a hallway. Enclosed."

"Yeah. Nice." The cop said and glanced down the hall with a scowl as if to accuse the place itself of criminal intent.

"It stinks." The detective kept his focus on Mort. "And so do you, Mort Phal. If that's your real name. I don't like being played. I don't like things that stink. You—"

"Then maybe you shower more often." Mort interjected. "The steam. It opens the sinuses."

"Watch it, wise ass." The detective glowered. "We're watching you. Your credentials are all new. Like the records just popped onto a hard drive at the same time. That makes me think you're hiding. Something. Maybe you're running. One false step—"

"Don't step on the skin." Mort spoke suddenly, even surprising himself.

"What?"

"Read the report. Forensics," Mort answered, with a renewed focus. "Enjoy your shower."

Mort glanced at both of them, suggesting a mutual experience was forthcoming.

"Hey!" both yelled.

Mort closed the door. He figured they wouldn't risk escalating the confrontation without solid evidence against him. If they had that, he'd be in handcuffs. Although even he wouldn't know why. Mort listened to them mutter and walk away. He smiled, and then massaged his temples. The TV was on. Mort was still standing, transfixed by the screen when his doorbell rang repeatedly, followed by an aggressive series of knocks low on the door. A small but confident boy stood in the hall with a plastic bin filled with goods. He took a breath to launch into his pitch. Mort cut him off.

"Kid, you know there's a no soliciting policy here."

"A what?" The boy feigned ignorance. "I'm not a pimp or a politician. I'm just trying to make a buck."

"Like a pimp. Or politician." Mort said.

The kid frowned. "Yeah. All right. But you look like a guy who eats chocolate. So why not—"

"You got any smokes?" Mort blurted out.

"What?"

"Cigarettes." Mort furthered, and then suddenly realized the question was wrong in this social context.

"No way! I'm a kid. Unless maybe you got some for me. I'll trade." The boy smiled. The grin left his face as he saw Mort intently staring at a shadowed bend down the hall.

"Dude, you okay?" The boy backed away from Mort and lifted his bin. He still stood within sales striking distance in case the weird guy took out his wallet. Anything else and the bin was ready to throw at him.

"Yeah." Mort finally answered. "Just don't go down that part of the hall. It's dangerous."

"Okay." The boy looked down the hallway at the shadows. He listened to Mort, and left.

Mort finally closed the door. He sat down in front of his computer. Web pages flashed like spinning fan blades in front of his eyes. In time, the doorbell rang again. No one stood in the hall. No cops, no boy, no lost pizza delivery person. Nothing. But the shadow was still there. Mort thought he could see something within the darkness. A translucent presence. Perhaps a giant spider that rings doorbells. He locked the door and switched off his doorbell. He switched off the radio, TV and computer. He kept the lights on, and went to bed.

The pulse of Mort's alarm clock was out of sync with the throbbing veins in his head. He focused, and prepared for work. Investigation. Data collection. Mort was good at his job. Or so he thought. He looked at the folders spilling out of his briefcase across the never-used passenger seat of his car and felt as if he was seeing something wholly alien. Then the information they contained began streaming through his mind. Another thought emerged from the flow, completely different to all the others. Some information could only be obtained from direct experience. He found a willing partner in sharing experience near his hotel's parking lot, and took her home.

"Did you have a good time?" Lahni, the prostitute asked Mort from the bed.

Mort paused as if to find some bit of hidden meaning in the question. "Yeah, sure. Why?"

"You seemed into it, but, um, like maybe it was your first time?"

"Hard to say," Mort said. He lifted a curtain and peered out the window as if to glimpse something lurking within a shadow. But it was night. The world was now a shadow. "My memory. It sometimes isn't quite what it should be. I think."

"Hey, no problem, Mr. Big." Lahni drew close to Mort and kissed him on the head.

"Ow!" Mort cried out. He grabbed Lahni by the shoulders to stop her from recoiling, but also to steady himself. "Sorry! Sorry. It's just—bad headache."

"I got something that might help." She smiled. "But it will cost extra. And probably, for you, another first."

"Probably," Mort sighed.

Mort needed to clear his head. He might always need to do that, he thought. He also needed to clear Lahni's something extra in case he had to fill a special plastic cup at work. Though the hallucinations proved interesting and distracting, some information was not to be shared. Mort ran for some rare exercise. His pulse increased. Endorphins flowed. Yet something was still chasing him within his mind. It amplified his fatigue. After a plodding mile, Mort slowed to a near crawl. He tripped.

Mort felt a constant throbbing become suddenly irregular. Sporadic. Then it stopped. The heart quit beating. The mind had died moments before that failure. Mort held his phone in one hand. In the other, he clutched the wrist of the homeless veteran whose body had tripped him. The man's body grew cold as if to merge with sidewalk where Mort knelt next to him. Mort had promised to call the man's daughter instead of calling for help. The veteran hadn't wanted help. He had wanted an end. Mort had listened to the man tell his story. One that ultimately brought him to his death along a city street. But it included nobility, service, war, disillusionment, sorrow, escape through narcotics, personal destruction and loss of social standing on every level. Finally, only a stranger knelt next to the man when he died.

Mort felt like a voyeur to the death. Yet he was also glad to fulfill the veteran's last wish. His promise seemed to provide the man a final solace, and perhaps release. He was going to die even if Mort had ignored him. And seeing death was something of human existence Mort needed to witness. He made the call to the veteran's daughter. Almost anyone else would have forgotten her number already. But Mort retained that information, all of the man's life story, the observation of his death, and all of human experience that could be recorded in mere weeks. So far, that was Mort Phal's life span. It was also coming to an end.

It was night. Soon, someone would be heard screaming. That someone would be Mort Phal. By morning, the place would be a crime scene. Now, Mort stood next to his car in the darkened park.

He could not resist entering it tonight. He felt a need for privacy. His pulse quickened. Mort felt as though something had finally caught up to him. No one was there for his last moments, not even a stranger. Mort did have one constant companion. His headache began to amplify to epic levels. Mort's skin began to spilt along his forehead. The pain was like a cutting edge, cutting through flesh to open up that place where all the information had been flowing. What emerged cut away Mort's screaming face until it fell on the ground with the tattered clothes, blood and shredded exterior of Mort Phal. It was all unnecessary, now. As was the attempt to scream through the smile of conic teeth riding on spider's legs. They weren't teeth, but light collecting cilia. The crystalline structures were better than human eyes in gathering light and visual information. They even saw the fluctuations between quantum filaments that allowed his kind to enter this universe from the next. That place was well known to the large, translucent, spider-like being whose physical structure had been folded within Mort's human camouflage.

The other information collector now strode out of the shadows where it had watched its colleague. Now there was recognition between them, not fear. They made a key from entangling photons gathered from the park's weak lights and reentered their universe through a crease in the night. The time would come when humanity would find such creases. The clues would come from data unfolding from collisions within great, circular machines. The collectors knew this, and gathered information to construct a parallel Earth to observe. This would expand understanding, and preclude some difficult moments during contact. Those moments were certain to occur when minds attempted to communicate despite being wholly alien to each other. Mort Phal helped to make such communication possible. A man who loved to gather information would become a source of knowledge. Mort would be reborn in that parallel, modeled Earth. He would live out a fully human life that would be, for most of the time, headache free. He would enjoy Chinese food and wooded parks. He would always be wary of scowling cops, and, somewhat ironically, shades of translucent blue within shadows.

36

OUT OF DARKNESS

I vaguely remember the stars as dull little specs dotting the brown, night sky. Now, night is forever, but starless, remorseless, and dotted with eyes lit with hunger. If you see those twinkling in the distance, scream. It's courteous to warn others, even today. I hear a sound and want to scream. It's only my alarm clock. Time to get up and go to work. I have a date with the things in the dark. My nametag reads: David Brindle, Licensed Exterminator. It should say terrified, professional runner. I rarely get to run, but when your species is now the first and only link in the food chain, it's nice to have the option.

It's 8:00 a.m. I nervously wait in the sick yellow light of the street lamps. Daylight perished when the sun disappeared behind a shroud of toxic ash. Among the shadows rose vicious patchworks of contamination and genetic vanity. It was as if the monsters were always waiting in our collective 'Sleep of Reason,' and we finally found a way to free them. I fill an opportunistic niche that exploits the fear of them. People dream each monster I kill is the last. We are still permanent. Or is that exploiting hope? Anymore, the difference is like night and day.

The company van descends and stops. I climb in. I feel the pull of the levdrive as the door shuts. I'll know where the job is when I get there. The van darts through and over the automated crush of humanity. I look out across the better parts of town. Monolithic skyscrapers shoot miles into the rolling black clouds high overhead. I've heard the buildings anchor to something even higher. I could never afford elevator fare to the second floor.

The van stops. I suit up. Metal slides over my sweaty coveralls. The whole world smells like sweat. I can't wait for them to finish those heat capacitors. Who would've thought dark clouds would make Earth hotter. I slide the door open. A small tenement house and a sea-box home sit besieged among the towers like doomed artifacts. A narrow alley separates them, but it's open and well lit down the center. Weird. Monsters typically like dark alleys. I withdraw my weapon from the rack. Outside my boss makes his appearance. A holographic bubble pops on outside the van containing his bloated, stubbled head.

"On time. Good!" Whatever-his-name says. "Client's in the tenement. Said she's heard screaming for a couple of weeks now.

No bodies. Figure it's transients walking through the alley and being bushwhacked."

"But there's no sign of a monster." I say sweeping my weapon's barrel across the alley to catch a reading. Nothing, of course. "The alley is clean."

"Then it must be below ground." The sage bubble offers.

"Who lives in the small home?" I ask, aiming at it.

"One really old woman still living in the middle of it all. She must be gonna die soon." Bubble-boy says with contempt.

"You sure? Maybe she can afford a reweave." I walk ahead and the van door slides shut.

"Then why the Hell would she stay here?" My boss snaps with sudden annoyance, probably because he can't afford to be rewoven himself, and he's stuck looking like that.

"Nostalgia?" I offer.

"There you go with the big words again, drop-out. Kill whatever creepy things you find. Flash 'em to the client and get going. I got three others for you before lunch. Move."

"Yeah." I give resigned compliance. It's easy for him, prion-brain. He never leaves his stool. I see him as less than myself, but ultimately he's my boss. I should have been the boss. I was Mr. College who would never have to be the grunt taking orders from a homogenous-gened neuroleptic. Our veiled insults mask the hate for each other, born out of our reversal of fates. I scanned clean at birth. Did he? Now he probably gets off more riding my ass than going home to his pig-faced wife. Then again, he might not even exist. He could just be some psychologically calibrated hologram the company thinks will instill the right attitude for the job. Maybe he isn't supposed to lift employee's spirits, but motivate us to kill by imagining him every time we pull the trigger. If so, it works.

I approach the alley. A young woman looks down from a fire escape on the tenement. Judging from her heart and respiration display it took all the courage she could muster to step outside. She seems frightened by me, a dull, armored monster here to kill the other one. I let her be afraid. That's a difference I can feel in myself. I used to be ideological, caring. Compared to the majority, I still am. But most philosophy was ripped out and eaten like my lower two feet of guts on my first kill.

I can still smell them on the monster's breath when it turned back for more. By then the pain was gone and the suit had dropped its screen to keep the rest from falling out. I had my gun ready and cut it into little pieces. I was sewn back together and docked a day's pay. All in four hours. I wonder if the woman looking down would like to hear the story. I'd want her to shower first.

Human blood. Traces of it litter the threshold and steps leading down to a dark basement. The tenement's narrow shadow hides the stairwell, but the center of the alley is well lit. How inviting to both predator and prey. I fire a probe through the door below. It flashes offline. Something broke it. I hate that. I walk down the stairs and feel the cool air across my metal skin. Lighting from my helmet and gun cuts into the basement dark. They run just ahead of the beams, a pack of them. Great.

Only the passive scans register the beasts. I switch to FRACDAR. My gut tightens. They're a meter in length when stretched. A new species of giant, grisly worms with jagged armor. They run and clatter on spikes tapering off the bottom of each hardened segment. Teeth, many long teeth, with eyes or something sweeping along their canine snouts that keep dropping open from their first, pointed segment. They must be full, or I just don't look tasty enough. There must be something universally unpalatable about canned food. So why are they massing at the exit? More of them to my left. A jab in the neck! Just the suit's needle. I'm calm. I take a step back to find the best possible firing angle. They're moving. Kill them!

I hit them with the torch, wide angle. Beautiful sheets of purple flame engulf the horrors. They writhe, burn, and scream, but most of all they get the Hell away from me. Damn! The automatic cut-off activates. The building's structure is getting too hot. Everything goes black. My suit's operating system is always a fraction slower than panic. Something hits my chest.

Think! Interface. I need the lights--no, the E field. The attacker jumps away as it sparks on. The FRACDAR finally hits my retina-screen. What I can see you I can kill. Explosive bullets rip open the survivors detonating on impact so only bloody fragments ricochet over the walls and me. Their attack dies. Most of the hideous worms were already scrambling into a small conduit to escape. My whole body sighs relief--until I realize where they're going. The things are crawling underneath a certain old lady's house. Yeah, I'll follow them. That first monster on my first day didn't bite deep enough.

I literally scrape through the conduit and slide into the old lady's basement. This place is ancient. Wooden beams run the length of the foundation walls. I can hear the worms under the stairwell. A little jump in output and the walls disappear like the darkness. Even more tissue traces are in here. This is their real nest. That old lady doesn't get down here much. Now, she can say goodbye to her unpaying tenants.

A missile cuts across the basement and strikes me. A monster dove through the wall. Its jaws penetrate into my gun. Feedback fries the beast, but its sacrifice renders me impotent. The other ten monsters attack. I vainly pull the trigger as they knock me into the wall. Suddenly the pinnacle of technology becomes a feeble club. Get off me you twisted--Ow! That damn needle. I could make it to the stairs. But then the old woman--! They knock away my gun, thrashing, twisting, and scraping off armor filings with their teeth. The E-field now just makes them pull tighter. I slam into walls and smash through centuries old wooden tables. Museum pieces, for sure. To Hell with them. Get off me! I bat and grab at them like a desperate boxer. If I stop fighting, they'll make it to my faceplate. I have to keep swinging. Look freaks, it's a draw. Let me go! Old woman I hope you can run. Light blasts from the top of the stairs.

"Stop!" The old lady yells, and they do. "What are you doing here?" She asks me.

"Get these things off me, or they die." I tell her, still pushing their jaws away.

"Yeah, right." She snorts, but then barks "off!"

The monsters comply and flow back into the shadows.

"Come upstairs," she offers. "Unless you'd like to stay down there."

The upstairs looks like a fusion of contemporary conveniences and old-century kitsch. The floor creaks in places. I stand where it doesn't.

"Okay," I say heavily. "What...what is...this?"

"Sit down," she says parking herself in a patched-up recliner. "Take your helmet off."

"Just fill me in, all right?" I become aware of my tone and modulate it. This situation is too strange to risk my life by being offensive. I see the recognition of its complexity in her eyes even through my geometric sight. She and I were in a battle for survival, mentally. The victor would walk away with a renewed future. The loser would become more ashes on the clouded sky. Or was there another option? Maybe she stopped the fight to save her property, or maybe to make a deal so I won't come back. This ancient woman was something different. She was older than the age of monsters, and myself.

"The only remarkable thing is that I managed to train them." She said after a moment, and swallowed.

I switched off FRACDAR and noticed how folded and slack her flesh appeared to my human eyes. That condition doesn't happen anymore, or so I thought. She moved easily, yet looked so weak. A typical form-fitting black jumper draped loosely over her bony frame. How could you live like this and survive? The monsters downstairs. Her monsters. If you can still think, I suppose you can do anything.

"At first, they were just bizarre little maggots in some black market meat." She said after briefly trying to peer inside my faceplate.

I decided she really didn't need to see my face, and kept it opaque. "So they act like--?" I said searching for a parallel.

"Dogs? Yes, a bit. But I don't pet them." She smiled.

"Uh, right." I said watching her just relax in the chair. She seemed to have no worries to vex her slackened face, just a curiosity about the future. I envied her peaceful acceptance. But what was I going to do? There was no page in the training manual, nor a memo on company policy for this situation. For once, I was alone to make a unique decision, and I didn't want to do it.

"Look, whatever you are." She said, as if sensing my bafflement. "The world is shot to Hell, and everyone who cuts through that alley wants to burn me. Those things keep me from being institutionalized, and euthanized. I don't have the graft to fight that in court if I did go to some, so-called, Safe Home. Here, nobody in an office gives a damn about me. The things only mulch the creeps that try something."

"They don't get hungry in the meantime?" I asked.

"There is hardly ever a meantime." She said dryly.

"Uh, don't the deaths bother you?" I felt queasy. It was the side effects of the drugs, I told myself.

"Well, they did jostle my sensibilities a bit, at first. But we all have to adapt to survive, now don't we?" She said smiling. "I stopped losing too much sleep once I became used to the screaming."

I stayed quiet. I wanted to leave, but only after I resolved this in my swirling head. She had forged an unspoken understanding with the monsters, the rulers of this new world. Between them, they formed the niche where both could survive together. And here I came, the young emissary of the old guard, the unwelcome judgment of the present.

"Look across the street," she said. "No one there has been chewed-up in all the time my things have been around. We coexist. Only creeps and other monsters do the screaming." She seemed to be soliciting my conclusion.

"Ah, I'll need to get my gun." I told her and saw her milky eyes draw a narrow stare at me. "I need it to turn in for insurance. They have us buy our own equipment."

"I'll have them bring it up." She said smiling again. "Would you like to stay for some cookies?"

"No." I said suddenly. She must be joking. "No, thank you. I have to get back to, uh, my job. Work."

"I understand." She said, and smiled wider. "Feel free to stop by after work. I don't get too many visitors through my front door."

"Right."

The van pulled away. Her house disappeared behind a thousand towers of glass and steel. I stand in the van while a mist of metallic lacquer heals the scratches in my suit. Coexistence. It was an interesting idea. It was locked in my head with that aged face and knowing smile. I hope it works. I had just bet mine and many other futures on it. We keep denying we are no longer masters of our world. But soon all of us will have to deal with the monsters in the dark. All of them. The hologram of my boss popped on inside the cab.

"What's up there?" he asks while looking at screens to his left side.

"Not much," I lie. "Just, stuff."

"World is falling into a pile of it." He says with certainty.

"Yeah?" I study his face. For the first time contempt isn't my only thought. "How's the wife?"

"Go to Hell." He answers blandly.

"Been there," I say. "There, and back."

"Huh. Day ain't over yet."

"No. Not yet. So, do you get out of the office much?"

"Like I'd ever want to!" the bubble barks.

"You should try it. It's a wild place out here. You might like what you find."

My boss stares at me suspiciously, but no insult gets spat before his hologram pops off. The van slows and descends. The doors slide open again.

OUT OF THE SUN

It was dead. The satellite up-link's screen displayed nothing but cold gray. Dr. Kimberly Vaughn moved her shielding hand. Intense sunlight reflected off the screen. Heat reflected off the sand, her head, and the dead rover. It was useless to know their exact point. This small spot on Sahara would be the universe until they fixed the vehicle. Sahara was an apt name for the hot world. The name originated from the largest, sandy desert on Earth. Now it branded an entire planet.

The sand pilling as a drift against the rover's sponsons built up urgency in Kim's mind. Matt, her assistant and occasional lover, failed to notice. Kim watched Matt look across the endless dunes to find--what? It was desert in all directions. It was a desert planet! And it was slowly burying them. Knowing the searing distance to the nearest, withering remnant of civilization would only inflame her anxiety. Kim imaged Matt saying that. If he did, for once he would be right.

She extended her hand to block the Saharan sun known off world by a dry, alphanumeric designation. Sahara had a similar mass and size to Venus, and thus similar gravity to Earth. The bright sunlight could fool a person to think it was as hot as Venus' molten surface, or the Sun itself. Sahara's sun seemed brighter than Sol, and more merciless to life unprepared for its endless desert. When it set, night here was a deep shock of opposing darkness. Away from the sole city and all light pollution, the night sky was an expanse of nebular waves, new constellations, and auroras of charged particles following Sahara's strong magnetic poles. Daytime was always bright, and hot.

Kim and Matt came to prove a lost ship of the Transcadian Corporation established a colony here. Even long dead, such a colony had legal ramifications in Federal court. However, it was of no interest to the scattered, desert populace. Their near ancestors were the only colonists that mattered to Saharan lore. More remote tribes began to doubt any human worlds existed beyond Sahara. Somehow, the notion grew, despite the dilapidated spaceport near the equator.

Matt looked like the stalwart adventurer from any time on most worlds. He was square jawed, with blue eyes staring purposefully from beneath the brim of his safari hat. Except, he was looking at nothing in no apparent direction, and doing nothing to fix the vehicle that was as important as water for long-term survival. Kim leaned beneath the rover's hood where their guide Ukud and his own helper Yozef probed the engine.

"Dr. Vaughn." Ukud began, struggling for restraint.

Ukud was always ingratiating. Although, his smile hung below other inscrutable and hard features. Hard, too, was his treatment of Yozef.

"I believe we can work best without you." Ukud continued. "Perhaps you would care to sift for some important stones in the sand."

"Let them handle it, Kim." Matt added, still looking to nowhere.

Kim was a lone woman among the small group. She had journeyed to a world dominated by testosterone, and right now, Matt offered little support.

"I'm sure Mr. Matt is quite right. Ukud is a very competent guide." The cultural attaché, Tariq Camus, spoke with seemingly genuine deference. Perhaps he was simply a more practiced liar. His need to mediate was a vestige from his formative years spent aboard an early colony ship. The few, conscious voyagers needed to be accommodating to each other, or be medicated, to endure the long journey. Camus kept wiping his forehead, though his perspiration evaporated nearly immediately in the heat leaving the salt.

"Doctor." Matt reminded Camus after he suddenly remembered his latest degree.

"Quite right. My apologies."

"My apologies as well," Ukud interjected. "The repairs will take longer. Yozef will set up shelter." A heavy slap to the back of the young man's head started him on the task.

"Did you feel that?" Matt said.

"What?" Kim asked. She stopped attempting to help Yozef after his meek protests.

"That breeze. It was cold. From between those dunes." Matt pointed, and then marched in the direction.

"Matt? Matt! You'll get lost!" Kim called after him.

"He cannot wander far." Ukud said. "Yozef will fetch him later."

"It will be night soon. Best prepare. In the morning, everything will be fine." Camus reassured.

Kim sat in the rover's cab in fatigue and disgust. Ukud and Camus exchanged furtive smiles. Yozef watched Matt's path with mounting dread. A low rasp from Ukud compelled Yozef to continue working.

Ancient Egyptians explained stars as holes in the curtain of night. Darkness was a façade. The true sky existed beyond the veil. Matt stood in the rush of cold air that seemed to be coming through the hot sand as light would through a punctured curtain. If the cold air rippling over him was real, it must be coming from a deep, sheltered place, such as a cave. A cave might allow access to Sahara's subsurface water. An initial colony would like such a location. So, perhaps this dune was a protective façade, a hologram. Matt wondered if the truth he sought lay beyond it.

Matt walked forwards, following the sensation over his skin and not his eyes. He opened them after colliding with a stone door. The breeze whistled through seems in the jeweled archway from a chamber beyond. Matt wondered if heat prostration was now causing delusions. Matt's mind became a tempest of questions. Could this be something the lost Transcadian colony built? If so, why would humans struggling to survive on an alien world, as yet without a terraformed and breathable atmosphere, spend time building weird, stone structures? They wouldn't. He ran his fingers over the decorative line work. Was it some unknown writing? Matt thought of Kim. She could translate anything. He needed her, now.

A clicking sound echoed. Matt turned to see a scorpion approaching. It was a very strange scorpion, and not one Ukud had described. It quickly crawled over the dune in the evening light. Was this also an illusion, or undiscovered, alien life? If it was real, it was larger than he was. Gigantic. It must be some trick of perspective. Nevertheless, Matt pressed against the stone portal as the creature neared. The door probably had not opened for millennia. It did not open for him, now. As the scorpion drew close, Matt could see each burnished segment bore the same densely swirling patterns as the archway. The tail and claws of the beast rose high. It was no trick of perspective. The monster was huge.

"They eat your flesh." Ukud said like a knife slash. "The sand spiders. They tranquilize your skin while you sleep so you will not bother their banquet. You would not want to find shards of your phantom colony, but lose your face. Wear the netting. It will give you a chance to awaken as they bite through it to reach your face." Darkness seemed to remove the veil of politeness from Ukud's face. His warnings to Camus and Kim seemed spoken with more contempt than concern.

"They're not really spiders." Kim muttered to herself.

"They're not even aboriginal." Camus added. "They came with the colonists. The species originated in Earth's deserts. Worse than rats. No one knows if releasing them was intentional."

Kim looked over at Ukud. She wondered if one of his ancestors tossed the flesh-eaters onto this planet to have a reason to sell netting to off-world visitors. Still, they needed him to survive. The idea of being stuck on this world seemed a death sentence for anyone who didn't conform to the now indigenous culture. Kim knew she could never do that.

"We will go find your partner, Dr. Vaughn." Ukud said. Another slap to Yozef's head started their hike.

Kim watched them appear to shrink towards the horizon. Only the stars and gravity betrayed the separation between the expanses of sand and darkening sky. She closed her eyes and fell into greater darkness.

Yozef stumbled ahead. Ukud's constant shoves made gripping the ancient rifle difficult. It was more a ceremonial piece than a survival necessity. Most life relocated to Sahara was small enough to crush underfoot. All indigenous life that survived the terraform was too small to see with the eyes. At least all life the sparse, nomadic population knew about. Yozef was from the single, spaceport city maintained by the freight conglomerates. More austere Saharans lived as nomads. Their people came here to practice a culture that was dying on Earth and other worlds. It was a harsh life, and the only one people like Ukud ever knew. They didn't wish to change it, and there was no one across a whole world that could make them change. Yozef thought it was an odd turn of history to see a culture look backward when that view was only possible from the advances of science. Still, Yozef wanted to learn desert survival in case the tenuous colonial connections broke. He certainly could not afford passage off Sahara. Ukud said he would teach him. However, Yozef now wondered if Ukud only wanted a thrall below him in the tribal order. Yozef had hoped to see the celebrations when the tribes united on rare occasions. Now he just wanted a way back home.

Yozef was never superstitious. Still, he had no way to explain the certainty of doom that clung to this place. He was certain Matt was another of its victims. Now they all would die for greed. Both men felt a cool breeze. Ukud shoved Yozef forward. This time he refused to move. He turned in defiance and faced Ukud.

"No." Yozef said.

Ukud bared his teeth and drew his curved dagger.

"No farther." Yozef added. He thought to use the rifle, but faltered.

Ukud spat and pushed Yozef into the dune. Yozef aimed the gun at Ukud, but faltered one last time. The rifle flew from Yozef's hands as Ukud knocked it aside. It was better if Ukud was his doom, Yozef thought. He lost that certainty as the curved blade opened his skin. Ukud's first slash assured Yozef would never scream. The following cuts crisscrossed Yozef's body in deep and savage patterns.

Kim awoke in the morning. Her face was intact. Kim saw Ukud through the netting that still wrapped her. Ukud sat calmly beneath the shelter Yozef had erected yesterday. Ukud drank slowly from an old, metal cylinder. The battered rifle was now propped ominously at his side. Kim removed herself from the sleeping bag, netting, and the slumbering Camus who had rolled beside her.

"Matt?" she called.

"He has gone out again," Ukud said. "He knows the way now. You will join him." The last phrase sounded like an order.

"What about--?" Kim began.

"He has found something interesting. Something that will make you rich."

"We aren't here for wealth, Mr. Ukud." Kim retorted. "Where's Yozef?"

"Close. There is no reason to be troubled. Today you will work." Ukud's tone was closer to how he spoke to Yozef. Suddenly, Ukud's eyes grew wide at something behind Kim. He stood quickly.

Kim heard a clicking noise and turned. Camus seemed to explode from his bedding as Matt walked into the camp. Matt's

48

face seemed glazed and his stride awkward. A cool breeze blew passed him.

"Matt! Where the Hell have you--"

"Uh, he is tired." Camus interrupted Kim while quickly walking to Matt. His naked feet burned over the already hot sand.

Camus and Ukud approached Matt cautiously, as if expecting a great revelation. Matt looked hard at the two men as if judging them. Camus and Ukud led him to the shelter with effort.

"He has worked through the night." Camus furthered after a harsh glance from Ukud. He led Kim away from Matt. The tremor in Camus' voice betrayed his surprise to see Matt alive.

"Get water!" Kim pulled her arm free from Camus.

Kim freed herself from Camus again, now with open animosity. Camus fell to the sand. The contents of the small, shaded table snared Kim's attention. The sat-link; survey scanners; old-school, handwritten logbooks of personal and professional notes lay strewn over it. She had left it all in backpacks in the rover's cab.

"Why was this tossed here?" Kim demanded. "Matt?"

"We needed to—well, Doctor—" Camus halted his sentence while recovering himself. Even standing, he lost his gift for explanations as Kim glared at him.

"You non-Saharan's will pay a great deal for our world's secrets." Ukud bumped Camus aside. "Camus promises me there is a market for Saharan relics. A black market, but a wealthy market. We true Saharans are here to preserve our culture, to live, not to wallow in the rubble of the dead."

"What?" Kim's anger evaporated from more intense shock. "You mean artifacts from the first colony?"

"No." Ukud shrugged and sneered. "From the dead culture before them."

"Alien?" Kim shrieked.

"Perhaps." Ukud frowned with disgust. "But dead. If you fools off Sahara want it, I will sell it. So long as you stay silent on where it comes from. It is my monopoly. And I will do anything to preserve it."

Ukud glared intensely at Kim. Kim was lost in the concept of an alien culture.

"Camus has the off-world contacts." Ukud continued. "You will find what we need. At least until your ransom is paid."

"Ransom?" Kim barked. "Camus!"

"The ransom is how I convinced Ukud to bring us here." Camus almost knelt before Kim. "He is very shrewd about risk venture. You see, the Saharan's believe this place is cursed. Many have disappeared here seeking arcane knowledge or treasure. The only reason anyone remembers the region is to shun it. But you are not superstitious. Fear won't stop you. No other competing archaeologists know of this place. This is actually an opportunity!" Camus ended with a joyful smile.

"Many robbers' bones—human bones—litter the borders of this place." Ukud said collecting his rifle. "If you work hard, you will not add to them."

"These are scientists--" Camus started.

"It does not matter!" Ukud spat. "We are robbers. So are you, now." He motioned the rifle barrel at Kim. "And it is time to work."

"Forget it!" Kim shrieked. "Get that rover fixed! We're-"

Ukud gave an unintelligible bark of anger and raised his fist at Kim, but the will to deliver the blow was severed. Kim glimpsed a huge, scissor-like claw flash in the light before the spurt of blood hit her face. Ukud's head hit the sand with a thud. The rest of his body fell to its knees with the fist still raised. The rifle dropped to the sand. Ukud's face was locked in surprise as dark purple flowed below it like water from a cracked gourd. Blood saturated the dry amber ground a moment before the desert breeze blew sand into the invading pool. It quickly sank.

Camus screamed. He screamed louder as he looked at Matt standing behind Ukud's body. Kim cleared her eyes, and then bolted from the pieces of Ukud. Matt turned to Camus. Camus violently flailed in the sand, attempting to gain his stride. His eyes grew even wider as if something far more frightening than a novice archaeologist approached him. Camus ran. Curtains of rippling heat seemed to sap the intensity of his screams as he fled. Matt pursued, followed by a clicking noise across the desert. His form flickered between man and giant scorpion in the ripples of heat.

Camus' screams waned to a low, gasping whine. He tripped over a shredded human leg. Yozef's body lay splayed on the slope of a dune. A grisly red jigsaw had spilled from below his ribcage. Sand spiders swarmed all sides of the body. The thick, segmented creatures on the corpse appeared to move as a series of ravaging, chitinous pistons. Other sand spiders climbed onto Camus. He found his lungs again, and screamed. He rolled from the horrific feast. The giant scorpion loomed over him. Camus kicked himself away while pulling the smaller monsters off his skin. The end spine of the scorpion's tail struck through his torso and spared him further bites.

Kim heard the new waves of screaming stop. She had reattached and initialized the rover's activation panel that Ukud had apparently torn out this morning. Still, the rover itself would not power up. Kim punched the dashboard. Its holographic interface and keypad were equally useless. Ukud was an expert saboteur. Kim frantically scrambled through the vehicle looking for some kind of weapon to use at the scorpion's inevitable return.

Clicking--!

Outside, it was already back. Kim slammed her door closed. Huge claws shattered and the left-side windows. The desert followed. The cab quickly filled with sand pouring through the holes. Kim dove from the rover. She ran hard through the mire of loosening sand. The desert itself sank. A funnel of churning grit carried her down. Kim closed her mouth and eyes before she was completely swallowed. There was pressure from all sides, darkness, and then cold.

The pressure ceased. Faint light met Kim's eyes as she carefully opened them. She pushed herself up and rose to her feet. Sand poured from her hair and clothes. It coated her skin with fine grains. She had rested on a long stone edged with a swirling pattern similar to ancient Earth's Nordic damascening if thrown into a storm. Jewels seemed to add punctuation. Kim cleared more sand from her face. She glanced around. Artifacts from human and perhaps other intelligent species spread before her. Cut amber rested on a small metal box with dials and plates inscribed in Hellenistic Greek.

"That's impossible." Kim muttered.

It was a historical exhibition arranged by an accidental curator. Kim stepped over the scattered remnants. Faint rainbows colored a chilled, stone wall. Hundreds of identical crystals sat recessed in an angled case. Light danced inside the crystals from facets somehow cut within the heavy, clear stones. Beyond them, clay tablets and chiseled stele lay carefully arranged into the distant shadows. Scrolls before them identified the collection for Kim. It was a library. Kim's heart raced. All these things were historic records. She was tantalized to the point of feeling a tingling across her skin. Kim wondered what people, or what form of life the records might reveal. She wondered what other, more exotic knowledge she could learn from it all.

The scorpion stood behind her. She turned to scramble over the crystals. Matt now smiled at her.

"You can read. Solve. Translate?" He--or it--asked in a strange, inhuman accent.

"Yes." Kim answered.

"I am too effective at one thing. Yet, I was built to be more than a guardian. I have killed so many who tried to slay me, those seeking plunder, that it has become all I am. Help me relearn all that I was. I will provide all you will ever want." It paused, and then added the deciding factor. "Either way, you cannot leave. That, I cannot change."

Kim paused. She glanced across the library. She glanced at Matt. She glanced at the scorpion. She glanced back at the tantalizing library. She drew a deep breath.

Kim steered the rover inside the massive archway, now plainly visible. The guardian scorpion pushed from behind. Kim traded one impressment for another. It was a matter of survival. This one at least held hope. As long as Kim helped the guardian, she would stay alive. Kim could establish the pace of its reeducation, and might even learn how to reprogram it. Alternatively, once they spoke a truly common language she might convince it to free her. And perhaps Matt, also. That was, if he still existed as a separate entity somewhere in the caves. Until then, it could manifest Matt's body, and perhaps his memories of what he was good at, physically. A cool breeze wiggled odd leaves on a tree similar to Earth's gingko as they passed the arboreal chamber. Whatever the future, she was glad to be alive, and finally out of the sun.

UNUSUALLY COLD

The thief felt the night wind across his back. The air was unusually cold for Summer. He suppressed a shudder, and carefully lowered the window frame. His foray into suburban burglary was a professional disappointment, all except for electronics. One last house, then home. He prowled in the dark. He froze when sensing sudden sound and motion. He turned. The heavy curtains billowed from a gust of wind behind him. The lack of constant city noise made him nervous. Out here, every sound seemed louder and at his back. He crept down the hall.

The curtains rustled again. Something heavy struck the floor beneath them, followed by sounds like heavy paws on carpet. This house had no signs of a guard dog. His heartbeat quickened. A sudden ringing drowned out the thief's pulse. An anniversary clock in a nook welcomed midnight. His satchel muffled the Westminster chimes. However, his heartbeat pounded on. Out in the room, more than wind rustled. He withdrew a long, thick screwdriver from his satchel. Quiet. His heavy breathing eased against his mask. Then, heavier panting echoed through the hall.

Dog! No, two!

They appeared at the hall entrance looking straight at him. Just dogs, he assured himself. Yet, each stood half his own height. They seemed to carry their own moonlight around them. One shined silvery-gray. The other, larger one was solid black. An odd glow reflected as crescents across its shoulders. The gleam from their eyes made them appear to float before them. Irises of coalescing red and green stayed locked on the burglar. His breathing hammered his mask, hot and wet. The breath of the big dogs-- wolves?--seemed to synchronize with his own. Their pants and his heartbeat became synchronous and rhythmic. They moved closer.

The silvery beast had an almost human smile as it drew back its lips across long, glistening teeth. The thief wanted to run, but the rhythmic breathing and heartbeats held him in a throbbing grip. Sleek masses beneath shimmering fur held his stare. He felt somehow attracted to them. The argent one stopped only a few feet before him. Both he and it tensed. A low growl of encouragement from the black wolf broke hesitation. He swung the screwdriver down as the silvery beast struck his chest.

A sound like an animal cry ripped away sleep. Harry wondered if the coyotes nailed another poodle. He drifted back into dreaming. A heavy thud against the floor woke him again. Another thud echoed from the hallway. Harry bought a house out here for the quiet and low crime. Cursing the real estate agent, he grabbed his gold plated nine-iron. Slowly he crept to the bedroom door.

Wet snapping and cracking noises grew louder as Harry opened the door and turned on the lights. He wanted to shut them off, immediately. A silver wolf crouched in the middle of the hall. Three wounds wept dark stripes down its shoulder. It licked at them and turned to look at Harry with an almost apologetic gaze. The black wolf tore at a man's arm and shook free a large screwdriver. The man seemed to be trying to scream through a paralysis of terror. The black wolf stopped the man from ever screaming again with a snap of jaws over his neck. Blood flooded the hallway carpet. Harry reeled. Nausea overwhelmed him. He slipped on the blood flowing around his bare feet. The gold-plated nine iron fell as the black wolf pounced and bit into the back of his neck. Harry managed to scream loudly, for an instant.

Bright red assaulted haggard eyes. It resolved into 12:08 a.m. Arnold focused on the clock. A sudden shriek had awakened him. It sounded familiar, almost like Harry next door cheering a touchdown. This scream was no cheer. It stopped suddenly, as if snapped off. Arnold wondered if it was a shriek from a dream. He felt the cold across his back. The covers beside him lay pitched off the bed. His wife was missing.

"Cynthia?"

Where was she? Arnold wondered. Not in the bathroom. Arnold stumbled further through the darkened rooms. The light to the bathroom went on behind him.

"Cynthia? How did I miss you?" Arnold asked shielding his eyes from the light.

Cynthia seemed to ignore him. She patted water off her naked body splashed from the running faucet. Finally, she smiled at him while putting on her silk nightgown. A breeze blew down from the opened skylight and wafted her long, blonde hair. The air was unusually cold for Summer. It did not bother Cynthia. She walked to Arnold at the door and caressed his neck. The gentle stroke of her fingertips soon moved in concert with Arnold's pulse. She

54

pressed more firmly to feel the throb of the artery. The rhythm of the blood seemed to arouse her. The press of her wet body had the same effect on Arnold. Cynthia left, abruptly.

Arnold stood bewildered. His wife had grown distant. Cynthia's marital disenchantment coincided with this increasingly strange behavior at night. It started after encountering that strange man at the last party. Arnold remembered his fiery, black eyes and oddly elongated smile looking down at him. The man was unknown even to the new crowd their city friends were ingratiating themselves within. Arnold recalled his odd jealousy at the bond his wife formed so quickly with this tall, odd person of unknown origin. If Cynthia had learned anything about the stranger, she didn't share it with him. It was just the exotic cocktails, Arnold thought. He shut off the faucet, and followed Cynthia.

She had opened the bedroom windows and slipped into bed. Arnold suppressed a chill, and climbed under the thin blankets. The curtains rolled from a strong breeze. He froze. Moonlight illuminated Cynthia's nightgown as it fluttered on the dressing chair. Three dark-red blotches stained its back. Slowly, Arnold lifted the covers. Three small scars near Cynthia's spine were visible in the moonglow, as if someone had stabbed her with an awl. Arnold stared at them. He couldn't look away. He nearly cried out when Cynthia rolled over to him.

Cynthia pressed Arnold against the bed and ripped open his nightshirt. The sharp spike of fear and confusion through Arnold's chest gave way to the frenzied beating of his heart. He stayed frozen as Cynthia slid over him. Her fingers followed wherever his arteries throbbed. Cynthia's breathing matched the beating of Arnold's pulse. She kissed him hard. A taste entered his mouth, something acrid and familiar. Her caresses became harder. Her nails scraped deeply across his shoulders.

"Ow!" Arnold cried, and bolted up.

Arnold suddenly remembered the taste. He hadn't experienced it since he slipped on the ice last Winter and cut his mouth. It was blood! He spit and probed his mouth. There were no cuts or mouth sores. Where did the blood--?

Heat curled across Arnold's back. Gusts of it followed the heavy panting behind him. He turned, slowly. Cynthia looked back at him with glowing red-green eyes. She was naked, but covered with fur. Wolf's fur. Her lupine features seemed to smile at him with long rows of knife-edged teeth. She grabbed the shoulder of Arnold's torn nightshirt in her powerful jaws and pulled him back onto the bed. Cynthia released Arnold. His back bounced on the mattress. Arnold thrust his hand under the pillows to the hidden compartment in the headboard. His hand gripped the handle of the .38 special.

A breeze parted the curtains. Arnold caught a glimpse of a now familiar, tall man looking down at them with a strangely elongated smile. His fiery eyes glowed just as Cynthia's did now. He twirled a golden golf club in long, slender fingers. Cynthia darted her lupine head towards the man entering the room.

"Do it my love." The man urged. "I cannot always be the one. I've changed you. Taught you. Now show me all you are. Be my bride. Devour your pathetic, human husband."

Cynthia turned her focus back to Arnold. He tried to speak, but her jaws clamped over his neck. Arnold tightened his grip on the gun. Even with Cynthia's monstrous teeth tightening around his neck and threatening to pierce his skin, he could not shoot her. He had lived to please her. It wasn't just because of her beauty, but because he could never think of loving another woman. He would not kill her. If he was to die, then let Cynthia kill him. Even if a monster had changed her into this beast, she was still his wife and his only love. He couldn't live without her, anyway.

Cynthia released Arnold's neck as if sensing his thoughts like a heavy scent through the air. She moved off Arnold who saw the look of shock burn across the tall man's face. Arnold looked back over at Cynthia. She was her normal, beautiful and human self. She looked at Arnold with a sorrowful gaze. He wiped her saliva from his neck and smiled back at her. A roar of a massive, angry wolf split the peaceful moment. It tensed to leap at Arnold. This time his gun flew from under the pillows. Six shots ripped through the black wolf. The force of the bullets and shock of the blasts knocked it backwards. The beast hit the dresser and collapsed to the floor.

"Will that kill him?" Arnold asked. He met Cynthia's curious stare. They shrugged in unison.

"Sweetheart," Cynthia said. "I am so sorry. I just—I made a mistake. Many mistakes. But I could feel your love." Cynthia swooned.

"I—how many mistakes?" Arnold pitched his left eyebrow high. "Oh, Hell. Never mind. We'll make it better."

Cynthia caressed Arnold's brow. It relaxed as he smiled and became lost in her loving gaze.

The dark stranger gave a low, human grown. His right hand grabbed the nine iron. He used it to push himself up while shouting foreign expletives in an ancient accent.

"I'll reload!" Arnold dove for his nightstand.

However, his target never stood. Cynthia's showed her ease at transformation. She leapt at the stranger and changed in flight. On impact, her jaws finally worked as her tutor desired, but against his own throat. Her savagery made Arnold's gunshots look surgically precise. The stranger's ravaged body collapsed to the floor, again. Cynthia stopped and panted. Arnold panted, too. The tall man with the oddly elongated smile laid shot, nearly decapitated, and ripped open. His blood dripped from the drapes and dressers and flowed over their expensive bedroom carpeting. Silver werewolf and husband locked eyes again and shrugged in unison.

Arnold stood at the door, in fresh pajamas. He told both police officers he had heard nothing. He and his wife had been sleeping comfortably. He was shocked about the deaths next door. He had always thought this was a safe neighborhood. The police thanked him in perfunctory tones and left. He waited until all the flashing lights disappeared from his street. Then, he and Cynthia dragged the bulging and bloody grocery sacks outside. They would need to buy more reusable ones the next time they shopped. Cynthia assured him all the neighbors were indeed inside and asleep. Arnold just accepted the information and didn't ask what heightened senses Cynthia used to confirm they were safe to act.

"Do you think this will kill him?" Arnold asked as he lit the fire of piled kindling, trimmed branches, phonebooks, oily rags, and anything else flammable they could find to incinerate the body parts of the tall, dark, werewolf stranger.

"I think so." Cynthia answered as the flames raced through their makeshift pyre. "I mean, how could it not?"

"Yeah." Arnold said. "I mean he might be resurrected if this were some schlocky horror film. But this is real life."

"Uh, right." Cynthia said. She hugged Arnold's arm.

They sat in the swinging lounger and watched the flames rise. They were at peace with each other and, once again, deeply in love. Nothing felt odd to them. They were simply a husband and wife getting warm by the backyard fire pit in the dead of night while also ridding the world of a murderous menace that ate two people next door and tried to separate them forever. The smoke swirled on the Summer breeze that now steadily grew warmer.

AT PEACE

Craig Miller entered the old building. The whole place smelled like formaldehyde. Craig thought the reek fit the old community college labs. The college had grown, moved, and locked up this place years ago. Now, renewed funding allowed the school district to rent it for a high school advanced placement program. Craig was one of its students. He volunteered to help his science teacher, Mr. Alvarez, reopen the place. He just wished it didn't smell like one, giant specimen jar. Every surface reeked. Even the dust. Craig hoped it wasn't all toxic. Formaldehyde's formula popped into Craig's mind. $CH2O$. Systematic name 'methanal.' These were only a few of his many memorized facts and formulas. Mr. Alvarez went to find the fuse box. Craig took the case of CFL light bulbs and wandered the dusty, tiled halls.

Horror movie scenes played in Craig's mind as he slowly walked through the darkened halls and into a shrouded lab. Then he saw it looking at him. Craig's pulse increased. It stared out from a glass dome capped with dust on a counter. The dome's sides were clear. The eyes behind the glass stared right at Craig. Beady eyes. A rat's eyes. Luckily, it was dead. Craig took a deep breath of relief and wished he hadn't after the smell and kicked up dust hit his sinuses. Craig peered closely at the specimen rat. It seemed to have a glint of life within the eyes, visible even in the shadowed lab. Craig put his case down and nervously moved even closer. The world seemed to explode into light.

Craig yipped like a poodle. Mr. Alvarez laughed as he flipped on the last light switches.

"Man, Craig! That was priceless."

"Thanks, Mr. A. I like heart attacks."

"Too young, too soon, my friend." Alvarez smiled. He pointed to the old light fixtures. "Replace as many bulbs with CFLs as you can. Do the reopened labs, first."

"Okay," Craig looked at the lights. Instead of a glass cap, each unit had a circular wire frame as if to trap the old incandescent bulbs inside. "Weird."

"This place is old." Alvarez said. "But we'll make it work. Can I trust you?"

Alvarez held up a set of keys to Craig. His honestly was why Alvarez had chosen him to help reopen the labs. Craig knew it and smiled. He took the keys. He would get to know these old labs and their secrets. He looked back at the rat. Even dead, it seemed to be studying him. Craig wondered what other weird stuff the cabinets held. Probably more dust. And bad smells. Maybe even some living rats.

The smell was still in the old labs the next day. Craig wondered if it would ever leave. Formaldehyde was a popular disinfectant and preservative, before its toxic effects were fully understood. Craig liked to think that science was always moving forward, but it sometimes seemed to make itself take a step backward. For the better, he knew. He peered down at the specimen rat. It still seemed to stare back at him with flat but knowing eyes. Craig wondered why someone would leave it sealed in this old place. He thought it might look cool in his own room. He shelved the thought and went to work. Mr. A. told Craig that he would only need some antihistamines to work in the reopened labs. However, Craig's mother insisted he wear a respirator and gloves after he had described the place to her. Craig tucked the gloves under his belt and the respirator hung around his neck. Technically, he was wearing them. He pushed a wide mop along the floors. He thought this was hardly a good use for his advanced placement intellect.

To make matters worse, Craig had loaned his earbuds to Janet Brooks in math class. The only noise to entertain him was the occasional squeak of the mop handle. After a circuit of the hall, Craig found himself back in the lab with the rat. He stopped. He wiped the dust from the glass dome with his gloves. He put them on, and lifted the dome from over the rat. It still stared back at him. Craig found it odd that the wire frame was outside the rat's body, as if it held the rat captive rather than support it. Craig flipped the tail. It moved easily, unlike a body part for a dried corpse. The lab was eerily silent. This rat was weird. Really weird. Craig fell deeper into his curiosity as if lost in a daze. A sudden voice knocked him awake. He hit the mop handle. It struck the tiled floor with a hard rap. Craig spun. A smiling man stood behind him.

"I say again, hello, young man!"

"Uh, hi." Craig squeaked over his pounding heart.

60

"You seem startled." The man said.

"Uh, yeah." Craig recovered the mop handle. He wondered if he would need it as a weapon.

"I'm Peter Dorral. Mr. Alvarez didn't tell you I was coming?"

"Uh, I guess it slipped his mind." Craig answered. "A lot of stuff does."

"Well, now. Ask him if he takes a statin." Dorral smiled. "He asked me to check out the place. I used to run this lab for the instructors. When it was a college." Dorral looked across the lab. His mind filled its emptiness with memories of students and colleagues.

Craig calmed down. He studied Dorral. There was an odd, flatness to his eyes. They seemed to be missing that sheen of tears that reflected light. Dorral's eyes appeared more like gray marbles set inside a wax sculpture. Craig guessed that was just another fact of being old. Really old. But Dorral seemed nice. Craig figured that when this guy worked here, he must have been at least as old as Mr. Alvarez is now. Mr. A. must be close to forty. And that's old, Craig thought. By now, this guy must be close to death. Craig hoped he didn't keel over while he was here. Craig had taken CPR certification as extra credit. But he didn't really want to use it on anything other than a rubbery dummy. Certainly not a man. A very old, old man.

"You've been busy!" Dorral broke both their reveries.

"Yeah, Mr. A, uh, Mr. Alvarez has a big list." Craig said. "Other kids were supposed to show up. But they bailed."

"But not you. Good work. Nice to see some work ethic out of the young. I'm not sure I had that when I was your age." Dorral looked at Craig with a grin and cocked his head. "That was about a thousand, ten-thousand years ago."

Craig smiled. He began to feel at ease with the stranger. After all, he hadn't blown up over the rat. Yet.

"Did they have the wheel back then?" Craig ventured a joke.

"Ha! Good one, kid. It was just out." Dorral chuckled. "I see you found Rex."

"Rex?"

"Yes." Dorral pointed at the rat. "Rex, as in king. Sort suggested by King Rat." Dorral looked at Craig but saw only a curious but lost expression on his young face. "The book. James Clavell?"

Craig gave a meek shrug.

"Kids. No sense of the classics. Even modern ones."

Dorral smiled. "That was true even when the wheel was new. Anyway, just be careful. Rex is about as old as this place. And you can guess that's old."

Craig thought of saying 'but not as old as you,' but in a moment of deference, he refrained.

"You, uh, worked here?" Craig asked. "As a teacher?"

"I only filled in for chem labs. I did all the work behind the scenes and graded lab reports. The instructors got all the glory."

"Old Rex there became our biology mascot. He originally belonged to a fascinating man. Dr. Leonard Carsters." Dorral looked to see any hint of name recognition in Craig, but he only shrugged again.

"Yep. Carsters." Dorral continued looking over the lab. "Controversial. Misunderstood. He had a career in academia, but like other forward thinkers, he hit barriers. But you would've liked him. He was a rebel. Kids still like to rebel, right?"

Craig nodded affirmation.

"He quit the ivory halls to teach in ones like these. He figured influencing young minds was as important as fighting entrenched thought."

"Is he still around?" Craig asked. He wondered if any other ancient ones would be joining them.

"Sorry to say, no. Heart attack. Kind of ironic." Dorral frowned and fell silent.

"Why?" Craig asked.

"Oh," Dorral paused. His ashen face flexed as he thought of his answer. "No reason. Today we know so much more about hearts, brains, and even rats." Dorral nodded towards the rat. "Don't let him bite you."

Craig did a half-spin to face Rex. He glanced back at Dorral who was smiling.

"I'll go see if I can kick on the air circulation." Dorral walked to the exit. "You'd like to filter some of this dust, right?"

"Yeah!" Craig nodded. That might mean less mopping.

Dorral left. Craig was alone again with Rex, the rat. He almost thought its eyes went from watching Dorral leave and focus back on him. Craig removed his gloves. He'd need his fingertips to start removing the wire frame.

62

"Uh, when are you going to be here, Mr. D?" Craig asked.

They both entered the parking lot. There was only one, old sedan. It was obviously Dorral's car. The bicycle was Craig's ride.

"You have the keys, Craig. I guess I'll get here only after you do." Dorral smiled. He turned and walked to his car.

Having the keys gave Craig a sense of security. He thought this old guy, Mr. D, was okay. Craig freed his bike and watched Dorral get in his car. He wondered if he should tell Mr. D about the rat. After Dorral had left the lab, Craig had carefully removed its wire frame. He had turned away from Rex to put the frame aside. When he turned back, the rat was gone. Rex had vanished like dust beneath a mop, but without even a fallen hair from its preserved body. It freaked out Craig even now. He felt bad over losing the lab's old mascot. He hoped Mr. D. wouldn't have some nostalgic crying jag over it. Rex was just a rat. A dead rat. A dead rat that disappeared as if it was still alive. Craig wondered if its limbs somehow had that same, weird animate quality in its eyes. To be dead, but move. A zombie. Craig began to think about Mr. D's flat, tearless eyes and ashen face. He pumped his bike pedals hard to get home fast.

The next day, Craig hurried to get the light bulb swap done while he still had some time alone. He had no way of explaining Rex's disappearance. He hid the wire frame and glass dome inside an empty file cabinet. Before Mr. D arrived, he hoped to unlock more doors, peer into old labs and offices, and maybe find Rex, the dead rat, partially chewed by a live one. And that rat would be dead from Rex's formaldehyde toxin. Maybe he could use it to replace Rex. That might work.

Craig now had a box full of old, incandescent bulbs to shove away. He tapped a cabinet door. It sounded empty. After fishing for the right key, he unlocked it. There was something inside. Old notebooks sat on the bottom shelf. He took them out. Rusting, binder rings had stained the pages. But the words were still legible. There was even a photo series on Rex when he was alive. In one photo, Rex clung to someone's arm who wore a lab coat. In the next photo, Rex was dead. In the following photo, Rex was alive again. Someone had made Rex a rat zombie. A typed note stuck to the last photo. Craig read that the subjects—he shivered that there was more than one—experienced a catatonic period similar to rigor mortis before mobility returned. A handwritten note read 'A coma for the dead?' Craig wondered if the immobility ever reoccurred. Maybe someone had later put Rex in that wire frame thinking it only a specimen. How many years had Rex stared out from under the glass until Craig freed him?

No way!

Craig thought he couldn't be reading this. But the penned and typed words confirmed that Carsters had made Rex a zombie rat. Now, that little zombie was now running free. Craig froze. He felt he was being watched.

"Hey, Craig!" Dorral's voice made Craig yip like a poodle.

Craig stood. His heart pounded again.

"Wow! That was some note you just hit. Must be scary reading. Can't be me, right?" Dorral smiled. "What did you find, there?"

Dorral looked at the notebooks. His smile ebbed. He seemed to know what Craig had been reading. Craig could see questions, concerns, and even fear light up Dorral's flat, grey eyes. A long, silent moment passed. Dorral broke the quiet.

"Wow. I didn't think any copies of Dr. Carsters' work survived."

"You know about this?" Craig asked.

"I was his lab rat. Um, assistant." Dorral said. "I helped him."

"Then you--you knew about Rex?"

"Well, it wasn't right, of course. But yes, we used animals back then. Now you can probably just write a computer model for tests. In the day, we were more direct. I'm sorry you had to see that, Craig. Obviously, things are better now. You okay?"

"Yeah." Craig drew a deep breath. "Yeah. I'm fine."

"Okay then." Dorral patted Craig on the shoulder. "Say, maybe we should put those notebooks back. We still have a lot of work to do. Right?"

"Right." Craig closed the notebook. "Yeah. Right."

The following day, Craig went right to the notebooks. They were gone. He wondered if Mr. D. still had an old set of keys. Maybe he had left an outer door open. Either way, Craig was glad he had snuck back and photographed all the pages with his mobile phone last night. Every bit of their data was now digital. No one could prevent it from going viral. The key to making zombies was only a few megabytes deep. And Craig owned it all. He hoped Mr. D would understand. Maybe now people didn't need to die or stay dead, not just rats. Craig remembered the horror film versions of zombies. He wondered if eating the living was something Carsters' test subjects ever did. He thought of Mr. D. and his ashen skin. How old would you be if you were older than forty when this lab was open, and you were still alive now? Craig thought the answer was: you'd be dead by now. And Mr. D. was not dead. Or maybe he was, just reanimated. Sort of like his Dad after a morning coffee. Craig wondered how far Carsters went in his experiments. Was Mr. D. a zombie? Would he eat Craig's brain? But he never tried, and he had plenty of opportunities. Maybe he just wasn't hungry. Craig wondered where his mop handle was. It was too late to find it.

"Hi, Craig!" Dorral said as he entered the lab. "You're early today."

"Uh, yeah." Craig closed the open cabinet.

Hours went by. Craig and Dorral waved when they crossed paths on individual jobs. Afterwards, they worked well together as a team restoring water and gas lines to the labs. Dorral was a kind and understanding teacher. Craig's concerns drifted from his mind. Then, as they were preparing to lock up, Dorral stunned Craig with a comment.

"I guess you're wondering why I took Carsters' notebooks."

Craig dropped his jaw but stayed quiet.

"I think you know." Dorral nodded slowly. "Just like you realize why Rex took off after you freed him."

Craig's heart began to beat hard, again.

"I was surprised to see Rex." Dorral said. "I guess he showed after I retired, had a coma fit, and someone wired him up. Weird, huh?"

Craig nodded.

"Don't worry, kid." Dorral gave Craig a gentle, understanding smile. "I am your friend. Really. I'd never let anything happen to you. It may sound a cliché, but young people like you are the future. You're smart. And you seem well raised."

Craig nodded.

"Do you, uh, do—" Craig felt his cracking voice lose volume, and then he lost the ability to form words.

"I don't eat brains, if you're curious." Dorral said. "I'm dead, so I don't need to eat anything. Just pump in some lubricants to keep everything moving, and I'm set for the day." Dorral flexed his arms. "You can't believe how much I save not buying groceries." Dorral gave Craig a wide smile.

Craig nodded. He swallowed and regained his voice.

"How did you die?"

"Heart attack. Right here." Dorral pointed at the floor. "It was after class. Only Carsters and I were here. It was a doozy. I was done for before you could dial nine, not all of nine-one-one. Don't smoke, by the way."

Craig's eyes locked on the floor. He nodded.

"I guess it was an act of curiosity as much as compassion when Carsters injected me with his formula." Dorral continued. "It worked. He was amazed. I was a bit perplexed."

"Did you see anything? When you died?" Craig asked. He and his own heart started to relax.

"I don't remember anything other than opening my eyes to see Carsters looking at me like I was either his newborn son or his means to stick it to his former colleagues."

"Did he?"

"He never got the chance." Dorral inhaled as if drawing a sigh of relief. "That's why it's ironic Carsters died of a heart attack. So did I. But no one was around to inject Carsters with his own formula. There was none of it left. He'd used it all on me, and he hadn't yet synthesized any more. I guess he waited too long to do both things." Dorral paused and lowered his head. "I blame myself for his death."

"Why?"

"I had asked him for time." Dorral looked plaintively at Craig. "I needed time to think. To adjust. And then, he was gone."

"But his notes!" Craig shouted, but stopped himself from revealing his digital copies.

"They can give clues as to how to recreate the formula. But Carsters was canny. He never fully revealed all his secrets. Not even to me." Dorral drew another deep breath. "I thought I had all the copies, until you found the early draft. I destroyed those, too. I don't think humanity is mature enough for everything it can do now. I don't know what would happen if death was less certain than taxes."

Craig paused. He drew his own deep breath. "I made copies."

Dorral paused. He sat against a lab table and massaged his forehead. "I see. Digital, no doubt."

"Yeah."

"What are you going to do with them?"

"I don't know."

"I'd like you to delete them. Destroy the drive they're on, too. I'll repay you."

"That's okay."

Dorral took a long look at Craig. "So, here you are. You have to make a huge decision without much life experience. I guess I have to appeal to your intellect, and any innate sense of ethics. I can't stop you from publishing Carsters' notes. But I would like you to think about the consequences if you do. Mostly, please think of me. I'm the only living example of his work. People will come looking for me."

"They don't have to know." Craig said. "I won't tell them!"

Dorral face took on that knowing smile. "People are smart. Even the evil and greedy ones. I don't know how the world keeps a balance between good and evil. Maybe we really don't. But they'll figure out who and what I am. I don't know if I even qualify for civil rights, anymore. No laws have ever dealt with the rights of the animate dead. And I'm too old to start protesting with signs again. Of course, it would be a demonstration of one."

Craig stared off in thought.

"I see you need a little more civics classes as well as the advanced math and science."

"No. I get it." Craig said.

"I'm glad." Dorral paused. He looked around the room, and slowly stood up from the lab table. "Well, there really isn't much for me to do. All the labs are up and running. Mr. Alvarez is going to come by and hook up the new computers and Wi-Fi."

Craig was confused, but nodded.

"I hope to see you again, Craig. As a friend."

Dorral extended his hand. Craig shook it. He felt Dorral's grip was firm but cold.

"Please consider what I said." Dorral said. He turned and left the lab.

A day passed. Craig and Mr. Alvarez took the Wi-Fi routers to the lab. Craig was hardly helpful. His mind was distracted by more than Alvarez understood. Alvarez sent Craig home believing his young mind and body were overworked. Yet there was a lot more for Craig to consider. He could change the world. He could destroy a friend. He wondered if one act would do both.

A day passed. Craig mounted his bike outside his high school and waited for the kids with cars to rocket out of the parking lot. He turned and was surprised to see Mr. Dorral approach him.

"Hi, Craig."

"Hi."

"I was curious." Dorral said. "Have you made a decision?"

"No." Craig dismounted his bike. He felt more adult with both feet on the ground. "It could help a lot. A lot of people, I think."

"Maybe." Dorral nodded. He looked to check that no one was within earshot. "It might change the world as we know it. Maybe into something good. Maybe not. Even the Earth consumes the land and renews it. Death is a part of ecology for a reason. I know that sounds odd, coming from me."

Craig nodded. He drew a deep breath. He looked at Dorral. He seemed more alive outside in natural light.

"Okay, Craig." Dorral looked to the side and slowly nodded. "I know it's probably too much to ask you not to publish those notes. They can set you up for your life even before your old enough to vote. Just get a good price."

Dorral turned to leave. Craig watched him take a few steps.

"I haven't decided!" Craig shouted.

Dorral walked back to Craig. "I know. And I trust you. But maybe it's time I went and found and ice floe, anyway."

"Ice floe?" Craig asked.

Dorral smiled. "Kids. No sense of the classics. Even the older ones. Take care, Craig."

Craig watched Dorral leave. He rode back home, slowly.

The coed screamed. Her blonde hair and other assets bounced as she ran. The zombies followed her into the warehouse. They shambled through every entrance and surrounded her. Grey and rotting hands grabbed at her limbs and clothes. She screamed and feebly attempted to push back the horde surrounding her. She fell at the center of the moving, dead mass. A sudden boom halted the coming carnage. Several shot gun blasts made the zombies flying puree. The hero continued to fire. He shot so many rounds that he paused to reload and restore an iota of plausibility. The zombies turned towards him with no sense of self-preservation. They advanced and the shotgun fired again, and again. Bits of gore and black blood flew liberally into the air as if pitched from buckets. The final zombic head exploded from a buckshot decapitation. The hero helped the coed to her feet. She was miraculously uninjured, other than the zombie teeth left in her scalp. She bit the hand that saved her. The hero screamed.

Craig ejected the old DVD from his laptop. He flipped the disk across his room. It hit a game cartridge that also promised "Guns Against The Dead!" His own encounter with a zombie was different. Mr. Dorral--Mr. D, had never tried to eat is brain, or infect him, or do anything else other than be nice and trust him. It was the trust that ate at Craig. He had a means to change the world. The photos of Carsters' notes could bring fame. They could bring fortune. They could also destroy an old man. Actually, a living dead man. A zombie. But a nice one. If Mr. D. survived the release of the notes, he could be like a strange uncle to Craig. However, this uncle's strangeness came from his odd existence, rather than how he behaved after too much holiday booze.

Craig sat and wondered about the future. Right now, he had homework. He had IMs and texts to answer. Maybe there were naked pictures of a young, female celebrity currently enjoying a scandal. None of it appealed to him. For the first time, he would neglect his homework and the other things that occupy a young man's mind. He simply sat in a dark room, and thought. The person he felt most comfortable talking with about this was the same person it could harm the most. Craig knew what Mr. D's answer would be. He didn't know his own. He sat and thought. Dawn and another day would come too soon.

The next day, Craig was stunned. He was getting tired of the sensation.

"I'm sorry Craig." Mr. Alvarez said. "I guess you two got close."

"Yeah. Sort of." Craig answered. He sat in the chair next to Mr. A's desk and tried to absorb what he'd just been told. Mr. D-- Mr. Dorral was dead.

"He died in his sleep." Alvarez said. "Peacefully."

Craig knew that was impossible, or so he thought.

"The body—?" Craig began.

"It's at the funeral home. Why?"

"How long?" Craig quivered.

"A while. So, why?" Alvarez eyed Craig with interest.

"Uh, I don't know." Craig slumped deeper into the chair. "It's just, just weird." And then probably not some coma fit like Rex suffered, he thought.

"I know. I'm still not used to death, myself." Alvarez offered. "I don't know if a person ever is. Would you like to go to the funeral? If you're folks think that's okay."

"Yeah." Craig said. "They will."

Craig's mother took him to the funeral. He wanted to see it all. The chapel service and the burial. Craig still didn't get how a zombie could die, not a zombie like Mr. D. Still, if anyone understood and could undo Carsters' formula, it would be Mr. D. The service had an open casket. Craig almost expected Mr. D. to open his eyes and wink at him. He suppressed a giddy laugh. At the graveside, Craig watched the same, closed casket lower into the ground. He suppressed a tear.

Another attendee was unseen by Craig. Rex felt an odd compulsion to travel to the cemetery. A rat was motivated by hunger, the urge to breed, and to fight or flee whatever tried to prevent either act. But those were the impulses of a living rat. Rex had been dead for a long time. He crouched beneath a car and wedged himself against a tire. The driver got into the car. Rex felt an impulse to run and escape, and a strangely equal sensation to stay and be crushed. He was uncertain which one to follow as the car started.

Craig read Mr. D's granite grave marker. It held the date of Peter Dorral's birth and the lie of his death. The dates spanned over seven decades. The phrase "Be at Peace" sat cut into the stone above them. It was meant as a wish for the dead. Craig realized it could also be a note for the living. And perhaps those in between. He made his decision. To be at peace with himself he would let another be left untouched. Quietly he withdrew his mobile phone and deleted all the photos of Carsters' notebook. If he ever saw Mr. D. again, it would be as his friend.

PUBLIC SERVICE

Cleanliness is next to affluence. Here, the white walls, floor, and ceiling are constantly cleaned. The cleaners are only seen by people who prowl the maintenance channels. Those unlucky few, like me. My ad and ID tells you I'm Joshua Grail. I've had other tags. The important part is my license to tag and kill monsters, and if I'm currently free for hire. The mall cleaners are always on. They're small, gliding disks emitting disinfectants, occasional bursts of gamma rays, and a pleasant, fresh scent. They kill stains and very small life. I kill bigger things. Things that make people disappear. And I typically leave a mess.

The modern opulence is sterility. Here, not even artificial plants violate the deliberate starkness. The only life is shoppers walking and floating between stores, and scurrying out of my way. This place indulges the new fad of actually traveling out to buy needless merchandise. So far, there are only a few places like this. However, monsters are everywhere. Hungry and powerful, they strike from shadow, oblivious to the pain they inflict. Only the vigilant survive, most of the time. Not so for some shoppers on level twelve. One victim was a politician's husband. So the bureaucracy hires me to find and kill the thing. I'm their revenge masquerading as public service. No mask could hide the obvious unease my presence creates. I am an unwelcome stranger in this sterile sanctuary. The bloody memories of yesterday stain my work clothes. The armored fabric doesn't completely conceal my weapons.

Most of the privileged shoppers and submissive storeowners hope I'll disappear like the monster if they avert their eyes and pretend to ignore me. They see little difference between me and the thing I'm hunting. Both of us are uncomfortable realities in this artificial world. At least I have a line of credit. More good news for them. My scans follow my quarry's path to the fire escape door mandated for public safety. It appears a monster has learned to work door locks. Bad news if I don't find it before lunchtime. Mine, not the monster's.

The door opens to solid black. A cone of torchlight reveals a flight of stairs. Something very heavy has left impressions in the landing. I emerge onto street level. Black yields slightly to shadows and yellow hues of aged street lamps. The coarse air vibrates with the noise of the global city, yet this block is desolate and eerily still. The monster may have driven off the local population, leading it to hunt upstairs. I stalk my target into an alley. Weapon's fire will not shatter the ominous still. The reptilian beast with dexterous claws and jagged teeth lies dead already.

A sudden presence meets the end of my gun barrel. The noise is only a man coughing. He's standing, but seems as devoid of life as the mall and this dim street.

"Kill me. I don't care," he says and coughs louder.

I become aware of others like him throughout the alley as my scanner dumps their locations into my brain faster than my natural senses. I lower my gun. The scan continues deeper into the man before me. Monsters take many forms. Like stains, some are very small.

"What's wrong with us?" A woman asks. She holds a small child balanced on her hip. Her eyes plead for an answer, even from a massive stranger dressed for violence. "It started about a week ago. Spread fast. I don't get it."

"You're all sick," I answer.

"Sick?" Many repeat the word like it's an unknown concept. It is, today. If you can access a medical kiosk and pay.

"You've been infected by a mutated segment of RNA, presumably from the monster. Its twisted biology probably created the same disease that eventually killed the rest of it." My answers only magnify the group's bewilderment. "Your own DNA is breaking down as your ribosomes unwittingly use the viroid in replication. Your genes are slowly being deleted. You're all dying."

The group stirred. They understood that concept, and most obviously didn't share the fatalism of the man next to me. It distracted them from wondering how a mere Monster Killer could interpret what his scanners recorded inside them, or why the settings would be set so deep.

"I'll get help. Wait here." I leave. Some will probably trust me and stay. The others will be too sick to move.

Monsters roam anywhere. Hunger breaches diverse forms of barriers and walls, so my Killer's access pass lets me into many restricted places. Deep inside a government tower, I walk a hallway nearly as wide as the mall. The photophores imbedded in all the surfaces are much older, making the light far dimmer. The sign proclaiming my destination is larger than the office itself. 'Health

Management Services' is chiseled from an imposing block of synthetic marble.

"You stumbled into a blank zone, Mr. Grail. Or do you prefer the street tag, Ice?" Director Schiff replies to my transmitted query as I enter and before I even speak. "It's marked uninhabitable, so it's been deleted from our service corridor."

The chromophores on her face broadcast colors like a diva's stage make up. Her hairstyle caps the display like an ancient helmet. She sits overstuffed in a uniform that fuses a doctor's coat and business suit. A cluttered blur of holographic citations and diplomas projects from the walls behind her.

"But there are people living there." I say. "I've spoken to them. They all need medical attention."

"People?" Schiff questions, and consults a projection. "They have no registration. No habitat. No means of revenue. In short, they don't exist."

"Is reality outside your service corridor, Schiff?" I have no chromophores, but my anger is obvious. "Those people are dying! The infectious agent may not stay in your blank zone."

"It is an unusual situation." Schiff shrugs, and her body threatens to burst from her uniform. "The plague will probably wipe itself out. Or we'll move when it affects a zone that warrants our intervention. One with tax payers, or under contract."

"That's what makes someone worth your time?" It became obvious more than her sterile desk separated us.

"We need to know that our services will have a return on expenditure," Schiff explained, calmly. "My office is a privatized contractor, Mr. Grail. We are alike. We both do a job for a fee. However, I buy the right to provide public service. And my shareholders expect a return on their investment. I do thank you for correcting the area's habitable status. I'm sure our affiliate agencies will do that as well."

Schiff smiles, and turns aside. Our meeting is over. I walk to the door. My frustration burns through.

"We differ in another way." I say. "My license gives me a lot of leverage. I guess killing monsters is more important a job than most. At least, today. I don't answer to shareholders, or almost anyone. I'll return for you later, Schiff. Be sure your own accounts are in order."

Schiff finally wears a concerned expression. Her chromophores dim.

I return to the alley. This time I'm armed with an old-fashioned inoculation gun. It's loaded with what I hope will rewrite these people back into existence. My medical expertise might reveal more about me than I want current reality to recall. I was a doctor once, when humanity ruled the world, not hungry freaks. Now, I stalk the shadows to elude the memory of my own failures. Perhaps those long buried monsters will come stalk me in my sleep. Yet, I have little choice if I want to remain human. The mother presents her little girl to be the first. Somehow, this woman slipped the effects of fertility inhibitors in the water and air. If I made the correct diagnosis this time, she will get to see her daughter live, at least a little longer.

Or not. I hear the whine of approaching turbines. Beams of white light lance by the alley entrance, and grow stronger. We rush to see the giant machine filling the street as it approaches. It's a huge version of the mall cleansers, a modern street sweeper. Our heartbeats match the vibration from scouring beams vibrating and irradiating the pavement and anything else before it. Civilization has decided to return. The real estate company's logo shines brightly on the huge machine's flanks. The technology of its automation and merciless function has changed, but the armored hull has lasted the ages. Even my weapons might not find a chink and stop it. All I can do is yell. Very loudly.

"Run!"

We all do. The corpse of the dead monster obliterates before the blast of the sweeper. The mechanical beast sucks up the fragmenting tissues into its blinding maw, then exhales sterile vapor through its grated top. I follow the last fleeing people. The sweeper detects our motion as it turns into the alley, and begins a deafening barrage of advertisements projected across its hull. But with no credit or ID signal, it won't stop.

"Please state price range!" echoes off dead walls.

The sweeper's sensors cannot hear my expletive reply. We run for a block and reach a street with working lights. Someone must be paying rent around here. The sweeper's lights flash in the distance behind us as it turns.

"What now?" the mother asks me while trying to quiet her crying child.

I hesitate to offer an answer. "I think there is a, well, a government office that could help." One without shareholders, I hope.

Members of the human caravan leave to disappear back into the shadows. Most of them make the pilgrimage from the desolate to the merely threatening. We ascend well worn granite steps outside the 'Office of Human Resources.' We enter through a hissing airlock. I did not expect to step out of it and into another world. Inside is a steep slope of equally worn steps. The noise from a thousand conversations breaks against our ears. We look across a vast beach made from multicolored, living sand. A small wave carried us inside, one of many to wash against this shore.

The smells of industry, food, and refuse drift up from a repopulated, ancient ruin. The new inhabitants pay no attention to the relics they surround. Only the latest immigrants notice the stalactites of dust and airborne sediment hanging from marble arcades high overhead. People flow or collect around the spiral columns supporting the inverted landscape. Human beings compose this sprawling, inner city, not structures. Thriving market places radiate out from two, tall doors before the actual office. This civilization is just the people waiting in the lobby.

"Here," I say to the mother. I drop a glistening capsule into her palm. "It's an infomere. It has games and an encyclopedia. I intended it for your daughter, but it looks like you'll need something to trade. Parcel it out."

"What about my daughter? See was born without a permit."

I draw a deep breath looking out across the lobby. "By the time you reach the office, she'll be tall enough so that no one will bother to ask questions."

I turn to leave. Some offer a fractured chorus of gratitude. Others question if thanking me is appropriate.

"I'm not finished, yet." I answer, and enter the airlock.

Schiff looked at me with surprise. Seeing someone over the same issue twice in one day was a complete unknown at her office. It has been a long day. It's time it was over.

Godforsaken, if anyone still prayed, that would be the word to describe where I've taken Schiff. The permanent darkness colors the air. Schiff nervously clings to a dying street lamp. The corroded metal stains her white coat.

"Monsters are everywhere." I tell Schiff, although the reality is suddenly quite clear to her. "They have many different forms. I used another kind of viroid to delete your files from this district's dataframe. You have no credit. No identity. Here, you don't exist. It won't be hard for you to re-establish yourself from a com-link uptown. All you have to do, is walk home."

The idea terrifies her. She tries to speak. Her face scowls, and then melts into a strangled plea. Her chromophores go as dark as the clouded sky. I enter the stairwell from the sidewalk. Behind me, the armored door slams shut. I, too, would walk through the darkness, but in another direction. Somewhere, hunger has penetrated again. There, too, the screams suddenly fall silent under the permanent shadows.

IMAGE OF VICTORY

Olive drab hung in front of the young Captain's eyes. The tent wall swayed from a gust outside. There was an intense storm of images within his mind. He was now a member of the Army's newest force that might be humanity's last hope. The briefing on the enemy was short, intense, and stunning. Still, he arranged his mental notes with disciplined precision. This was the first invasion inside the US since 1916. However, these marauders didn't run back across the border. They popped through a split in thin air to rip up a chunk of American heartland. A big chunk. It was bitten away by towering, carnivorous things that walked on their teeth and spat invisible acid from their eyes, or whatever those things were bobbing at the end of the dozen stalks on their cephalothorax. Standard warfare did not apply to these causality-violating aliens eating Kansas. This division's orders were to find tactics to kill and repel the invaders. It was so secret it had no name. The Captain did. It raised an eyebrow on the General's aide outside the command APC.

"Your name is really Captain Bobo?"

"Affirmative, Lieutenant. Problem?"

"No, sir."

The Lieutenant's tone was slightly flippant. He respected Bobo's rank, but gave a questioning gaze to the man. Bobo knew it was because his own time fighting the invaders was yet to come. So was the shock that awaited Bobo inside the armored vehicle.

"Be warned," the Lieutenant said. "He's just back from combat. Against the Creeps."

"Don't worry. I'm ready." Bobo said confidently.

"Right. For the Creeps, maybe."

The Lieutenant left as Bobo entered. The General stood looking over maps on monitors. He was a mud-spattered and bloody clown. Literally. Big, squeaky orange shoes and a red, light-up nose that flickered from overuse opposed his digitally rendered camouflage uniform. Bobo stared with shock at what looked like Patton in bright, comic face paint.

"Something funny, Captain?" The General growled and looked up.

"N-no, s-sir" Bobo slowed his words to suppress his laughter.

"Of course something is funny! Your CO is dressed like a clown. Don't lie, Bobo!"

"No—I mean, yes, yessir!" Bobo snapped to attention, hitting his head on the steel ceiling.

"Bobo. Hmm. I guess the name adds to your qualifications for this assignment." The General pursed his red painted lips.

"I'm ready, sir."

"No you're not. The General pointed his puffy, gloved hand at Bobo. "So shut up. Listen. We discovered this tactic when a Creep recon attacked a circus. Wasted the elephants and the crowd. But the clowns escaped. One was a former Ranger. She had a rifle in her trailer and killed a few aliens. It's the way to fight these freaks. Dress like a clown. Fight like a soldier."

"Understood, sir."

"Probably not. I sure as Hell don't get it. But this get up makes the aliens freeze. They hate clowns. And in close combat, we need the edge. Me, I'd love to nuke 'em. I'd blow up Kansas to kill them all. I'd rather blow up Wisconsin, but I don't get to choose. Problem is we can't get a missile, shell, tank round, or spitwad to hit their base. Their dimensional shunts redirect our salvos. Sometimes back at us. We need a new strategy. One that doesn't make me look like an ass. You like looking like an ass, Bobo?"

"No, sir!"

"Good! Or bad. Because you're going to. In make-up."

"Ass. Yes, sir."

"Watch your mouth."

"Sir, my briefing described the dimensional shunts the enemy—the Creeps use. They act like trans-temporal shields. But when they use them to redirect our fire, the ordinance reappears in a predictable timeframe and a rift occurs between their shields. We can fool them by positioning dummy assets for them to target with redirected fire. And then—"

"Then we use that time frame to deploy at the rift and pour through it to kill them. Kill them all!" The General yelled and his nose popped free and hit the screens. "Rifles, grenades, sidearms. The way God intended combat. Up close. Man to man. Or, man to alien."

"Clown to Creep, sir?"

"Shut up. But your plan is brilliant, Bobo. If it works, you're promoted. Now, get ready. Grab some make-up. Get a fright wig big enough to puff out of your helmet, but not fall into your field of vision. And floppy shoes. If you can, get the orange ones. Don't ask me why, but orange shoes stun them for a split-second more. And that's a half clip into the monster trying to fry you. I want you fully outfitted for this attack. Your attack."

"When is that, sir?"

"Now. Right the Hell, now."

Bobo didn't have much time to meet his own combat unit, but they were following him into history. He clutched his MK17 SCAR-H rifle in the back of the charging APC. Bobo's plan fooled the Creeps. Now mechanized armor thundered full throttle towards the opened rift. The Creeps would no doubt reinforce it with their own acid-spitting soldiers. It would be heavy combat, weirder than a Vegas naked magic and fish-juggling act seen on 'shrooms. But he was about to fight for his country, fight for Earth and all humanity. Even so, he hoped to God there would never be any photos of him in face paint with purple lips, blue fright wig, and huge, orange shoes. There was a bump, then a feeling like sudden frostbite. They were through the rift.

"All right!" Bobo yelled. "Noses on! Deploy!"

His unit's bulbous, plastic noses lit up. All the clown combat units sprang from their APCs and into an explosion of carnage. Rifle muzzles glowed red-hot. The world was a close quarter Grand Guignol of searing skin, spurting blood, blue grue, alien eyes, face paint flecks and the occasional burning fright wig arcing thru the air. Automatic weapons fire made a single deafening soundwave as alien blood splashed under bright, oversized shoes.

Traditionally, Victory is personified as a winged angel with her sword held high. For Bobo's battle, Victory wore a flashing red nose over purple lips and clutched a roaring assault rifle in puffy white gloves. Victory was a soldier willing to do anything to save his planet. Victory was named Captain Bobo.

IT'S A THEORY

The Interrogation Room's smell was that of a soggy cigarette butt left to dry on the side of a ditch. The deputies starred at the suspect with hate in their eyes. The handcuffs and chains were deliberately too tight, and nearly pulled the small, grimy man into a ball in his metal chair. Sherriff Billups sat across the table. His eyes held no sympathy. Neither did the return gaze of the suspect. Billups sat in front of a large window of one-way, mirrored glass. But no one was behind it. The only people in the building on this late night where in the regrettably scented room. That was just as planned by the Sherriff and his two deputies, but also by the man they thought they controlled.

"Fitz," said Billups.

"Pardon?" The suspect asked.

"The name on your shirt." Billups continued. "Fitz."

The suspect looked at the name stitched on his bloody shirt. "Oh, yes. Right. Tonight I'm Fitz."

"Fitz, what?" Deputy Parmenter asked.

Parmenter stood to the left of Sheriff Billups. Deputy Sorento positioned himself next to Fitz and readied to slap him if no answer came.

"Obviously this is not my shirt. Not that it matters." Fitz answered.

"Those boys mattered." Billups said. "They mattered a lot to me and everyone in town. And you killed them all."

"There were only five men, Sheriff." Fitz answered. "But I suppose it was a dent in your small county's already questionable gene pool."

Sorento raised his hand. A glance by Billups averted the blow.

"I know you killed them." Billups said. "I just want to know why."

Fitz smiled. Sheriff Billups was still fit but passed retirement age. His deputies, Parmenter and Sorento, were overdue for a chance at the top. Uncommon loyalty kept the three men close. Something else kept Billups on the job. Something more than local prestige and free coffee. Billups glared at Fitz but saw no sign of intimidation. He saw a man capable of calculation, manipulation, and despite a bony frame, bloody violence. What made Billups almost fear his chained prisoner was the stranger's look of complete calm. Fitz acted as if he knew something. His knowing gaze said he could use that something to expose or exploit them. Few men acted as if they were in control when chained and bent over in a small, fetid room with armed men. Billups needed to find out what secrets this man knew, and quickly.

"I didn't kill them." Fitz said, breaking their stare.

"That's their blood on your shirt, freak!" Sorento flipped the collar of Fitz's blood-flecked shirt.

"It is." Fitz replied. "Bodies tend to spurt with repeated blows."

Sorento slapped Fitz across his ear.

"Sorento!" Billups shouted. "Get a coffee."

"No. Don't order him out. Please." Fitz asked. "It will mean I have to spend more time here. I'd rather not."

"Son, you are never leaving this county." Billups answered. "Not until you go upstate. For execution."

"Really? You'd let me get plugged into the system?"

"Why wouldn't we?" Parmenter asked taking a step towards Fitz.

"You need something from me." Fitz smiled up at Parmenter, and then looked back at Billups. "Information. Otherwise you boys would shoot me trying to escape."

"We might do that anyway." Sorento added.

"Probably not. But I also hold on to the concept of hope." Fitz smiled towards Sorento. "You can, too. For a little while."

"Look, we know how this is going to end." Billups said. "It's a matter of sweat. And tears. Your tears, boy. So just tell me what I want. Either way you die, here. In my parish."

"And so will you." Fitz suddenly dropped his smile. "And soon."

Sorento slapped Fitz again, hard. Fitz took the blow without even a slight jerk of his head.

"Don't worry, deputy." Fitz said looking at Sorento's reflection in the window. "I won't leave you out."

Sorento drew his gun and raised it to pistol whip Fitz.

"Sorento!" Billups yelled again.

Sorrento slowly holstered his gun. "Let's just take him out back."

"No." Parmenter said. "Take him to where he killed our boys. Spence was my cousin!"

"Why don't you take me to Mulderhill road, near the tree stand?" Fitz added, and smiled again. The three men froze. "It's surprisingly close to the highway. There's a coffee shop en route."

"What the Hell do you know about--?" Sorento halted his speech.

"Actually, the question is: what do you know, deputy?" Fitz smiled even bigger. He looked over at Billups. "But, you, you're the Sherriff. I suppose it's really a question of why you never stopped it."

There was no reply. Only the sounds of deep breaths as the Sheriff and his men exchanged shocked glances.

"Okay, boss. We just got to kill him." Sorrento finally uttered.

"Wait." Billups raised his hand to Sorento and leaned over to Fitz. "How, boy? How do you know?"

"I know a lot of things," Fitz answered. "Through the years you gain experience, knowledge. You develop a sense for things. Bad things. I've been around a long time. And you, Sherriff Billups, Deputy Sorento, Deputy Parmenter, have been very bad."

Again, there was only silence and exchanged glances.

"But not as bad as your cousin, Spence, who you so gallantly wish to avenge." Fitz looked up at Parmenter. "No, he was far worse. Young girls. Boys. Folks of all types and ages, as long as they were from out of town. I guess you could say he was a real people person. A serial-killing freak. But I guess not so bad once you got to know him."

"Shut up!" Parmenter yelled. He sprinted to the bound Fitz and shook him at the shoulders. "You just shut up!"

"No! No!" Billups rose from his chair. "We need to know how he found out."

"Why?" Sorento asked. "Just kill him and it goes away!"

"Nothing just goes away now a days!" Billups barked at Sorento. "Maybe he posted this on the internet. Maybe he's looking to blackmail us. We need to know what he's done with the information. It could go viral and then we're all dead!"

"Wow," Fitz said calmly. "Look at the codger schooling the bucks on the modern world. I guess there's a reason you still have the big chair and these boys just race around your heels."

Sorento knocked Fitz over. He hit the floor on his right side with a thump of his chair, chains, and skull bone hitting linoleum.

"Sorento, damn it, knock it off!" Billups walked over to Fitz and looked down at him lying sideward and tightly bound. "Now you tell us what you know."

"It's a long story," Fitz answered.

Billups kneeled next to Fitz. "I am old. Patient. And one way or another I going to learn everything you found out. How you did it, and what you've done with it."

"You'll be happy to know, not much." Fitz shifted and rustled his chains. "I don't need to lift a finger. I just wait. And watch."

"Watch what?" Billups asked. He stood and motioned for his men to lift up Fitz. They reluctantly complied.

"Watch death happen." Fitz said as his head swung upright. "Awful death. Bodies being crushed. Limbs snapping."

"So you admit you killed them!" Parmenter yelled.

"No. I'm saying I saw it happen." Fitz sighed. "I can't look away, unfortunately. It's part of the curse."

"Curse?" Billups asked.

"Now this is getting crazy!" Sorento snapped and drew his gun again. "Let's pop him and go home!"

"Did you kiss your wife tonight, Sorento?" Fitz asked.

"You shut up, filth!" Sorento stuck the muzzle of his gun in Fitz's face, but Fitz kept staring directly at Sorento. "She's got nothing to do with this!"

"Good. Then she'll live to see morning."

"So will we, punk." Parmenter added.

"No." Fitz drew a deep, labored breath. "He's already coming."

"Who?" Billups asked and pushed Sorento's gun from Fitz's face.

"I'll call him Bert, so your men can follow along." Fitz answered.

"OK, boy. Who is Bert?" Billups leaned against the table.

"He, rather it, is the reason I'm barred from any lasting relationships. With people, at least." Fitz said. "Too bad, because I'm also a people person. Now I'm forced into solitude. Alone."

"Boo, hoo." Parmenter said with disgust.

"It's you I cry for." Fitz said.

"Oh? Why's that?" Sorento asked and flicked Fitz's reddened ear with his gun barrel.

"First," Fitz said, "because you are a stupid thug."

Sorento slapped Fitz with his empty hand and then punched him. Parmenter joined in before Billups pushed both of them back.

"Second," Fitz continued and spat blood on Sorento's shoes. "Because you are all going to be crushed like bugs."

Billups held his hands up to keep back both enraged deputies. "OK. Like bugs. Now, who is Bert, son? Is he your partner waiting in a truck outside town to give you a ride and take his cut?"

"Well," Fitz shuffled his body to find the most comfortable position chained to a cold metal chair. "I can't really describe him in terms of a 'who.' More in terms of a 'what.' Bert is a force. A spirit. Like a poltergeist."

"A what?" Parmenter asked.

"Poltergeist," Billups answered. "It's a ghost."

"Noisy ghost." Fitz added. "This one is violent. Against people. Sinners."

"Sinners?" Billups asked. His genuine tone surprised his deputies who looked at each other with concern. "Those boys—" Billups continued, but was cut off by Fitz.

"Men. They were men, Sheriff. The word 'boys' implies innocence. And they were far from innocent. Like you."

Billups was silent. Both deputies took deep breaths and grew uncomfortable as their boss considered their prisoner's words as more than a freak's ravings.

"Here's my idea," Parmenter began. "You fed them something. You drugged them. Then you took and ax and a hammer and went to work."

"Sick freak!" Sorento added.

"You meant to steal their wallets." Parmenter continued. "Their guns. The truck. But you spaced out yourself. Just sat there instead of running. And got caught. That's my theory. You did this. And we're going to hang you for it. Or just shoot you out back. Knees first."

"I'd prefer the hanging." Fitz said in a cheerful tone.

"Sick—" Sorento started.

"Freak," Fitz finished. "Yes. You're close to the truth, deputy."

"Is that a confession?" Parmenter asked.

"No," Fitz sighed. "I've already told you. Bert killed them. And he will kill you all. Soon."

"Don't try to get inside my head!" Parmenter leaned forward and put his face in front of Fitz's bloodied smile. "It's been tried. But I have lots of experience dealing with--"

"Murderers?" Fitz finished.

"Yes." Parmenter said. "Scum like you."

"Like yourself." Fitz added.

"No way I'm like you. No way I—"

"You're all like me." Fitz cut in. "Your cousin did the killing. You've been covering it up. Family ties. They make a tribe strong but also cause it to protect its sinners. And now you share that sin. You're all, what would the modern phrase be? Oh, yes. You're all accessories after the fact. Accessories to multiple murders. How many has he killed?"

All three glanced at each other and then looked away in shame.

"You should have stopped it." Fitz stared straight at Billups. "But none of you did. And more innocent people died. That's a lot of bloodshed, and bones hidden in shallow graves."

"He must've just found one over there," Sorento piped up. "Tripped over a bone, or—"

"Shut it! Shut up!" Both Billups and Parmenter yelled in unison at Sorento. He flinched with his gun still in hand.

"You can shout over the truth, gentlemen." Fitz said. "Silence the screams. You can never really silence the sins. They are always loud and clear within your mind."

Fitz no longer smiled but looked at the men just as a disappointed parent might regard wayward children.

"For an innocent guy, you sure sound like a killer." Parmenter said.

"I didn't say I was innocent." Fitz countered. "I was once a very evil man. I used my social skills to climb ladders and drop people from great heights. Eventually, those who could, cursed me. A real curse. A strong one. For a long time now, if I find people like myself I can never form lasting bonds with them. If I do, what I've called Bert arrives. You see, it isn't death I fear. Now I would welcome it. I fear being alone. And the torture, the vengeance, the curse is for me to find people, ingratiate myself to them, and then see them pulverized in front of me."

Fitz stopped and fixed his stare back on Billups as the Sherriff slumped back against the table. "Yes, that is what happened to those men. You see it!"

Billups looked away from Fitz and went back to his chair. Fitz smiled again as the two deputies looked at their boss and began to wonder how many loose ends they would need to tie up tonight.

"I'm drawn to evil," Fitz continued. "Evil is in all human hearts. But those that sense my evil and turn me away are spared. They save themselves, if unknowingly. And I am alone again. The wicked who give me their company are the ones Bert destroys. Crushes. Part of the curse is that I have a week stomach. Can't stand blood. And so Bert causes blood to be freed, like a tsunami. It's truly awful. I get sick just thinking about it."

"Sick. You're that, pal." Sorento said.

"So, what about now? You've been here a while. Where's Bert? He doesn't like jails?" Parmenter asked.

"He can go anywhere," Fitz answered. "He's here right now. That cold jolt. You'll feel it."

All three men exchanged glances. Their eyes grew wide as they each shuddered from sudden cold.

"Right," Fitz said. "That's him."

"Boss, you're not buying any of this, right?" A nervous Sorento asked Billups.

"I saw the bodies." Billups answered. "I was sure one man couldn't do that. Now I know there was another."

"But you don't think it was, well, what he said." Parmenter jabbed a finger into Fitz's shoulder.

"I saw the bodies." Billups continued. "Even two men—I don't know. I'm getting tired of all of this."

"Too bad that's too late." Fitz said. "But I understand regret. After a time I repented. I'm sorry for what I did. And yet I'm still cursed."

"Any way out of it?" Billups asked Fitz.

"I'm trying." Fitz looked at Billups with an understanding gaze. "I'm trying to gain favor with whatever can lift this torture."

"How?" Billups asked.

His men shifted their attention from Fitz to their boss as they struggled to grasp why Billups now seemed to seek guidance from the monster in chains.

"I began to use the curse to implement justice." Fitz explained. "Seeing evil was a skill I've always owned. Now I seek it and let Bert mete out punishment. I still must watch his actions. But in the end, evil is destroyed. Justice is visited upon those who escaped temporal law. Now isn't that something that any divinity could respect? If I use this curse to end evil on Earth, then maybe I can be a force of justice, and ultimately be forgiven and released. But, so far, it's just a theory."

Fitz lost himself for a moment in memories. A grin curled across his face while looking at Billups.

"It's not a very good theory," Billups sighed. "That smile shows me you've grown to like it."

Fitz paused. His broad grim became a wry smile.

"Now that is the first real blow you've landed, Sherriff." Fitz nodded in salute to Billups. "Congratulations. And, good bye."

Sorento gagged. He slapped his gun on the table and clawed with both hands at something unseen crushing his windpipe. His entire body shot up into the air and slammed into the room's upper corner. Bert began his work. Billups and Parmenter gawked at Sorento. The pressure kept constricting around his throat. His gagging suddenly stopped but his body began to spasm violently against the ceiling.

Parmenter looked at Fitz. Disbelief and shock flashed into rage. Parmenter drew his gun and fired two shots into Fitz who convulsed with each shot but remained alive and kept a calm expression as the bullets ripped through him. Parmenter screamed as he was hurled against the table. Billups bolted from his chair as his deputy rolled across the table's surface. Parmenter's body looked as if it was being crushed inside an avalanche of invisible, jagged rocks. What fell off the other side and splattered against the floor was more raw meat than man.

Billups turned for a moment to lock eyes with Fitz who looked up from eying his bullet wounds and shrugged. Billups shot into the air and slammed against the mirrored window. Bert pinned him against the glass like a body across a vertical coroner's table. Billups struggled to yell as the glass began to crack. The window shattered. Years of keeping fit tore away in seconds as his body flew into the next room inside a whirl of shards that spat out crimson ribbons. Sorento's body fell. Fitz blinked as blood spatter struck his face.

"Now, I really need a new set of clothes." Fitz groaned. "And a new set of friends. But mostly, I need to find the keys." He jerked the chair in short hops towards the indistinguishable remains of Sorrento or Parmenter. "Who said the life of a fiend was easy? I suppose I did. Once."

88

The man known this night as Fitz kept muttering to himself. The only replies came from the creak of his metal chair and the clink of chains dragged across aging linoleum. It would take him a long time to free himself. He had the time, and no one to interfere. Once again, he was completely alone.

WHAT REMAINS

Samuel Troy looked into the opened can of meat paste. He could eat it. More accurately, he could eat them. He would spit out the shards of bones and chunks of tough skin, but the nans in his system could neutralize the toxins and adjust the proteins. What was once a sentient person could fill his rumbling gut. The smell of processed Sevitt made him nauseous and broke his sickening deliberation. Troy dumped the remains of a farmer, or a scientist, or a physician into the sack below it. Such specialized individuals typically made up a colonial force. However, no spacefarer ever intended to suffer the fate waiting on CoOr Nome 27585.

Force was not an accurate word to describe the Sevitt colonists. Even Troy's current employers did not raise soldiers, but the Sevitt could have learned from the calculating human descendants that sent him here. The Voren were a civilization with dwindling reserves and an acute paranoia about losing control of technology. When they needed to immigrate to a potentially hostile world, they bought a living reconnaissance probe bred for endurance, survival, and aggression. Samuel Troy was a cheap and contained option sent to test the planet the Voren targeted as their new home.

Troy's mission had proved a prudent measure. He dubbed CoOr's aborigines the Canners after their main industry. Canner factories took a technological sprint after the peaceful Sevitt arrived with entreaties of beneficial coexistence. The Canners welcomed the alien émigrés. However, each culture saw the Sevitt's promise to end the Canners' famine in far different terms. Sevitt translators labored to interpret the multiple nuances of the Canner word for "welcome," and place it in context. But the Canners' primary goal is to satisfy hunger, quickly. Now the hulls of Sevitt colony ships served as converted, stench belching slaughterhouses for the bodies of the bewildered aliens that brought them. At least the Canners stopped eating each other. That was one small, moral victory for the missionary race dripping from the sack on Troy's floor.

Troy wondered how the Canners managed to digest an alien race without nans. Eating Sevitt should have killed them. Perhaps it still will. Just not quickly enough to aid his altered mission. He took his dagger and opened another can. The contents of this one slid out easily, and splattered against its compacted peers. It was beyond Troy how the Sevitt guerrillas were going to separate the remains. The Sevitt had not engaged in combat for several hundred years, and the raid against the stockyard had cost nearly as many Sevitt as the cans they stole. Still, they had some remnant of the carnivore spirit, and they wanted their dead back. Troy wanted the metal that entombed them.

Troy's hard landing had damaged his ship. Magnetic chambers still trapped their atomized stores. For food, Troy choked down the indigenous algal filth and moss. The nans converted it all into sludge his body could use as fuel, tissue, and sweat. Troy set the repair program to make the fabricators first priority. He needed specific tools more than appetizing food. He placed the last can into the slag chamber with two alloy nodes. The hatch slammed shut. Inside, the metal liquefied under the pressure. He started to assemble the waiting projectiles by hand. He needed to finish the weapon quickly. Time was disappearing as fast as the Sevitt hidden in the forest.

The Canners had nearly slaughtered all the Sevitt too terrified to run or fight. Naturally, the demand for fresh meat increased with the declining supply. Soon, the Canners would have a new source for their slaughterhouses: the Voren. Troy's nausea returned. The Voren were descended from humans. He wondered if the word 'descended' included bioengineering and grafted tech like his own. Still, Troy could still see a common ancestry even in their elongated features. Yet the Voren stood no better chance than the Sevitt on this savage world. And they were still on course for CoOr. Troy concluded their ship must be damaged. No one acknowledged his warnings. From orbit, CoOr was a beautiful, emerald world covered in mossy pastures and oases of trees. In one spreading stain lived a growing population of the ultimate butchers and flesh eaters.

Troy would need to warn the Voren directly on their arrival. Until then, he would do to the Canners what their factories did to the Sevitt. The rifle cooling in the fabricator was merely a tool to achieve a greater, more destructive end. Troy planned nothing less than the complete destruction of the Canners' butchering industry. Maybe they would start biting away at each other again. His own useless stores would finally serve a purpose. Once away from their power supply, the magnetic fields would weaken and the teeming

91

contents would release at once. The resulting, violent expansion should be just as effective as the explosives Troy used on other, less verdant worlds.

He could time the strike perfectly. The quivering crystal in his head ticked off the seconds directly into his brain. The explosions would wreak chaos among the Canners, and give him time to warn the Voren. Troy and the Sevitt survivors could then board the Voren ship and leave this cannibal's paradise.

However, Troy felt a tinge of regret with this calculated massacre. Denigrating his enemy was part of Troy's psychological conditioning. Yet the illusions were never as strong as he would like. At no time since his arrival had the Canners attempted to eat him. Instead, they asked him into their city with gifts. Gifts of carefully dismembered Sevitt, and a platter of vegetarian nightmares. As a sole entity, Troy was something unique. Perhaps he also lacked the fat to make his meat tasty. Still, Troy wondered if some part Canners' psyche sought kinship. Perhaps they were truly curious about the second alien species their brutal culture had encountered. If the Canners really did want to understand him, perhaps he should contact them before he started killing them.

Troy had fought on the wrong side before. He had always followed orders, regardless of bureaucratic or moral momentum. Now, he served as a private contractor. Now, he could think multilaterally. A thorough exchange of information could be worthwhile. But, what kind of information? Recipes for the bodies of pacifist races? The Canners demonstrated great adaptation. If these fast breeding monsters somehow ripped out the files for weapons and tech in his greydrive, they might spread their hunger beyond this moonless world. There was danger in whatever action he took. He had a duty to his employers who sped here, unaware of the horror in this false Eden. Several Canners would likely survive his strikes. With enough survivors, you can always rebuild a civilization. Troy had seen it done before. His own planet had made it a cyclical event.

Troy had marched across several planets where he had encountered various, distinct cultures. Nevertheless, the similarity of some simple customs always amazed him. There was a knock on his ship's hatch. His screen showed the lone Sevitt standing outside. The creature warily eyed the brush along the edge of the ship's impact crater. Of course, it actually had no eyes, but their

92

bluish flesh puckered around black orbs that always faced him. He preferred looking at them instead of the constantly flexing orifice that sensed every atom in the air. Sevitt heads reminded Troy of Earth's sea anemones without the tentacles, and with the addition of those obsidian orbs. Otherwise, the shape of Troy's allies was much like a kangaroo, except for the tail. It was more lobster-like and faced forward. Even in this gravity, the Sevitt could spring several meters when retreating. The messenger clutched half of a Canner's lower jaw. Its large bone and heavy teeth undoubtedly worked well to crack living skulls. The primitive weapon looked battered from use. Troy no doubt greeted the Sevitt equivalent of Achilles.

"Come on!" shrieked into Troy's ear. He also felt the vibrations across his body. The translator converted the low sonic component of Sevitt language into broken phrases. Troy did his best to interpret the corresponding scents they emitted. The Canners also had exceptional smell. Therefore, this Sevitt wisely restrained both its methods of expression.

"Plans. Fast! Fast!" The Sevitt hissed.

Troy darted into his ship to collect his new weapon. When he exited again, the Sevitt had advanced and raised his jawbone club. Four others appeared from the brush around the edges of the ship's crater. They were determined that Troy would go with them.

Sevitt within the brush screamed. Troy slid the magazine of miniature warheads into their launcher. Two Sevitt fled like manic rabbits. Their braver two comrades stayed, but quivered and twisted in fright, uncertain if they should also flee. The Sevitt Achilles turned to face the attacking Canners. A small group bounded with deliberate speed over the crater's edge and hurled razor edged disks at the Sevitt. They slashed Achilles, but the Sevitt warrior still charged. The two other Sevitt ran towards Achilles. They were swarmed by Canners that leapt from the brush.

A great nose like a rhino's horn projected from the Canners' armored skulls. Visible alveoli flailed inside huge nostrils. Below them, snake eyes as big as a python's head squinted with savage glee at the Sevitt. Wide, flexing mouths held rasping tongues sliding over tapered, slashing teeth and bone-breaking molars. Long, grasping arms shot from the heavy, ruddy bodies and ended in two talons. Two shorter arms branched from their double shoulders that clutched wide knives and cleavers.

93

Canners were swift and practiced butchers. Their blades slashed in unison. The two Sevitt appeared to explode into uniform chunks of meat and severed bone. Crude arrows shot from the left of the ship and struck the flanking Canners. Troy aimed his rifle. He could opt to do nothing. The Canners would probably invite him to join them. The Sevitt Achilles scored one well-placed blow, and then screamed. Heavy blades hacked away its arms. Troy felt instant, intense remorse. He opened fire. The Canners convulsed as explosions rippled across them. Their bodies spread into a pocked, dark field of bloody fragments across the crater's slope. Achilles was also gone.

The archers revealed themselves. One shot an arrow towards the setting suns. They fled back into the brush. Troy reloaded, and followed the arrow's path. There would be no going back to the Canners.

Troy pushed silently through the alien forest. The rough vegetation grew in angry tangles. There were old traces of animal trails beneath the dense brush. Nothing had walked over them in a very long time. Amongst the tall shoots and winding limbs, the Sevitt surrounded Troy. He made no aggressive moves. They turned their backs to him with their weapons facing outward. They were protecting him, at least in gesture. One Sevitt entered the ring of his people through the brush. His skin sagged. Grabbing sprigs pulled its folds.

"Your ship...functions?" The Sevitt asked.

"It was damaged on entry," Troy replied. "Otherwise I would have left after assessing the surface conflict. And aboriginal aptitudes."

"Repairs?" The Sevitt furthered.

"Underway. I have limited on board functions."

"Motors--thrust!" shrieked in Troy's ears from several Sevitt.

"I can execute a sub-orbital hop. But we couldn't--" A strong musk odor nearly suffocated Troy.

"Coordinates. Specific. Hop to...location?"

"I could perform a limited burn and controlled descent to a target area. Cor--"

Shrieks and a confusion of odors assailed Troy.

"Yes!" the Sevitt squealed. "Location. Specific."

Troy returned to his ship. The old Sevitt and two others joined him. He suppressed his unease at the odd creatures jammed with him in the ship's cramped interior. Troy diverted his computer's efforts into deciphering the pearl-like data node the Sevitt gave him. The Rosetta Program was the largest file on Troy's computer. It converted the configuration of Sevitt data into a visual context. It was no library record. The data was recently recorded. Somewhere the Sevitt must still have a power source and technology. The screen displayed an orbital view of the Canners' city. Graphics overlaid the image. New lanes and buildings stretched to enclose the Sevitt's former ships. They were also Troy's future targets. A red dot centered between the converted slaughterhouses.

"I won't sacrifice my ship as a missile. Nor will I commit a suicide raid. I'm--"

"Unnecessary." The Sevitt interrupted. "Your proposed bombs. Improvised. We will take them within our ships. You leave...back. We are willing to die to do this."

The clarity of the last Sevitt idea struck Troy. He would ask them how they learned of his plans later.

"Also unnecessary," Troy said. "No one needs to be a martyr. I'll take your volunteers back with me. Let's see if you grasp the concept of a commando raid."

The inculcation of combat technique into the Sevitt volunteers had taken precious time. Troy regretted the loss of Achilles, and hoped the volunteers would be as brave. Troy was uncertain how successful his tutelage had been. There was no time for analysis. He and his allies stripped almost everything out of his ship for more room and less mass. The improvised bombs would be the last things removed, and only at the target site.

Sevitt engineers waited to do that task. Troy's hastily trained commandos stood beside them. Each team brandished its new rifle, modified for Sevitt limbs. Troy entered the command. His ship roared upward. He hoped the descending engine's heat would scatter the Canners in panic. Yet, Troy had never seen a Canner in panic, even with arrows in its skin. Troy grasped at the ancient concept of luck. It would be over soon. It had to be. The Voren ship was near orbit above CoOr.

The Canners did scatter as Troy's ship dropped from the pale orange sky. Sevitt shrieked, and quickly freed the magnetic chambers from the bulkhead. The hatch popped open. The weird, blue people quickly hauled the deactivated cylinders outside as

Canner roars grew loader. Nearly all of them did their part. Two quivered and stayed in the ship. Razor-disks sank deeply into the one closest the hatch. It tumbled out. The furious reports of rifle fire surrounded the ship. Troy watched with pride as bloodied Sevitt hauled the canister bombs up the ramps and into the converted charnel plants that were once their homes. His communications screen suddenly flashed to life. The elongated face and silver eyes of a Voren man looked blankly at the startled Troy. Troy drew a breath to shout his long anticipated warning. The Voren spoke first.

"Your messages have been received, probe Samuel Troy. Our scans inform us that your ship's engines have thirty percent function, with forty-six percent fuel remaining. Fire the engines to achieve a sub-orbital arc. Your shielding will protect you from the electromagnetic pulse. The hemispheric leap will project you far outside the blast radius.

"Blast radius?" Troy shouted.

"Yes. CoOr Nome 27585 will be pacified within one hundred and forty six seconds."

Troy fell silent. He realized the Voren must have bought more than just his services from off world militaries, and were now preparing to launch those weapons on his location.

"My people can't get inside that soon!" Troy shouted. "And the Sevitt in hiding--"

"Samuel Troy, your actual people are seventy-four thousand, eight hundred and twenty-eight light years away."

"My people are my allies. You should have told me your plans! Why--!"

"There was no need. The course of action was obvious after receiving your first report. The missile is in the planet's atmosphere. Detonation will occur in ninety seven seconds. Leave now."

The screen went black.

Troy felt paralyzed. The Sevitt too frightened to join his people now slowly left the ship. Troy understood he did not want to be the only one of his kind left on this harsh world, however safe it would soon become. Bewildered Canners stared at the lone Sevitt as it calmly walked toward the bodies of its fallen brethren. The other Sevitt soldiers still fought inside the canneries. They were brave, and doomed. Troy lifted a cold, shaking hand and closed the hatch. The ship's computer read the telemetry sent from the Voren ship, and fired its engines.

Troy felt nothing until the momentary weightlessness at the top of his ship's arc. Heat from the thermonuclear blast momentarily seared away his emotions. Then the shockwave hit. Troy and his small craft shook violently. The shockwave passed, but Troy continued to shake. He was over seventy four thousand light years from anyone who could understand why the intensity of his rage grew as his alien allies became less than dust as radiation flared across his ship's hull.

When the blast site cooled, the Voren forgot Samuel Troy. He became an extraneous variable lost in the calculations to reshape their new world. They didn't scan to see if he made it through the radiation. Only his reconnaissance data was of any value. No monuments would be built for his sacrifice. No memorials made for his service. No data of him in machine code or RNA would need to exist. Their terraforming would commence without a backward glance. Or so they had planned. Samuel Troy had other intentions.

Troy had already accomplished the first step in his new mission. He had survived the explosion in an injured ship. He touched down far from the Voren and the blast site of their highly efficient and final solution to the Canner threat that also annihilated the Sevitt. Step two would take much longer. Troy set out with little resources. His main asset was a bitter desire for vengeance. It drove him through a four month trek across half the wild planet. At the edge of the Voren camp, step three and his entire mission was close to completion.

The Voren forgetting Samuel Troy was a fateful miscalculation. He entered their landed colony ship, undetected. Shortly, he solved the arming sequence of a second warhead. He imagined horrified Sevitt looking up from the Canners' city at his fleeing ship. They burned across his mind. He rested his hand on his makeshift detonation trigger. He imagined that after the ebb of the thermonuclear heat, two glassy craters would be all that remained as unnamed monuments to three sentient races, and one tired and angry man.

Troy flexed his hand over the trigger. He thought the Voren would appreciate his choice to enact vengeance, even if they didn't understand the motive. The bomb would be efficient and complete. Annihilation in seconds through the epic application of heat and force. Genocide, once more. The word cut through Troy's mind. Genocide. It was the act he was about to commit.

He paused.

Slowly, he released the trigger. He carefully detached it from the bomb. He then disarmed the bomb itself. He continued and disarmed all the Voren warheads. Afterwards, he sat on the cold metal floor. His mental images of the Sevitt came to the front of his mind. They were alien, and thus inscrutable. However, now the ones in his mind no longer showed an imposed human look of betrayal, but one of peace. Even though they were alien, some of their actions were clear. They had wished to liberate the Canners from hunger, and then their own people from a horrific fate. Troy could not imagine them squeezing the bomb's trigger. Death was not liberty.

Troy placed the trigger, minus a few key components, out in the open where it was sure to be found. The Voren would understand what it was. He hoped they understood what he had done. They and Troy shared an ancestry. Perhaps his actions would not all seem completely alien, or simply insane. He thought he would never know. He gathered his tools and a few others he liberated from Voren stores. There was a virgin planet to explore further. He would set foot into places no human of any kind had ever seen. He had the liberty to do that. A few Voren ventured to watch Troy as he walked among their domes and from their camp. They stayed silent. Troy had left all he had to say in the bomb bay. No one followed him into the wilderness. Once again, he was alone.

Several nights later, Troy enjoyed his nighttime ritual. The surrounding, smaller fires burned well. They would deter any predators from venturing too far up the ridge, at least for a few hours of night. Troy settled near the main fire. His eyes darted back down the ridge. Smaller fires approached. The height of the three torches told him what species neared his camp. Unless another tall, intelligent alien group had dropped from the sky. The fact they were not artificial lamps but poorly built torches told Troy why they came. He waited.

Three Voren entered his camp. They looked young. They seemed to wait for a signal from him. He motioned to clear space around the fire. They stuck their torches into the ground at the perimeter and walked to the fire. They sat, and instantly realized their knees were too close to the flames. After a graceless scrambled of elongated limbs, they sat farther back and looked over at Samuel Troy with returned calm. Their spoken syllables, unaltered by machines, sounded like notes from an oboe. Troy guessed it was from the Voren's very long larynx.

"Our efforts, on this world, are not as effective as calculated." Voren One said.

Voren Two, whom Troy guessed was female, immediately picked up Voren One's train of thought. "Our people will face greater hardships than was planned."

Voren Three, another male, continued. "We are not of this world."

"Neither are you." The train returned to Voren One.

"But you have survived," said Voren Two.

"We must survive." Voren Three added.

The Voren chorus paused. Troy stayed silent.

"Teach us." Voren One said.

"We wish to adapt." Two added.

"We must adapt!" Three said with emphasis.

It was the first sign of emotion Troy had seen from any Voren.

"All right." Troy said as he exhaled, slowly. "Start a fire. With no tech. No tools but what you see here." Troy pointed at a set of flinty stones. "Geology. The very first human tool was probably a rock. It's a good place to start."

"You already have fire." One said.

Voren Two put a stone on top of the largest piece of flint. Voren Three added another. Voren One placed a forth stone on the column. The short pile teetered and fell. Voren Two looked at Voren One. Her thin lips curled at the corners of her mouth and her sinus slits flared. Troy considered the expression one of reproach. Voren Three rolled his shoulders perhaps as a shrug. He quickly reassembled the column. All three returned their gaze to Troy.

To him their wide, triangular faces were strange, alien, and almost unreadable. Still, their large eyes held irises similar to Troy's own. Their narrow eyebrows rose as if asking for further direction. Troy nodded at his three, unexpected students. They nodded back. All four of them smiled as one group. That mannerism survived reengineered biology, and a vast separation in culture and space.

Troy's mind flashed through his life on this planet, and considered his life to come. Despite changes through time and experience, he knew humanity remained in both forms sitting at the fire. It, like the rocks, was something to build on.

THE LITTLE BEAR AND THE THREE LOCKS

The little bear found the trailer. It was new, but not strange. Now, more people lived where bears and other wild creatures roamed. His ursine claws easily peeled up the metal skin. Inside, there were three similar scents of the missing occupants. Three chairs sat around a table. There was nearly three of everything. Most of it did not taste good. But the kitchen had things that tasted just right. He found a soft, yellow substance rich in fat. It could help a young bear thrive in an uncertain and darkening world. The little bear ate it all.

His stomach full, he slept. Then the three Locks came home. Forest foraging was not a typical job for young women in the modern world. However, the world was no longer modern in many ways after the latest and deepest financial crash. The three Locks did what they could to survive. The oldest was Aurelia. Next was Argenta. The third was Copernica. Her sisters considered her the most foolish. Such is the fate of the youngest. Copernica screamed at the chaos inside their small but once orderly home. It woke the little bear.

"What happened?" yelled Argenta. "Were we robbed?"

"No!" A furious Aurelia answered. "It's an animal. A bear. It ate all our food and destroyed our wares. And it's still here!"

The three Locks stared at the black, furry thing looking back at them in the kitchen.

"What should we do?" Argenta asked. "It looks confused."

"We're making it afraid." Copernica said.

"Good!" Aurelia spat. "It's made me angry!"

"Me, too!" Argenta added. "We have traveled far to find some peace. And this little thing has wrecked it all!"

"But it's only an animal," Copernica said. "We can't blame it for acting naturally."

Her sisters, who glared with anger at the bear, turned their hateful stares at Copernica.

"I only mean that it didn't act out of malice." Copernica offered meekly.

"The effect is the same." Aurelia said. "Now we have a thing in our midst and no food in our stores. Two problems that weren't here when we left."

"But Aurelia, we are three and it is one." Argenta thrust a finger at the little bear. "We have overcome a lot. Surely we can beat this thing into running out the door."

The small, black bear grunted warily in reply.

"Oh, but look at it." Copernica said and stepped forward to the little bear. "It's rather cute. It can't be long out of the nest. Perhaps we can use it. Perhaps as a pet."

Her sisters' angry looks fixed again on Copernica. She grunted warily in reply.

"I only mean there may be a way to use this creature for good." Copernica knelt down and stroked the cringing beast. "It's soft. It hasn't bitten me. I think it likes being stroked."

"It certainly liked our food!" Argenta barked. "And all the butter, too! Butter isn't cheap. Nothing is anymore. And this beast ate it all. I'd like to kill it. For revenge if nothing more."

"Revenge is wrong! You both told me that." Copernica said. "It's only a lonely creature. It doesn't have sisters like us."

"It has a full belly, you foolish, little imp." Aurelia said.

"I'm not little anymore." Copernica countered.

"And once that thing grows, it can eat this trailer, not just the insides. We must act to save ourselves, now."

"I don't like the sound of that at all!" Copernica cried.

"You are right about one thing, little sis. It can be of use to us. Even after all it did all this." Aurelia said, coldly.

"Yes, there is a way to get back some of the goodness it stole." Argenta added. "Although it will be difficult. It has sharp claws and teeth."

Copernica shared a glance with the bear. Its eyes were black and glassy. Copernica's were lit with fear.

"Yes, but beyond the claws, beyond the teeth, there is a fat little roast we can cook and eat." Aurelia said, licking her lips. "Bring out the spices to seal in the taste. A fat little bear will be juicy. Bring out the spit. Light the fire with haste!"

"Run, little bear! Run!" Copernica pushed the bear. Her world became only one sight and only one sound. She heard young bear claws hewing scratches in the trailer floor over her sisters' painful glares that cut as sharply as bramble barbs.

"Get a mop to hold it, a knife to flay it!" Aurelia shouted, following the confused, small bear as it bounded.

"No! No! No!" Copernica cried.

"Shut up, sis!" Argenta spat. She dug through a drawer to find what Aurelia demanded.

"You cannot kill it!" Copernica wailed.

"If you keep this up, there's more room on the spit!" Aurelia screamed. "For a sister or a creature. Best shut it and help!"

Copernica drew her deepest breath, ever. Her sisters surprised her, and terribly so. The shock inside her cooled her breath to a frigid mist. Whatever words she could speak while frozen, she would never know. The cornered little bear gave out a terrified cry. The three locks held their collective six ears. The two sisters' aggression split into terror as the wall of the trailer shuddered and tore away. Massive claws entered. Then Aurelia's life was torn away. It was as if night had become a rippling thing that cut through their home and then the sister. Argenta raised the knife and screamed at the black mass. The blade did little good against the angry mother bear. Huge jaws clamped over Argenta's face. Her skull made an awful sound. The knife dropped without screams.

The little bear ran back to Copernica. She fell to it from shock and a need for compassion. Her sisters were gone, and the bear's mother roared again with anger. A giant wet nose smacked Copernica's face. A smaller snout seemed to plead with the giant in rage. The carnage stopped. The little bear stayed with Copernica. Its fur was warm, but black as the events of the night.

Morning came, and a new life dawned. Copernica watched the little bear run to its mother. The massive bear looked at the last Lock and grunted quite loud. The little bear yelped. They turned and walked deeper into the woods. Copernica looked at her shattered home with an empty larder. She turned and followed the bears. She was uncertain of the future, but alive and hungry. She was one of three again. A single, golden Lock, and two very black bears.

JULIET, BY ANY OTHER NAME

Spring came, and along with it a spider. Muted blue and steel gray painted her body. She worked at night to build her deadly architecture and collect its prizes. The web stretched from the eaves to the cement path below. It centered in front of Montgomery's window. As a young boy he loved insects and spiders, especially large ones like this spider. Less innocent now, he kept his window shut. However, he looked out at her each night at the center of her enormous, and to everyone else, invisible web.

The afternoon sun cast the shadow of the towering fir tree across the street, linking the empty house below it to Montgomery's home in a bridge of darkness. The neighborhood considered the property abandoned. One day a small storm of girls, seemingly all the same age, and their generously rounded mother moved in. Just as suddenly, it was quiet again.

"Renters," Montgomery's mother said it like a curse from behind the closed curtain. "How odd. No father! And all the girls look identical. Are they some kind of quads or sextuplets? Terence, did you hear if they were sextuplets?"

"No, Phyllis," the erect newspaper and gripping fingers answered. Montgomery watched it lower over the plaid shirt and reveal his father's bemused face. His eyes still seemed focused on the missing pages.

"And did you see their clothes?" Phyllis finally stepped from the edge of the window. "Those dresses were as dated as the station wagon. Station wagon, Terence!"

"Yes, Phyllis."

Montgomery kept quiet and sipped his soda. He was mowing the front lawn when the feminine invasion occurred. All the girls did look identical. All seemed a few years older than himself. One was slightly smaller than her sisters were, but just as shapely. She was the one who caught Montgomery's glances. When she stopped to look back, Montgomery decided he needed to turn the mower around and empty the catcher. The red had cleared from his cheeks. Now he rested and pondered the somewhat uncomfortable possibilities offered by the blonde hair and dark, very dark eyes now living across the street.

It was good that the girl arrived during Spring break. At least Montgomery avoided his friends pressuring him to 'do something' because she lived across the street from him. The goading would be especially intense if they shared at least once class. For Montgomery to see if the girl shared a similar interest in him would mean being bolder than jumping into an abandoned backyard and braving the tall grass. Although his curiosity was now greater than stealing glimpses at his father's hidden magazines, Montgomery did not feel that bold. Not yet.

Adolescent fear of embarrassment made life difficult for Montgomery. His father grew tired of his reluctance to perform his chores in the all important front yard. The mail he could fetch quickly. However, mowing the lawn meant exposure outside for long minutes. He caught glimpses of the focus of his distraught desires from behind his own curtains in his room. At night, light shone from the two floors of the sisters' rooms. He watched their lithe shadows move across the lowered blinds. The spider became a mere silhouette. It didn't matter what room held the smaller girl. The fantasies were all the same. Sometimes though, weird shapes slashed at his reveries like sickles darting before the lamps. Montgomery thought he might be confusing the spider's movements with the feminine shadows.

It was different in day, when the sun seemed trapped in golden hair. Montgomery had an eerie feeling the girl knew when he spied her. He did so only for a few seconds. He felt certain she turned to look straight back at him, even after he shrank below the window.

Night came again. This time the girls' rooms stayed dark. Light flickered around the edges of the hastily draped picture-frame window. Swift, violent motions cut the rays. A low screeching accompanied the weird action. Across the street, it all fed Phyllis' snooty disapprovals.

"What a time to do housework." Montgomery heard his mother say through the wall.

Even the spider withdrew from her web to the eaves. Montgomery crawled into bed, falling asleep to the sound.

Montgomery bolted awake. Early morning sunlight shined through the curtain seams. At first, he cursed waking too early. Then he remembered last night, and slowly approached his window. Spherical rainbows hung in dewdrops on the spider web. The girls' house was quiet. He looked to each window. Nothing--the big tree! Broad, gauzy tendrils rippled in the wind from its highest branches. The towering, upper half was wrapped like an evergreen mummy. Glistening sheets of silk arced in the breeze all the way down to the Bowen's house. A long arc broke away. It became nothing more than mist in the air. The tendrils from the high branches were no more. It was evaporating under the sun like the dew. Seconds of panic and awe held Montgomery.

"Dad!" he cried finally.

Montgomery shouted again. He met his father in the hall who pulled up his pajama bottoms in a groggy trot. Montgomery dashed to the front door and threw it open. Remnants of the gossamer still clung to branches.

"There!"

"Huh," his father muttered, relieved there was a good reason for his son's outcry, yet underwhelmed by its cause. "Must've been some damn parachutist get lost. Sheriff's probably on it."

"But it's evaporating!" Montgomery retorted.

"No," His father countered, and turned away. "Its scraps are just getting tossed by the wind."

"But--!"

"Son!"

Montgomery shut up and watched his father walk to the bathroom. To press further risked his allowance being cut off for good. Most of his friends had already suffered that fate. He looked through the plastic window of the screen door at the vanishing silk. Perhaps this would be an icebreaker with the blond girl. Now, even her backyard captured his fascination. Thinking of her, Montgomery stepped back and closed the door. Not yet.

Soon, another mystery captured the larger fascination of local gossip. The girls' mother seemed missing. Although, no one knew her well enough to inquire about her at the door. The girls were missing, too. Montgomery kept this to himself. Everyone else would notice soon enough. Weird thing was, he caught glimpses of the slightly smaller girl still haunting the house and his young man's fantasies.

Montgomery's fears about the results or failures of meeting her were impaled on the gaze of her very dark eyes. She stood in the center of the front lawn, circled by the concentric arcs of mown grass. Montgomery summoned the courage to shut off the mower and croak out a hello.

"Hello, back" she said.

Her accent was like her blue dress with gray flower pattern. It was familiar, but only from an imagined memory. Montgomery did not expect her to speak with one. A sudden, cool breeze fluttered lace trim against her knees. She moved closer to Montgomery at an angle between him and his front door. Montgomery held his position and grip on the mower.

"What is your name?" the girl asked cocking her head and smiling.

She held her dress at her sides with both hands slightly swaying. Montgomery remembered his much younger nieces doing the same thing when asked to speak to unfamiliar relatives. Perhaps she was nervous too. Maybe not. The ebony stare under the cocked eyebrows and curl of her lips into a piercing smile bound Montgomery in place.

"Uh...Montgomery." He suddenly remembered.

"Mont-gom-er-y" She repeated each syllable as if probing for a soft part. "Monty!" She shot at him with eyes wide open.

Montgomery resisted jumping back completely, but lost his sweaty grip on the mower's handle. He hated that nickname. His obvious distaste was visible on his face. Yet, he didn't want to blow this and end up looking like a chump. He became more afraid of one of his school pals appearing and shouting jeers than what he faced now. However, he wanted to get out of everyone's sight. Maybe he could get her to the side of the house.

"Yeah, I guess." He said, and lifted the catcher off the mower with one arm. "But, nobody calls me--"

"I like your pet," she said pointing to his window. The barely visible web gently wafted before it.

"Pet? Um..." Montgomery wondered how she could possibly know about the spider. This was as close to the house as she had ever been. Wasn't it?

"I see you looking out at her at night. Sometimes I only see your left eye peeking out. Peeking."

Montgomery's courage began to bleed away. He felt naked with all his secrets exposed. His face began to flush. He was sweaty. Naked. Exposed. The catcher became very heavy.

"I don't look at her every night." He said humbly, and somehow maintained eye contact with the penetrating dark eyes partially hidden behind wind tossed bangs of gold.

"Do you have a name for her?" She asked twisting her torso as if pulling a fishing line. "Monty?"

"Uh, yeah." Montgomery paused. He might as well tell her. She seemed to know everything, anyway. Suddenly he wanted to have that serious talk that his father offered two years ago.

"Juliet," he volunteered.

"Why?" She turned to look at the web.

Montgomery drew a deep breath. "Because she lies outside yonder window." He lowered his head and the catcher. "It's stupid."

"My name is Juliet." She said strangely, softly, and walked next to Montgomery and took his hand.

Montgomery found his hand guided toward the blue dress. He thought she was inviting him to make the first move. The sudden reality of her closeness overcame his fear. He rose to the occasion. His lips met hers in front of the entire world. Caress of lips grew to exploring each other's mouths. Her arms snaked out and grabbed Montgomery's with vices of five nails. There was a strange taste like medicine. His tongue became numb. And something else. Her teeth seemed to enlarge inside her mouth. Montgomery turned his face aside, but could not break free. His universe was two unblinking disks of black with no pupils. His heart raced for different reasons than seconds earlier. Freedom was the sound of his mother's voice.

"Dear?" Montgomery's mother continued. "I said dinner is almost ready. And who is your friend?"

Montgomery found himself free. She, Juliet, stood next to him smiling at his mother.

"Juliet," she answered over Montgomery's unintelligible, breathless mutter.

"How nice. Well, Juliet, how is your mother?" Montgomery's mother got straight to her inquires. "We haven't seen her out in some time."

"That would be four days." Juliet answered with certainty. "Our mother provided well. There was much to her. I am smaller than my sisters, though. I did not get as much as they did. I am still a little hungry."

"Oh, how unfortunate." Montgomery's mother offered. "Would you like to join us, dear?"

108

Jolts of fear and realization shot through Montgomery like something savage tugging his skin: the idea of sitting across the table from Juliet; his mother dropping innuendoes for the rest of his life about what she had just interrupted; about four days ago that silk enshrouded the fir tree.

"No. Thank you." Juliet answered.

Montgomery remembered not being able to move despite his mother's harsh gaze until Juliet was on her way across the street. He didn't remember emptying the catcher, nor dinner, nor going to bed. He regained full awareness when noticing the weak light on his ceiling reflected off his curtains. Dreadfully he pulled one back. The spider hung in her web. There was one room lit in the house across the street. The blind was up. Juliet stood centered in her window. She stared purposefully back at Montgomery. A strange, white texture coated the walls behind her. He dropped the curtain and stood, waiting for dawn.

Morning came. The sun lit everything, including the bodies wrapped in white shrouds that littered the bottom of Juliet the spider's web. Montgomery studied the desiccated corpses of moths, flies, and stranger victims outside his room. He remembered what the other Juliet had whispered before departing: I love you. The words scratched inside his brain like something scuttling across a chalkboard. He was certain this spider had loved these reluctant companions as well. She gave them a silk bed to die in as she ate them. Juliet was still a little hungry. Arousal. Montgomery remembered the sensation. Fear he remembered, too. Montgomery came to fear darkness most of all.

The next night Juliet was not in her room. Later, Montgomery heard something outside his window. His heart threatened to hammer itself from beneath his ribs. Slowly, he looked out. The spider worked to repair a large portion of its web. Something had torn away its symmetry. Afterward, even in the day, Montgomery felt a presence behind him, about to strike. Inexplicable arousal always flared with the fear. He shunned sleep and standing near shadows.

Montgomery forgot to get the mail. He had become derelict in most of his duties outside. It was getting dark. The mailbox was a few house-lengths down the street. He bolted back through the front door gasping for air, and not from his run. His sweaty hand slapped the mail into his father's chest. And then he had to mow the lawn.

Back and forth, he pushed the roaring mower across the rectangular yard. Perhaps he should have tried to explain to his father. He would still have to mow the lawn. Quickly, back and forth. Montgomery pushed through the wet grass. He trampled the clumps leaking from the overstuffed catcher. He stopped.

The tool shed blocked the weak moonlight from the lawn for several feet at its north wall. The shadow hung like a solid black pyramid thrown to its side. Fear and the strange arousal made Montgomery vibrate more than the mower's old gasoline engine. Something moved.

Images collided in Montgomery's brain: A mother spider injecting herself with her own venom; the spiderlings swarming her body to feast; the sated children sailing from the nest by catching the wind in broad strands of silk cast from their spinnerets; remnants of silk shrouding the fir tree; fantasies of Juliet; the bodies of bugs gathering below his window; the thing tensing in the shadows.

Montgomery drove the mower straight into the black. It hit something. The mower pitched up. A hideous shriek killed the din of the engine. The spinning blades choked and stopped. The night was silent, except for Montgomery's frantic panting. He fell into his house. Confusion and fear twisted his face. Without words, Terence followed his son back outside with the expensive flashlight used only for emergencies. Nostrils flooded with the scents of gasoline, cut grass, and something like crabmeat left out of the refrigerator. The intense, white beam cut into the black.

The lawn mower sat pitched atop the body of the giant spider. Dark blue fluid seeped into the lawn around its body. The same inky grume coated Montgomery's shoes. Irregular kidney shapes in juxtaposing shades of light gray colored the mutilated thing. The eyes and fangs lay mauled underneath the mower. Eight articulated spikes flanked the gas-powered killing machine. Each was nearly as long as Montgomery was tall. The left set of legs laid whipped back against each other. The other four on the right still seemed poised to jump. Translucent spines projected from the segments of each leg that ended in intricate masses of curving spines. Revulsion climaxed as the beam lit the smooth abdomen behind the mower.

110

Other than color, it appeared to be a massive oval of young, human skin.

Montgomery finally vomited. His father gently placed his hand on his back, while keeping the beam focused on the spider's body. After Montgomery could stand up, they covered the remains with a tarpaulin.

Early the next morning, Terence called the police and reported hearing screams and seeing a man with a possible gun around the house across the street. The family watched the heavily armed police enter the unlocked house. Even from a distance, their horrified expressions were visible when they exited. Montgomery and his father went to check their secret.

Wind had tossed the tarpaulin half off the body. The stench nearly overwhelmed them. The sun had burned away the dew, and done likewise to the exposed arachnid corpse. Terence looked at his Montgomery. He wondered if his act constituted murder. He resolved to protect his son. Montgomery at last had a partner in this incomprehensible horror. He followed his father's lead. They took the tarpaulin off the body, and lightly covered the rotting mass with lawn clippings. They went back inside.

Montgomery's mother was already talking with the police. Montgomery overheard the description of what lay in the house across the street through the coughs and cracking voice of a detective. At first, the interior looked like it hadn't been dusted in centuries. But the sticky cobwebs throughout the house began to disappear as each room was opened and lit. Stranger still was the once plump mother's body found ravaged by dozens of apparent stab wounds. She appeared mummified, or at least sucked of all bodily fluid before the body began to disintegrate. Montgomery slowly walked to the bathroom, and stayed kneeling in front of the toilet for most of the day.

The strongest thing to linger from that horrifying Spring was the unspoken bond between Montgomery and his father. Montgomery grew to tolerate his name, and many annoying things in life. However, he avoided taking biology until his senior year after the Summer when Rebecca Swanson showed him where the stem of her rose tattoo ended. Montgomery would never feel comfortable around large groups of young sisters. He would never like the term World Wide Web. For clothes and all woven things, he preferred synthetic fabrics. And, no matter how hot it became,

Montgomery always slept with the windows closed. One issue he never overcame, nor ever mentioned to anyone, was the fear that Juliet's sisters or their children might seek him in the night.

THE LITTLE GIRL AND THE SHADOW(S)

Noise. Beth awoke. A dragon charged down the hill outside. Its roar was the angry shouts of people pierced by howling dogs. But dragons didn't exist. The roar died away. A presence remained. A breeze rippled the curtains. Beth noticed a very dark shadow against the wall. This shadow looked back at her. Beth clutched her doll and looked away. Her heartbeat fluttered her nightdress. She pulled Darby the bear from under the pillow. The shadow did not move. It seemed afraid of the street light bleeding in rigid streams through the curtains. Soon, Beth began to play quietly on her sheets.

"Your doll is very pretty. What is her name?" The shadow's voice was a soft whisper.

Beth paused. Her fear ebbed to wary acceptance. "Mae," she offered coyly. "She's angry."

"Oh, dear. Why?"

"Darby takes up too much room." Beth plunked the bear on her lap. "Mae wants to sleep with me by herself."

"There seems to be room on either side of you." The shadow offered. "Perhaps each could have its own space."

"No. Mae doesn't want Darby here at all." Beth voiced the doll's case like a prosecutor.

"Then perhaps Darby should eat Mae."

Beth found the idea bizarre. Teddy bears didn't eat anything, did they?

"But they're friends." Beth retorted.

"Then they should cooperate. Their universe is only a small bed, with a child for a god."

Beth did not understand. Perhaps the shadow would explain. It moved closer, and had form now. It was a lady with dark, dark eyes and needles where her teeth should be. But she was nice. More importantly, she was willing to play with Beth. Darby and Mae liked her, too.

Suddenly a fist thrust through the curtains holding a brilliant white flare. The noise of the dragon roared behind it with a thousand angry eyes. Beth screamed. The shadow lady shrieked and writhed against the wall. Her sharp fingers slashed at the torch. A man screamed and the torch went away. Beth's mother threw open the bedroom door and reached for her. A living tornado of yelling people knocked her aside. They ripped Beth's new friend from the wall. She shrieked and snapped her sharp teeth. A leather hood swallowed her head as they tugged her away. Deacon Murray followed the mob, seemingly pulled by their wake. He spouted nervous prayers lost in the verbal carnage. Beth's father shouted at the mob thundering in the parlor. The shrieking died. There was a horrible smell of something burning, then silence. Father shouted again. Slowly the murmur of the dragon bled back into the street.

Beth collected Mae's shattered body through her mother's gripping arms. Darby still lay on the bed. Beth stopped crying. She would rarely ever cry again. She and Darby would stay awake at night for a shadow to visit and play. Years later, Beth ventured into the night itself to search. One night she found a young and very handsome shadow, and left Darby all alone.

AMID THE DEEP

Don felt the aft deck roll. It was a stronger pitch than when the ship was docked. The waves would get bigger. They were moving out to deep water. He looked back at the harbor with remorse and anger. His ship left it for the final time. It was also the final moments of the city, Nomos, and anyone still alive near it. He hoped to stop the end of human life, but that could happen if the ship sank. Humanity had claimed this world, renamed it Emerald, and then remade it for themselves. Then a plague came that twisted humanity. Corpses rose to rend the flesh of the living. Soon after, cities burned as they had on Earth and other worlds. The night sky and banks of drifting smoke were flat black. Don looked back at the burning chaos that had been an industrial harbor. It all burned. He felt an urge to run from the smoke and screams drifting out to sea, even though the ship could move faster than any human could swim. The ship turned and the edge of the last standing city came into view. It glowed like a massive ember.

They had to launch their self-contained rescue mission before the next wave of refugees arrived and also demanded passage on a ship already overcrowded and short on supplies. It ate at Don. He couldn't save them. Some people started a riot when they saw their hope moving into deeper waters. The riot spread like an instant plague and rolled back through the city. And then the wave of flesh ripping monsters flooded the streets. Don's homeworld called the monsters 'chomps,' 'greeze,' or the far older and more traditional tag: zombies. On his new planet, Emerald, they called them rippers. All worlds knew the scenario too well. The animate dead attacked and ate living people. If enough of a victim's flesh clung to its bones, the plague that spawned them added one more to the collective horror and the apocalypse got worse.

Live images illustrated the distant screams Don heard. Cam-drones still broadcast video. They still flew like dutiful, mindless things showing pictures of living people ripped apart by wretched, dead, and mindless things. Don saw the video played directly across his eyes. He watched a walking horror with vacant sockets wander and snatch at any moving thing. It collided with a fellow ripper that was once a human female and began biting its shoulder with impossible savagery. The victim ripper thrashed violently and tore itself free as most of its remaining deltoid muscle came off in its attacker's teeth. The victim became the attacker and bit at bare cheekbone and a partially fleshed neck. The fighting corpses folded in on each other and fell. Don hoped they wouldn't serve as a visual omen of life on his ship, with or without a reanimating pathogen. He pressed his subdural sphenoid switch and cut the video.

Don looked with unaided eyes at the destruction that became more distant. His former life as a colony administrator burned among the cinders on shore. The ship was Don's grand project. She ran silent while under power and dark while still near the shore. Both steps were defensive. A horde was still a threat while close to land. If zombies came aboard, the crew and every living thing would fight them off, but the risk of infection meant one bite or splash of putrid blood could annihilate all hope. With contact lost with Earth and the other worlds, survival here could be survival of the human species. Don heard sharp noises between the ship's side and the shore. He stepped over and gripped the deck rail. He had to take a moment and steel himself to look down at the dark waters. He could see nothing in the low light from the distant inferno. The sound was almost as if masses of limbs slapped against the water just as one would expect from a large group of people trying to swim out to a passing ship. Those people might be living, or otherwise. There were no voices, no cries. Don told himself it was the wash of the thrusters as the captain maneuvered the ship.

The weight they carried to sea was heavier than intended. Far worse, there was even more pressure to find a cure. News of a big boat under construction spread faster than a virus. Survivors followed. Some brought skills suited for the mission. Others brought vacant eyes focused to desperate stares when they saw the prospect of escaping a horrific death and wretched afterlife. Although everyone screened plague-free, more people meant a greater chance of spreading other infections and causing total failure. Some of Don's lieutenants wanted to bar any human overflow. They argued that fighting a mass of living, hungry mouths was no different to facing a zombie horde. Don pointed out that in today's environment, crowd control needed to be passive. You couldn't truly kill an onslaught of people, just slow it down. The plague would reanimate the dead, and they would become an even worse threat. And harder to kill. Don knew that if

116

the ship didn't take extra people, they could destroy the project. A violent horde wasn't always made of zombies. Living people would riot just for food for one more day. The city inferno was that fear realized, but he felt no vindication. The ship was completed and loaded with the scientists' equipment. But even with extreme rationing, the additional mouths would suck up supplies and mean less time at sea away from zombie jaws on land.

Don called his scheme Project Emerald Tide. He hoped that sounded hopeful and uplifting. Even if it didn't, he just wanted it to work. The plan was to build on existing data and find a vaccine to stop the plague. If they could stem the outbreak and turn the tide of death, civilized life could return. In the very least, a vaccine would create the chance to fight the hordes without fear of becoming zombies. There were stockpiles of guns and bigger weapons on land. All they needed was willing, living trigger fingers. People would face death with more enthusiasm if dying meant you wouldn't try to eat your mother or son. Don didn't have anyone to fear losing or eating. He just didn't want to be eaten. And he wanted to be able to sleep soundly without fear on solid land. It surprised him that his plan was the best and now only chance at having that simple future. All others had failed. The deck pitched again. The burning shore was now farther away.

"Beautiful night for a sail." Dr. Narren said as he left the superstructure and walked out on deck towards Don.

"Beautiful? Right." Don said still watching the city ember become more distant.

Don looked over to Narren who grabbed the rail. The scientist and physician's narrow features stretched between his sharp chin and wide forehead. He made himself look weirder by wearing eyeglasses with thick, black frames. Such accessories were odd for Don's interplanetary culture. Discreet ocular caps adjusted vision or shielded eyes from intense light when necessary. Narren took to using age-old spectacles when ophthalmology became a lost art on Emerald. Don and others found Narren's reactions more odd than his appearance. Don never knew if Narren's smiles while looking away during a conversation were from a strange sense of humor, or mocking fatalism. Narren smiled a lot. It unnerved Don, who hardly ever smiled. Unknown to Don, his own demeanor got him dubbed 'the Glare' behind his back. Yet before the plague he was

117

thought of as very amiable. Narren was considered weird even then.

"Well, we might as well take pleasure while we can." Narren said.

Don looked at him with a raised eyebrow, and glare.

"With all these extra people," Narren continued, "we are already doomed."

"You think these people will stop you from completing the vaccine?" Don said as a compressed hiss as old aggravations instantly hardened his mood.

"Oh, no! Don't get me wrong, Admin Keenan—or should that be admiral now?"

"Answer me." Don demanded.

"Sorry. I will do my best." Narren took in a deep breath. "So will Dr. Sast and all our colleagues we could save. We won't stop trying. It's just that with all the—"

"All these decisions were debated already, Doctor." Don cut in.

"That they were." Narren nodded and looked out across the ocean.

"If you thought we would simply fail, why did you come on board?"

"I had a pass." Narren said blankly. "A valid pass. It's a good plan. Or was." Narren paused. He made his characteristic smile and stretched out each syllable of his sentence as he spoke again. "But the al-ter-na-tive? Yee-ah!"

"Just do the work." Don said over the sound of waves rolling against the hull. "We need this to come together. And fast. You have the resources. Just work faster."

"Well, I shall get hard at it tonight, sir." Narren nodded. "But right now I'll take some soon to be vanished personal time and have a smoke."

"A smoke?" Don asked. Narren's comment baffled him.

"Yes," Narren withdrew a small, paper cylinder filled with dried foliage from his pants pocket. "Of the indigenous *Ardens pulmone*. I like the older traditions we humans have put aside. Space travel impacted our culture. But we aren't in space, now." Narren grinned and looked toward the red glow of the city.

"No. But we still have rules to follow." Don glared.

Narren smiled at Don, and then pulled a small surgical laser from his pocket and lit his makeshift cigarette. A puff of white smoke curled from his mouth and blew across the deck.

"Isn't that harmful?" Don asked.

"Well—" Narren paused as the ship gently swayed. He smiled again. "Yee-ah."

Don looked at Narren with narrowed eyes and a tightening brow. He left Narren and entered the superstructure. His brow was still knit when he entered his cabin and went to sleep.

Morning found Don on the bridge with Captain Ruiz. Several screens swept along a crescent against the forward bulkhead. Most were blank. A small column supporting a panel of levers stood in front of them.

"I really wanted a wheel." Ruiz said as he stared at the lever panel. "She was built from scrap and hope, but you'd think finding or making a small ship's wheel would be easy. How long has humanity known the wheel?" Ruiz shrugged and looked at Don.

Don wondered how long humanity would last. The captain's mild rant over an esthetic control surface was not of interest.

"You said something was important. What?" Don asked.

"Yep. We have no nav aid from above." Ruiz answered and pointed skyward. "Contact was lost with the commercial and colonial satellites just after we launched."

"Why didn't you tell me then?" Don almost shouted.

"She's a new boat, and she's had no shake down." Ruiz answered with calm. "If I called you up here for everything, you might as well never leave."

"This is something big!" Don grated.

"This is a big ship, Don. It's my job to see she stays afloat. Now that we're at sea, I need to focus on doing that. I run the ship. You run the people. But without my boat, there are no people. No hope."

Don considered Ruiz's words. He wondered if this was a coup, or just a formal division of labor. Either way, Don had to make this relationship work. Without Ruiz, there was no mission. He was possibly the last captain with true ocean sailing experience. He was as necessary to the mission as the scientists. Don resolved to keep him happy, or at least shown respect.

"Okay," Don took a deep breath. "So, both the commercial and civilian signals are gone?"

"Aye," Ruiz nodded. "It's not my hardware, it's the birds. Do you have an admin code to switch Emerald's own satellites back on?"

"No. They shouldn't have stopped. The commercial sats probably stopped when the lease on their feeds ended." Don paused and shook his head. "But the feeds should be permanent, now. We activated our colonial distress beacon at the first outbreak. All planetary networks should be in emergency support mode."

"Someone forgot to tell that to the satellites' OS." Ruiz frowned. "I don't think we really controlled any of them. They all ran the same software."

Both men paused in irritation over the rented infrastructure of their planet, and contemplation of what to do without it.

"Even if they've become electronic zombies," Ruiz said. "We are navigating by stars, charts, math, and hope. We'll still get wherever we need to go." Ruiz ended with a confident smile.

Don thought he liked Ruiz's smile better than Narren's version.

"We never formerly named the ship," Don glanced around the bridge.

"The Iris," Ruiz said. "That's her name. After the flowers that bloomed in springtime on Earth. It's a sign of renewal. I ordered a plank with her name hung on either side. That's the best we can do until we come across a floating can of paint."

"I like it," Don said. "It's better than 'the ark.'"

"What does than name mean, anyway?" Ruiz asked.

"It was some big ship." Don answered. "Or part of a circle. Part of a sextant maybe?"

"Good enough for me." Ruiz said.

"Ru, we need to keep the satellite failure, quiet." Don nodded as he sought his Captain's agreement. "I don't know if anyone among the extra people has a gadget that can tell them the satellites have quit, but I know there is a belief among them that we have a secret system that will save us. It's becoming this community's lore."

"Stories get told if you make them or not, but they can also be hard to control." Ruiz cautioned.

"This story can help us. It's based on hope. Right now that's a more limited resource than food." Don breathed deeply. "We launched already in emergency mode. I don't want us to fall into desperation mode. People will become restless and doubtful of both me and you if too much goes wrong too fast. Doubt becomes despair. That will be a threat to the mission, and perhaps humanity."

"I understand." Ruiz nodded. He then smiled. "Our government just made its first official secret."

"We need to keep the people orderly." Don steadied himself against the edge of the blank screens as the ship swayed. "For now, we need to keep them curious about where we're going, not that we're fighting just to stay afloat."

"We'll stay above water." Ruiz nodded, but his eyelids widened. "Just understand there is a lot ahead of us that's unknown. They mapped out shipping lanes that were never sailed. Outside those lanes, my charts might as well say 'here be monsters.' Honestly, I don't know if there aren't any. This is still an alien world."

"I thought the prospect drones scanned Emerald's entire surface!" Don rocked from surprise, not the roll of the ocean.

"Land, maybe." Ruiz said. "But not all its oceans. They were too deep for the initial probes, and deeper scans weren't done before colonists arrived."

"I wasn't told that." Don sighed.

"No one was told everything." Ruiz slowly shrugged. "There was a push to get people on livable worlds. Almost like someone knew a plague might spread on some of them."

"I doubt that." Don took a deep breath and wasn't sure he believed his own last sentence.

"Well, I never thought the last bits of humanity would see apocalypse on a cruise—on an alien ocean! But here we are."

"Yeah." Don's eyes opened wide at Ruiz. "And you just made me leery of even using a life raft."

"I'm pretty confident. Cure or not, we are going to save these people, Don. No worries."

"No vaccine is not an option," Don groaned.

"Then I guess you better make sure the scientists and doctors are doing their jobs." Ruiz raised his eyebrows.

"Roger, that Captain." Don replied.

"Saying 'aye, aye,' might work better, now." Ruiz smiled.

"True." Don nodded. He took a moment to look out at the light green sea rolling before the bow of the *Iris*.

Vall Kuenen enjoyed a breeze and slight ocean mist on the deck outside. The moment of joy ended as 'Admin Glare' appeared at the top of the stairway next to her. Vall felt like a school girl caught outside the classroom. Don's typical, narrowed gaze didn't help. Yet, Vall knew she had no reason to spin in sick bay without patients. Plus, she hadn't seen an hour of free time outside of scant sleep since signing on to Emerald Tide. Vall assured herself she was guilty of nothing. She considered Don as he came down the stairs. He was relatively young. So was she. She hadn't thought of pairing up on this ship. She never had time to pair with anyone after the outbreak. If the plague couldn't be treated, the other carnage still needed stitching. As the living population shrank, Vall saw other women seeing pregnancy as a potential responsibility. If the vaccine worked, new humans would need to come from somewhere. Don was relatively attractive. Possible sex aside, he was also the best source of information on the ship and thus everyone's fate. Having his friendship would be a boon by itself. Vall took the initiative.

"Admin, good morning." Vall said.

"Same," Don answered.

Vall saw his stare as indication he thought she should be somewhere else, but he began to walk away as he left the stairs. She stepped back towards him. He stopped.

"Should I use the old form of address, or do we get new titles out at sea?" Vall smiled.

"My name 'Don' still works. Even rusting in this sea air."

Vall was surprised at his stab at humor. "It does smell differently, doesn't it?"

"As opposed to?" Don asked.

"Earth seas. They smell of salt. And on a beach, you can get a good whiff of drying seaweed."

"I've never been to Earth," Don said. "But I had to pull a lot of weeds back home. From dirt."

"Home?" Vall asked.

"Cayley," Don said.

"One of the old colonies." Vall nodded to herself in thought. "I'm sorry what happened there."

"It's happened here," Don said.

"Maybe they have a last hope mission, too."

Don looked to the deck and suppressed a sneer at the thought of 'last hope.' Yet he knew that was true.

"I hope so," Don said. He looked back at Vall. "Shouldn't you be working doctor?"

"I'm on shift." Vall raised her hands along with making a coy smile. "I'm medical, not research. So far, no one is sick."

"Can you help with the research?" Don asked.

"Yes. But tell that to Narren and Sast. They have a lid on their equipment and limit anyone just looking at it."

"I'll talk to Sast," Don said.

Vall wondered if she now had even more work handed to her.

"All right then." Don nodded to Vall and walked on.

Vall smiled as he halted for quick moments to steady his gait as the ship swayed. She allowed herself one more breath of sea air, and went back below decks, slowly.

Later, Vall sprinted back up. The medical staff had yet to elect their chief. Vall seized another opportunity when Don summoned division supervisors to the bridge. A crewman opened the hatch for her. Inside, Don glared at Narren.

"I asked for department heads!" Don barked.

"Well, not everyone got your order, admiral!" Narren shrugged and looked around. "We did, and Dr. Sast is sorry. She felt her research was—"

"All right!" Don waved him off and looked over at a preoccupied Capt. Ruiz.

"Don, what's going on?" Vall asked.

Narren raised his thin eyebrows over his glasses at Vall's informal address to the man who was presumably the highest official alive on Emerald.

"We have contact with other survivors out here." Don answered.

"Another ship?" Narren asked.

"Something that floats." Ruiz said. "We'll see. They had no current maps and drifted out too far. It should be coming into cam view." Ruiz pointed to his right eye.

All instinctively tapped their under-skin, sphenoid switches to see the images sent from a drone. A huge raft came into view. It looked as though a giant, water-logged mat drifted on the green ocean with small, decaying buildings torn free from a city and dropped among shipping containers. The faces of densely packed, desperate, but living people stared up from the raft at the circling drone's camera.

"We should help them," Don sighed.

"Um, ah, with what?" Narren asked.

"I'll put their captain on speaker." Ruiz said and taped at his keyboard flipped up from the lever panel. "It's on a separate radio frequency."

"Like I said," a man's voice spoke over static. "We've cleansed any infection. We're clear, Iris. Please assist. I repeat, we are adrift."

"What does that mean?" Narren shrugged. "Cleansed, how?"

"It's meaningless if they've been in contact with rippers." Vall said.

"Everyone here has seen rippers up close," Don looked over at Vall.

"That's true," Narren said. "But we were all cleared of the virus. Even if they currently have no signs of infection, they could be incubating the plague. We just can't afford contact with them."

"For all we know, we are they only ones that can help them." Don countered.

"For all we know, we could be they only surviving humans." Narren said.

"This disproves that." Don pointed out to sea in the raft's direction even though all saw it in feed from the drone.

"Maybe not." Vall said. "Dr. Narren is right. They may be already infected."

Don glared hard at Vall. She felt as though their budding relationship got pitched overboard.

"I'm sorry," Vall sighed. "We can't risk contracting the plague."

"Tell them we will sail to their location and asses if we can give aid." Don told Ruiz.

"Okay, Don." Ruiz gave a slow nod. "But we keep a safe distance and engines on." Ruiz double tapped the side of his head and spoke again. "Raft captain, this is the Iris. We will come to you and offer aid."

"Can't you take us onboard?" was the immediate reply over the static.

"Negative." Ruiz answered. "The best we can do is shuttle over supplies."

The only reply was static. Everyone refocused on the drone's images of the raft.

"Do you copy?" Ruiz said. "Come in."

There was another long moment of static, and then a reply.

"We read you." The disappointment was obvious even across the poor radio link.

"This will also put my people and ship at risk." Ruiz said.

More static crackled before the raft captain replied, again.

"I suppose if that's all we can get."

There was a 'click' as the raft cut the channel.

"This is a mistake." Narren said flatly.

"We need to know what's out here." Ruiz said and clicked off his drone video. "This is a recon as well as a mercy mission."

"I'd call it suicide." Narren smiled and shrugged. "But—"

"Okay. We made our points." Vall said to Narren as they all shut off the video feed.

Narren left the bridge with his hand fishing in his pocket. Vall looked over at Don starring out to sea.

"I'll check medical inventory," Vall said to Don. "Maybe we do have something extra."

Don nodded while still looking out. Vall turned with a nod to Ruiz and left.

The deck pitched at steeper angles as the *Iris* sailed towards the raft's coordinates at the fastest speed Ruiz dared. An hour later, the raft came into view of the starboard decks. Ruiz dared to sail within forty meters of the craft that caused both fascination and fear. It looked more pathetic rolling on the waves than in the drone's camera. Don stood with Ruiz on the starboard walkway along the bridge. People on lower decks called to the raft. Their efforts were lost in the distance, wind, and waves. Still, Don wondered if people were attempting to communicate with relatives or friends they thought were lost. Those on the raft seemed almost devoid of enthusiasm. Only a few waved toward the *Iris*. Don wondered how long they had been at sea. Perhaps they could tell them how to survive better. A scent of smoke drifted over the ocean. At first Don thought it was a lingered memory from the city's death. He was wrong.

"Captain!" The First Mate stepped from the bridge and called to Ruiz. Her voice has high and stressed. "They just radioed. They have a fire. Their screaming for help!"

"What caused the fire?" Don asked.

"They didn't say, sir!" The First Mate answered. "But there was shouting behind the voice on the radio, and then it—Geez!"

The First Mate pointed toward the raft. Ruiz and Don looked over. Flames shot like sudden, red fins between the decaying structures. Screams rose with greater intensity. People began leaping from the raft in the direction of the *Iris*.

"Back off! Back us off!" Don yelled in panic.

"Take us away from the raft!" Ruiz ordered.

The First Mate dove back into the bridge.

"Hit the alarm!" Ruiz yelled again.

A klaxon sounded as the ship lurched and her bow swung away from the raft. There were screams from the ship's lower decks. A few people that leaned too far over the rails fell from the sides and plummeted to the ocean. Ruiz grabbed the rail. Don fell backward, but someone caught him. He was shocked to see it was Vall. They both steadied themselves as the ship swung away from the conflagration and cries of the raft. The cam-drones stayed steady and shooting. The tallest structure of the raft fell. Flames exploded from its foundation. The raft split. Bodies were visible among the split structures. Many were burning. Some were motionless. Others displayed the unmistakable stagger of a reanimated corpse seeking flesh. Even as the raft burned and broke apart, the zombies lurched with purpose towards any living person still on each bobbing fragment. Some of the living pushed off biting attacks, even as flames consumed the deck. The same occurred as the ocean swamped the other half. It vanished from direct view as the *Iris* kept her swing away. The view on deck became empty ocean. The video feed was cut and the drones recalled. The raft and its people, alive or both forms of the dead, disappeared in the distance. Another group's last attempt at survival burned and sank. Those that fell were lost among the burning flotsam. The *Iris* sailed on.

"That was horrible." Vall said.

"Yeah. Again." Don added.

Narren entered the ship's laboratory. It had been a spacious cabin. Now, computer nodes, nanoscopes, gravi-fuges, and

126

seemingly primitive syringes and pipettes were massed on almost every surface. The visual interface with their eyes spared them the need to take up more room with monitors. Narren took a beaker filled with green fluid from a lab table. He sat in a shockingly empty chair across from Dr. Nyla Sast. She rested on a small desk. Sast appeared to occasionally wave her hand at nothing and ignore Narren. The last part of her behavior was true. Images of the ship's manifest cross-referenced with each person's medical files occupied her apparent blank stare.

Narren watched her with a gaze that would make anyone uncomfortable. That was, if they cared they were being watched or about the watcher. Sast didn't care at all. Narren sipped the green fluid and continued to ogle Sast. He found her beautiful. She was the frequent object of his lustful fantasies. Yet he was intimidated by her, not from an inability to act on his attraction, but from the fact she was possibly smarter than he was. Much smarter. Sast was in control of their venture. Still, even Narren's sexual fascination and intimidation couldn't stop him from making his quirky smiles and gibes. He was more socially aware than he let on, but liked to unsettle people as his own secret sport.

"Well, I wish I'd seen the raft completely sink." Narren sipped and allowed the awkward silence to become obvious. "All those people. All the potential data just ss-un-kk."

Sast took a deep breath. She sighed and answered, but kept her focus on the virtual information floating in her field of view. "I didn't see it at all. I didn't care."

"Too bad. It was a fairly interesting event."

"Interesting?" Sast queried. "How?"

"If the raft's population wasn't keeping an outbreak secret so we would come aid them, then the outbreak occurred after our communication."

"So you think the infection had no incubation." Sast finally clicked off her visual link, but still didn't look at Narren. "You theorize the reanimation was immediate."

"In-stan-tane-eeous." Narren said almost in song.

"Rubbish." Sast said. She darted a glare more cutting than Don's at Narren. "They obviously were hiding an outbreak. Occam's razor."

"But, if not?" Narren shrugged and smiled as he looked away. "We need to consider such a mutation. If it exists, it would further complicate our efforts, here."

"Wherever here is. We are always moving on this damn yacht."

"But this boat has all the equipment we need." Narren sipped his beaker again. "You have to tip the hat to our Admin for that." Narren raised his beaker.

"All I have to do is—no," Sast stood and took Narren's beaker away from him. "All you have to do is get to work. Look through the sequencing we already have and seen if such a mutation is possible. Now."

Narren clicked his visual link and began waving his hand in the air to move virtual screens of data. Sast looked at her own right hand, but not as a tool to flip invisible pages. She eyed the region between her thumb and index finger as if peering into her skin.

Vall's hunch was correct. Don stood holding the rail and looking out on the starboard deck. She walked over to him. Starlight lit his brow. His skin was showing a tendency to wrinkle. Vall knew that could mean he was in his seventies and just needed a quick trip to a cosmetologist. She sighed that no such place or perhaps even profession existed, anymore. Don turned to her. He nodded.

"Hello, Admin." Vall said and joined Don at the rail.

Don sighed to himself. "Even out here, we've left another cinder to burn."

Vall dropped her head for a moment as vivid images of the burning raft replayed across her mind without the need of recorded video.

"It was ominous," Vall said. "But I don't think it was an omen."

Don was quiet. The noises of waves breaking against the hull were heard bellow. Voices on lower decks also came to ear when the wave noise subsided.

"At least nothing is chasing us, or burning here." Vall said.

"True," Don nodded. "We live another night, and will see another dawn. I've seen a lot of dawns. I want to see a lot more."

The personal comment surprised Vall. She hoped that the damage done on the bridge by her agreeing with Narren was not permanent.

"It's a bit ironic that people now live longer than ever, but the ravenous dead are the biggest enemy."

Don was quiet for a moment. "The plague is the enemy. The dead are its victims."

"Well," Vall cocked her head while looking at Don. "I stand corrected, *doctor.*"

Don raised his eyebrows wide and slowly turned his head to face Vall. Vall playfully put her hands on her hips. Don pursed his lips. They suddenly became a smile. Vall smiled back. They drew closer and enjoyed the stars of an alien sky. Both knew the constellation that held Earth's star. In the past, that knowledge brought colonists comfort. Comfort now was in the quiet moment.

Several moments later, the dawn came and Vall was a physician in action. After cries for help and shouted orders, Vall knelt beside her patient. The 'hospital bed' was only a blanket thrown of the ship's inner metal deck in the cargo hold serving as sick bay. Small ovals detached themselves from the young man's naked chest. They floated to his left side and dropped to the defibrillator unit. Vall rested her fingers on the round housing of the vein-shunt attached to the man's right arm. The vital signs she saw were only flat lines. No pulse. No neurocerebral activity. Vall knew there was no use in wasting additional drugs. Her patient was dead. She resisted the impulse to bolt from the fresh corpse. The reaction made her nauseous, but it had become an understandable reaction to death.

"Should I detach the VS, Doctor?" Call's nurse asked.

Vall nodded affirmation to him, and stood. She clicked off her view of his vital signs. She folded her arms, and began the pathological examination in her mind. Vall had become an infectious disease specialist after the outbreak in addition to her specialty of internal medicine. Emerald was still a mostly alien planet. However, the disease was a well-known retrovirus. It was lethal if untreated, but it normally had a much longer incubation. It should also have been in his constantly updating medical files. An injected spy monitored everyone onboard. Something was wrong beyond this patient's odd death. She glanced at him again. He was still unmoving. She was almost ashamed that she was glad for that.

Days later, Vall grappled with stronger mixed emotions while looking up at a sort of layered sky. Clouds floated over the light green sea. Towards the horizon, thick cumulous clouds appeared to reach into the evening sky while tilting backwards. Vall was too tired to review the science of Emerald's terraformed atmospherics and their odd effects. She knew the layers had differing refracting qualities, but would one day resolve into a visually unified mixture. Then, clouds would float as humans thought they should from some shared memory of sky watching that spanned between stars.

If Vall had children, their sky would be different than hers. Terraforming meant children knew a different world than their parents. The grandchildren saw yet another one, until the visible changes were complete. Mere generations experienced a collection of seeming geologic ages. Vall knew physics and geochemistry remade a dying Earth into a habitable world. Yet, she wondered if the planet Emerald could think, would it feel simply altered or infected? Even so, she wanted the human changes to last. She wanted to live. However, her own life seemed to be at risk now on the ship as when she faced ripper hordes on land. Vall was at another funeral for another patient, and even more were becoming sick. She looked back down among the people gathered for the burial at sea on the aft deck. She wondered who to trust. Trust or betrayal was life and death.

Crew members lifted a rigid stretcher to slide the white-shrouded body overboard. The small crowd dispersed. Vall saw Narren walk to the rail and look to the sea as if following the body. Vall went and also looked over the rail. The body of her nurse was already several meters behind the stern. She expected it to be closer. The engines were off and the *Iris* was using ocean currents to save fuel. An odd, rotting scent wafted to her nose. She thought she saw a dark mass in the distance. It was hard to be certain from the white crests of the waves. The body was lost among them.

"I'm surprised we're not doing this more often." Narren said over the ripple of winds across ears.

"Why?" Vall asked and turned to him.

"You're a doctor. Of internal medicine, anyway. You know when people get densely packed, as on this boat, infection spreads rapidly. It's, well, natural."

"In that case, shouldn't it be spreading even faster?" Vall arched her left eyebrow.

"Well, we are a well-inoculated lot. Perhaps the pathogens are mutating at a slower rate without more susceptible hosts."

130

"An interesting idea, Dr. Narren. You've obviously been thinking about this."

"Well, I'm an interesting guy." Narren gave his characteristic look-away smile.

"How is your work?" Vall asked.

"Coming along well. Although there are days I think Sast will throw me overboard."

Narren waited as if wanting Vall to protest the imagery. She didn't. Narren gave a quick nod and focused back on the ocean. He gripped the rail as a thrilled child would do.

"I'm also interested in catching a glimpse of some indigenous Emerald life." Narren said. "At least life that's surviving the terraform process. We're moving into deeper seas. Some just has to be out here. I was hoping the light would last long enough while I was allowed on deck. I've caught glimpses of giant jelly fish, but those are seeded Earth alters. I'd love to see something truly alien!"

Vall glimpsed Don and Ruiz walking toward the super structure. She looked aft toward the dark mass. She couldn't spot it, but thought it might be useful to her.

"I saw something large behind the ship. Maybe if you look straight off the aft—"

"I will! Thank you!" Narren chirped.

Vall watched Narren almost sprint to the aft of the ship even as the deck pitched. She turned and saw Don and Ruiz talking by the superstructure. She carefully walked over to them.

"Doc." Ruiz greeted Vall.

Vall was silent. Her gaze was pleading but also one of confusion.

"What is it?" Don asked and waited. "You can tell us."

"I really have no one else to tell." Vall said. She paused and took a breath. "Okay. The deaths. They're not natural. The initial infection is a retrovirus. Like I told you. But it's been artificially mutated."

"And you asked Narren and Sast for help?" Don asked.

"Yes." Vall answered. "Sast said the deaths are caused by multiple pathogens. She's wrong."

"You're sure? They're supposed to be the best." Ruiz said.

"That's why I know the error is willful." Vall glanced to her sides. "I just needed them to verify my conclusions. But instead both added and obscured facts. Why?"

Don furrowed his brow and frowned so intensely his face muscles quivered.

"Could they be right?" Ruiz asked.

"No." Vall slowly shook her head. "I'm certain the reason these people died is due to the same initial pathogen. It allows other diseases to assert themselves once the patient's immune response is compromised. But the retrovirus—"

"Makes a good cover," Don interjected.

"Have you challenged them on this?" Ruiz asked.

"No." Vall said coldly. "I don't want to die."

"What?" Ruiz barked and then looked across the deck to ensure they were still alone.

Don eased his scowl and focused with intense interest on Vall.

"I don't know how they're administering the—" Vall began.

"Wait. Wait!" Ruiz nearly hopped as he spoke. "You're saying Narren and Sast are murderers?"

Vall and Don looked at Ruiz as if that conclusion was foregone and understood.

Ruiz threw his hands up. "Look, this is serious stuff!"

"I'm hoping it is them and not either of you." Vall sighed. "Like I said, I want to live."

"So do I." Don nodded. "So we keep this quiet."

"What? We can't—" Ruiz began.

"You want this ship to live?" Don asked, grimly. "Then we need to keep this wrapped until we can prove it. People are still reeling from the escape. They still remember the raft. Now we have these deaths. I don't want a panic—a riot!"

Ruiz's eyes widened and he rubbed his forehead.

"We don't know how they're doing this." Vall said. "The method is very sophisticated."

"Okay. I get it." Ruiz said.

"Right now, we stop them." Don grated. "Gather some security officers and we go to their lab and tear it apart!"

"And their research?" Ruiz asked. "If they see us coming? They might burn it to spite us."

All three looked at each other for answers. All seemed to be swayed back and forth by more force than the roll of the deck. Finally, Vall spoke.

"I have an idea."

On land, Jaelen had been good at running. He knew to keep pace with any group of people while the rippers chased them. He always ran to the front as they got closer. He would then sprint out ahead with all speed his legs could produce when the screams and sickening sound of tearing flesh began. He was faster than most people. He knew groups of rippers always fell on one slower person just to get one mouthful of living skin instead of his whole sprinting body. Groups of people were his shield. Then he came onboard the *Iris*. Every space, even the latrines had a mass of asses and heads to wade through. He couldn't run anywhere. If a plague broke out on the ship, there wouldn't be a need for rippers to chase anyone. It would be like hitting the 'chop' button on a blender with dead teeth for blades.

Time outside the packed spam deck was strong enticement to follow Dr. Narren to his boss' quarters. He didn't know what Narren wanted him to do. He didn't care. Apocalypse wore away many taboos. Still, he was glad Narren sought his skills with computer systems. He was happy just to be in a small room with only two people. One of them, Dr. Sast, didn't seem to really be there as she focused on her work. How Narren knew he was a sapper, Jaelen didn't know. The term 'hacker' had been around for centuries, but fell out of favor because it also suggested someone who torn off parts of things. Or people. That was something rippers did, not smart people. They ran. Jaelen didn't really like the replacement term 'sapper,' but it was better than 'convict.' That was a title Jaelen removed from his current identity so he could get on the boat.

Jaelen knocked back the last of the vodka or whisky or whatever Narren had fed him. The room was hot, but his chair was comfortable. Jaelen whirled his fingers in the air as he worked a virtual screen. His eyes saw the red banner ACCESS DENIED almost as quickly as a strobe effect across various access screens. Jaelen sighed. His fingers finally rested.

"I'm sorry," Jaelen said. "I can't pop the seals."

Narren and Sast were silent, but Sast clicked her eye-feeds off and looked over at Jaelen. He found her narrow stare disturbing.

"Are you sure you can't do it, Jaelen." Narren asked as he crouched next to him. "I mean real-lee sure?"

"Yeah," Jaelen said. "The bio-spy OS has some security I've never seen. It wasn't part of the original security system. That

133

looked as strong as steam. Pathetic. I guess whoever was hired to amp the seals didn't look for sub-admin systems like you guys have. It was probably a machine. They're pretty narrow minded. Your keys let you give the sub-sys commands, but not alter the programming or data feeds."

"For that data we didn't need you." Sast sneered. "We want you to give real-time locations on individuals."

"Yeah. Sorry," Jaelen said with a quick shrug. "I mostly used a tool kit, and made a few tweaks. I didn't do much code writing. I mean, it was hard to keep up on new saps and seals running from rippers, anyway."

Sast stood and leaned over Narren. She spoke with a mocking impression of his quirky speech pattern. "And this is the best you could do, real-lee?"

Narren smiled and looked away.

"Can I go now?" Jaelen asked. "You guys are still going to pay me, right?"

"No and no." Sast said through clenched teeth.

"Hey—!" Jaelen started.

"Shut up!' Sast barked. "Narren, now!"

Narren reached over and tapped a button on a small key pad.

"What's that do?" Jaelen said and then felt a slight tingle in his feet.

"The devices we wanted you to access are in every person on this ship." Narren said. "I just blocked the feed for yours."

"Okay. Nice" Jaelen nodded.

"Yee-ah," Narren continued. "Also nice, the manufacturers make micro-med delivery vessels. Of course, those are supposed to release curative drugs." Narren looked away from Jaelen and gave a big shrug. "But they come in handy for other chems. Such as the paralytic released by the one you swallowed with the alcohol."

Narren looked back at Jaelen with a perverse smile. That would be bad enough for Jaelen without the weird spectacle things he wore distorting his eyes. Sast also glared at him. Jaelen felt uncomfortable having two weird people starring at him. The tingle had now reached his knees.

"I get that you guys don't really work for the Admin." Jaelen said.

"Nope." Narren replied.

"Who?" Jaelen asked. He noticed he had difficulty raising his legs, but wondered if he could work an angle with Sast and Narren's real boss. "I mean, everyone alive from corporate or government is one this ship. Right?"

"Not everyone," Narren smiled. "And not everyone is on Emerald. Or alive."

"Who? Where?" Jaelen shrugged with an effort. "Wait! Para-what?"

"Yes," Narren nodded with a quick, irregular head bob. "It is a-maze-ing. It's so concentrated it only requires a picogram to interact with—"

"Narren!" Sast shouted.

"He's noticed the effects," Narren said. "I'll bet you have an urge to run, but it isn't working out, is it?" Narren stood and fished his hand through his left pants' pocket. He withdrew a small white cylinder and laser scalpel.

"What are you doing?" Jaelen asked. His anxiety was rising but his heart was slowing down.

"Smoking." Narren lit his white cigarette with the laser, and exhaled the smoke at Jaelen. He offered the unlit end to Jaelen's mouth. "Would you like to try it? You can still inhale. For a few seconds."

"No!" Jaelen screeched and kept moving his face as if trying to propel himself by thrusting his cheeks forward.

"Just seeing if you wanted a new experience before you die." Narren shrugged. He pushed his glasses back up the bridge of his nose.

"What?" Jaelen screeched again.

"True," Narren said and took another puff. "It's a bit late for that. You might like it, and then what? Oops!"

"Don't torture him." Sast said with disdain to Narren. "Why are you even still talking to him?"

"I like a two-sided conversation." Narren said and flicked cigarette ash over Jaelen.

"But he's going to be dead." Sast growled.

"D-Dead!" Jaelen uttered as his body began to quiver.

"Yeah," Narren said to Jaelen, then flicked more ashes on him and focused back on Sast. "Well, then soon it will be like our conversations."

"P-puh—!" Jaelen now convulsed between Sast and Narren.

"You're getting to be a prick, Narren." Sast said with a sneer.

"A prick!" Narren chirped. "Good one. It's what I do for you without ever doing it to you."

"Juh-Geez," Jaelen managed to utter through violent spasms. Even in his altered state, it was obvious Sast and Narren had spent too much time together in too small a space. He could see that now their personal taboos were ripped away. "Yu-you guys should g-get—*KLAAGH!*"

Jaelen's eyes rolled back. Froth dripped from his open mouth and spattered against the floor.

"You should get a dose of respect, Narren." Sast said. "Fast!"

"You should get a towel." Narren jabbed his cigarette at Jaelen and then took a long drag.

Sast clenched her teeth and dove into the narrow closet that served as a lavatory. She leapt out with a small towel in her clenched right fist.

"Put that goddam thing out!" Sast howled and slapped Narren with the towel. "And *you* mop this up! Now! You've made one Hell of a mess already you stupid, little man!"

"I did what—" Narren stopped and plucked the broken cigarette from his mouth and pushed his glasses back on. "I did what any rational individual would do. I'm a physician and a scientist. I acted to save lives."

"By killing more people!" Sast screeched and pitched her right hand backward to ready for another towel swat.

"There were too many onboard when we launched." Narren looked at his broken smoke and extinguished it on Jaelen's shoulder. "We've virtually eliminated the chances of a ripper outbreak. So, gradual reduction of non-essential population seemed logical. And the evidence all goes overboard after a cursory autopsy. I've already increased our chances by three percent with fewer mouths draining food and resources."

"But they don't need a whole body to link these death to a single, artificial pathogen, you idiot! They only need some blood. We only needed a few subjects for tests, not population control. If we can't hack the spy-bots, we won't know what the Captain, Admin, and security are doing behind us! Someone like Vall could piece together your little RNA-retrovirus. She has specialty in infectious disease!"

"Well, that wasn't in her personnel file." Narren shrugged.

"Well neither is the fact that you're now a serial killer, man-bitch!"

"You didn't tell me what you knew." Narren rocked his head back and forth as he considered his actions and what he should do now. "I mean, I shouldn't—"

"I shouldn't have to tell you anything!" Sast screamed. "You should just follow orders! I was the one assigned to infiltrate this project. I brought you in to work for me. But thanks to you, our employers—*my* employers—might cut us and this planet loose. How are we going to survive then? How?"

"Well," Narren lifted up his palms to the ceiling in an exaggerated shrug. "May-be, act-you-al-lee making a vaccine. Maybe a cure. Just an idea."

The towel hit Narren's face with enough force to knock off his glasses and send him to the floor. Jaelen's body rolled from the chair and fell across him. Narren stayed on the floor covered by the corpse as Sast slapped the walls, chair, and air with her towel bludgeon. He was there for a long time.

A room built as a small cantina for engine workers now served as a secret morgue. Plasscreen sheeting and bioseal on the doors trapped in any infection, and Don and Vall. Don stood in protective jumpsuit with a clear cylinder for a helmet. He watched through the portal sealed between the kitchen and serving counter. He looked like a customer at a sterile but macabre café. Don thought there must be some irony or dark humor in the dead examined in a food service setting when a plague of zombies stalked over the planet. He was glad these bodies were motionless and he was not on the menu. Vall was alone in the kitchen area and sealed in her protective bio-hazard suit. She conducted a set of autopsies with technology in place of scalpels. One male and one female body pulled from the funeral rotation lay naked on separate tables. Vall observed the virtual feeds from her portable medlab console. From the small machine, Vall guided the scanner disks currently floating over the corpses, and the microscopic probes that roamed the still veins, arteries, and cavities of her subjects.

"You think all the evidence we need is in these bodies?" Don asked.

"In the blood," Vall said. "Or its residue. I just need to find the right glob for the right molecules."

"No small feat." Don said with a tight smile.

"Oh, 'the Glare' is a funny man, now." Vall said while still focused on data in her field of view.

"Will you be able to pin the evidence on Sast or her team members?" Don asked.

"They might do that, themselves. I'm guessing anyone sophisticated enough to construct this virus from a lab will have an ego large enough to smile when confronted with the evidence."

"A smile?" Don said as he thought of Narren.

"Yeah." Vall looked over to Don through her face shield. "All I have to do is isolate the virus genome."

"There isn't any whole virus?"

Vall smiled. "You think it's like some little bug running around, but it's actually the genetic structure that plays havoc inside the host cells. The closest thing to a bug is when the virus is still contained within its capsid, a protein shell. A virus is not alive. They're sort of a natural molecular zombie. It just wants to make copies of itself, and without the awareness of an urge, or the sensation of an impulse. They can't even move on their own."

"But a ripper can." Don said.

"Yes. And they spread their virus. But its genome doesn't account for all the aspects of ripper reanimation. And we haven't detected a capsid that contains the virus. The genome doesn't contain information to make one. But it's too complex to not have a shield, or else it would break apart in the environment." Vall sighed. A puff of breath condensed to cloud her face for an instant. "That's why a vaccine has never been created. We need more information. For that we need more time. But the human population was so large, the plague spread faster than we could gather all the data to stop it."

"Do we know what causes the running around and biting?" Don asked.

"Yes. No." Vall answered. "It's the virus, but plus something we haven't detected. We are, or rather were getting close. The reanimation occurs after the victim is dead, so they don't make new antibodies to help us identify the agent. For that we need to scan an active ripper."

"So? Did anyone do that?"

"So, yeah, go ahead." Vall turned to face Don. "Scan a ripper."

"Point taken." Don frowned and nodded.

"I guess we will, someday, somehow." Vall refocused on her medlab's visual feed. "But I was hoping Sast and her team would get a viable treatment and render the need moot."

Vall suddenly turned to look at the female body and then jumped back from it.

"What?" Don asked.

"This, ah, body—" Vall halted and took a shallow breath.

"Is what? What?" Don yelled with concern.

"It has plague."

"The retrovirus?" Don asked.

"No. Plague. Ripper plague."

Don jumped back from the portal. Both of them remained silent as if not to wake the dead and be chased.

"Then why isn't it trying to eat us?" Don stepped back to the portal. "The plague isn't, ah, active?"

"No." Vall breathed. "It looks like the virus has infiltrated the corpse, but it isn't reanimating. Okay. Yeah. Weird."

"Are we safe?"

"I think so," Vall answered. "We aren't at risk of infection if we don't come in contact with its fluid or tissues. But this body has both the retrovirus and the plague."

Vall turned and cut her video feed. She stepped to the portal and looked straight at Don.

"Don, did you allow Sast to bring plague samples onboard Iris?"

Don was silent and stared passed Vall at the corpse.

"Don?"

Don took a deep breath. He looked at Vall. "No. Only virtual models. Not physical cultures."

"Well, someone either reconstituted the plague from those models or, more likely, they smuggled physical samples onto the ship."

Don was silent again. His plan to save the world and the human species had been doomed by lies, and for what he didn't know.

"So, we found the one-to-one relationship." Vall said. "The murder virus and the plague in the same body. We know who was working on the plague. Don, I know we need to do this carefully, but those people can't be allowed to be free on this ship. Or anywhere."

"Then we're dead." Don said with audible bitterness. "We just wait for the end, here, in the middle of an unknown ocean." He paused. "They were supposed to be the best minds to find a cure."

"Maybe they are," Vall said. "But they're still murderers."

Don clenched his right hand into a fist so tightly it felt as though his wrist tendons would snap. He stared at his gloved fist and watched it quiver.

"We're not done," Don said quietly, and then he yelled. "Damn it, we are not done!"

Darkness. At times it was a stench, not the absence of light. Orra looked out at the total black of the ocean night and smelled the other form. They sat in the sharp crease of deck steal that bonded to the aft bulkhead. Her children had never known another planet. Orra wondered if they ever would. She knew they were tired, and now enjoyed the view from the aft passenger deck. She did, too. It let her think they were putting distance between themselves and the threatening land. Now she felt darkness chasing her at sea. It was time to move.

"Let's go." She nudged her son Jarren and nodded to his sisters beside him. "Now."

"What? Mom!" Jarren protested. "You know how long it took to get this spot."

"I know. But we need to move." Orra stood and gathered her pack. It was light and carried mostly objects for her children, and her own shiv cleverly hidden in the strap. "Come on."

Orra's children slowly moved aching muscles to follow their mother. She had lead her family across this world as rippers and vile forms of living humans tried to destroy them. Her children knew it was wise to follow her, even if their bodies followed their brains only reluctantly.

"I'm not going back in the spam deck." Jarren groaned.

Orra looked at her son as he stood. Soon he would be old enough to make tough choices on his own. Not today. The wind blew strongly across the ship's aft and carried the stench with it. Jarren turned to look towards the blackness. He reached down and quickly gathered his pack. He wasn't alone. Others were beginning to sense what Orra already knew and also collected what little they had. Something was coming close. Most of them had also fled death for so long that they didn't question the impulse to run, even if it was just the other end of a ship. It was time to run. Orra lead her family away from darkness, again.

Don and Vall entered the bridge. Ruiz had summoned Don, but was surprised to see Vall with him. Ruiz didn't know they were just pealed from protective suits and wondered why they were both sweaty. Normally that would have made him smile. Not today.

"Line 2." Ruiz said and pointed to the right side of his head.

Don and Vall clicked their sphenoid switches. A black expanse of sea was all they saw, but there was movement.

"This is live-wave LIDAR," Ruiz said.

Don and Vall felt sudden nausea and the impulse to run. The image of the black sea became a rolling field of horror. A collective mass of giant jelly fish and the planet's approximation of seaweed bound together bits of charred raft debris. The movement wasn't only from the roll of the waves. Arms legs and torsos bobbed. Some of them moved on their own. The mass was mostly reanimated human corpses. Rippers were floating in the waves. Some of them clung to and fed on the remains of shrouded bodies dropped into the ocean.

"It's like a zombie Sargasso Sea that fell into the same current we're using," Ruiz said. "And it's damn close."

"Speed up!" Don yelled.

"Oh, you think?" Ruiz snapped.

Don turned his head toward Ruiz and cut his video feed. Ruiz stared at him. Don waved his hands in a plaintiff gesture.

"Yeah. I'll gun the engines if it comes closer," Ruiz said. "But we've been traveling on the currents for a reason. I need to conserve fuel for the storm."

"Storm?" Vall said as she switched off the feed of the zombie Sargasso with a shudder.

"A big one," Ruiz replied. "It will overtake us, no matter our speed. I need the fuel to maneuver the Iris and minimize the impact. We're going to be hit with big waves."

"Will the ship be okay?" Don asked.

"Will *we* be okay?" Vall asked with a high tone.

"Oh, yeah." Ruiz said. "I'm too good and the Iris is too strong for this storm to sink us. But with this squeeze play of drifting rippers and approaching storm, I'm worried about what's going to go down onboard. Have you got the evidence you need to nail the killers?"

"Yes. We—" Don started to answer.

"Then if there's going to be a conflict, I want it on calmer seas." Ruiz cut in. "I don't want a loose killer running free, someone starting a panic, or even a damn poker game going on when I'm steering us away from one horror and through another."

"Poker game?" Vall asked. "What's with poker?"

"I like to play." Ruiz replied. "I don't want to miss out."

Vall cocked her eyebrows.

"Okay," Don said. "Let's get this done."

The ship was already pitching hard from the occasional large wave that rolled out from the closing storm. Even so, the warning signal Narren installed on the walkway to his cabin still worked. He enjoyed looking out passed the edge of the rail and at the waves breaking over dark green ocean. His was a choice, shipside view with a big porthole. He enjoyed it a little longer before he saw Ruiz, Don, and Vall approach. They were obviously coming for him. An unexpected wave of peace flowed across Narren's mind. He sat in a tattered but comfortable chair and placed his right hand on the handle of a large, upright cabinet once intended as a wardrobe. Narren wasn't sure of the occasional bumps of metal were from the roll of the deck jostling the cabinet or what was inside it. The ship made a lot of noises he wasn't used to. He felt life in general was an odd experience. He wondered how much longer his own would last. There was no knock. Ruiz unlocked the hatch and walked right in. Don and Vall steadied themselves as they followed him. Narren smiled and never released his grip on the cabinet handle.

"Welcome." Narren said. "Please make yourselves—"

"What's with the steel cabinet?" Ruiz asked.

"What, this?" Narren rattled the cabinet handle. "I had it moved up from the lab to store specimens. We scientists are always at work, wherever we are. Right, Doctor?"

Vall said nothing. Her focus was on the rumble inside the cabinet.

"So you found the retrovirus." Narren said and raised his eyebrows over his glasses as he focused on Vall.

"Yes." Vall said.

"Good work," Narren nodded. "I apologize for not thinking you had the intellect or knowledge to back trace my work."

142

"She's a doctor and you didn't think she was smart enough to do that?" Ruiz asked.

"Well, there's smart and then there's *smart*, Captain." Narren answered.

Ruiz raised his own eyebrows as he stared at Narren and wondered at what level of *smart* the odd, spectacled man placed him.

"We also found the plague." Vall added.

"But not a reanimate corpse. Neat, huh?" Narren smiled wide.

"No." Don said. "Not at all."

"Wait, did you say 'no'?" Narren questioned. "Do you have any idea what a technical feat that was?"

"You have any idea the trouble you're in?" Ruiz asked.

"Well, let us just see mon cap-ee-tan." Narren gave a one-shoulder shrug while still holding the cabinet handle. "I'm on a planet overrun with zombies and on a makeshift ship that's about to be hit by a storm. Trouble? Yee-ah!"

"If I allowed weapons onboard, I just shoot you right now." Ruiz spat at Narren. He looked at Don. "Can we just throw him overboard?"

Don wrinkled his forehead in serious consideration of the act.

"Before you do," Narren slid his free hand into his pants pocket.

As Narren fished in his pocket, everyone tensed. Don expected Narren to put a cigarette in his mouth. Instead He pulled out a small data stick and handed it to Vall. She didn't take it immediately.

"What is it?" Vall asked.

"Well, safe for one." Narren said as he still held out the data stick with his left arm and gripped the cabinet handle with his right hand. "For another, it's the fulfillment of a promise."

Narren looked at Don and gave a nod free of sarcastic smile or physical quirks.

Don took the data stick. "Just, why?"

"The research. And that's it." Narren pointed to the data stick. "And to try and save us. Well, save the human race."

"You've got to be kidding!" Vall sneered.

"I know our methods are different." Narren raised the palm of his free hand at Vall. "But understand our work was not just for here on Emerald. Sast and I were working for interstellar concerns."

"The Inter-colony Commission?" Don asked. He handed the data stick to Vall.

"Nnno," Narren answered. He reached down to the floor and retrieved a brimmed hat. He propped it loosely on his head and smiled. Above the brim a motion-decal played a company slogan above its star logo in bright, friendly letters: From the Sun to every star. One purpose. Transit. UNI-SOL. "I stole this hat from Sast. The bitch."

"You're some kind of spy for a C-class shipping firm?" Ruiz said in disbelief. "That's an automated enterprise. It's a bunch of machines running machines!"

"Think about it!" Narren chirped. "Who needs humans more? A shipping company needs things to ship, and humans are a self-generating cargo that expands the number of places to ship things to. And if there are no humans—you get the point. We die, their function ceases. They aren't programmed for much adaptation."

"You actually work for machines?" Vall asked as her face pulled into a confused scowl. "Machines!"

"We all work with machines, of a sort." Narren countered. "This boat. Our medical equipment. You can describe it as *for* or *with*, but it's really all the same. We all fill a niche. That's all Sast and I did. We filled a niche. At least I still do."

"What do you mean?" Don asked.

The ship rolled. Ruiz stayed standing fast. Don and Vall grabbed each other to steady themselves. Narren pressed his arm against the cabinet's handle to keep it shut. A loud *THUMP* came from inside it.

"Weh-ell," Narren said. "Sast is toast. Expired. D-E-A-D. In capitals."

"You killed her!" Vall shouted.

"I wish!" Narren retorted. "But, no. She killed herself. It was actually quite funny. You see she had these microtubules in her hand that held plague samples. It's how she smuggled—anyway! She gets into a rage and starts whacking everything with a towel. Geez, she flipped. Anyway! She griped it so tightly she broke the tubules. Can you imagine?"

Narren broke into a spasm of laughter. The hat fell off, but he never lost his grip on the cabinet. The others watched him thinking a stretched mind now snapped.

"So, so the bitch killed herself." Narren wheezed. He composed himself and looked up at the horrified stares of Ruiz, Don, and Vall.

"Obviously we share a different appreciation for irony." Narren wiped his brow with his free hand. "See, she flew into a blind rage and—never mind. I hope you'll let me continue my work." Narren hoped his manic moment had gained him enough pity to press for lenience. It did not.

"With more killing?" Vall spat.

"Hey, wait—!" Don started to say and looked at the cabinet seeing it was large enough to house a person.

"We did that for the benefit of the majority." Narren said and adjusted his grip the cabinet handle. "I'm sure you can see the greater good once you read my research."

"I see you in my brig, jackass!" Ruiz shouted.

"I'm sorry, then, for you all. The incubation period is, doubtless, long over." Narren said.

Narren thrust his hand gripping the cabinet handle down. His hand just slid off from his sweaty grip. He dove from his chair to grab it again as Ruiz, Don, and Vall collided with each other as they rushed to grab Narren. They were one fraction of a second too late. The doors swung open. What had been the multiple PhD holding Nyla Sast hissed as the cabin light hit her dead eyes. The lack of muscle and skin elasticity kept her face pulled back as if stuck at high velocity. Her hair was already falling out. All she needed was her eyes and teeth. The teeth sunk into the back of Narren's neck as he tied to push up from the floor. He screamed. So did Ruiz, Don, and Vall.

Don jumped up as Ruiz and Vall scrambled back from Narren on the floor. Don lifted Narren's chair and swung it into Sast's zombie. A tear on the back of Narren's neck spurted blood as his attacker fell back. The ripper bounced inside the cabinet and then fell across Vall's legs. Vall screamed, squirmed, and thrust herself to escape from it as it rose on its arms. A tooth-bared death mask looked up at her with strip of Narren's flesh between teeth. Don's heel smashed into the zombie's face. Narren gripped the back of his neck and rolled away. The zombie's violent flailing kicked his eyeglasses across the floor by. Don pummeled it with the chair amid undead kicks, clawing swipes, and frothing gnashes.

"Run!" Don shouted.

Ruiz and Vall bolted through the opened hatch.

"Come on!" Vall stuck her head back in and yelled at Don.

Narren stood while clutching his bloody neck. Don finally began to tire from his relentless beating of the seemingly unharmed ripper. He threw the chair onto it and ran. He hit Narren who also headed for the hatch. Narren fell against the bulkhead. Don leapt to the walkway and almost over the rail into the sea. Vall grabbed at his arms to pull him away from the hatch. Ruiz was gone. Klaxons sounded. Immediately all the hatches locked. Narren's hatch automatically swung closed and locked, just as he stumbled out with the ripper clawing his ass. Vall and Don bolted to the bow. Narren ran to the aft. The ripper chased its former colleague and partial meal.

Narren reached the top of the stairs onto the open aft deck. Sharp, cold wind buffeted him in bursts. They felt good against his neck wound. He looked up instinctively and strained to see the constellations. He wanted to find the one that held the Sun and thus Earth. There were only dark clouds.

Narren took the laser he used as an improvised lighter and cauterized his neck wound. The scent of burning flesh was horrid. He cried out and grimaced, but finished the job by feel and his unwanted experience as a field medic. The wound was fairly superficial. It alone would not be lethal. But he could feel the other pain of the changes unfurling inside his body. Inside him, recently reprogrammed surgi-bots slowed the plague's effects. The information he gave Vall would enable her improve on that programming and save him. That was, if he lived long enough and Vall cared to save a mass murderer. He wondered if he should push the laser to burn deeper. The hiss of the Sast ripper broke his macabre reverie.

Narren aimed the small laser at the zombie. A small piece of Sast's disfigured face began to burn. It slowed its shamble towards him. He once found that face attractive. Now he wanted her whole body to suddenly ignite. He smiled at the irony, but did not look away. A wave rolled the ship. The laser's power ebbed. Jaws opened wider as Narren struggled to maintain his balance and escape the ripper.

146

"Hey!" Don yelled.

The ripper turned. Vall and Don were crouched behind Ruiz and two ship's officers. All of them looked like they wanted to be on another ship or, better yet, another planet. Ruiz stood ahead of them all with a small cannon aimed at the monster.

"Just get down!" Ruiz yelled.

Narren hit the deck. The ripper turned to charge the fresh meat. Ruiz squeezed the trigger. There was a loud blast and an instantaneous cloud that engulfed the zombie. It froze as instant crystals jutted out from its mass and through it. It stood frozen as a jagged statue.

Narren pulled himself up along the rail. He took a deep breath and started to laugh. The deck rolled sharply. Narren felt his body rise from the deck and press against the rail. He saw the dark ocean as if the deck and the sea were at right angles. And then the wave struck him.

The sudden mass of sea across the deck slid Don, Vall, Ruiz, and the officers toward the superstructure. It rolled back and drew them toward the rail. The seawater spared them. It flowed back through the scuppers without taking any of them. Except for Narren. The wave washed him and the frozen zombie overboard. Don shook his wet head. He blinked and looked at Ruiz who somehow still held his small cannon.

"A rip-freeze?" Don said as they all began to rise back to their feet. "That's military tech. I thought you didn't allow weapons onboard."

"It's not a weapon." Ruiz said, and coughed. "It's a security measure."

"I like it," Vall added.

Clean and dry, Vall sat at her work station inside her small cabin that didn't have a nice view. She inserted the data clip from Narren into her computer that was no bigger than the clip and activated her video link. She stole her nerves at what she might see. It was indeed unsettling. Narren's face appeared in close focus.

"If you are watching this file and you aren't me editing it, again, then I'm out of the research picture." Narren's image said. "If I'm dead, then Sast probably killed me. Or, one of our research subjects somehow animated and ate us both. Of course, in that case you may also be dead from an outbreak. But, if you're not and can make sense of this data, allow me to proceed. Or you can shut me off. Whatever."

Narren's image smiled and looked away in his quirky style.

"Okay," he continued. "We were able to separate the elements of the plague. We dissolved the virus' DNA and analyzed what remained. This had been done before, but we had new screens, better computers, and a new perspective. We knew something had to be there, and not something typically correlated with a virus. We found it. It was protein. Dense protein. Yes, it was prions.

"These were a unique and undiscovered prion form. They were more complex and exhibited behaviors beyond just acting like an enzyme. In fact, you could describe these structures as prion-like, in that they are made from dense protein but work differently. I wanted to dub it Narrentien, or perhaps the prions Narrenoids. Cumbersome name, yes. But if I'm dead—dead, dead, I hope. Either way, indulge me.

"So the Narrenoids—oh, Hell. The prions take the place of the virus capsid. Neat, huh? Explains a few things. The virus inhabits folds in the prions. The prion and virus is a commensal form. Both use each other to allocate resources and replicate. Mutual evolution in non-living forms."

On the video, Narren took a moment to shake his head. He looked at the viewer. Vall found herself also shaking her head in agreement and instantly stopped.

"Yeah." Narren's image continued. "The prion unfurls and releases the virus. The prions then begin converting human proteins into the reanimatory structure, bonded to the corpse's nervous system. The re-ambulant corpse is then guided by impulses given to the brain and nerve tissues by the virus. Okay, at this point, you get it, you get it. If you do not, then why are you watching this? Find someone who does. But here goes, very, very basically: the prions make a spring inside the corpse and the virus gives it the direction to bounce. With teeth.

"In the past, we isolated the virus, but not the prion because we simply weren't looking for it. By the time it was active we were either blowing the corpse to pieces or it was ripping off our face. A pretty good hiding strategy. But it's over. Now we can, or I hope have, built on this data and created a cure.

"I don't know what you know about me. Just realize—oh, Hell. Whatever."

The file ended. Vall switched off the visual feed. She began to analyze the data. She was certain all Narren's research could have been done without causing a chain of events that lead to his own death and cost many other lives. She recalled the ancient Hippocratic oath of physicians that bade them 'first, do no harm.' Obviously Sast and Narren forgot that, or didn't care. And they both died and left the final steps of the cure to be discovered and created by others. What did they think they were doing? Accelerating the research? Vall wondered. In truth, they only accelerated their own, horrible deaths.

Narren woke. The storm had passed and he rolled along gentle, emerald waves. He lifted his head and saw the smooth expanse of ocean stretch to the horizon. The *Iris* was far away. He was alone. His appreciation for irony came to a fine point when he noticed what he gripped to stay afloat. It was the plank with the ship's name carved into it. It must have ripped away in the same wave that took him off the ship.

He noticed a stinging pain, but not from his neck. That still throbbed, but this was a new burning pain in his legs. Large jellyfish floated around him. They were clear and not all seemed alive. His own flesh was still living, mostly. The plague was slowed by the microscopic machines at war with the prions in his tissues. Still, the virus lurked in his blood. He looked up at the partially cloudy sky. A breeze wafted the smell of rotting flesh. He turned his head and saw a large, dark mass floating nearby. He knew what it was. The engineered jellyfish would not be what killed him. Narren parted their membranes around him and looked into the deep but clear ocean. He hoped to see something truly alien before he died. He did.

It swam several meters below him. It was a long black spine with several, large cilia beating in rhythmic waves along its sides. Large, oval structures appeared to be like eyes before forward facing gills or a tiered mouth. A sloshing noise broke Narren's concentration. The dark mass was closer. He could see the zombies bob among the flotsam. They also saw him. Some left the dark mat and did an undead version of the dog paddle swimming stroke towards him. They were unlike any rippers he's seen. The elements and ocean had bloated and ravaged their bodies. But they still could move. They were obviously hungry, and heading for him. Narren imagined being ripped to pieces and the sea water flowing into his wounds and searing his insides. He hoped the alien creature was a predator. He dove down and wanted it to kill him fast.

Through stinging eyes, Narren saw what he thought were large cilia shoot way from the central, black spine. They darted towards him, but then just as quickly back to the spine. He wondered if they sensed he was something alien. He wondered what he saw. The cilia now looked to swim on their own. They reformed around the spine and resumed their synchronous rhythm. Was it a polymorphic form of life like jellyfish? Were the cilia actually young and the spine the mother? Or was it a form of life that somehow controlled its limbs without physical attachment? Perhaps it was some type of magnetic life. Maybe it was a machine. Burning lungs ended his theorizing. The creature dove into the depths.

Narren lost his hope of a swift death. He swam deeper and gulped sea water in an attempt to drown. Something grabbed his ankle. He wasn't as deep as he thought. A cold hand, certainly human pulled him up. Several other cold hands yanked him back to the surface. Narren felt teeth bite him from all direction. He tried to scream but only gurgled out seawater. His blood washed over him and colored the ocean dark red.

Don's hunch was right. He found Vall looking up at the stars as the *Iris* sailed into calmer waters and under clearing skies.

"Company?" Don asked.

"Sure," Vall smiled at him.

"Think we're alone?" Don asked as he joined Vall looking skyward.

"Odd how once that question was about alien life," Vall observed. "Now it's a question if humans still survive on other worlds."

"Maybe the other colonies are keeping silent out of fear the plague." Don said. "Maybe they won't once a cure is known to exist."

"It will," Vall nodded. "Soon. Various anti-prions were developed on Earth decades ago. He can do what they did on this ship. And no one needs to die."

"I'm glad," Don said and heard his voice quaver with the thought of his plan actually succeeding.

"We will turn the tide." Vall smiled and looked at Don. "But I don't think the journey ends there."

"Oh?" Don looked at her with curiosity lighting eyes.

"This is still a changing world." Vall said. "We will also have to change to live in balance with it, and in balance with ourselves. We may be the last of humanity, but also the first generation that gives rise to new, intelligent life."

Don said nothing as he considered Vaal's words. He felt the deck pitch as the *Iris* rolled with the alien ocean. Before they made landfall again, he knew they would need to travel out into deeper waters.

TRADED FAVOR

Estelle sat at the bar. No matter how evocative she was dressed or the fact that she sat alone, no one came near her. Anyone who did was warned away. The big thugs down the bar didn't need to stand. Estelle's sharp glances cut off any opening lines and large chunks of ego. Her only companion was a tumbler with ice and bourbon. Her drink was a prop, although poured from the best under the bar. She only came into the club to remind herself where she'd been, and vowed to never return. Estelle glimpsed Nona and some of her old associates raising the spirits of a few men with heavy wallets in a booth. The girls were dolled up and showing skin. The wallets would open wide to see and feel more. Estelle took a sip to wash away memories of herself and Nona. She rolled an ice cube into her mouth and crushed it between her nice, white, and remade teeth. She looked at a long spine above the racks of bottles. It was also a tooth, but from a mouth that could crush bones and whole bodies. The spine was a trophy of the bar owner, Seaton. He owned almost everything Estelle could see, including all of Estelle's time and favors when he called. Estelle stared at the spine and thought about changing her world, and how to own it.

"Thought you had a private room?"

Estelle glanced to see Nona sliding onto the next stool.

"I thought you were busy." Estelle said while focused on her next frozen victim in the tumbler.

"Yeah. A bunch of slugs. I might as well be doing Maws, tonight."

"Keep talking and they might be your only johns, real soon." Estelle took another pull of bourbon.

"You were cool before, 'Stell. Now you're a glacier. Loosen up." Nona said.

"The glaciers are gone. You should be, too." Estelle stared over to the bottles behind the bar.

"I see," Nona sighed. "You can't hang with the help now you got an office on the bosses' lap. Cut your friends a break. You were one of us not long ago."

"I don't care if it was yesterday, or an hour ago." Estelle kept staring at the bottles. "I can hear the favor coming before you ask it, and I'm not screwing over what I got for you. Just do your job. I did."

152

"I guess you did the right job enough times."

Estelle cast a hateful glance at Nona, but she was already slinking back to the booth of slugs.

"You are kind'a cold." Now LaRoy dared to speak to Estelle, but not by sitting next to her. That would be obvious. His voice came from the jack hidden in Estelle's crystal earring.

They kept their affair hidden by necessity. Seaton knew Estelle had lovers. So did he. But even in a world of the illegal and illicit, the lie of fidelity still held cache. LaRoy was freelance muscle who worked for Seaton's various lieutenants. It meant he could roam between rackets and keep Estelle informed on Seaton's business and competition. LaRoy was her spy with a nice set of abs. He had her private number and almost her trust.

"If you don't have info, shut up. I'm thinking." Estelle whispered while watching Seaton's thugs watch Nona and her crew work the slugs.

"I can't call to say hello? To check on you?" LaRoy's words of care were sarcasm. On the other end of the line, he knew Estelle's silence was more cutting than the harshest expletive. "Okay, c'mon, 'Stell! I may be your beef on the side, but you need somebody, girl."

Estelle's continued silence made LaRoy nervous. She released his anxiety with a question.

"How would you wax Seats?"

"Seaton? Hell, I wouldn't."

"Gutless prick." Estelle crushed another ice cube.

"Look, if he gets popped, then somebody gets paid to pop the popper. If nobody sees the shooter, there's gonna be a lot of people getting chopped just on spec they were Seaton's killer. That's not to mention people killing people to take his turf. You pop him, you pop the world. At least all the world we can see, sweetie pie."

Estelle was silent again.

"I know you got your fingers into everything," LaRoy continued. "Just don't get them bit off. And that advice is free."

"That's what it's worth." Estelle answered.

"Be cold. But you know I'm right. I've been around a while, too. And not just because I got better aim than most."

Estelle looked at the trophy spike. The freak it came from must have a brother. Or sisters. Or whatever they had as family. With family you had bonds. Bonds meant emotion, even if you didn't walk on two legs and had giant spines for teeth.

"Keep in mind, ol' Seaton's been around a while for a reason." LaRoy cautioned. "It ain't because of the gene twist, or whatever it is that keeps his face pulled tight."

"It's not just his face," Estelle said. She heard LaRoy grunt. "You pick me up around the corner. Now."

Estelle slammed her tumbler against the bar and walked to the doors. Two goons stood to follow her. She waved her right, middle finger backwards at them. They sat back down.

The next morning, Estelle left again. This time it was from the apartment Seaton rented for her. She had left LaRoy in his car after she ditched the bar. Luckily Seaton stayed in his own home all night. Estelle walked out onto the street, but not in the way she did in her past. She smiled because she wasn't selling doses of vice, or anything else she proffered in the past, such as herself. Now she had money, respect, and a major asset in fear. No one touched her if she didn't permit the privilege. Estelle's physical assets endowed her with a lot of capital since adulthood, or just before its official start. Even after the age of 19 had long come and gone, she still drew eyes when in a tight skirt. Estelle hated tight skirts. She also hated most people, including Seaton. Nevertheless, he did serve a purpose. For now. Seaton's thugs would beat down anyone at her signal if they annoyed her, or she was just in a wicked mood. Some people hated her for that reason. It didn't bother Estelle. Despite owning several mirrors, she didn't spend much time in personal reflection. As civilization eroded, she was building a secret empire. Estelle figured people abhorred all powerful queens. So, she was in good company.

Today Estelle walked alone. She relied on the disguise of plain clothes and the short barreled .357 in her pack as protection. She told her unit of Seaton's goons that she went to visit her mother and didn't want her scared by thugs. What she really sought was more frightening than brutish men wearing guns and strong cologne. Most of Seaton's thugs could drop anybody. The thing she wanted to find had dropped from the sky. As humanity fought to keep a grip on a changing planet Earth, space let loose a shock near Albuquerque, New Mexico, USA. A group of alien freaks dropped in and stuck around. They didn't come as saviors or invaders. They didn't bring any tech toys for scientists and thankfully no mega-plagues for everyone else. They rolled out of an interplanetary taxi that took off without a glimpse of the other aliens that flew it. There was no ceremony. No world leaders gave speeches. No one in the military knew to flip a bird let alone pull a trigger. No media had a chance to pander panic or awe. The one person who saw them arrive ran a lonely desert gift shop, but no officials or freaks came in to buy even a postcard.

The mass of coy aliens seemed content to let humans deal with them however they chose. They were all the same type of monster, and became known as "Mitigants" because of arguments for their rights through mitigating circumstances. The term stuck. It was better than "Maws." People called them Maws for the same reason Estelle sought one out. Their mouths held the spines where Seaton got his to hang in the bar. Despite having mouths that could eat a cow, Mitigants roamed free. Mostly. They kept to zones sanctioned by law and local attitude. Those were mostly on the fringes of human civilization. There were more fringes as cities contracted. Estelle wanted Earth to hold together long enough for her to get what she wanted. It could go to Hell or get eaten by Mitigants after she died an old, rich hag. Maybe sooner, if she got bored.

Estelle cursed having to walk so far, but was glad she opted for boots over heels. They allowed for mace and a knife, in addition to her .357. Her nice car would draw attention near the edge of town. Attention would kill her plan to kill Seaton. To succeed, she needed a Mitigant. It would not only kill Seaton, but also remove questions about how he died by just eating him whole. The absence of his body would support the lie that he was away for a time just long enough for Estelle to take control and avoid a blood bath that might drown her. A Mitigant would be assassin and disposal, all in one. Getting one interested wouldn't be hard. Seaton once raised enough firepower to kill one of the Mitigants. Estelle was sure one of them would like to return the favor. Mitigants liked favors. That was part of some code of honor among them. One of their smaller groups lived outside Seaton's turf. Estelle only needed one for her plan. Once Seaton was gone, his rackets and muscle would be her own. Seaton would be a meal. Favor for favor.

At the city's edge, foliage reclaimed what had been a residential neighborhood. Estelle was finally out of range of Seaton's spies and probably mobile phone range, for any phone company still in business. A few human drifters pointed out where she could find a Mitigant through a small ring of trees. That was after each made lewd comments and gestures to Estelle. They paid for that through kicks to the crotch or gun barrel blows to the face. Estelle made her way through the trees. In the center was a small dale covered with grass. Estelle appreciated the natural beauty. She didn't get to see many places like this one. Although other places like this didn't have a tentacle that looked like a shaft of dark, liquid glass erupt from the ground. A globe like a giant cuttlefish eye oozed up through the tentacle and popped out at its top.

"You seek me?" The voice came from bellow the ground. It was a low rumble felt through the soles of Estelle's boots as much as heard in her ears.

"Uh, yeah." Estelle answered, considering the eye. She was sure it was an eye. It looked like things she saw sticking out from Mitigants' faces, or at least the parts that held their huge mouth. Whatever this thing was, it faced her. She had an eerie feeling it could see a more than it should. It was just flat out weird. "You're a Mitigant. Right?"

"One could safely deduce that fact," was the vibrated answer. "We are the only alien species on your planet. And, I assume what you see is not the norm in human to human conversation."

Estelle wasn't sure if its tone was condescending or humorous. It didn't matter, as long as it did what she wanted.

"I want you to eat somebody." Estelle shocked herself by blurting out her goal so soon.

"You?" the rumbling asked.

"No!" Estelle shouted. She stepped back and slid a hand towards her gun. She knew it couldn't kill the thing. Seaton needed several crews of shooters with heavy guns to kill his Mitigant, but her hollow points might hurt it enough to let her run.

"You won't need to run," the rumble sounded calm and assured.

"What?" Estelle took another pace backward as she wondered what she had stepped into.

"And, no, I can't read your thoughts."

Estelle stayed quiet and glared at the eye thing.

"You humans make it easy to discern your intensions. However, you have no reason to be afraid. At least from me."

"Huh. Yeah. Okay." Estelle took a shallow breath. "So we can deal?"

"It depends. Who do you want me to kill for you?"

"But you'd do it?" Estelle's voice rattled with anticipation. "You'll kill a mark for a favor?"

"Who?" The Mitigant's asked with a stronger pulse that vibrated up through Estelle's legs. Estelle worried it was getting irritated. She thought it was time to get the meeting wrapped and over, even if all she did was run.

"Seaton." She spat out as the eye moved closer to her.

"Ah, the gangster. The great Maw killer. The little human who commands the region just South of here. And you must be his moll, Estelle Norris."

"How the--?" Greater confusion cut short Estelle's spoken thought. Her hand now gripped her gun's handle.

"As I said, human intensions are easily discerned. I understand your goals. You wish release of your station as his asset. Does he require that you offer your body for more than his own gratification?"

"Ah, no. Not anymore." Estelle blinked to suppress her slashing glare at the eye.

"A loss for that market, I am certain."

Estelle wondered if that was a compliment. She didn't think this thing could be interested in her body. At least, not if she wasn't a meal. She had looked forward to making one deal when sex wasn't an issue. Estelle remembered what Nona said about doing Maws last night and instantly dismissed the thought. She scrutinized the unblinking eye in front of her. Estelle thought that it must be the Mitigant's way to disarm her or ease tension. She realized it understood negotiation strategy. It was being nice to gain an edge. She was surprised. Mitigants might be better at business than she thought.

"I want his assets, his markets," she said. "You get that, I'm sure."

"Yes. And, yes, I will kill Seaton. That will benefit collective interests. This pact we make will allow me to act without harm to my clan's honor."

"So you'll do it." Estelle said with a deep release of held breath and tension.

"I will act as I say. Yes."

Estelle now found the Mitigant's voice vibrations almost soothing.

"Before we formalize our pact," the Mitigant continued. "You realize this will make you part of my clan's cycles."

"Cycles?"

"The rotations of our pacts, our contracts."

"I'm not putting anything in writing!" Estelle squinted at the ever-staring eye and anticipated disappointment.

"Nor will I. We Mitigants have never needed to make a physical manifestation of an agreement. What I mean is that you will be subject to the arc of benefits, and any turns of cycles linked to this pact. We Mitigants trade favors. They can be exchanged just as you humans trade assets."

"As long as Seaton disappears," Estelle said. "You need to take him out without witnesses."

"That will be difficult."

"I don't care if you need to kill anyone else, just do it as quiet as possible. And so no one knows I ordered the hit. I mean, why would you tell anyone, right?"

"I would not. But I can exchange my pact with you to another Mitigant. You understand?"

"But he—the other Mitigant would eat Seaton?" Estelle took a deep breath.

"It would be honor bound to do so."

"And then what would you do?"

"Whatever was required of the favor I accepted in exchange."

"Such as?" Estelle became anxious to close the deal.

"I don't know. Imagine a scenario. Do you know of anything that could be tied to this pact between us that can influence its execution?"

"No one knows about this but you and me. And you won't try to use our contract to muscle me for a cut of what I'll take from Seaton?"

"No. That is outside our pact. I will not." the Mitigant droned. "In any event, you have almost nothing to offer me. Personally, or professionally."

Estelle thought she felt a shrug under the ground as much as the voice's vibration.

"Then just do the job, and we're fine." Estelle sniffed and flexed her shoulders.

"I was honor bound to explain that we Mitigants trade favors."

"Look, I don't care about honor!" Estelle paused, but the Mitigant made no effort to exploit her remark. "Just do what we agreed. Kill Seaton. Got it?"

"Your emphasis is noted, Estelle Norris."

"What do I call you?"

"You seek my name?"

"Only if it doesn't cost me anything." Estelle sneered.

"It will not. I will make a sound that will be the closest thing a human could approximate as my name. Call me *RAAL*."

The name vibrated the ground and rattled inside Estelle's head just as a bee or hummingbird did when buzzing too close to her ears. She realized she didn't see either of those small things flying around, anymore. She shook her head and looked back at the eye.

"Okay, Raal. I think we're done."

"We are." Raal's eye lowered to emulate a bow.

"You need word on Seaton's movements?" Estelle asked.

"No. I'll hunt him in the traditional manner."

"But hit him stealth," Estelle moved close to the eye and glared at it almost point blank. "Do it quiet."

"As quiet as possible. Now, step back, my new cyclic. I'm going to move."

Estelle felt a stronger rumbling, but Raal's voice was silent. The ground spilt around the tentacle and it rose higher. A strong odor like rotted oysters hit Estelle's nose. Finally, she took Raal's advice and ran back to the edge of the trees. She understood Raal's concern on killing Seaton quietly, and wondered how Seaton, even with a small army, could kill anything like what burst from the ground. All the photos, graphics, and videos of Mitigants never really made the alien creatures real. They were a part of the news, and the news was always other people's business. Now, Estelle was in business with a completely inhuman thing that seemed to like instilling awe.

The ground over Raal rose like a dome and cracked as Raal pushed up from its hidden pit. The dome spilt and chunks of earth broke into cascades of dirt and small rocks as they fell. The shaking ground caused Estelle to fall down. She felt a jolt and electric crackle as Raal moved free of the collapsing earth. Raal was shaped was like an armadillo, but an armadillo on steroids put on more steroids. Sunlight glinted through the deep gray sections of shell free of dirt. Estelle thought the effect was like giant, ugly sapphires. Fully exposed, Raal was as long as a bus and as high as one chopped in half. As Raal moved passed Estelle, she looked to see its face. Even armadillos had faces. Mitigants only had a front section covered by some membrane or thick ooze that held the eyes. Their eyes weren't attached by a tendon, nerve, or vein. They just rolled in the ooze like bowling balls in syrup until a tentacle formed. Below that were bulbous plates that pulled back to open their spine-toothed maw.

Estelle recalled video of a Mitigant eating a cow. The spines pierced the body and pulled it in as others farther in sliced it into blood steaks before it all disappeared horrifically fast. The steaks didn't need to be small for a mouth that big. Estelle thought of Seaton becoming bloody steaks. The joy of that idea didn't ease her nausea. Raal moved off between the break in the trees without another word. No legs moved Raal's bulk. A swarm of oddly fast slug feet swirled between the edges of shell and the ground. An energy field took the place of slime. That was one small favor, Estelle though, even if the energy crackle made her nose bleed. It was either that or the smell. Estelle move towards the edge of the Raal's pit. She wanted to look into it. The stench made her stumble backwards. She started walking home. Back in the city, she said to Hell with secrecy and called for a cab.

"Say, ain't you famous? Like an actress or something?" The cab driver smiled wide at Estelle in his rearview mirror.

"No." Estelle said and tried to keep her breakfast down. Raal's odor was still strong in her nostrils.

"You look cute like an actress. You should be one!" The driver beamed.

Estelle pulled out her gun and placed it on her knee with the barrel aimed at the driver's back. The rest of the ride was nice and quiet.

The nightclub was loud. There was more bass tone booming from speakers through floor than music reaching ears. It reminded Estelle of her meeting with Raal. She pushed the thought aside as she watched people push their way to the bar. She was at a private table. Servers brought her drinks and they were all on the house. The low light and dark walls hid the club's small size. Strobes exposed the truth in staccato flashes every few minutes. The joint was only a front. Most of the building was an illicit warehouse and distribution enterprise owned by Finn Halverson. He was Seaton's main competition, failed hit target, and best friend. Tonight they negotiated the distribution of a haul of fish stolen by Seaton. Fish. Estelle though of scales and slime. She ordered another drink.

Estelle swirled the ice in her tumbler, looking for a victim and then looked up. In the low light, Seaton almost looked good. That was until the strobing revealed his face. It looked glued on to older skin that squeezed into a seam of wrinkles from his surgically lengthened chin and up to his ears. Seaton was pieced together on the surface and deeper down. All to stay young, if not beautiful. For that he had Estelle. She looked at Halverson. He was either afraid to risk negative side effects or still not quite rich enough to buy the gene-twist that rewrote your age at the ends of your chromosomes, or some other place. The noise and strobes made it harder for Estelle to think more than the alcohol of her cocktails. She decided to go all in, and ordered a Manhattan.

Estelle knew Seaton and Halverson saw themselves as kings. Estelle saw them as marks. One she arranged to erase. She tried to listen to Halverson and get a sense on how he bargained. She cursed the loud bass, instead. She glanced over at LaRoy. She hadn't told him about her new pact with Raal. If Raal did as promised, she would make LaRoy her main squeeze, just as she currently served Seaton. LaRoy was working for Halverson, tonight. At least Halverson thought so. Seaton paid LaRoy to spy on Halverson's operation. LaRoy took the job knowing Halverson would only trust him to whack people. That way he'd never be forced to compromise either boss but could still cash their checks and live to spend them. With fewer bosses than before, a good shooter became a commodity that could ask his or her own price. It would be an expense she would try to lessen by keeping LaRoy happy otherwise. She ordered another Manhattan, with ice.

Later, Estelle could feel the effects of bourbon and maybe a cracked tooth from biting ice cubes. She held her balance even in the stiletto heels from years of practice. They stood outside in the club's rear lot waiting for Seaton's car. It was late. Estelle's practice at reading Seaton told her the dragging night was not the only thing making him tense.

"What's wrong?" She asked.

"The car's late." Seaton spat.

He looked around the lot as if expecting something. His two guard thugs heard the tension in his voice and slid their hands toward hidden guns. Estelle looked at the one on her left, Bandy. He was her first choice of side toy until LaRoy showed up. Bandy gave her comforting nod, but then looked across the lot with obvious anxiety. He eyed a shipping container that sat at the end of the lot.

"What's really wrong?" Estelle asked Seaton.

"The negotiation went well. Halv made the deal in my favor. But too easy. Something's up."

Seaton's mobile rang. He snatched it from his pocket. Halverson edgy face flashed on the screen.

"Hey, Seatie!" Halverson chirped with a nervous nod. "I just wanted to let you know it was nothing personal. We're friends and all. But these Mits, the Maws, they got more muscle than you know. They've been quiet, but they got angles. They got one on me. They say I owe them a favor. But, geez, I just don't want them rolling into my joint, you know. I mean you killed one. You know it's hard to—"

"Shut up you gutless filth!" Seaton screamed at Halverson's image. Spit flecks hit the screen. "What have you done?"

"I just got you here, Seatie. That's all." Halverson continued through the speaker. "I mean, it's not like I pulled the trigger. We're friends and all."

"Aw, Crud!" Bandy shouted.

Raal entered the lot from behind the shipping container. His bulk now moved in near silence, and a weird approximation of grace. His eyes were low on his front plate and obviously focused on Seaton. Estelle was shocked at Raal's stealth, and more shocked by Seaton's display of concern for her. He turned and yelled at Bandy.

"Get her out of here!" Seaton barked. He turned to his second thug, Soles. "You go in there and you kill Halverson! Do it!" He shoved Soles towards the club.

Soles looked at the approaching Raal and decided he'd rather die in a gunfight than get spine ripped and eaten. He ran back to the club.

Seaton tore a custom machine gun from under his jacket. Estelle had never seen it before, and never knew Seaton carried it. It was thin, compact, and suddenly loud. A flame spewed from the small barrel as Seaton fired a burst at Raal. All bullets, either twenty or two-thousand scattered off his front plates without taking a chip. Seaton then worked the keys displayed on his mobile phone.

"Stupid!" Estelle let slip.

A gust of rotting oyster stench hit everyone's nose as Raal began to open his maw. Spine teeth erupted and stabbed the night air.

Estelle felt a strong pull on her arm. Bandy tugged her away. They fled around the corner to the alley. Bandy leaned flat against the filthy wall holding his shiny .45 in his right hand. Estelle reached in her purse and ripped out her .357. Estelle heard Seaton screaming something and in tones of high-pitched, naked fear. Bandy dropped his jaw in horror but stayed still. Estelle smiled. Bandy looked at Estelle. The fear stretching his face compressed into confusion, and then hardened into accusation as he realized she had a part in the hit. His accusing face broke into blasted skin and shattered skull flying skyward and across the alley wall as Estelle shot him point blank in the face. Estelle threw her empty piece onto Bandy's body, and then pulled out her back-up, semi-auto .40-cal. She kicked off her stiletto heels. There was no more screaming or gunfire from the lot. Estelle figured Raal was done. She ran, fast.

Estelle rocked back in the plush leather chair of the bar's office. She only got to sit in the chair when Seaton's lap was below her thighs. Now, all of Seaton was gone. Only Soles knew just how he disappeared, and he was killed just walking back into Halverson's club. Bandy was just another victim of mob violence. The threat of revenge was more capital for Estelle to exploit. Halverson would trade a truce with Estelle for her keeping quiet that he was a Mitigant shill. The set-up wasn't perfect, but Estelle's plan was working. Despite a lack of legal papers, Estelle took control of the Seaton's bar with LaRoy, two loyal goons, plus her own intimidating glare. Other gigs would follow, soon. She felt she could relax. Maybe go buy a suit, or another pair of stiletto heels. And a bigger gun.

LaRoy came in later with a plan of his own. Estelle wasn't buying.

"It's just a romantic drive. Geez!" LaRoy shrugged. "You like sex, but why not a little romance to go with it?"

LaRoy smiled wide. Estelle looked at his brilliant, handsome grin. She smiled, too. The sensation surprised her. The emotion was genuine, just as when she smiled in the alley before killing Bandy. This time, no one died. She took a breath and nodded approval. LaRoy drove her to a park on the edge of the city. Its grounds were not yet completely overrun by weeds and vagrants. Still, Estelle was slightly nervous. This was Mitigant turf. Estelle recognized a long sedan with darkened windows parked in the cracked parking lot where short walls of grass hid patches of asphalt. The two loyal goons, Cigs and DeeDee, leaned against the sedan's hood.

"They just made the place safe. Made sure no one was—"

"I get it," Estelle said.

Cigs and DeeDee nodded as Estelle looked them over as she got out of LaRoy's car. LaRoy retrieved an old fashioned picnic basket from the rear seat and joined Estelle. He looked at her and smiled, but his eyes looked ready to dart behind her. Estelle spun as she heard a door on the sedan open. Cigs and DeeDee casually held their guns in front of them. Seaton stepped on a wall of grass.

"You, muther!" Estelle screamed at Seaton.

"Babe, that's my line." Seaton shrugged.

Estelle turned towards another rustling of grass. Raal moved swiftly through dense foliage like a juggernaut. Estelle didn't know if she should be happy or afraid. Raal stopped beside the sedan, facing Estelle. A cloud passed in front of the Sun. The glare vanished from Raal's huge shell, but made his cuttlefish-eyed stare more frightening.

"Looks like you've seen this thing before." Seaton said.

Years of time spent in police custody had taught Estelle to keep her mouth shut when confronted. She held her lips closed tight.

"Favors, favors. They spin around." Seaton spun his right hand in a circular motion. "I can see why you guys call it a cycle."

Raal answered with a low tone as his eyes rolled towards Seaton.

"Each turn is an angle on someone." Seaton started. "Or, today, some *thing*. You see—"

Estelle turned and clawed LaRoy's face as revenge for his obvious betrayal.

164

"Ahhh! Geez!" LaRoy grabbed his slashed cheek. Seaton waved away any reprisal as blood welled between LaRoy's fingers gripping his face.

"What the Hell do you want?" Estelle yelled at Seaton. She darted her eyes at Raal, hoping for recognition and a sense of allegiance.

"Hey, I just want to live. And a new main squeeze. I guess Nona is up in rotation.

Estelle's nails nearly ripped open the seam of Seaton's face, but he darted backward. A deep tone from Raal stunned everyone into stillness.

"You're good at keeping your mouth shut, I'll give you that. If it wasn't for flipping Halverson before I waxed him, I might not have guessed you set up the hit. So, bravo, 'Stell. Of course, it means a bad day for you. A bad end."

"We had a deal!' Estelle shrieked at Raal.

"We had a pact." Raal's voice vibrated the ground. "I traded my favor I owed to you. I told you of such conditions before we formalized."

"Traded with who? For what?" Estelle screamed at Raal and nearly clawed at the giant monster.

"You can guess." Raal replied.

"No one knew the reason I whacked that Mit—sorry!" Seaton looked up at Raal.

"No offense taken, little speck." Raal droned.

"So, yeah," Seaton continued. "I whacked the Mitigant because they asked me to. Not this one, but another. At least I don't think—"

"It was not me." Raal said. "But it was an arc decided by my clan. The clan member Seaton killed for us was acting out of proportion to our goals. His aggressive actions risked making our long-term plans obvious."

"So, you are here to take over Earth?" Estelle said. She then looked over at Cigs and DeeDee in a solicitous manner. She frowned as both men looked away nervously.

"No." Raal answered. "But like your species, we need sport and occupation. In proportion, naturally. Our numbers are small, in comparison to Earth life. Thus, even if we are hard to kill, we need to be little threat to you humans, or else you will kill us all out of fear. So we maintain a low profile, while still taking what we need. Mostly we need entertainment. And food."

"Entertainment?" Estelle asked, and took a deep breath. "So, I entertained you, right?"

"You did," Raal answered.

"So that's a favor. And one I can trade that for my life." Estelle relaxed, but took a step towards the front seat of LaRoy's car where the purse holding her gun sat.

"It wasn't part of our pact," Raal seemed to vibrate a sigh through his low tones. "So, no, you cannot."

"You've got to work out the details, 'Stell." Seaton said. "When you called me stupid I was opening the signal file I was given as a pass if one of the big boys came at me."

"The file played a frequency that verified that favor owed by my clan." Raal added. "It omitted the chance of a lie. Something your species can craft quite well."

"So why did you shoot at, at him?" Estelle carped.

"Well, he was coming at me. Why not?" Seaton shrugged. "That reminds me. I have some issues with the gunsmith. She said those bullets would work on their hides. Anyway, you know the cred' I got from bagging the one Mit. If I could bag a second one—? You get the picture." Seaton smiled, then quickly looked at Raal with his hands up. "No offense!"

Raal answered with a short, low tone of unknown intent that made all the humans glance at him nervously.

Estelle turned to dive for the car door. Two sudden stings stopped her. Small metal poles pierced her blouse and skin on her back. She shook with convulsions as Seaton pressed the trigger on the stun gun. Estelle hit the cracked pavement.

"Evidently they got to clean up the ends, themselves." Seaton leaned down and spoke to Estelle. "That keeps the cycle closed for their own clan. Sorry, babe. But he says he's gonna eat ya slow. I guess that's better."

Estelle saw Seaton's wool slacks and black leather shoes disappear behind tall grass. She fought to push herself up. She rose to stand, but her legs were still too shaky to run. And she wore high heels. She reached to grab the car and steady herself, but Seaton or his thugs had dragged her away from the cars. A gust of horrid air smelling of rotted oysters blew over her. The two sections of Raal's vertical jaws were already at her sides. The

166

longest spines pierced and slashed her thighs and shoulders. Estelle saw her blood spurt across her expensive Lantouche' blouse. It was silk. That stain wouldn't wash out. She felt several stabbing pains as more spines drove deeper into her legs and abdomen. Spines slid between her ribs. She tasted iron. Estelle's head rolled backwards as Raal closed his jaws. Estelle tried to shake the blood from her mouth and bite the spines flicking down towards her face.

LaRoy watched Raal move forward and engulf his former lover. He took a few steps back and leaned against his car behind, Seaton, Cigs, and DeeDee. All three were locked in horror or fascination at the sight of someone they knew get eaten by a giant alien. LaRoy winced as he took his hand from his face and looked at the blood. We winced again as he heard crunching noises coming from Raal.

"So, Halverson is dead." LaRoy mused. "Estelle is getting whacked—"

"Chewed." Seaton corrected.

"Yeah, okay." LaRoy shrugged and held growing nausea at bay. "So, with you dead, it's open season."

Seaton jerked his surgically altered head as LaRoy's words shifted his focus from the carnage committed by Raal.

"One problem!" Seaton cocked his gaze at LaRoy. "I ain't dead!"

"No, but if you do drop, and soon, anyone, or *anything* can take your territory. You work angles, man? So do they!" LaRoy pointed a bloody finger at Raal.

Cigs and DeeDee grunted affirmation.

Seaton paused to consider LaRoy's point. He saw some of Estelle's hair caught by the wind that was sliced away from her scalp.

"You got a point, LaRoy." Seaton nodded. "A good—"

The silence at his back made Seaton freeze. He slowly turned his head to look behind his back stretching out his wrinkles at the seams. Cigs and DeeDee had their hands up. LaRoy had a gun in each of his hands pressed hard against their necks.

Seaton's fingertips touched his compact machine gun.

Raal moved on without a glance at the loud blasts of gunfire coming from the cars. Even if it would take a much larger caliber to hurt him, prudence was a cultural trait of his clan, or at least among its surviving members. Raal had eaten Estelle. Therefore this arc of the cycle was finished, and in ample time for the clan's spawning. The arc of favors with the humans had lessened the danger to the clan's crèche by paring down warring factions in the city. The little specks had essentially eaten themselves. Their willful killing of each other eliminated those capable of threatening his clan's coming young. For a time. Other humans as ambitious as Estelle would rise up. They would be entered into another cycle. The clan would not deal with humans until then, unless boredom made such interaction alluring. Humans did have a lovely flavor.

THE DRIPPING, RED PRIZE IN HER TEETH

"C'mon, Craig! Quit messing with that." Stu admonished his friend as he passed him while carrying a load of boxes.

Stu was more annoyed that Craig dared to look through the boxes of private belongings than by Craig's lack of lifting them. All of the packed boxes and bins belonged to Stu's new girlfriend, Layla. Stu wanted to surprise her by having them all moved to her new apartment before she came home. Her job at the doctor's office seemed tiring enough. Craig had promised to help. Instead, he snooped as Stu worked.

Craig was curious. He wanted to know what type of metal container he had found. He was even more curious about what was inside it. The metal box looked like a small safe, but it was comparatively lightweight. It was about the size of a cooler that could hold a six-pack and sub sandwich. It weighed only as much as bowling ball. The lid and its main body seemed cut from the same rectangular block of metal. Only a barely visible seam separated them. The lid had no dial for a combination lock, but it did have an inlaid keypad with six buttons. It wasn't like any safe or tool box sold at the hardware store. It was weird. It was also weird that Stu's girlfriend Layla owned it. Craig thought that maybe it wasn't as weird as the more-normal-than-normal Stu having a woman like Layla. She was also fairly weird. But hot.

Craig thought the metal box's keypad seemed to be old technology, like Stu's computer. Poor Stu, Craig mused. He had old tech, an old TV, and a hot GF that dressed like an old maid. Craig realized he had never seen Layla really relax and bust loose. But bust was a word he often thought of when considering Layla. She had a super-model's body, but with an even better front deck. Too bad she kept that front deck covered with business suit jackets and blouses. Those blouses always had a frilly collar nearly up to her chin. Craig thought that she should give the guys a break and sport a plunging neckline. It would be nice to see, even if her face was always sort of grayish. Her long and straight black hair probably made it look paler. Maybe her whole body was grayish. Maybe it wouldn't be if she got more sun. Craig thought of Layla in a bikini with her front deck laid out on a beach. He liked the idea so much he stopped pressing keys for a moment. Craig then realized Stu was the only one of them likely to see that front deck outside the frilly blouse. Craig sped up his tapping in a half-realized act of defiance spurred by jealousy.

The loud, furious tapping irritated Stu who came back inside Layla's apartment. His annoyance with Craig's probing hands and idle feet grew.

"What box did you get that from?" Stu asked.

"No box," Craig answered. "I found this in the bedroom."

"What?"

Stu felt sudden, parallel lines of panic. In one, he questioned his choice of friends. In the other, he wondered how soon Layla would kick him out of her life once she knew Craig and pawed through her intimate possessions because of him.

"Put it back where you found it!" Stu yelped. "Geez! Then follow me down."

"First, you want me to—"

"Just do it!" Stu screeched "The moving! Grab a box, not your ass."

"Don't you want to know what's inside it?" Craig held up the metal mystery. "It's pretty weird."

"I can ask Layla." Stu wiped his brow.

"What if she doesn't tell you?" Craig asked.

"She would."

"Just because you're helping her move?" Craig looked at the metal box.

"Because she's my girlfriend, dumbass!" Stu yelled. "Put that thing the Hell down and grab a box. Christ!"

Stu muscled up another stack of boxes and headed out again.

Craig had never seen Stu angry. He knew he should put the little vault down and actually help Stu. Stu was sure to buy them beer and a burger, later on. But right now, Craig knew Stu was stuck hauling a bunch of Layla's precious boxes down flights of stairs. This metal thing was pretty cool and very weird. Craig felt he could crack it open if he hit the right sequence of numbers. He had fast fingers and typically good luck with popping locks and finding pin numbers and passwords. He sat on the boxes he was supposed to lift, and then madly typed way on the keys.

Craig jolted as the seal on the metal box released. He saw the gap under the lid was now wider. He thought he must have hit a partial code. Maybe completely unlocking the box needed more than one code. He opted for brute force over more random tapping. Craig strained to pull the lid open. He couldn't open it, but his nose caught a perfumed scent from the popped seal. Craig would've identified it as being like rosewater, if he had ever smelled rosewater.

"Craig! I said leave it!" Stu shouted as he reentered the apartment.

Craig jumped. The metal box flipped from his sweaty hands and sailed into the bedroom. A heavy *THUNK!* came from inside the room.

Number Eight awoke on impact. She could feel the sudden waft of cool air against her exposed skin, but she stayed still with her eyes closed.

"Calm down, bro!" Craig waved his open palms at Stu. "It's all cool!"

"No it isn't!" Stu retorted. "What if you just busted that thing?"

"We don't even know what it is!" Craig shrugged.

Stu glared at Craig, and then sighed and walked into the bedroom. Craig eyed the opened front door and thought of bolting. He heard Stu scream. Craig knew he should run. Instead, curiosity compelled him to stick his head into the bedroom. There, Stu stood frozen. He stared at the metal box. It was now wide open. Craig wheezed as he saw what was nestled inside it. It was Layla, or at least her severed neck and head.

"Geezus!" Craig yelled and gripped the door frame.

Stu let out an unintelligible high-pitched noise. Craig pushed passed Craig to enter the bedroom. He looked to see if something had grabbed Stu's face. It was clear of anything gripping it, and also of all color. Stu felt Craig put a supportive hand on his left shoulder. Stu felt his pulse slow down. He looked at Craig's face staring at the potential decapitation result in the metal box. Craig looked composed. Stu thought that maybe Craig was the right friend to help him, after all. And then Craig spoke.

"Layla. She's dead, man!"

Stu shook his own head. The one in the metal case looked real, but Stu knew it couldn't be. He knew he'd talked with Layla a mere hour ago. Why would a killer slice off her head and put it in a special case in her own apartment? Plus, not even a homicidal nut could work that fast. The head in the box was just a really good fake. Stu thought that Layla never showed it to him because she didn't want to freak him out. They were still in the early stages of their relationship. He hadn't even seen her naked, yet. That fact he'd keep from Craig. Stu knew that Craig had imagined her naked several times. Craig was probably doing it right now, even looking at what appeared to be part of her corpse. Stu vowed to get better friends. Right now he had to deal with this one.

"Okay." Stu inhaled. "Okay, let's just calm down."

"Hey, I'm calm." Craig said. "Weirded out, but calm. You're the one who squealed. I mean, I guess that was a squeal. It was weird. Dude, you make weird sounds."

"So do you after Mexican food," Stu retorted. "But just keep clam."

"Clam?"

"Just shut up." Stu sighed.

"What are you going to do?" Craig asked and leaned down to look at the exact copy of Layla up from the shoulders. Craig wondered if Stu had killed her. If he did, Craig thought he should actually shut up.

Stu stepped in front of Craig and reached down. He gathered the metal box with care, but kept the head and neck at arms' length as he examined it and its container. It all seemed to have survived Craig without damage. He closed the lid. The box sealed itself as tightly as before.

"Did you touch it?" Craig asked.

Craig's question nearly relit Stu's anger at him. Stu opened his mouth to shout again. He took a deep and he exhaled instead.

"I'm sure it's just rubber. Or latex." Stu set the box on the fringed pink quilt that covered Layla's bed.

Inside the metal box, the walls muffled Stu and Craig's conversation. The head and neck known as Number Eight rustled. She flexed her cheeks to press hidden controls. A green LED light flashed on from a small panel beneath the synthetic skin that held and nourished her. She then heard the conversation, clearly. She didn't feel in danger, but she would monitor the moronic males that found her. She coveted their mobility, but not their brains. Her own was obviously superior. At least they had revealed a need to improve the locks to the cereculum that held her. Number Eight questioned her sister's involvement with the one man called Stu. Both of them didn't seem useful for much, save for one purpose that could only be temporary for the male form. Number eight relaxed and listened.

"Layla works for doctors in some fancy, high tech clinics." Stu continued. "This is probably some after hours experiment. Something made from a three-D bio-printer, or something."

"It sure looked bio." Craig said. "I mean, maybe she made herself a spare self."

"It's not real."

"Then why hide it?"

"You think Craig, that maybe because some people poke around where they shouldn't?" Stu glared at Craig. "It scared me. And you. That's why."

"Well, next time you're poking around with Layla, ask her." Craig nodded to affirm the virtue of his own idea.

"Yeah, Craig." Stu slowly rubbed his forehead. "Yeah."

Stu quivered. He hoped he wouldn't break out in convulsions as he spoke to Layla right after she got home. At least they were sitting on the couch if he collapsed. Stu knew he needed to tell Layla the truth, but the truth required him to relate how much he failed her and how much of a failure he and his friend were. Stu knew Layla was not a failure. She was smart and probably more successful than the men she knew, socially. That included Stu. Yet, Stu realized he was the only man and only friend that Layla seemed to know. There were no photographs of anyone in her apartment. The only likeness Stu had ever seen in her home was the head identical to Layla. It was the subject of his current apology. Stu found it strange that Layla remained calm as he spoke of Craig's violation of her most private space and their subsequent strange discovery. It was almost as if she somehow knew what had happened, and patiently waited for Stu to finish telling her. Stu ended his confession and pleading with a sigh.

Layla lowered her head. Stu expected her to cry. All that followed was a long, icy silence. Stu couldn't even hear her breathe. The lamp light reflected off her black hair that flowed down over the padded shoulder of her blue suit. Stu had never seen her wear anything else, even when they went out on dates. He could wear a T-shirt and shorts and Layla would wear one of her business suits and a blouse with a high collar.

"What you found was a bust of Reyna."

Layla's words startled Stu after the cold silence. She looked up at him.

"It's the only thing I have left of her." Layla continued.

Stu paid close attention to show Layla his sincerity, and also because he sometimes strained to hear her. Her voice was low, almost weak and with an odd flutter.

"Reyna?" Stu asked.

"She was my twin sister. That bust was made as sort of a death mask after a car crash." Layla paused and took a breath. "You can imagine that even though she was my sister and I want to remember her, I don't like looking at what could also be my own death mask."

"Right. Right!" Stu nodded. "And I am so sorry. I—"

Layla lifted her palm to Stu to stop him from speaking.

"You won't have Craig over, anymore." Layla said as a command.

"No. You got it." Stu nodded more vigorously. "Not here or your new place. He's history!"

"Okay." Layla stood.

"Well, I, um—" Stu stopped and nodded to himself. He thought he should be glad things had gone as well as they did and not hope for more.

"You can stay," Layla said and gave Stu a slight smile. "But you behave yourself."

"I will! I swear."

Stu felt a sudden calm. The danger was over. Layla didn't kick him out. She said he could stay. He watched Layla walk to her bedroom, no doubt to check the metal box and Reyna. She came back out walked to the bathroom. She smiled at Stu before she closed the door. Stu wondered if he should order pizza. He heard the slight squeak of the bathtub valves turned open and spray of water from the shower head. Things were going very well, Stu thought. Layla was now comfortable enough to take a shower with him in the apartment. The hiss of the shower spray grew softer accompanied by the splash of streams cascading off a body. A Craig-like thought struck Stu's mind. He realized Layla was now naked. And wet. Stu hoped that his time spent on good behavior would end soon in a shared shower with Layla. He sat back on the couch and mused further. A beep interrupted his salacious reverie.

174

The tone sounded again. Stu thought it was an alarm clock or tablet dying from low power. He'd just check it out and swap the batteries or plug it into a charger. Layla should consider that good behavior. He could still hear the water falling on the bath mat and paused to imagine it flowing down her bare curves. Another beep sounded. And another. Stu found the noises coming from the bedroom. His thoughts of Layla warm and wet cooled as he considered the room, and what he knew was inside it. The beep sounded again. He was sure Layla wouldn't mind if he was stopping an annoying sound. Plus, he didn't want a sudden tone interrupting anything going on between them on the couch tonight. He could smell the coconut oil conditioner wafting from the shower. He entered the bedroom. The tone sounded, again. His warm thoughts of passion chilled. The beeping thing was the metal box. It was still on Layla's bed. Craig must've damaged it after all. Stu picked it up and looked for a panel to a battery compartment, or just an off switch. He studied the small keypad. The lid hissed and popped open. Stu groaned long and deep. He opened the lid to slap it back down, hard. He screamed. The head, Reyna, was smiling with sinister glee and staring right at him.

If Number Eight could laugh, she would have as she looked at Stu in shock. Her plan had worked, perfectly.

Stu felt locked for eternity inside a spinning bedroom and staring at a severed head in a small metal vault that stared right back at him with menacing delight. He mustered the strength to slowly put the opened box back on the pink bed. He could hear the water falling from Layla's body, but this time in heavy drops and not a flow. The shower was off. The dripping was loud, and right behind him.

"Stu!"

He turned to face the naked and angry Layla with as much fear as looking at her identical stare from her decapitated twin. Stu finally saw Layla freed from her suit and high-necked blouse. It was as shocking as the thing in the box. Her grayish complexion ended at the same terminating line as her decapitated twin's likeness. Layla's neck was a shade paler than the curvaceous form that glistened down passed the clavicle. A seam or suture ran at the bottom of Layla's neck where it attached to the body coveted by Craig. Stu remembered putting airplane models together when he was younger, and how his brother's surgical incision was closed without stitches. In both instances, the pieces were glued together. So, it seemed, was the top of Layla. Fully revealed in either all her glory or horror, the two section of Layla looked slightly mismatched. Her stare was harsh and precise. It aimed straight at Stu.

"What have you done?" Layla cried. Each word shot at Stu like rifle rounds.

Stu's thoughts unspooled in his mind. He tried to find a line of thought that would steady his brain and shaking body. He thought of that awful moment in an adolescent boy's life when a mother, or perhaps worse, a sister discovers him doing something that suddenly becomes shameful when exposed. His friends had told him about that horror. Stu had never experienced it. However, this moment of his naked, human chimera girlfriend and her twin's head glaring at him must feel as humiliating. Actually, Stu realized it was far stranger, and far worse.

Layla and the head stared at him as if waiting for an explanation. Stu realized that the head in the box had framed him by luring him into the room. This situation was weirder and more awful than Craig's transgression, yet it was not his fault. Stu felt he should defend himself. He could only summon an unintelligible noise and shrug. Stu made another yip when he saw the head now moving its lips as if to speak.

"She can't speak without air moving through her larynx." Layla said pushing though her own disappointment and Stu's shock. She unhooked a bathrobe hung behind her bedroom door. She put it on and sat on the bed next to the head in the box.

Stu was surprised that Layla looked at the head with as much accusation in her stare as when she looked at him.

"Hhu--! How does she breathe?" Stu finally managed to speak.

"We don't need to breathe." Layla answered. "But we like to. The extra oxygen in our brains is sort of a, well, a rush."

"Uh, uh, what are you?" Stu rubbed his forearms with his palms to generate heat. He saw that even wet, Layla wasn't cold. His shivering was from shock.

"I wanted to be your girlfriend." Layla considered Stu for a moment. "We need experiences to adjust to normal life. Human life."

"Are you, um, some sort of alien?"

"Not to Earth." Layla turned her gaze to the identical face looking up at her from the box. "Just to normal life. We are new to it. We just want to live."

Stu tried to fathom their relationship. He tried to fathom just what and how deep this situation was, and just what the Hell was going on.

"I just wish you didn't betray me, Stu."

Stu gasped as Layla looked back at him.

"I, uh, I'm sorry." Stu offered.

"Is it so hard just to respect people?" Layla asked.

Stu's eyes opened wide. He had never thought to define his own concept of 'people.' Yet he was sure Layla and the twin thing in the box wouldn't fit one. Then Stu realized that Layla was identical to the twin thing not just in appearance. Her body was obviously not original equipment. Maybe they traded the body. Maybe the head in the box was what he had first met and asked out. Maybe there were more boxes and more heads hidden in the apartment. Maybe he was about to faint. Maybe he needed to run to the toilet and puke for an hour or more. Maybe he should just run. Now.

Layla saw that Stu was tumbling ideas in his head, and that obviously none of them included herself as a person. The same thoughts also ran through Number Eight. Layla had lied when she said her name was Reyna. And Number Eight knew Layla was Number Five. Both of them fixed glaring eyes on Stu that burned with reproach and disgust.

"I think I should just go." Stu said as he backed away from them both.

"Think?" Layla spat. "You should've thought before you— Ahh! I trusted you! Is it too much to ask for a normal life? Is it too much to trust?"

Stu felt cut into pieces himself. He still found the strength to back out of the bedroom and flee the apartment.

Layla stared at the doorway. She heard the front door slam, but kept looking where her normal boyfriend had stood. She lowered her head and caught the eyes of Number Eight fixed on her. Eight's gaze was both knowing and accusing. Layla gently caressed the lower edge of her twin's neck as if to smooth away friction between them. Eight raised her eyebrows to illicit Layla's next action.

"No." Layla replied to the unspoken prompt.

Eight narrowed her eyes and pursed her lips. Even without a voice, her scorn was strong.

"Stu is good." Layla said. "Even after this, he deserves his life."

Eight frowned. She then opened her mouth in a silent but passionate expression of rebuke.

"No. I won't do it." Layla stood as if to stop something from escaping.

Eight focused clearly at Layla's body, and then back up to her eyes. Layla's instinctively gripped her hands around her neck as if to keep it attached.

"No!" Layla took the lid and began to close it.

Eight quivered as she raged in a voiceless cry of frustration and defiance. The lid shut. She was in darkness again. She flexed her cheeks and worked the controls inside her small, dark home. A red LED light began to flash.

Stu dragged his feet as he approached the door of Craig's dingy first-floor apartment. The hedges beside the door were always well watered, but so was the mildew under Craig's carpet. Stu didn't have anyone else to commiserate with. He wasn't sure what to tell Craig, if anything. If he said that he just broke up with Layla, that might be good enough to explain his glum mood. Stu knocked slowly on the hollow-core door with its number missing. Stu's mood sank further when he realized Craig wasn't even home.

"No luck?" a familiar voice asked.

Stu turned. The shocks of his evening continued. Layla smiled at him. Behind her stood Layla, or maybe Reyna? Behind them was another Layla. Stu's legs grew weak as he saw that this third Layla attached to a muscular man's body. The first and second Layla were the wrong height. One was too tall, and none, especially the Layla-man, had 'front decks' as impressive as his now ex-girlfriend.

"Ow!" Stu grabbed his butt after a sharp pain stabbed from it. He looked to his side and saw a forth, short Layla stand from a crouch behind the hedges. She held a syringe. It was a big syringe. Stu felt suddenly aroused, and then stiff. The collection of Laylas guided him to a large, old sedan. They must like big things, he thought. Stu liked the sedan. It must be a custom job to look so clean when it was so old. He admired the intact upholstery as his face smacked into the backseat. The car drove off. Stu couldn't cry out to anyone or reach his mobile phone. The Laylas owned him.

He focused passed the drugs washing over his mind and found the clarity to become terrified.

One, all-female Layla left them. The other three Laylas drove for unknown minutes. They stopped and then dragged Stu to the front of the sedan. They pulled him across the wide hood. From the small movements Stu could manage, he saw the road shoot off to flickering lights he knew was the city from a great distance. The other direction looked like the barren edge of the world. There was just pale dust extending to the darkening horizon. Pale, just like Layla's face. All of her faces.

Stu hoped a plane or drone or even a crow would fly over and see him. There was no motion, other than the small collection of Laylas. Stu wanted nothing to do with them, but they keenly focused on him. Stu knew his whole system and thoughts were slowed by the drugs shot into his ass. If they weren't, he was sure his heart would have flown from his chest by now.

"Can I, uh, I talk to my Layla?" Stu managed to say through the effects of drugs and a dry mouth.

"She's not here," Tall Layla answered and patted Stu's chest.

"In a manner of speaking," the Man Layla offered. "But we are her. Also, in a manner of speaking."

"Confused?" Tall Layla asked.

Stu wanted to nod his head, but could only utter a sound odd even to him.

"You should be." Tall Layla continued. "But imagine being us. You wake up and you don't even have a body. All life is a bad dream. Not just one day, like the one you're having now."

"Wha-wha--?" Stu uttered.

"What are we?" the Man Layla finished Stu's thought. "Oh, even you can guess."

"Aaa-aliens?"

"Oh, Hell, no!" All the Laylas answered in near unison.

"More like a group of clones used in reanimation experiments." Man Layla answered in a matter-of-fact tone.

"Partial clones. More sophisticated than simple spare parts. We're made this way." Tall Layla explained and then stroked her collar bone where her pale neck fused to the long body beneath it.

"Born! We're born!" Short Layla shouted.

"We certainly don't want to stay this way." Tall Layla lifted up a metal box like the one in the bedroom.

"You're—" Stu struggled to speak and move. "You're zombies, without bodies?"

"Well, most of us do have bodies." Tall Layla to said and put the metal box next to Stu's head. "We weren't made—sorry, born with bodies. But we adapt them for us. We've gotten good and quick at it."

"So long as they're fresh." Man Layla smiled at Stu as if waiting for him to realize something.

"Fresh, fresh, fresh!" Short Layla laughed to herself.

"You'll get the idea." Tall Layla said.

"Well, not really." Man Layla shrugged. "The part that will get it isn't the part we use."

"Too bad." Tall Layla sighed.

Short Layla held her mouth and giggled manically. Stu shared a moment of unity with the other two Laylas as they looked with arched eyebrows at the smallest one as she laughed.

"Two bad." Short Layla said regaining a semblance of composure. "Get it?"

"We should've left you behind, Six." Man Layla sighed.

"A truly funny thing is," Tall Layla leaned over to look into Stu's eyes. "Number Five really did like you."

"She'll be mad at us." Short Layla said behind her.

"Yes. For a day or two." Tall Layla replied and stroked the arteries in Stu's neck. She took a scarf and rolled it up as a small pillow and then tucked it under Stu's neck.

"She wants a normal life. We want to live." Tall Layla again met Stu's gaze. "Sometimes that's not one in the same. At least, when you're escaped experiments on the run."

"Run, run, run." Short Layla said as if she was becoming afraid, herself.

Stu heard the whir of an electric motor. It was more shrill than a power tool, but not as high-pitched as a dentist's drill. Stu didn't have the intense spike of fear as when he last went to get a filling. This was much worse. Short and Tall Layla pressed Stu's shoulders flat against the car's cold hood. Short Layla looked away, but Tall Layla smiled as the whirring tool came into view in Man Layla's hands. Stu saw the amped-up electric carving knife and managed to scream. Hands covered his mouth as several slashes per second sank into his neck just above the collar bone. A deep red wave leapt from where the blades disappeared behind his chin. For a brief moment, Stu felt lighter and in a dream-like state. He saw the two Layla's that held him pull his headless body from the car hood. They, Man Layla, and his new shirt were wet from the massive gush of his blood. Stu felt a sudden, new spike of terror as he realized he was now like them, but unlike them, his severed state couldn't last. That was quickly followed by darkness, and then no sensation at all.

Man Layla set down the blade and opened the metal box next to Stu's severed head. Bloody hands lifted Number Four out from the box and carried her over to what of Stu was still alive.

Craig could feel his head swim. He knew he needed to be careful, or else he'd be cut off at the bar. For a second he thought the sight of Layla was an alcoholic mirage. He looked around and wondered if he should talk to her. Then Layla turned and looked over at him. She smiled as she sat at the bar.

"Okay," Craig said to himself.

"Hiya," Layla said to Craig as he sat next her.

Craig's pushed his brain to think through the effects of beer and bourbon. He guessed that Stu must not have mentioned the events at the apartment, especially with the small vault.

"Um, you seem taller." Craig said trying to eye Layla over again as she took her drink from the bartender.

"Oh, I am." Layla smiled. "It's my heels. They work even when I'm sitting."

Craig was confused, but shrugged it off.

"Um, have you seen Stu?" he asked.

"No. Not in a while." Layla took a long pull from her cocktail. "Sometimes I wonder if Stu wants to stay with me."

"Oh, he does!" Craig chirped and was glad to see a free drink put in front of him. "He always says you had a great body."

Layla looked at Craig and raised her eyebrows.

"Geez!" Craig leaned back. "I guess I shouldn't have said that out loud. Sorry."

"No. I'm not offended." Layla took another long sip. "It's funny, really. I always thought the same about you."

Craig was stunned for a second, and then managed to smile back at Layla. He knew he should walk away from his best buddy's girlfriend. But, things seemed to be going well with her. And, Stu wasn't around to protest. His thoughts drifted elsewhere. He thought it was odd thing that Layla now didn't seem to have the same 'front deck' endowment he coveted. He adjusted where his intoxicated eyes had drifted.

Layla smiled. She fondled the high collar of her blouse, and winked.

Craig knew he really, really shouldn't make time, this kind of time, with his best friend's main squeeze. Actually, Layla was Stu's only squeeze, and he was Stu's only friend. Flirting with Layla just felt evil. Yet, he was doing so well. Tonight, Layla was acting very differently. She had never looked at him this way before. She really did seem to like his body. Her black eyes ran up and down his torso. It reminded Craig of all those videos about sharks he'd watched. He knew he really should step back. This was wrong. He saw Layla smile even wider. Her teeth gleamed in the neon beer lights behind the bar. A clear and strong image popped into Craig's mind. It felt almost as if it was a premonition. He imagined blood dimming the ocean as a thrashing shark ripped away a big, important chunk of its prey.

Layla lifted up the small, plastic sword that pierced the cherry in her drink. She slid the cherry off the small blade with her tongue, and caught the dripping, red prize in her teeth. Craig wet his lips with his tongue as Layla smiled and carefully cut the cherry into pieces in her mouth. She then gently, slowly drew the cocktail sword across Craig's neck. It was wet, and tickled. He knew he should leave. He swallowed. He just knew he should leave. The second round of drinks arrived. There were more cherries.

BLEEDING HEART

Life itself is essentially assimilation, injury, violation of the foreign and the weaker, suppression, hardness, the forcing of one's own forms upon something else, ingestion and--at least in its mildest form--exploitation.

So wrote Friedrich Nietzsche in <u>Genealogy of Morals</u>.

Old Freddy N. is dead, now. Even so, his thoughts live long after he was ingested by the ground. Contrast that to the thoughts of most living people that seem as enduring as coffee through kidneys. Ideas like that came to my mind while watching hardened shoppers push through the weaker ones across the shopping mall. Nothing like half-price sales to stir the exploited herd. But I smiled through my contempt. It was part of my job. I welcomed all at my temple marked 'Information Booth'. Mostly my supplicants were irritated mothers asking what happened to their children. Smart phones or the internet, I would offer. I would smile at their perplexed expressions before telling them security is in the West wing.

I was a smart ass. Cocky. I worked out between classes and watched the dwindling middle class spend too much and move too slowly at the mall. My biggest concern was if my shoulders were noticeable through the dress shirt at work. One day I thought they must be when I saw one woman who could easily have walked from a fitness magazine cover. She looked at me from halfway across the mall. She was tall, sleek, and blonde. Gorgeous. Somehow, everyone avoided bumping her as she walked a straight line to my booth. All pick-up lines became nothing more than a hard swallow when she leaned against my counter and smiled. I really hoped I didn't need to tell her security was in the—South wing?

"Excuse me. I, ah, was wondering what you do after hours." She said cocking her head and smiling wider.

"I, uh, I'm open to suggestions," I coughed up and cleared my throat.

I shouldn't have been surprised the line worked. I could have said nothing. She wanted me and was in control. I took the sparkle in her eyes as the effect of some expensive contact lenses. Mistake. The glint in her eyes and high-wattage smile still held me while I fumbled with my keys at my apartment door. I got a bigger surprise once we were inside and the door closed.

She threw me hard against the wall. I got up and thought: she likes it rough. Then, okay. I could try and get into that. I saw the stupid Halloween picture of my former roommate and myself wearing drag and in a beer-induced, near kiss pose. I slapped it down so she wouldn't—

I hit the wall again. Hard. I tried to playfully wrestle with her. I hit the opposite wall. Next, I flew across my weight bench and iron plates. The pain wasn't fun. It finally hit me that this was not foreplay. Still, I didn't believe even a fitness queen who maybe juiced before work outs could throw around me so easily. I looked up from the floor and wiped away blood from my lips. It wasn't steroids giving her unnatural strength. What I saw wasn't possible.

The gorgeous blonde was gone. Standing in her place was a beast in the same dress. Even her suddenly jagged teeth seemed to glow from beneath the burning, hateful eyes. I ran. I made it down the hall. I threw shut my bedroom door and dove for my nightstand drawer. She--it--came through the door in a storm of wooden shards. I aimed the revolver I bought on a bet. I had always been more afraid of the gun than what I might use it against. Not this night. The thing charged me with jaws open. The gun held five rounds. I leveled it at the charging thing and flinched at the coming booms and flashes.

One!

Two!

Three!

Four!

Each bullet ripped through her, but all failed to stop her. She tore the gun out of my hands before I fired the last round. The fifth shot exploded into my chest. The bullet hit my sternum and grazed my heart. I didn't die right away. The thing knew what she was doing with the gun, and the demonic weapons protruding from her mouth. She needed me alive a few seconds longer. Teeth bit savagely into my neck. Pain burned my consciousness black, and then the darkness burned into something else. An empyreal dimension split open and sucked me in. Screaming elongated faces on sheets of twisted skin spun like an accretion disk around a black hole. At the center of this nightmare, a horrific entity consumed them, the terrified souls. People. Their minds tore apart like butchered flesh eaten by the malevolent, surging mouth. It was destroying them, totally.

I fell rapidly towards the swirling horror. I screamed and fought. I fought against the pain of being shot, against my blood being sucked out, and against the threat of total death. And I didn't die. At least my soul stayed intact. Pain and anger tore me out of the spiral. I broke free of the vampire's grasp.

I turned to see the Vampire writhe in pain while holding her head. I clutched my neck and chest. Both were warm, throbbing, and torn. It didn't just want my blood. It was a portal for that vacuum monster eating the souls. I didn't get sucked in, so it punished its thrall. That gave me a little time. The glass ripped open more wounds when I dove through the bedroom window.

I wanted to go to an emergency room. Instead I collapsed in a nearby drainage ditch and died. Except, I woke up again. Luckily before full sunrise. Sunlight hurt. I watched my blood mingled with sewer water, and followed the current. I crawled inside a culvert like a frightened spider. I wasn't able to comprehend what had happened, so I just waited with the rest of the detritus to flow out into the night.

Darkness. I slid out and wandered an empty stretch of urban highway. This used to be the business district before the freeway took most of the traffic, and then the mall sucked everyone into its void of asphalt and bright lights. Now, this place was desolate. Dead. So was I. Sort of. Some wounds healed, such as my neck and cuts. Others didn't. My chest kept bleeding in some impossible way. Why? The whole universe seems different, transparent. Something else was just beyond a membrane in the night. Yet it stayed unfocused and shifting.

I wondered why that once-gorgeous thing attacked me. A broken silver chain dangled from my right hand gave and me a clue. It attached to a small prism pendant imbedded in my palm. The vampire must have worn it. I had ripped it from her and kept clutching it. I suddenly remembered my roommate George wore a larger one of these after joining that church, or cult. Weird. I wondered if Georgie ever met my bad date.

As I wondered, I staggered. I was like a zombie for hours. I felt physical changes. I spit out my fillings as they painfully popped out of my growing teeth. Blood too. My tongue kept getting between their sharpening edges. At least my blood had color. My skin lost any hint of pigment. I didn't look good in ashen grey. I was becoming a vampire, but without bloodlust. How interesting.

How? Well, so much for me ever being the source of information. At that moment, wet, wounded and afraid, I suddenly understood the angst of the mothers' looking for missing children. I was lost, myself. For me, there was no kind security guard to give a reassuring nod, and then click the radio for a check the food court and arcade while mom tried again to get her kid on the phone. There was no one I could call. I was alone.

My apartment had a lot of guests. I guess my bad date was heard through the thin walls of the building. Someone called the cops. Too bad for me, and lucky for them, they were late to the party. Almost a day later, they were still sipping coffee while their technicians swept for clues and through my old roommate's porn collection. Yeah, of course it was his. I'd get to blame old Georgie for a lot of things. I wondered what clues they found. I wanted to go ask for help. But I don't exactly match my driver's license photo or pictures on social media anymore. Plus, looking like a walking fright fest with a bleeding heart might get me shot. Again.

I was patient, for once. At night I slid passed police tape and gathered a biker jacket, jeans and a t-shirt. The old snake design on the shirt might have different meanings for different groups since it first appeared in the American Revolution. I thought the words "Don't tread On Me" beneath its scales had special meaning for me. Besides, the blood from my chest obscured the images soon after I put it on. Weird wound.

I wandered again. I came up to a house where a storm of light flickered through the window. I looked in like a moth from Hell. Inside a dozing man in boxer shorts had let his potato chips dump across his belly. He sat in front of a fancy, huge monitor and ergonomic keyboard. Who knows what he'd been surfing for earlier? I was just glad he wore boxers. And then I looked at the screen.

An avalanche of emotion fell inside me. I recognized who was on the screen even though I had never seen him in human form. By aim or accident, the man in boxers and chips had clicked a link to a live feed from the Church of Universal Light. Its leader gave a sermon. I wanted to scream. His sinuous, bearded face looked straight at me. His eyes glared from the shadows of the hood woven from his braided hair. I felt his hunger and heard the cries from the tempest of souls again. I felt him claw at me through the digital cloud and ethereal force beyond the membrane of night. He

186

tried to pull me back into the spiraling horror his thrall sent me to in my apartment. The vacuum monster at the center of that horrific black hole had a name: Devon Koenig, beloved cult leader.

I punched through the window. Glass shards showered the terrified man. I crushed his monitor above my head and cried out in defiance. I screamed Koenig's name. I left the man cowering on the floor among smashed potato chips and glass fragments. I knew he could get a new monitor at the mall. He also needed better internet habits, and new boxer shorts.

I focused my mind. I had a new purpose. Kill the thing that wanted to eat me. Even without all the answers, that seemed like a good idea. I thought of someone who could help me. Even if he didn't want to help, I had the power to make him. I concentrated on my old roommate and CUL member George. My senses flew over the thickening mixture of commercial buildings and suburban housing. I found this a handy skill. I also knew it would be a bitch if the things like the vampire thrall and Koenig could do it, too. Then they wouldn't even need the blood I dripped from my chest to find me.

I was happy my own prey didn't see me when I found him. Although, I think George sensed something. I felt a tug from him. Maybe he heard the metal roof of the welder's shed creak when I moved across it and then along the outer walls of the warehouse where he and his friends did business. Maybe he heard the gentle pats of my bleeding heart hitting the cement. Georgie had moved up in the cult world. His clean, skin-head looked nice. I wondered who his friends were. There were armed goons by George's side, and by the guy he spoke with. This was not biz you did at the mall.

Near the men I could see white powder in clear sacks packed in loose grocery boxes. It didn't look like the produce for clean living. I wondered why the CUL needed black market narcotics when the cult had legal sanction for other drugs. They must be floating something extra into the followers' pipe dreams. Georgie's business partner still took hard cash but no handshake. Cold bastard. The powder-seller and his goons walked to their car. I was faster. I slipped snake-like inside their ride. The seats were real nice, real leather. One goon opened the back door.

"Hi," I said.

His face erupted dark red under my jagged knuckles. I found I was a bit stronger now, as well. And quicker than the goons. Goon number two swung his machine-pistol up, but not before my shin and knee found his groin and head.

"I was wondering," I said as I grabbed their boss' throat and ripped his gun away. I lifted him off the ground and then lowered him to my burning eyes. "Could you do me a little favor? Scream."

With little finger pressure, he screamed. The cult goons ran outside. Georgie slowly followed. I wondered if he glimpsed me shooting into the warehouse. He let his goons deal with the distraction. Back inside, he returned to find his laptop missing and replaced by a small prism pendant in a large drop of my blood. More drops hit across his face. He stumbled back into grocery boxes. I went back outside to arrange the players for our own meeting.

George came outside for his goons. He wiped my blood from his face. I greeted him with a smile of my magnificent new teeth.

"Hello, Georgie. It's been a while."

He turned paler than me as he saw me kicking my heels against the drug dealer's car. The dealer's goons, the dealer, and George's boy were in a neat pile beside the car.

"You look, ah, look different." He said.

I was surprised he could still recognize me.

"My hours have been pretty long, lately." I answered "You don't look well yourself, pal."

"I, um. I've been away from my I.V. line."

"Nasty habit, that. I never understood why you needed hallucinations to see the truth. But that's just me, and recently, reality hasn't exactly been my forte either. I guess you knew that."

"No. No! I didn't! They were just going to recruit you. Uh, what happened? Am I hallucinating?"

"No pal. Hard edged truth." I say and click my sharp fingernails together. "Want to feel?"

I gripped his shoulder with my nails. He didn't react.

"You can't hardly feel much, eh?" I asked. "Brain not in total sync. So how do you run this, then?" I waved the computer in front of him. "One of your boys help you?"

He nods yes.

"And I have a window of guidance, when Devon is with me." George explained. "And the drugs are less strong."

"Well, this is some old school tech, but it will help me learn some of Devon's secrets and schedules." I said and tucked the laptop in my waist belt.

George managed an expression of fear.

"There is one thing you can help me with." I said to George. "Do you have a spare gas can?"

"No," he said and made a failed, half-hearted grab for the computer.

"I guess I'll just have to use what's in this tank." A satisfying crunching noise came from the asphalt as I rolled the car inside the warehouse and left a trail of broken glass and plastic. I rested the car on its side near the boxes with the white powder and tore open its gas tank. Fuel splattered across the floor. I splashed gas across the boxes.

"What are you doing?" George shouted. "You'll ruin it!"

"You grasp the general idea. With the help of those old acetylene tanks I plan to blow it all."

"No! That is the fluid of our umbilical to *him*. He is everything. Embrace him and you'll know!"

"He already tried to embrace me. Sorry, but total death is not my idea of a good hug. And so his candy here goes boom." I withdrew a match box from my pocket.

"No!" George yells and picks up one of the scattered guns. "Stop! That's our vehicle out of the world of ego and its lies. You will never know his love if you can't surrender yourself to something greater."

"Your guru has turned me into something decidedly less than what I was." I withdrew a match and closed the box. "Be seeing you, or maybe not. Depends on how your boss handles your failure."

I raised the match to the box. The report of George's gun was a loud staccato, but he was shooting at a shadow. The ricochet sparks and hot brass worked just as well a match. The brilliant orange fire ball struck the warehouse's flimsy, corrugated walls and blew them off their frames. Heat added a little color to George's face before the ruptured sheets of metal fell over him. Later, I watched the rescuers pull him out. He was alive but stunned. That seemed his permanent condition anymore.

I kept moving. I found a universe in the shadowed roadsides. Sometimes I sensed something, and moved faster. A sense of desolation became my strongest sensation. It's what you feel after life is sucked out of you. I felt rage grow to replace life's spark. I felt it was time to strike another match. I found something to burn one late night. I looked down across an alley where three of Koenig's men entered a large van. Beside it stood a large man holding an assault rifle like it was part of his arm. Inside the van were crates with more rifles and assorted other power favors displayed by the rifle-man's partner.

"Hey, Vic, close the doors!" The man inside the van called.

No response. No Vic.

"Vic?" His partner called again.

All the men looked suspiciously to the open doors and pulled out their guns. Vic's gun didn't help him much. On the van roof he struggled nice and mightily in my grip, and used up his oxygen like a good thug. Koenig's men watched Vic's partner pensively as he leaned out and aimed his gun ahead of him. Vic's heavy body slammed into him and they both struck the asphalt. I remembered gravity fondly. Koenig's men shot blindly through the roof. The noise was annoying. The metal screamed as I jumped through the bullet-perforated roof and into them. The strongest one of Koenig's men crawled out. I helped him off the ground, by the ankles.

"Don't worry, I don't bite." I assured him as his head dangled over the ground. "But your boss does. Tell him it was me. He'll know who I am." I flick some of the blood from my chest across his terrified face. "And say hello to George."

I dropped him beside his car. He scrambled inside and floored the gas to speed out to the old highway leaving me to pull his pals out of the wrecked van. That proved a good idea. The diesel engine of the van still worked and chugged noisily as I drove it across the traffic lanes where I parked it to block traffic. As I got out, a delivery truck screeched to a halt in front of me.

"Hey dipstick! Get that out of the road!" The belligerent driver yelled. His angry face melted and seemed to flow towards his chin as I leapt up to his cab and smiled.

"No problem," I said.

Behind me the timer clicked to zero inside the van. The fireball roared across the highway and rocked the delivery truck. The crest of the shock wave blasted out the CUL pamphlets I'd packed next to the bomb. Some of them twirled and floated back to earth. Most fell like burning snowflakes.

In the morning I dared to enter my old apartment, again. They hadn't fixed that window yet. The police tape was no real barrier. I considered calling the building manager, but I didn't want to complain and loose my security deposit if I hadn't already. Plus, I wasn't sure if they'd hike the rent due to my semi-death. I wondered if I should move to a nursing home. At that thought I mentally apologized to my grandmother and turned on my old television with the sound really low. On the screen, a female reporter held up a burned pamphlet.

"The cult again seems linked with these bizarre acts of terrorism." She squawked. "CUL leader Devon Koenig responded to the charges:"

"These are merely acts of an injured soul bent on destroying our sacred mission." Koenig said in a clip. He stood calmly before a cluster of microphones. Even in a recording he seemed to stare straight at me. I wondered how he managed to cope with sunlight.

"However," Devon continued on the TV after a reflective pause. "We bear the perpetrator no hate, and would embrace him."

The camera shot panned out and showed Koenig flanked by his identically dressed acolytes. All wore purple velvet robes that Elvis would probably wear if he were still around. It didn't look too bad on George. Koenig addressed reporters in front of his stripmall church: the Vatican in aluminum frames of tinted glass for all lost, suburban souls and vacant minds.

"You're cult grew exponentially after the courts allowed your ritual use of narcotics." A reporter said. "Isn't this violence linked to drugs?"

"No." Koenig firmly answered. "My *church* is dedicated to peace. Violence has bled away from our being. These acts only illustrate the need of our mission." Koenig extended his arms as if offering to embrace to the assembled. "This new and unfolding millennium can be a path beyond humanity's present, animalistic level. It can be one of evolution of universal understanding that waits within. Bless you all. And to whoever is responsible: I forgive you."

If he could see my reaction, I hope he noticed my middle finger an inch in front of his recorded face. I kicked off the television, and stretched out to nap on the ceiling above the door.

It was a good spot for ambush or quick escape. Hours passed. I woke when someone actually knocked. I lowered to the peephole like a spider. It was Valerie from the 'We 'R Books' store that somehow stayed open.

Val must have wondered where I went. I sensed she liked me, even before I could sense her blood pressure change and smell the hormones flow in her healthy, young veins. Throb, throb, throb, went her heart. Too bad for her I was dead. Well, sort of. She turned and left with a cute little furrow across her brow. I bid good bye to Valerie. I thanked her for picking me over Erik in the vitamin store. All my smug reverie vanished when I sensed something move within a shadow.

The stairwell door closed behind sweet, ignorant Valerie as I threw the Vampire down the hallway. Maybe she--it--never left. I kicked it into my apartment and slammed the door before Mrs. Henderson peeped in the hall. Inside, she threw me against the wall again. This time I slammed her back. It seemed to pull the air out of the room as it shot down the short hall to the bedroom where she killed me. I followed her out the shattered window and to the roof. We moved like lizards chasing each other up a cliff. On the roof we slithered on the night breeze. At the center of the roof she stopped and turned to me. Her eyes burned intensely. A mask of shadow cloaked the twisted cover-girl face. She spoke.

"I can end your pain, and tell you what you are."

"Koenig?" it was Devon Koenig's voice I heard. The shadow mask became his face.

"I'll teach you to grow stronger." Koenig continued. "That's what you want, isn't it? To be strong."

"What I wanted you've stolen!" I yelled. "Now, whatever you have I'm going to destroy!"

His laughter thundered in my head. "Bold words little one. And you are still so very little. Try not to scream again."

Koenig's face vanished from his thrall. The Vampire instantly became its more monstrous form and moved with incredible speed. It tore a length of cable from the stairwell housing and wrapped it tightly around my neck. I grabbed at the cable. It wasn't trying to strangle me. It was trying to cut off my head. I flipped the Vampire hard against the roof. It slashed at me with razor claws. I grabbed it. There seemed no limit to its stamina, but neither was there a limit to my rage. I hurled the snarling thing into a cell tower

192

attached to the roof. It quickly burst from the wreckage. It was bigger, less human, and wielding a long metal shard. My body also swelled as my wounded heart pounded. I salivated in torrents, and felt a hunger swell inside me. I caught the Vampire's arms in mid-swing and shoved the shard into its ribcage. The twisted metal took a deep and winding path before erupting through its back. It finally collapsed. I stood over it and watched it bleed. The foul, dark blood was lost against the black roof tar.

"I'd like to say I'm sorry," I told it. "But there are many urges I'm fighting right now."

It leapt up screaming. I grabbed its face and stopped its teeth just short of my face. I could no longer hold back. My own teeth sank deeply into its neck. A dark spurt filled my mouth. The transparent membrane of reality ripped open and the images become clear. I felt the vortex again. This time, I was its center. The screaming soul of the Vampire spiraled into me, feeding me. Its last cries were of a hateful woman lost long ago to a more powerful monster, and then kept as its slave and assassin. Now she was gone forever. Her soul was consumed by mine.

Free of the force that sustained it, her body cracked and fractured into crimson shards. The shards splintered into drying filaments as thin as dust. As I watched, waves of pain exploded inside my head. I had severed her link to Koenig and the backlash snapped in my mind. I fell among her remains.

Her body was just a vessel for Koenig's will and a conduit for him to feed through. By consuming her, I ripped away a piece of him. I heard him screaming. I just laughed. He'd failed to kill me a second time, and now I was twice as strong as before. I reached up as if to bite into the sky and roar in victory, but a wind blew the Vampire's dust into the air. The roar died in my throat. There wasn't even a ghost left of the person she had been. I realized this little war had become bigger than just fighting Koenig. It needed to end.

I had destroyed physical aspects of the cult. I had attacked the altar. Now I needed to kill the god. Maybe I hadn't tried by then because I needed to nurture the hate that focused my life after death. The truth was that I needed to destroy both Devon Koenig and the hate he created in me. Otherwise, I'd nurture my little war while the victims were eaten across the battlefield. No more. In the distance, Koenig's image glared at me from a billboard.

"You'll know where to find me." I said over the ashes on the wind. I knew, somehow, Koenig could hear me.

I waited at my old job in the mall Information Booth. It was long after closing hours. Even the security guards were home and peacefully asleep. I stayed close to the counter, waiting. Koenig came alone. I thought: How brave; how arrogant.

"An interesting location you've chosen." Koenig said and circled the counter island.

I found it strange that he avoided eye contact in person.

"And now you seek information?" he said. "You must have many questions."

"There are a few blank spots," I admitted. "I sense a pull from some people. But they are rare. I was one of them, wasn't I? And that made me a target for you."

"Yes." Koenig smiled.

I could see the fire in his eyes even with his face turned. He still avoided looking into mine, and still circled.

"You have the spark that, magic or evolution, whichever you choose, kindled within you." He said and gestured as if to a crowd from muscle memory. "It can burn intensely, fed properly. We, and now you, harvest this spark to become stronger."

"Like parasites!" I spat.

"I prefer the term: hunters." Koenig said with chilling encouragement to my anger. "Nature creates balances. We are the dark side of the scale."

"But I wasn't born with fangs. You made this!" I gesture my talon-like nails towards him.

"Yes." Koenig smiled wider. "You escaped death, and your spark ignited around the dark influences grasping your soul. It is how we are all born. You were a trifle premature."

"Then we're abominations! Freaks!" I bark.

"No. Lions and hawks! There is an expression: 'whatever cannot harm you makes you stronger.' Compared to humanity, we are invincible!" Koenig gestured as if conducting an orchestra of demons.

"So that's why we scud around in shadows and suck blood like bugs." I said as if trying to spit out my fangs.

"Blood is not the goal, only a means to weaken the prey so they release their soul."

194

"And you use the drugs on your followers so you don't even have to do that." I said. "How slick."

"I think so." Koenig said with pride. "I'm actually doing this community a service. Think of how many stronger minds now operate fast food restaurants. Ordering a quick, greasy meal is faster than ever. Speaking of which--"

Koenig finally faced me. His eyes glowed brilliant red with each showing the vortex roiling within them. "You have your answers, boy. Now, come to me."

He gestured toward me. I felt the pull and pain like a thousand leeches rioting over my skin. I squeezed the handle of my Army-issue security blanket hidden beneath the counter. The electric motor of the twenty-millimeter Vulcan mini-gun shrieked to life. It purred loud and violent. The gun's discharge devastated the mall wing and Koenig's body.

So much for invincibility, I thought. I took out another keepsake from the van. Holding the shotgun ready, I walked over to the collection of bloody ribbons and shredded velvet that make up Koenig's body. He actually began to stand.

"You forgot to mention that stronger vampires, or whatever, enslave others to feed from. How many slaves are you sucking up now to stay alive, killer?"

The bloody scraps launch at me. I blast him into a display of chattering teeth in front of the novelty shop. He still tried to get up. I shot him again. And again. The echoes of the blasts rolled through the whole mall. Koenig finally stayed still, but he wasn't dead. He drew life from his victims to stay in one, semi-living piece.

"So what can't harm you makes you stronger." I barked as I quickly reloaded. "You're hurt plenty and you can't even die. I wonder what Fred Nietzsche would have made of you, Devon? Get ready to ask him. In person!"

I didn't have enough ammo. Koenig needed an even more devastating shock to his system to leave his mortal coil. I needed to end him and his life-sucking reign in one, explosive act. I tied up the shredded beast. It was a wet and filthy job. I could see him actually healing as strips of skin knit together as I bound him. I traded the million bungee cords I stole from the mall department store for a stolen spool of heavy chains at a hardware store on the old highway. I also pocketed a book of matches. And I took a metal bird yard decoration. I liked it.

I carried Koenig on my left shoulder bound in chains. We entered his cult's stripmall inner sanctum. A few of the cultists watched us in a hallucinatory haze. They all sprawled out on thin mats on the floor. Tubes filled with some white fluid snaked out from ports in the walls and floor and buried themselves in the distended veins of the cultists. I once would've called them pathetic, just parts of the herd getting thinned. But when you've had something stronger than you tearing into your neck, you suddenly get empathy. I was a sort of an ass when mortal. I learned consideration for others as a vampire. The irony bit hard. But a person can grow in weird ways, even after death. Maybe that's why souls are immortal. Or at least, they should be.

Maybe I should've thanked Koenig for the lesson. No. I wanted no sympathy for this devil. I just wanted him to burn. Koenig was depriving people of the chance to become more powerful, themselves. They were his food. There was nothing mild about this exploitation.

"I can see why your followers worship you, Koenig." I was certain he could hear me. "Once you get them hooked, they don't move. You still do."

But some of them did begin to stir. They didn't move to get up, but slowly squirmed as if their bodies were suffering cramps-- or something was eating them from inside out. Koenig's body seemed to be getting heavier. I realized I might've accelerated his healing by bringing him closer to his body bank.

"No way, Koenig." I said. "The pain you're causing is waking most of them. Let's see if I can inspire them all to a higher level."

I threw Koenig against the wall and hurriedly struck a match. I moved it too quickly. It went out. Now Koenig squirmed. Some cultists moaned. Others now didn't move at all. My second match burned brighter. I held it under a sprinkler head. A rain cloud exploded inside. The surviving cultists roused and moved in slow motion but with a single purpose: escape the inside downpour. They instinctively fled and snapped their chemical leashes. Their dripping blood and the white fluid mingled with the water pooling on the floor. The fleeing mob bunched up at the double doors, and then fell forward as they swung open. I figured that even at that speed the survivors should save themselves. I hoped this brush with death would be their last for a long while. I went to finish what I came there to do.

Water collected across the thin carpeting. I saw it flow through seams and reveal a square in the floor. I smashed through the hidden trapdoor, and then hauled Koenig behind me down the stairs and into the basement. Near the stairs was a swank lounge without walls for the king monster and his thralls. I wondered where George was hiding. Koenig had prepared for our encounter at the mall. A small gathering of devoted followers had fallen in a circle like logs kicked out of a fire pit. Their blackened and split skin looked similar to burned wood. The char mark on the basement ceiling revealed something like an electric arc had shot out of the cultists. I assumed the one at the center was George, acting as a new conduit. I had wanted to free him. Now his body just spiked my resolve.

I found the main water valve and turned it closed. The plush couches and fluffy carpet didn't block access to the pipes and utility systems. How practical. I rolled the squirming Koenig aside and focused on the large canisters marked 'FLAMMABLE!' I ripped out the lines of the pumping system to the upstairs pre-morgue of IV lines and mats. White paste squirted back at me in defiance.

"Nitric-cannabolin." I read on the canisters. "My chem Prof said this was explosive stuff."

I glanced at Koenig. He looked remarkably more like himself than the shredded carcass I had carried.

"What you're planning isn't a very heroic act." He managed to say through his ventilated throat.

"Depends on your heroes. Thor killed giants in their sleep. At least I let you wake up. He was a god, too, by the way."

"Aren't you tempted to try and consume me? You've seen my power."

"No. I've seen the size of your ego," I said. "I'd probably be crushed beneath it."

I rip off the top of a canister and dump it. The contents wash over Koenig in a small wave of milky white. He flexes harder against his chains.

"But I'll bet there are others, even older and more powerful than you. That's what this cult was about. You were trying to beef-up before someone could eat you. Juicing for the major league."

"And without me, you stand little chance of survival." Koenig sounded a little nervous as I tore another canister from the pipes.

"And with you? Sure. Hey George," I said to my old roommate's fried corpse. "Explain to me the good sides of the cult again."

Koenig manages to shrug within the chains.

"You did teach me one thing, Devon. There are things greater than my own ego, things worth fighting for greater than revenge. But, actually, I learned that myself. So there really isn't any point to you, mister messiah."

A bitter hiss rose above the sound of scrapping chains against the concrete floor.

"Except for one last question. What if the body dies before you suck up more souls to heal, or whatever?" I asked.

"You'll haunt the area where your body falls." He answered matter-of-factly, and oozed blood through the chains by flexing against them.

"And if your remains are scattered, then your soul stretches tightly across where they get spread." I dumped the remaining canister on the floor. "Am I right?"

Koenig thrashed like an angry shark on a boat deck. "You are dead! Dead! Deeaaad!"

I walk back up the stairs. Koenig writhed at the bottom step and bared his extended, hideous teeth. His burning eyes cut glowing ribbons in the shadows.

"There is still much you don't know, little man!" Koenig screamed. "Ignorance is weakness!"

I stepped out of the stairwell. I knew he was probably right. He was also my greatest threat to staying intact. I opened my match book.

"If you denied me life, I deny you death." I struck a match and let it ignite the whole book. "At least a final peace."

I dropped the burning matchbook through the shattered trap door and the shrieks of the chained thing below.

I escaped before the explosion, barely. The stripmall temple burned hot and fast. There wasn't much fire crews could do. There was nearly nothing for the cops and fire techs to sift. Everything was ash. Everything. Although my nose could sniff out what I needed from under their boot prints, after it all cooled.

Some miles away at a cemetery, I reflected on what I had done. I didn't have a funeral of my own. I wasn't sure what the living world would do with the remains of my past life. I'd left that chaos for others. Among the graves, there was peace. Really, it was only stillness. The endless fields and hills of grass were dotted with small metal plaques. A single dash between two dates summed up whole lifetimes. A small bank of old tombstones sat on a hill surrounded by trees. Near them, a more recently built but now dated spire stood alone. The styles shaping the stone and steel seemed mismatched. I smiled that it wasn't just good and evil that clashed. The spire faced the interstate freeway that always roared like ocean surf even late at night.

Koenig was much lighter. He was only ashes. No chains held him, just glass. I opened the Mason jar that served as his urn. I cupped a handful from the jar and threw an arc of black ash skyward. His ashes drifted back to earth under the backdrop of stars. I wondered how many lives Koenig destroyed to make himself a dark messiah. Probably as many as the grains in the jar. I wondered if this was justice for those souls lost to him. I didn't know. Maybe I never would. I left that to a higher judgment, if there was any. In its absence, this would have to do. My own dash between life and death would be the story of how a monster tried to eat me, but I bit back.

Nietzsche looked to the violence in nature to describe the dynamic of life. Some might equate the will to think for yourself with the will of the lion, and that it's all just a game of brute power. If that were true, I'd have been nothing but cat food. Yet, I survived. There may be dark powers out there, but they're not eternal ones. They can be fought, and stopped. I was forced to move within shadows, but I wouldn't rot in a grave. I knew it would be a different future than I imaged, but I would live on. So would others. I'd adjust to the new job and odd hours.

Another arc of ashes disappeared into darkness.

A MORE BEAUTIFUL WORLD

A young woman sat in a metal chair, nearly motionless. She could be any female student. Her blank expression was the same as one of utter boredom. Widened eyelids hinted at a buried will to escape. The reality of being trapped dulled the urge. Her expression was identical to many young faces in classrooms at any place and point in time. The same expression and same event occurred in many rooms at this campus, and other campuses worldwide. An almost clear screen in an eye-shaped frame sat before the young woman. It rested on a thin column that rose from an oval desk. A single cable attached to the screen's frame from a port in the table. She didn't notice the occasional throb through the line that made it appear more similar to an artery than a wire. Her blank stare finally rested on the screen. An enthusiastic but sterile narrator's voice began the lesson.

"Greetings. You are now of age to enter the world. We will impart this important memory strand and data helix to you. Observe your blank in front of you. You will use it to interact with our world. That world is changing. We must act to make it better. To move forward, we must know where we came from. This history abstract will impart the key moments of our shared experience."

The unseen speaker became quiet and let the information flow within the student's mind. The history lesson unfurled as a succession of media clips. Engineered memory-RNA and sensory stimulus imprinted each scene as if it was directly experienced. An introduction header flashed before each clip.

Education Helix
History Arc. 1.00.1
Event Strand .01
Start...

The first images were from a well-produced commercial. The setting was a bright, tropical hotel. Beautiful people frolicked in minimal clothing on a beautifully styled veranda under a beautiful blue sky. Lush palm trees overhung the nebulous, happy scene.

"Hey, there!" The male voice over was excited and buoyant. "Beauty may be skin deep, but now all of your skin can be beautiful. Beautiful with Synthaskin!"

The camera's view zoomed into a lineup of bare female arms and legs and fit male torsos. Each close-up area of the actors' skin held a translucent, oval patch that was hardly visible. The beautiful actors circled their Synthaskin patches to point them out to the viewer.

"Synthaskin is not an artificial covering or cosmetic veneer." The buoyant voice over continued. "It's real tissue. Not just hypoallergenic, it's hypo-all-genetic. Synthaskin can be used by all people across the globe."

The camera's view moved back and focused on the smiles of the various actors from different ancestral backgrounds. They all smiled with perfect and uniform white teeth.

"It's safe for them, and you! Like them, are you someone with a scar? Blemish? Psoriasis? Boring tattoo?"

The camera zoomed back to the patches on the various actors' perfect parts shown to have Synthaskin patches. The patches vanished to reveal scars, discolored blotches, and crude flower and anchor tattoos on the actors' otherwise flawless bodies.

"Now, nothing on your skin will ever embarrass you!"

The Synthaskin patches returned to the actors' skin. The collection of tattoos and afflictions disappeared behind them.

"Improve your appearance with Synthaskin!" the voice over beamed.

The actors all leapt about as if hit with a wave of absolute joy.

"Erase those marks and embarrassments of the past. Synthaskin covers what you don't want the world to see. Be beautiful. Use Synthaskin and take the future!"

A slick, Synthaskin sales package floated into view in front of the dancing actors. There was no sight of the actual product within the molded plastic outline of an androgynous human being that either supported or raised its arms in praise of the 'Synthaskin' emblazoned hemisphere over its head. The smooth packaging and its bold lettering changed color as the unit oscillated slightly.

"The world will be a more beautiful place with Synthaskin! No matter where you go, Synthaskin covers the world!"

The commercial ended. The second file began.

Education Helix

History Arc. 1.00.2

Event Strand .02

Start…

Images from a red carpet event featuring a train of celebrities flanked by their amassed fans, paid gawkers, and the incessant flash of paparazzi cameras appeared. The voices of a male and female reporter duo spoke as strobes flashed intensely at someone approaching the scene.

"You're with Jeannie and Larry again on the red carpet." The male voice chimed. "It's one exciting night, Jeannie baby!"

"Sure is Larry-poo!"

The view zoomed closer to one young starlet whose heavy application of face make up covered more than her backless, glitter-festooned gown that seemed to be in a state of constant cascade, yet never actually fell away as she walked with a tuxedo-clad companion who was never fully framed in the shot. Her legs darted in and out of high splits in her gown.

"Newest Hollywood sensation Darly Karren shows her skin, Larry!"

Darly Karren stopped on the red carpet and parted the right side of her dress to fully reveal her leg and a seashell tattoo on her upper, right thigh.

"I'll say! And not all that skin is hers. Or at least she wasn't born with it. It's the new rage of self-slapped tattoos. A new product called Synthaskin has upgraded to sport tats or even fake muscle lines or macho-man scars!"

"You could use those last two yourself, Larry!"

"Ouch!"

Darly moved her exposed leg to all the eager phones and traditional cameras gathering like a school of piranhas behind the velvet ropes and fences.

"Just kidding, Lare! You look great. But I hear the makeup world and many plastic surgeons are not happy with this new skin app."

"You're right, Jeanie, about me and that Synthaskin is causing waves. The product is apparently real skin, or the best fake equivalent to come out of the labs. It's alive and it's hip, just like Darly. Show us more, young lady!"

"And she's up for an award tonight, Larry."

"So is that great tattoo!"

Darly winked and then dropped the sides of her dress like a falling curtain. The flashing strobes died away. The scene of the red carpet event ended and the third file began.

Education Helix
History Arc. 1.00.3
Event Strand .03
Start...

Rough video from a shoddy phone showed the interior of a dark tavern. The view zoomed from a close up of a half-empty beer bottle toward shouts coming from a booth. On the booth's table, a recently opened 'Synthaskin Plus!' package sat torn open. Two women were engaged in a tug of war with their joined forearms. The women with the brightest blonde hair screamed as their arm tugs became more violent. The camera zoomed in on their forearms as they slowed to rest between tugs. A dove tattoo seemed stretched on a patch of Synthaskin partially bonded to both of their forearms.

"It's mine, damn you Cherry!" The most blonde woman screamed and renewed her aggression.

Her less-blonde rival gnashed her teeth and rose up to throw her body weigh backward. The skin of her rival's arm split at the edge of the dove tattoo and her skin pulled away. Blood erupted across the table. Both women screamed in horror. The phone operator yelled unintelligibly. The tavern images stopped. The fourth file began.

Education Helix
History Arc. 1.00.4
Event Strand .04
Start...

A nicely framed but still cheaply produced video started. A man in a silk shirt swayed on a stage inside a shopping mall. A rhythmic bass drowned out the rest of the music track. He moved with the music as nearly naked models came and danced with more grace at his sides. Three women in bikinis swayed with a single male model. All the models wore several, bright Synthaskin tattoos across their bodies. A large rack of Synthaskin products stood behind them.

"No matter what you've heard folks, Synthaskin is totally safe." The man in the shirt announced to a gathering crowd.

"Yeah! And expensive!" A belligerent male voice called out.

"You got to pay for the best, my man." The man with the models answered. "Synthaskin is the best. Look at these lovely people. You think I'd let them wear something that wasn't real, true, and safe?"

"Then where's yours, jackass?" a heckler challenged.

"Right, here my brother!" The man pulled off his shirt to reveal a nipple to nipple phoenix tattoo. "Synthaskin is on me, too. It can be on you. It's true it's not cheap, but Synthaskin is—"

A thug in black leather rushed the stage. The presenter instinctively leapt to protect his product, but the thug knocked down the male model. Two of the women in bikinis screamed as one rushed to aid the male model now on his back. The thug pushed her down. Two other leather wearing thugs leapt up to hold down the male model while the first thug pulled a knife.

"That spider tat is coming home with me, you pretty prick!" The knife brandishing thug barked at his victim.

The presenter threw the product display onto the thug with the knife and knocked him off the stage. The crowd's shocked murmur increased to a roar of outrage. Some people reached up and grabbed the other thugs pinning the model.

More people rushed the stage. The camera fell to its side and began to automatically adjust its focus amid the riot. The camera focused clearly on a cracked package of Synthaskin kicked in front of it. A clear fluid oozed from the plastic container. A translucent patch of Synthaskin followed the ooze from the package, and continued to move on its own until it traveled passed the camera's view. The scene from the mall ended, and the forth file began.

Education Helix

History Arc. 1.00.4

Event Strand .04

Start...

The view held planet Earth seen from space. The buoyant voice from the first Synthaskin commercial returned to voice over a new one.

"Synthaskin! It's worldwide and on the stars!"

The view of Earth descends to a young, taut female posterior clad only in a tight bikini bottom and sporting a rose tattoo. The woman, Darly Karren, stood covering her bosom with her arms. Vivid, thorny stems illustrated her crossed arms. The stems end in red roses on the backs of her hands. Darly winked.

"Our family of products now includes ones for your entire family!" The buoyant voice announced.

The image cuts from Darly to a family of mixed complexions all fully clothed but copying Darly's crossed-arm pose. The actors playing the father and mother flanked a son and daughter set. A rose-stem tattoo pattern ran across all their arms and ended with two roses on the hands of the mother.

The image cuts to the dad smoothing a lotion on his sports car tattoo.

"With our new multiplying agent, the tat on dad can be one for his son!"

The image cuts to the son as he beams showing off his own arm that now has an identical tattoo sports car tattoo. The dad grins with pride in the background.

"Looking swift is now a family affair! But don't stop in the home."

The view jumps to a kick drum on a stage bearing an axe-shaped guitar logo. The view quickly leaps out to show all the band members sporting the same image across their chests.

"If you can dream it, draw it! We can let you duplicate it. Look good as a group! Look hot! Kick it with Synthaskin!"

The view jumped to pan down a long line of chorus girls. Each girl kicked their right leg in succession, and then they all bent their legs with their thighs held up as the camera ran down their line. All their thighs sported the same tattoo of a line of chorus girl legs. The identical tattoo encircled each thigh like a wide garter.

"The multiplications are unlimited!"

The view continued along an impossibly long line of happy chorus girls that extended out from Earth's surface. The girls began to kick in unison as their line continued out into space and across to the moon.

"Synthaskin covers the world! And with our multiplier, it can reach to the moon!" The eager voice over continued.

The chorus line ended with the family at its end. The four of them jumped with joy in slow motion on the surface of the moon.

"Join the Synthaskin ascension!"

The commercial ended. The fifth file began.

Education Helix

History Arc. 1.00.5

Event Strand .05

Start…

Grainy video played from a security camera positioned on the ceiling of a hospital emergency room. Two doctors were visible in the camera's overhead view. They flanked a hospital bed concealed by curtains that held a motionless young woman. The sheets were pulled down to their female patient's feet as the doctors examined her. She should have been naked. Instead, Synthaskin patches covered her skin in layers like scales. Each patch has an identical but obscured flower image on its center. Oxygen and intravenous lines attach to the comatose woman. Copious amounts of surgical tape secured the IV line in her left arm. A few Synthaskin patches wriggled as the doctors spoke.

"Was this on purpose?" the doctor on the left asked and shook his head.

"I think it was some failed attempt to mass produce her Syntha-tat," the right-side doctor answered. "I guess it was pretty popular at her health club. She was selling them."

"She must've bought every vile of splitter lotion in town." The left-side doctor sighed. "This has got to be one for the journals."

"I just need a way to get these things off her. They're drawing on her tissues to feed themselves. She came here already in shock. It was hard just to push through the tat patches and reach her own skin for the IV! There are so many of these things." The doctor shuddered. "Her whole immune response is shutting down."

"The inhibitors?" The left-side doctor asked.

"Yeah, the trans-genetic properties. I mean, I don't even get how they trick the immune system not to attack them." The right-side doctor gripped his face in confusion.

"Maybe try a chemo protocol." The doctor on the left offered.

"I guess. The company hasn't called back, yet."

A nurse entered and spoke. "Doctor, the family is here."

"Okay. Okay." The doctor on the right said and drew the sheet back over the patient.

The grainy security camera feed ended. The sixth clip began.

Education Helix

History Arc. 1.00.6

Event Strand .06

Start…

A clip from a TV news broadcast appeared featuring a red-headed anchor woman. A super-imposed video loop of a brunette woman clawing at her Synthaskin-covered face played at the

206

anchor woman's left shoulder. The title "Soldado Assassination?" gleamed below the video. The horrific images of the brunette woman repeated as the anchor calmly read the story to viewers.

"The world was shocked as video of Corrine Soldado's death went viral." The newscaster began. "Ms. Soldado's murder was broadcast live through her own webcam. Her Synthaskin patch, or lucent, quickly covered her face and prevented Ms. Soldado from breathing. She could not claw it away before collapsing from lack of air. The FBI's forensic labs confirmed that a pheromone mixed into Soldado's herb tea lured the patch to her face. It then adhered tightly after Soldado stopped using the tea after at the onset of suffocation.

"This murder is also a potential assassination, as a shunt virus was found on Soldado's computer that would give access to proprietary technologies of her employer to unnamed accomplices. Ironically, Ms. Soldado worked for Gen-Path Pharma, whose own competitor to the Synthaskin line, Feel Cleer membrane, has yet to reach the open market. Neither company could be reached for comment."

The newscast video ended. The seventh file began.

Education Helix

History Arc. 1.00.7

Event Strand .07

Start…

Video of a press conference focused on two men at a podium. One man wore a shiny suit. The other stood in a bright white lab coat. The Synthaskin logo blazed on the front of the podium and beamed large on wall behind them. The man in the lab coat spoke first.

"I'm Dr. Erwhen White. This is my colleague, Synthaskin division head, Wilson Sprenner. The unfortunate event involving a Synthaskin malfunction has led us to improve the Synthaskin brand. We are making the patches, the lucents, smarter to prevent this from happening." Dr. White ended.

"Smarter how?" a reporter called out.

"Ultimately that's proprietary," Dr. White answered. "But the lucent will be able to link to the nervous system of the consumer." Dr. White stopped as Wilson Sprenner leaned in.

"We have a new line of products for the consumer to communicate with their lucents." Sprenner said. "It will make the

Synthaskin line far more symbiotic. The link of lucent and consumer will become far more intimate."

Sprenner ended with a broad smile and nod. He glanced at White who also smiled and nodded.

"And they'll detach on command?" a reporter asked.

"They'll move." White said.

"But will they detach?" The reporter pressed.

"We are making the product safer." Sprenner smiled.

A rise of simultaneous question grew into a loud clamor as Sprenner waved farewell and lead White away from the podium. The images of the press conference ended. The eighth file began.

Education Helix

History Arc. 1.00.8

Event Strand .08

Start...

An interview on a cable television news channel played. The show's middle-aged, Caucasian male host sat at an impractically large, glassy black desk on the neon-red and black set. His suit was rumpled grey. The younger male interview subject sat pensively at his off-set location. His image was broadcast on a flat screen hung to the left of the show's acidic host. The televised guest bent his shoulders toward his torso as if his arms threatened to bump thin walls just off camera at his sides. A static background of Washington D.C. sat behind the guest, even though the title on the screen below his face said: 'Albert Winterbourne, PhD. Live from San Antonio, TX.' The host looked at the viewers from across the expanse of black desktop where he lounged with room to spare.

"Welcome back to 'Best Guess Live,' I'm your host, Robert Guess." He turned to the screen displaying his guest. "So you were saying doctor, not to worry about the skin patches, I guess they're calling them 'lucents', but not to worry about them infecting *us* with *their* genes? Incredible."

"No. That's not what I said." Dr. Winterbourne answered on the screen. "I said I'm less concerned about genetic transfer from the Synthaskin lucents to their users, and I'm more concerned over the ability of the individual patches to exit without a host. They can do this in the lab. Thousands or more were bought and discarded before the self-replicating agents were sold. I'm worried they may become some new form of parasite."

"Parasite?" Guess asked, dryly.

"It could happen." Winterbourne said. "They're built to store energy reserves. Off a human body they're something like a flat worm. Except these things are artificial worms."

"So?" Guess shrugged.

"So? Okay. So, they have properties of natural life, but they're artificial." Winterbourne's hands came into view at the bottom of the screen as he gestured with passion. "If enough are lost into the environment, we can't guess what they might evolve into!"

"Evolve?" Guess pursed his lips and slowly rocked his head. "Doctor, hasn't evolution been disproven?"

Winterbourne's brow furrowed at Guess' comment. He stared into the camera in silence and shock. The video of the interview ended. The ninth file began.

Education Helix
History Arc. 1.00.9
Event Strand .09
Start...

The natural sights of a diary farm in daylight appeared. A distressed farmer addressed a reporter who stood off camera. An isolated cow chewed grass behind him. The cow was predominately white with patches of black across her heavy sides.

"I don't know what the Hell that is, but it's not something that should be on a cow!"

The camera view zoomed beyond the farmer to a closer view of the cow. One of the cow's dark patches had a round shape and perfectly even edges. It distended off the cow's hide like a shallow blister. Its tint was dark brown instead of black. It rippled on its own. The scene cut from the cow and pasture. The tenth clip began.

Education Helix
History Arc. 1.01.0
Event Strand .10
Start...

Images of suburban America appeared. An angry man stood by his front yard as three children played in the drive way behind him. All three children walked around in a loose circle while focused on small screens held tightly in their small hands. The man addressed a female reporter who nodded almost in sync with the man's points.

"My neighbor said he saw a bald patch on his dog!" The suburban man screeched. "But it wasn't mange, it wasn't a bald patch. It moved around."

"That disturbed you." The reporter said.

"Of course!" The man snapped. "Do you know what the Hell's on your dog, today? Your cat? Hell, what's got stuck on your neighbors? Do we even know?"

The reporter nodded. The scene jumped to the eleventh clip.

Education Helix

History Arc. 1.01.1

Event Strand .11

Start...

Internet video uploaded from a phone's camera showed a wriggling gold fish in a tabletop fishbowl. The goldfish swam with difficulty. It turned its body. A small Synthaskin patch covered is opposite side and gill.

A hesitant male voice spoke as the goldfish labored in its bowl: "I don't know where it came from. I know I didn't put it in there."

The scene cut from the confines of a fishbowl to the sprawling majesty of the Grand Canyon as the twelfth file played.

Education Helix

History Arc. 1.01.2

Event Strand .12

Start...

The Grand Canyon shot panned out from an observation site built to give an epic view, but the images darted away from the sprawling vista. The photographer found a site more to his liking. The camera became still while focused on a ventrally well-endowed young woman in a tight, Summer top. She was enjoying the other view.

"Hi!" the photographer said. His voice was that of a young man.

"Oh! Hi." The surprised young woman replied as she noticed her camera-armed admirer.

"You like my hat cam?" the photographer asked, and a momentarily finger jabbed into view from bellow.

"It's nice." The woman replied while still taking in the canyon.

"It sends a live feed!"

"You should be filming the view." The woman pointed across the canyon, but didn't look at the young man. "It's beautiful."

210

"Yeah, it's beautiful. Not as beautiful as you."

"You're sweet." The woman finally looked again at the young man and glanced up at the camera. She immediately looked back across the epic geology stretched out before the small crowd of tourists.

"Thanks!" the young photographer said. "How about a flash?"

"What?" The woman turned to frown at her now intrusive admirer.

"Just a quickie!" he said. "Flip up your top. They're hot!"

"You little freak!" the woman made a fist and cocked it.

"Whoa! Hey, I—"

The image became jostled from people running passed the young man and woman.

"What the--!"

The young man aimed his head and camera angle to follow the running group. An awful noise came closer to him from behind. It sounded as if an animal suffered fear and sudden suffocation.

Hnnnnnngh!

Hnnnnnngh!

Hnnnnnngh!

The young woman screamed as she saw what made the noise. The young man flipped his point of view and collided with someone as the sounds became the loudest. The camera view jerked back. It showed a park ranger's face engulfed by rippling flaps of skin. A flap leapt over and covered the hat-camera's lens.

"Geezus! Oh, Geezus!" The young man cried out. "Ge-*hnnngh!*"

The Grand Canyon scene went black. The thirteenth file began.

Education Helix

History Arc. 1.01.3

Event Strand .13

Start…

Video shot at the bottom of a city canyon between skyscrapers played. Smoke drifted across the glass-plated sides of the high-rise buildings. Shouting echoed down the street. The camera's view lurched to show a street barricade made from cars, tires, and parts of the urban landscape smashed into debris. The top of the barricade exploded. The camera's view ducked among several police officers and soldiers behind an armored car marked

'NYPD'. Burning fragments fell around them. The muzzle of an assault rifle jabbed into view.

Another, louder explosion sounded. The soldiers moved from behind the armored car. The camera followed. A seemingly dazed man holding a rifle staggered from the barricade as its top collapsed to the street.

Behind the camera a loud voice yelled: "Freeze! Freeze!"

The loud, sharp pops of assault rifles sounded and the man fell. The camera followed the soldiers towards the dead man. It stopped and panned down on him. Taut, translucent skin covered his face. His eyes were visible behind the membrane and locked in shock. The camera lurched around the shattered barricade and revealed the smoldering bodies of a small unit of armed people. Synthaskin patches also covered their faces. Some of the patches rippled and others slid off the corpses.

A voice yelled behind the camera: "Burn 'em! Light 'em up now!"

The camera angle dropped suddenly. The ground came into focus as the camera swayed. The view rested on the black service boots of the camera operator. A Synthaskin patch was visible climbing the right boot. It formed a tip and quickly probed its path ahead as it climbed the laces. The camera's view rose back up. The rising lens slowly passed the corpses. It stopped at a sweaty, angry male face capped by a Kevlar helmet glaring at the bodies. The angry man turned and looked passed the camera at its operator. His face lit up with shock.

"Ah, geez! Frank!" The man in the helmet yelled.

The muzzle of an automatic pistol appeared. The image went black. The fourteenth file began.

Education Helix

History Arc. 1.01.4

Event Strand .14

Start...

Coverage of an impromptu press conference with a four-star General flashed on. The General faced a dense, half-wreath of microphones and mobile phones in a sparse hallway. A loud, dissonant barrage of question came from behind the mics and phones.

"We don't know if the people afflicted are even in control of their actions." The General said to one questioner.

"That suggests the mutated lucents are in control." A reporter off camera said. "Are you saying the lucent patches are controlling, not just altering the hosts?"

"They can think on their own?" Another reporter furthered.

"I'm saying this is not a war against rebels," the General answered. "This is a war for human survival, at least the humanity we know now."

The General began to push through the reporters' barricade. The video ended. The fifteenth file began.

Education Helix
History Arc. 1.01.5
Event Strand .15
Start…

Video from a helmet camera at another combat scene played. On the top of an armored personnel carrier, a sleek assault rifle rested across legs clad in the latest color-reactive camouflage. The heavy fabric changed its pattern as the vehicle moved between tracts of trees with Autumn leaves and abandoned residential houses. At the end of the soldier's legs bobbed contrasting and timeless black combat boots. Brakes screeched. The personnel carrier lurched. The boots hit pavement. The view panned across a crumbling neighborhood. The view showed the backs of a unit of soldiers well-equipped with body armor and technology. They sprinted to rusting cars for cover.

In the view ahead was a house where people rushed out. All carried differing styles of rifles. They ran to a revetment built near the street. A man ran out the doorway and exploded into a cloud of red mist and bone fragments as deafening blasts sounded from the heavy machine gun on the armored personnel carrier. The vehicle's engine revved as it moved behind the soldiers. An invisible chain saw appeared to cut the house apart as the machine gun continued to fire.

The sharp *whizz* of bullets cut through the air above and around the soldiers as return fire came from the revetment. The view zoomed to a close-up of a haggard looking woman among the militants from the house. They all wore salvaged and miss-matched combat gear over normal clothing. The militants' muzzle flashes popped in the direction of the camera. A cross-hair flashed on the woman's face. Her head erupted as dark red when a quick salvo of bullets ripped her skull apart. The people around her suffered the

NIGHTMARES AND OTHER VICES

same fate. The gunfire stopped. The crack of falling beams sounded from inside the militant's shattered house. The camera swung to the victorious, but silent soldiers. Under their color-reactive helmets rippled layers of Synthaskin that puckered around a lens in the center of each soldier's face.

The combat scene ended. The sixteenth file began.
Education Helix
History Arc. 1.01.6
Event Strand .16
Start...

The image jumped to a darkened chamber. A stark light flashed on to reveal the flat metal bed of a modified coroner's table. Six uniformed guards in executioners' hoods lifted a scowling male prisoner from the shadows. The prisoner wore a bright orange jumpsuit. His head was completely shaven. A plastic gag bound the prisoner's mouth. Three men in suits and hoods stepped to the head of the table. Each man carried a small canister in their hands. They observed the prisoner strapped down to the table. The guards stepped back in unison. The men in suits placed their canisters around the prisoner's head. His eyes glanced around with a defiant glare.

The canisters popped open along seams down their sides. The seams rolled back like lips. Clear fluid erupted from the canisters. The ooze flowed slowly toward the prisoner's head. It touched his skin. He thrashed his head and neck. His violent motion flicked some of the fluid across his face. He bit against his gag, and uttered a long, defiant grunt. Synthaskin patches slid out of the canisters and toward the prisoner's head. They inexorably gripped his skin, despite his thrashing. They traveled up his shaven head, checks, and neck. His thrashes become spasms, and then his body became limp. His defiant glare relaxed into a blank stare as the Synthaskin parasites fastened to his skin. The one adhering to his shaven skull rippled.

The prisoner's file ended. The seventeenth clip began.
Education Helix
History Arc. 1.01.7
Event Strand .17
Start...

Images played of several people moving in slow but orderly rows inside a skyscraper's entrance lobby. Evenly spaced and straight lines of pedestrians also filled upper level tiers and a wide, transparent staircase. All visible eyes carried a blank stare. Most of the walkers were bald. All had faces have with an extra layer of thick and occasionally moving skin. Several skin patches had tattoos. Other than the noise from footfall, the scene was completely silent.

The voice of the original narrator from the classroom returned and said: "Thus, order was restored to the world. Our order."

The images of the orderly walking masses faded and the series of clips came to an end with a final header.

Education Helix

History Arc. 1.0 Stop

Event Strands Complete

End.

The student's awareness was again the reality of the single-desk classroom.

"We cover the embarrassments of the past." The voice spoke again in the classroom. "We make a more beautiful world. Now, take your blank, and move forward to maintain our beauty."

The tube connecting to the screen detached. The screen's membrane slid down from the oval frame and moved toward the seated young woman. A sudden *SNAP!* sounded as metal restraints trapped her in the chair. She slowly shook her head as if just waking. The translucent patch of Synthaskin coiled like a viper, and shot onto her face. Behind the membrane, the young woman's eyes widened and her mouth opened as if to scream. She flexed hard against her restraints and thrashed her head from side to side. Her motions slowed. The translucent patch flowed behind her neck. The young woman's face was again blank, and now even more lifeless. The restraints released. The young woman's body rose from the chair with legs that fought to stand as if feeling gravity for the first time.

"Remember, you are beautiful." The voice said. "You are one of many who are the future. No matter where you go, Synthaskin covers the world."

OUTFALL

The weather was cool, but nice for late Fall. Nevertheless, Floyd Welker frowned. His stomach wanted to pitch out the large omelet and bad coffee he had at the diner this morning. He resisted. The spew would further violate the grave where something had made a meal of a buried corpse. Floyd liked greasy food stuffed with cheese. He didn't like chunks of skin and lumps of gelled blood, especially when he had known the rest of the person recently buried in his cemetery. Caring for the dead was his livelihood. Now both their bodies and his business were under threat.

The sod of the freshly filled grave lay thrown aside. Something had dug out the fill dirt and strewn it to the sides in chaotic piles as if by hand. Large hands. The expensive casket sat ripped open. Shreds of clothing littered its padded interior. Dark stains and small, waxy fragments stuck to the casket's silken padding and congealed on the grass. The casket had been heaved out of the concrete crypt at the bottom of the grave, and then used as a cafeteria tray. The entree was the loved one of Floyd's last client who was not left to rest in peace.

"Is that a tooth?" Grady, Floyd's grounds foreman said as he pointed to a small chunk near the piles of dirt.

"Oh, geezus, Grady I don't—" Floyd stopped as he glanced at the lump. "Yeah, an old-school, gold crown."

"We should save it." Grady said.

"Yeah." Floyd nodded. "But leave everything as is for the Sheriff's people."

"Crows?" Grady asked.

Floyd sighed but was relieved to look up.

"Yeah. True." Floyd watched some of the black birds gathered in the trees at the cemetery's edge. "Post someone to scare them off. And keep looking."

"For?" Grady asked.

"For whatever."

Floyd looked again at the aftermath of grisly hunger sated by brutal focus and great strength. He knew that neither human nor animal did it. He was glad the culprit wasn't still around, but Floyd knew it would be back. Life wasn't so simple as to give one, quick if horrific problem and then have it disappear. This was going to involve far more than just calling the cops and enduring the bad press. He would have to find a way to explain to his client's survivors that something ate their buried loved one, and that there was no refund.

"It's got to be some sort of 'Chant." Grady said as he turned towards his groundskeeper truck on the car lane. "But I don't think it was our shorty friends. I like them."

"Me, too." Floyd said.

He certainly hoped it wasn't the 'shorty friends' Grady mentioned. They were business partners, now. Many of their exquisitely carved headstones and granite plaques identified Floyd's immobile tenants. It was one good thing to come from this new, weird era. Floyd didn't think eating corpses was in their nature. He suppressed another urge to bring up his omelet. He was amazed at Grady's constitution, but saw him lean against his truck for moment before grabbing his radio. Floyd reached for his mobile to call Sheriff Danridge. Although Floyd wanted answers, he hated investigations. One by the Department of Ecology forced him to spew out money to redirect the water drainage from his cemetery into a catch basin. The outfall ran into a local stream long before the birthdates on many of the older headstones. Salmon could rot in streams and weed killer from neighborhood lawns could flow freely, but clean rain water from a green cemetery was banned. It seemed to Floyd that was more about psychology than ecology.

Psychology effected more than mortal laws. After humanity multiplied and dominated the Earth, its surge of minds diverted the flow from that strange dimension often associated with magic. That diversion pushed more ethereal forms of life to become more lore than living presence. These beings called that era the Reclusive Age. In time, enough power flowed back to these enchanted species. They now walked the Earth as easily as human beings, and demanded rights from the world's once unchallenged masters. Enchanted beings were collectively called 'Chants by mortal humans. Not all were as calm as Elves or as beguiling as fairies around a hummingbird feeder. This new age was named the Reascension. For Floyd it was a time of adapting his brain and business to the new reality. He wanted to bury the dead, if for a small profit. Death remained a typical, mortal concern. But something was treating his cemetery as a macabre buffet. Whatever 'Chant had ate the recently departed was a monster.

Glynis Welker went on her hike through the local park. She shoved her phone into her jacket pocket. It was her lifeline to friends and media, but at three months old it was a style fossil horribly outdated. Her parents were not moved by her pleas for a better phone, or for a better everything. Her Mom worked in insurance, and her Dad owned the local cemetery. That might be a dark stain on her popularity if the town had much more to offer on its social tiers. It didn't. Owning a cemetery was a better job than what her pal Barb's father did. Still, there were enough septic tanks in town that needed pumping out. Barb had a newer, better phone. Despite the promise of her mother's actuary tables, there were never enough dead people for her father to bury so her family could become rich. For a moment, Glynis wished for more death. She shook her head when realizing that was an awful, macabre thought, even if the result meant a better phone. She shoved her mobile deeper into the pocket. She didn't want to lose it in the thick brush of the park trails. This park was more a forest than a stretch of walking paths. She liked to charge through it alone, despite her father's protests. She had a feeling there was something to be found in these woods. Today, something found her.

Glynis walked into the woods. She saw someone ahead of her on the paved pathway. It was old Mrs. Channing. That was weird. She didn't even have her cane. Mrs. Channing looked at Glynis with a vacant stare. She turned and started into the woods on the rough trails that branched off the paved walking paths. Glynis thought that odd for an old lady. Mrs. Channing would probably trip and fall. Medical alert ads of old people collapsed on their floors popped into Glynis' head. She followed the old woman. She took out her phone, certain she would need it to call for help. Glynis hiked the rough trail and saw Mrs. Channing was already far ahead. Glynis wondered how she could move so fast. Glynis moved quicker in an effort to catch up to her. Then a thought struck her. Her Dad had just buried Mrs. Channing. She was dead.

Glynis was chasing a ghost. An icy cold spread across her chest. Glynis stopped. She should snap a photo of the ghost. She couldn't keep the rules straight on what creatures liked to be recorded, and what ones hated their images caught on tech. A human ghost would be okay. She hoped. Glynis crept forward. She held her hand out in front of her with the camera phone ready to shoot. She walked to the edge of a slope where the trees grew more

218

densely and it was dark even in the Summer. A hand snatched her outstretched wrist from behind a tree. The flash from the phone's camera popped off repeatedly. The thing grabbing her leapt out and roared. Glynis shut her eyes as a gust of hot breath and sewer stench hit her face. Glynis screamed. She thrashed around, but couldn't free her arm. The hand gripping her wrist was not some old lady or her ghost. It was a large hand with strong, dark blue fingers. Glynis glanced at the thing grabbing her. She saw a shadowed face with no nose and yellow eyes set deep into a skull like dim lights near the back of a culvert. Glynis screamed louder. The trees rustled with no wind as if they heard her cry for help. The blue hand released her. She fell back towards a thick cedar, but her impact was soft as if its low boughs reached down to catch her. Glynis massaged her wrist. The thing was gone. It had taken her phone.

Floyd watched another police cruiser leave, this time from his home's driveway. He was frightened. It was the awful fear of a father's realization that he can't protect his daughter all the time, and that strange horrors stalk the world. He resisted barking an 'I told you so' to Glynis.

"Mrs. Channing?" Floyd asked and shook his head recalling what his daughter Glynis had told the police. He remembered the traces of carnage at the violated grave. The grave belonged to Mrs. Channing.

"Yeah. Mrs. Channing." Glynis answered, still massaging her wrist. "Or her ghost or something. Or her ghost *and* something. It was gross! It stinked!"

"Stunk." Floyd automatically corrected.

"Floyd!" Floyd's wife Dorene cautioned him.

Floyd didn't look at his wife but knew she glared at him with her characteristic, wry frown.

"And it took my phone." Glynis added with a sudden jolt.

"But at least you're okay, sweetie!" Floyd enveloped Glynis in a genuine, fatherly hug.

Glynis spoke muffled words from her face crushed against her father's chest.

"I'm sorry, what?" Floyd asked and released his daughter.

"Can I get a new phone?" Glynis asked. "A better one."

"Hey, look. We're glad you're okay." Floyd tapped Glynis on her shoulder. "Maybe stay out of the park for a while. Or just stay home. Forever."

"Yeah, sure." Glynis said. "But do I get a new phone?"

"She might as well." Dorene sighed. "We'll still be paying for her line and the minutes."

"Yeah. Okay." Floyd's shoulders slumped. He slowly reached into his suit pocket and then handed his phone to Glynis. "For now, you can use mine."

"But it doesn't have my apps. And it's even older!" Glynis sneered as if being handed a piece of moldy bread, but took the phone anyway.

"So am I, after the stress today." Floyd said. "And, probably, so is that thing that took your phone. Really old."

"Yeah. Okay. Thanks." Glynis said while already texting on Floyd's phone.

"We've got to do something about this." Dorene leaned into Floyd and nearly hit her face against his head. "We can't live in an area where creatures steal phones."

"Geezus, Dorene! I just hope that's all they steal!"

"Watch your language, Floyd."

Floyd took a deep breath. He knew it wasn't Glynis' ears that Dorene worried could overhear him. Other things might be listening. 'Chants weren't always visible. Floyd became nostalgic for when it was only the government listening. Now, something in the air might take offense, and they didn't need technology. Floyd assumed the government didn't need technology to spy now, either.

By the next day, the police had gathered whatever evidence they could at Floyd's cemetery. The small scraps of Mrs. Channing had been gathered with as much care and as few crows as possible. The family was comforted, and thankfully never asked for a refund. Restorations were a company expense. The casket was repaired and what remains could be returned to it were lowered back into the grave and the cement crypt resealed. For all the good that would do, Floyd thought. Whatever had dug up the grave could easily do it again. The cops and their guns gave Floyd the idea of hiring armed security. But what would a gun do against something that could tear open cement? Life was complicated, and so was keeping the dead safe. Floyd leaned against an old-style tombstone. He didn't think Charles and Norma Whaley six feet below his polished leather shoes would mind. He looked up from their birth and death dates. Several eyes were looking back at him from the other side of the stone. They were all very large eyes.

Floyd smiled. The 'shorty friends' had returned. The group of five Rock Folk stared at Floyd with eyes wide open. Their bushy eyebrows collided with the thick waves of hair that dropped from under tight, knitted caps and metal helmets. Bulbous noses were the only area of skin visible on their bearded faces. Floyd assumed even their women were bearded. They seemed too solid to be 'Chants, and made from more flesh and blood than even humans. But they were Floyd's favorite kind of ethereal being. Their height was oddly uniform, as were their stocky bodies. All were about half as tall as a typical human male, but unlike most men Floyd knew, these Rock Folk all appeared to work out. Floyd knew they cut through earth and rock without machines.

Floyd's association with Rock Folk came when his crew was excavating a grave, only to uncover a Rock Folk tunnel. Floyd's apologetic overtures appeared to forestall any unpleasant interaction with the creatures peering out from the bottom. The Rock Folk left their intimidating pickaxes in the tunnel and came out of the ground. Floyd attempted to be a genial tour guide of the cemetery, but the Rock Folk were more interested in the gravestones. They retuned underground and soon after reappeared in Floyd's office with drawings of their own headstone designs. Floyd was annoyed at the gaping hole in his floor, but agreed to an initial order. When their stone work arrived, Floyd and everyone who looked at them were stunned. The blunt hands of the Rock Folk had taken lifeless stone and made it appear to move. Their artistry cut hypnotic ripples in marble as layered as clouds seen from an airliner's window, and lines cut along grains of granite that created the illusion of waves that looked more dynamic than real ones crashing on a beach. Floyd thought the Rock Folk could not be dark, devilish creatures. They must be some form of earthly angel. People were willing to spend at a much higher plane to have their dearly departed memorialized by their work.

Floyd was unsure if the Rock Folk were a form of compressed Elf, or perhaps true Dwarves. Maybe they were boulders made living through magic. Speaking to them was almost like talking to stone. Their eyes were human-like, but hardly ever blinked. They were always staring. It never felt like a threat. Still, to have such huge eyes focused so keenly and constantly was unnerving. Floyd was glad Rock Folk was easy to remember. Keeping track of the proper names for all the 'Chants a person could see and those just beyond sight gave him a headache. Misnaming an ethereal creature could cause offense and bring an unexpected curse plus a very tangible fine. Floyd made sure the word 'band' never followed Rock. But their name did conjured mental images of his grandfather's Kingston Trio albums. Floyd thought of asking them to join the Chamber of Commerce. Perhaps they would see things more his way with their enormous eyes than the other, mortal members. Although, he figured that getting them to speak up at meetings might prove a challenge.

"So, how are you guys?" Floyd asked.

There was a moment of silence, and then Rock Folks at the head of their group pointed to the remade grave of Mrs. Channing.

"Yeah. Just horrible." Floyd said. "Something, um, something violated the grave. The body was—well, it was horrible."

Ten huge eyes fixed on Floyd.

"Um, yeah." Floyd took a breath.

Floyd pondered. He didn't want to suggest an association with this grave raider and the Rock Folk. However, he figured that 'Chants were likely experts on other 'Chants. Maybe his stocky business partners knew something. They obviously came to investigate on their own. It might be worth sharing information. He resolved it was worth risking offense. Plus, they were good listeners, and he wanted to vent.

"I guess you guys might have some insight to this kind of thing." Floyd started. "I mean, I hope nothing has ever violated yours graves this way. If you have graves. If you guys ever—any way. This happened, and then some creep in the woods attacked my daughter. But she saw Mrs. Channing in the park before that happened. I mean, it can't be a coincidence. Can it?"

The Rock Folk jostled. They turned to look at each other. Floyd heard a low groan. He wasn't sure if it was a sound of recognition between them, or just the creaking of their thick boots. They turned and focused their stares back at Floyd.

"I'll figure this out, I promise." Floyd said. "Even if that thing comes back, I won't let it ruin my business, or our partnership. We all love your work. I'll get to the bottom of this. Not the bottom!

But to a solution. I mean, I know you guys live in the bottom--I mean in the earth. The rocks. Just know I won't let this stop our business. Trust me."

Floyd's breathing increased. He felt his pulse throb in his neck. The Rock Folk just stared at him. He wasn't sure if their silence was for solidarity or rebuke. After a long moment of silence and shallow breathing by Floyd, he saw the closest Rock Folk give him a hint of a nod. Maybe.

"Ghouls." The single word from the lead Rock Folk sounded like a long note from a tuba in an underwater cave.

Floyd jumped back as the Rock Folk spoke. He then side stepped off the Whaley graves.

"Ghouls." Floyd repeated, more shocked by the Rock Folk speaking than from the information.

"Ghouls," Floyd said again as they turned to walk away.

The Rock Folk ambled off as the idea of his grave robber sank into his brain and hit realization. Ghouls ate dead flesh and he owned a cemetery.

"Crap! Oh, crap! Ghouls!"

Later, Floyd sat and flexed his toes inside the Sherriff's personal office. He wasn't sure how typical it was to have once bought shoes from the man who went on to be elected the county's highest law enforcer. But it was good to have contacts who sat at important desks. Still, Floyd decided he liked Paul Danridge more in business suit than a Sheriff's uniform.

"So let me get this straight." Floyd inhaled through a crush of exasperation from his talk with Danridge. "You knew. You knew there were ghouls in town."

"Ghouls openly exist. This clan laid claim to some available real estate near your neighborhood."

"Near my cemetery." Floyd hissed.

"Floyd, look, they have rights. The Reascension code was signed by a council of Elder Spirits and human officials. It's the law, now. The ghouls have a right to move into an area of their choice."

"And you don't think it's suspicious that flesh eating monsters chose a spot near a graveyard. You knew your people came to my cemetery where something chomped Mrs. Channing. Ghouls can take the image of the dead they ate. That's evidence! That's what attacked my daughter!"

"Yeah, I saw her file. Sad thing, that. I'm glad she's okay." Danridge nodded.

"So, are you going to arrest the ghoul?" Floyd asked.

"When we can narrow it down to the right one. Sure. But there are a lot of them."

"How many?" Floyd hopped in his chair.

"More than a few." Danridge shrugged.

"Can you get a court order to search their guts?"

"Probably not." Danridge frowned imagining how forensics would gather the evidence. "Why?"

"The one who ate Mrs. Channing probably—never mind." Floyd shook his head and shuddered. "Look this is bigger than just what happened at the cemetery. They're ghouls. They eat people!"

"They eat the dead. According to the files." Danridge said pleased with his mastery of the fact. "I understand your stress, Floyd. But try to get mine. I enforce mortal law. I have some jurisdiction over 'Chants when they cross a line. But I can't just charge into a 'Chant camp and roust them because of circumstance. I don't have the manpower, or any other kind of powers to invoke. I have to stay in the law, and who knows what I'd be stepping in if I try to muscle some dark ethereals."

Floyd leaned back and sighed. "But you still give out speeding tickets to mortals. Do you give out speeding tickets to ghouls?"

"Yes. If they drove."

"And if you saw a body in the back seat?" Floyd pressed.

Danridge shrugged. "It may be a zombie. The black magic ones have the same rights as ghouls."

"What it had teeth marks?"

"Look," Danridge threw his hands up. "The act of biting might've been consensual. I can't judge what dark 'Chants do! Hell, I don't even want to know what they do!" Danridge froze. He gripped the edge of his desk and looked to his sides. "Sorry! I didn't mean to say that word." He spoke to someone or something other than Floyd. He leaned over to Floyd and uttered a harsh whisper. "You're getting me in too deep here! I have to walk a fine line!"

"Tell that to my daughter!" Floyd barked without caring if the deputies outside the office or anything else heard him. "We're not talking about some angry pixie kicking over garden gnomes and ripping up flowers. This is about ghouls. They eat us!"

224

Danridge flopped back in his chair and took a deep breath. "There are no teeth marks on you right now, Floyd. Go home. This will sort itself out."

"What about the rights of my clients? What about trespassing? They didn't have a right to rip up a grave or walk across the cemetery to do it. You could at least get them for trespassing."

"That's quasi-legal, at best. A cemetery is almost a public place. I mean, I can't ticket you for going to a diner if you walked across another café's parking lot to get there."

"What? Are you kidding me?" Floyd gyrated and caused his chair to squeak as he ranted. "I own a cemetery, not a slow food restaurant! Did you sell a lot of shoes with logic like that? When did you start being such a, a freakin' cop out?"

Danridge sighed. "Puns are infractions against the county code. It offends the humor spirits, and that leads to bad weather, somehow. I'm going to have to cite you."

"Great. Ghouls can eat my client's loved ones, but I can't speak freely."

"I don't right the new laws, Floyd."

"No. And you don't enforce the old ones."

"Floyd! You have the right to remain silent. Use it!"

Kerry Nguyen liked driving at night. This proved a bonus when he signed on at Eddelston Limo & Hearse and was put on the night shift. He would drive the dead from hospitals or nursing homes for what was likely their next to the last car ride over the lonely back roads. After each funeral, the hearse at Welker's Cemetery & Funerary Services would take each body to its grave. Kerry shuddered as he recalled what the receiving crew told him about what had happened to the body in the raided grave. The news didn't spell out everything. Kerry wished he only knew what the news reported. Still, Welker's was the only grave site in town. So the bodies kept rolling—

Kerry hit the brakes. Hard.

"Zombies!" he screamed.

Five menacing figures blocked the darkened road in front of him. The headlights lit up the corpse-like figures. They started toward the hearse. They didn't shamble. They came at him with purpose. Their yellow eyes burned more intensely than the glare of the high beams. Each had skin that looked tie-died in blue. He grabbed for his phone with a suddenly sweaty hand, but realized it was in his jacket across the hearse's cab. He shoved his hand deep into the space between the seats. They were at the hearse too quickly. A massive blue hand slapped against the driver's side window like a spider. Kerry opened his mouth to scream. The window exploded. Kerry spit out small chunks of safety glass and shook his head. Blood welled inside his mouth. He thrust his left arm to throw the gear shift back into 'drive', but never got to reach it. Powerful hands grabbed his arm. He frantically searched between the seats while fighting to free his captured arm. And screaming.

"Keys!" a loud, rasping voice bellowed outside. "Keys!"

The hearse shook. Kerry heard steal and plastic buckle as more blue freaks yanked and finally tore open the rear door. His shirt sleeve was ripping away and he could feel his tendons, muscles, and bones begin to fail as pain exploded through his left arm. His right hand at last grabbed what he was required to carry in his day job at Eddelston Armored Car Service. He shoved the .38-caliber revolver at the shattered window and fired. The sharp pain of gun blasts inside the cab cut into his ears. All six bullets blasted the thing tearing his left arm. Through the ringing from the blasts, Kerry heard it cry out after the last shot. But it sounded more of a yip of annoyance than death knell. He heard a loud thump behind him. They'd pulled out the transport casket that held the fresh remains of Samuel Rollinburg.

Loud cries of pain and gurgling noises sounded from the rear of the hearse. There was a muffled sound similar to a tree branch snapping, and then a noise like mud hitting the side of the hearse. Kerry pulled his wrenched arm inside the cab and kicked open the door. More weird sounds as if sharp spikes were hitting the road rang out from behind the hearse.

With one hand, Kerry flipped open the revolver's cylinder. Spent shells hit the worn asphalt. He winced as he gripped the hot gun with his left hand. His trembling fingers managed to slide in new bullets from an ammo box hidden beneath his seat. He snapped the gun closed and cautiously crept, barrel first, around the end of the hearse. Samuel Rollinburg's corpse was back in the transit casket. The vinyl body bag had been ripped open, but then carefully folded back over the body. It was as decent as it could be after its violent rip from the hearse.

Something moved.

Kerry aimed the gun at something moving on the ground beside the ditch. It was a blue arm, severed and twitching. Kerry heard a rustle. Passed the thickets and inside the woods he saw several eyes staring out at him. They were all large eyes and had the same eyeshine as owls. Most importantly, those eyes didn't glow yellow. Their owners probably beat off the blue zombie things. Kerry hoped they would stay close by. It would be several minutes before the cops would get there. He was glad for the help from his unknown allies. His arm throbbed badly, but it was still attached.

Floyd stood outside the Breeze Thru motel lobby and office. The electric hum of the red vacancy sign seemed to grow louder as his annoyance from the meeting grew. Floyd thought the Chamber of Commerce should meet at a more prestigious location until they had offices of their own. However, even if the motel owner had yet to join the Chamber, her place had free coffee. If one called it coffee. It was about as palatable as the other gelatinous horrors Floyd had seen, recently. He grimaced. It wasn't from his gut ache. One more attempt at getting help against the ghouls had failed. The local business owners were closer to working class heroes than magnates and millionaires. Floyd had thought he would get help from people who saw the direct effects of local issues, both real and ethereal. They happened in the community where everyone lived and worked. Nope. Floyd considered a new social attitude: my backyard, but not my problem. Unfortunately, M.B.Y.B.N.M.P. didn't create a clever sounding acronym.

"Sorry that didn't go your way." Dale Perrin said walking up to Floyd.

Floyd shrugged as he considered Dale. Unlike himself, Dale owned more than one business. In addition to the local burger joint, the shop that was Dale's most envied enterprise was the L.A. Lingerie Boutique in the next town over.

"Everybody's a bit twitchy." Dale offered. "The Reascension and all."

"Really?" Floyd sneered. "I hadn't noticed."

"You've been to the policy meetings." Dale shrugged.

"I've been to the policy arguments."

"See what I mean?" Dale thrust his opened hands from his sides with an entreating nod. "Everybody is worried. Not just about ghouls. We're afraid for our livelihoods in this new market. Who knows if sweatshirts, lube jobs, or burgers are going to sell in the near future. What type of competition are we going to face from the 'Chants if they go commercial?"

Floyd kept quiet as he considered his own deal with the Rock Folk.

"Will they even pay taxes?" Dale continued. "You may come out ahead, Floyd-o. People are always going to die. I think."

Floyd took a deep breath and spoke as he exhaled. "I'm paying out, right now. Ghouls eat the dead. No one is going to burry grandma where she's going to be lunch for monsters. You think you'll have problems selling see-through bras to elves?"

Dale shrugged. He turned to the motel as its front doors opened.

"And there's the Tran scram." Dale said as Ernest 'Larry' Tran left the motel in swift stride to his BMW.

"Sorry, guys. Clients. A lawyer's work is never done." Tran said without stopping. "But it was good to see both of you. Take care and keep in touch!"

Dale and Floyd watched Tran walk away.

"So Danridge ran for Sheriff." Dale said. "What do you think our chairman will run for?"

"President." Floyd said.

"Something smaller, probably. At first." Dale said and smiled.

"Governor?" Floyd offered.

"I was thinking major, but if he's got the cash, why not?"

"District attorney, for sure." Floyd said. He wondered what goals Dale harbored. Dale now owned Danridge's shoe franchise, and maybe looked to step into politics himself.

"Why do we even meet?" Floyd's eyes narrowed at Dale. "Everyone's already decided the agenda and number of bathroom breaks through text and vids before they drive here."

"Tradition." Dale shrugged. "A chance to get out of the house and office and hang out with like-minded people."

"Not too many people like me, right now." Floyd rubbed his acidic gut.

"It's not personal. It's this ghoul business. Everyone likes fairies and elves, not so much gremlins and ghouls."

"But we have to deal with all of them. Some of them are threatening more than cash flow. A lot more! I thought we watched each other's back."

"We watch. But if we all make a noise and mark this town as 'Ghoulville' we kiss off cash coming in from the rest of the county. That's most of our business. One wrong step and—"

"Oh, just save it." Floyd cut Dale off with a quick wave. "I got enough circuitous excuses from Danridge."

"You're going about this all old school." Dale sighed. "The law, the Chamber. You need help, but we're old world. You need a solution in the new world."

"I should become a Pilgrim?" Floyd flexed his shoulders.

"No, but this isn't a normal fight. So look outside the normal world and laws." Dale offered.

"I should buy a bunch of M-16s and go action hero on the ghouls? That would work. Or not." Floyd shook his head while looking at the cracked asphalt of the aging parking lot.

"Ah, no. It would be AR-15s. But, ah, do you want to buy a few? I have a cousin in sporting goods. We could cut you a deal."

"Sounds great," Floyd didn't bother to mask his sarcasm. "Do you have a surplus Russian a-bomb, too? How about nerve gas? I mean, I might as boost my business as well as take out the ghouls. Right?"

"Okay, Floyd. You're pissed. I get it. But, here's a lead." Dale took out his wallet and handed Floyd a worn business card. "My brother-in-law went there for some sex advice. But maybe they can handle your situation."

Floyd looked at the card. The word 'witchcraft' caught his eye.

"Maybe they have an app for ghouls." Dale smiled.

"Maybe," Floyd nodded.

Nearly twenty hours and twice as many antacids had passed when Floyd tried to find help again at the address on Dale's card. He entered Tobar Segais Hall through the Plexiglas doors. It used to be Chubby's Pizza Plant before the bank yanked in credit lines once extended to small businesses around town. Floyd missed the Mass o' Meat deep dish he would order and eat under Dorene's sharp glare. He thought of meat and then the ghouls. He became nauseous. He frowned at himself for making such an association in his mind. The bright, remodeled interior now only partially smelled of hot pepperoni and cheese. Florid candles and a new ventilation system spread the aroma of flowers and spices. Two young women met him at the door. They also smelled like flowers. Floyd hoped he smelled good. He'd bought a discounted case of musk deodorant at Cost Pro, so he'd be smelling this good or bad for a long time.

Without a word, two young women at the front counter came around and led him beyond new walls built inside the old dining hall. Beyond them was another chamber entered through an arched doorway. Inside it, there were even more candles and a stronger smell of flowers, spices, and what Floyd guessed was an expensive perfume wafting from the middle-aged woman seated towards the back. She sat on a wicker throne resting on a platform hidden by flowers and fake moss. Above her stood several old tree boughs woven together to form a naturalistic arch. Floyd hoped the woman, her throne, and the arch were all well secured. It all looked as if it might topple down on him if the imperious woman on the throne moved suddenly. The two young women bowed to her and departed.

"Hello, I'm—" Floyd started.

"Floyd Welker!" The woman said and opened her eyes wide as she stared down at him.

"Yes. I called ahead." Floyd said. "I need—"

"I am Cerridwen! You have entered and are now in my coven's domain."

"Right. Sorry." Floyd nodded. "Nice to meet you. So I—"

"You have a problem beyond your ken. From beyond this world, and far beyond you, mortal man!"

"Um, pretty much." Floyd said. He waited for Cerridwen to continue. After a moment, he began again. "So I was hoping—"

"Hope!" Cerridwen barked. "That eternal spring. It is good for ephemeral men to hope. But it can be a curse if the hope is not supported by action."

"Right. So I—" Floyd stopped himself. He waited for a shouted sentence from Cerridwen to cut into his own. When she didn't, he continued. "I'm hoping for some help. You guys—sorry! You ladies—"

A narrowed stare and flare of nostrils stopped Floyd.

"Excuse me. So, your coven is like a bridge between the human world and the, uh, other places now crossing through. Right?"

"There was never a time when magic was elsewhere, or elsewhen, little man."

"Okay. So you can deal with this stuff on its own level. Right?"

"Correct." Cerridwen looked aside as if in contempt of Floyd's comprehension. Floyd wondered if it was the musk deodorant. Then he wondered how she could smell anything other than the suffocating smells form the candles and her own perfume. Still, she could probably help him. It would be worth using up all his prescription nasal spray. He took an instinctive deep breath before speaking again, and coughed.

"Sorry. Um," Floyd bowed his head. "May I please have your help? I'm trying to save my business and family."

"You have a daughter?" Cerridwen asked with interest.

"Yes."

"Is she a virgin?"

"Well, I certainly hope so!" Floyd screeched. "She's barely a teenager!"

"Then bring her to us." Cerridwen smiled.

"Um. Why? She not much of a joiner."

"No." Cerridwen looked at him again with contempt. "We need her not for our coven. We need her to assist you."

"Okay. Great. Um, how?"

"We need her so that she can be sacrificed."

"What?" Floyd barked and nearly jumped at Cerridwen.

Cerridwen moved back in her throne from Floyd, the angry father on the floor below her.

"How could that even be legal?" Floyd howled.

"It's legal if you sanction it. We have the proper forms."

"Are you kidding? I thought you were the good guys. Crap!"

Cerridwen sighed. "You're morality is only of mortal concern. There are greater forces here to appease and redirect. You must trust us. You must give us your daughter. And, of course, you must sign the paperwork beforehand."

"I will not!" Floyd waved his arms and nearly spun around. "I won't even give you our goldfish!"

Floyd realized he would actually give them the family goldfish. It was sick anyway and its bowl stank like a grave's bottom. He thought of Glynis, and his anger returned.

"No! Forget it." Floyd shouted and wiped spit from his chin. "No way"

"Then I can't help you." Cerridwen shrugged and looked to her left.

"Fine!" Floyd sucked in florid air and coughed. "I mean, Geezus!"

Cerridwen shrugged and leaned down at him. Her regal air was gone as if she was an actor breaking from character.

"Hey! Look, mister! You've made your point. It was a test. You failed. Now, just get out!"

Floyd's left eyebrow arched. An idea popped into his mind. He composed himself.

"No. Okay." Floyd said and dropped his shoulders. "If you really need my daughter. Then, Okay."

"Really?" Cerridwen brightened and nearly smiled.

"No!" Floyd shouted. "That was a test! Geezus, lady!"

"Kiss off, creep!"

Cerridwen took a branch from her arch and swung it at Floyd. He dodged it just as he had ducked back-hoe arms swung by inexperienced operators.

"Fine!" Floyd barked. "Just—geezus!"

Floyd stormed out of Cerridwen's chamber and straight to the glass double doors.

"Wait!" One of the young women called to Floyd from behind the lobby counter.

"You must still pay for the time spent here and the advice given."

"But it was lousy!" Floyd shouted.

"Nevertheless—" The young woman flipped a pen into the air. It defied gravity and slowly drifted back down to her hand. Floyd knew Cerridwen was not the real power behind the coven, but real power lurked here, somewhere. Perhaps it was in the form of a young woman flipping a pen.

"Crap," Floyd said, and pulled out his wallet.

"That will be forty-nine ninety-five" The young woman said, and smiled.

Floyd suppressed a sneeze.

Elsewhere, there was a scent of scattered blood. The smell was strong to nostrils unhindered by the flesh of a nose. To eat other flesh was the sinister purpose of a ghoul. Newly, dead flesh. None of the sniffing ghoul's clan had caught the scent. The prize in the road was its alone. Its clan had traveled to this new land seeking abundant corpses to sate their dark and cursed hunger. There were so many mortals now, unlike the shadowed past. It seemed certain that their meat would glut the ghouls' infernal bowels. But the mortals had unexpected allies. Foreign magics welled and flowed through this alien land, not just the ghouls' dark power. The ghoul king needed more information and a strategy before unleashing the full force of his hungry legion. Some had tasted mortal heart and limb, but for most it was an unfulfilled promise. This petty feast in the road was a creature unknown. Yet, it was fresh, dead flesh.

Black finger nails on bony, blue fingers worked the crushed possum free from the crevices of the asphalt. Its fingers felt a vibration. No metal carts or beasts traveled the road in this late hour. Fewer passed now that these abodes were know as the lairs of ghouls. The vibration came from the earth. The ghoul pondered the vibration only for a second as his plaque encrusted teeth began to crush the road kill more completely than truck tires. Another ghoul jumped from behind and bit into the possum. Two sets of jaws on ancient nightmares tugged the remains of the small animal between them with savage fury.

Splat. Splat. Splat. The next night, Floyd watched the red, fibrous bits hit the sink as he emptied the blender's pitcher. The pulpy remains of fruit and berries flowed slowly to the drain. It was a nice evening at home. Dorene was enjoying her fresh smoothie. Glynis sat at the dining table ostensibly doing homework. Floyd was glad to see the five canisters of mace he bought her close at hand. She seemed engrossed by her reading assignment. Although Floyd realized that with the myriad electronic devices employed by youth, a parent would never know all they saw. He may pay for them, but he didn't know what flowed through them. For all Floyd knew, it might be a digital spell harnessing minds of the youth like a psychic bot-net. He shuddered at the thought and the fact it now seemed possible. Floyd assured himself it was actual homework mesmerizing his daughter. He never remembered having so much homework as a kid, himself. He wondered if his daughter's course work taught her how to deal with Rock Folk and other, less desirable 'Chants. If so, he wanted to read the notes.

"What are you working on?" he asked Glynis.

"Karma and similar concepts," Glynis answered. "Something like continued good acts and positive effort leading to good outcomes. Sometimes where you don't expect them."

"I guess philosophies like to cover their bets." Floyd said glimpsing her tablet's screen.

"Yeah. I guess." Glynis replied, moving her tablet.

"I'd like it if trying to do the right thing paid off where you could see it." Floyd took a rhetorical sigh. "Like interest at the bank."

"Yeah. I guess."

Floyd parked himself next to Dorene on the couch where she read an old-style book of paper and printed ink while sipping her smoothie. Floyd liked reading over her shoulder. He liked her shoulder. He liked this life. Now he wondered how long it could continue, and what he could do to keep it going.

"We've had a good, life. Right?" Floyd asked his wife.

Dorene stopped her reading. She took deep sip and looked quizzically at her husband.

"What?" Floyd asked his staring wife.

"That almost sounds like you're about to tell me it's almost over, so I should buy a grave plot & casket. I assumed I'd get the set for free." Dorene smiled.

"Okay. Sure. But..." Floyd searched for words to finish his query.

"You in need of a sales pitch, sailor? A pep talk?" Dorene asked.

Floyd smiled. He liked it when Dorene used pet names. Although he knew rising displays of affection now would not have the same result as it did over a decade ago when Glynis was conceived.

"Yeah. We've had a good life." Dorene continued "Why?"

"I just want it to go on." Floyd said.

"If everybody's life went on, you'd be out of a job." Dorene offered.

"I could always pave the graves and open a strip mall." Floyd offered.

"Skate park." Glynis said at the table.

"I thought skate parks were passé." Floyd said.

"Nope," Glynis said, still focused on her tablet.

"Okay. A skate park."

"But paving graves might not be good karma." Dorene said, and focused back on her book after another deep sip.

"True." Floyd said. "And we need that."

"I need a new smoothie." Dorene said and handed Floyd her empty glass.

Floyd took the glass, and smiled at his wife's playful nudge that followed.

Karma. Good Karma. Floyd kept repeating the idea in his mind now that he was in a very different and darker circumstance than a pleasant evening at home. He thought there was only one avenue left to him to solve the ghoul issue. It was the direct approach. It was also the most terrifying option. He now went to meet with the king ghoul. He hoped all 'Chants respected reason. He also hoped it was true they didn't eat the living, and that he would remain living through this meeting. As he walked up to the dwelling that served as ghoul headquarters, he thought he felt a slight rumbling beneath his feet. Floyd was certain it was just nerves. Even if they were frayed, he wanted his nerves to stay connected to his brain and spine for at least the immediate future.

He was relieved he wasn't approaching a stygian castle or haunted mansion. The ghoul clan lived in a group of duplexes. It all looked so ordinary, save for the fact that the dank air around the houses seemed to leach away most of the light from street lamps and stars. That seemed fitting for the seat of power of flesh eating monsters, even in suburbia. Floyd pressed the doorbell button at the front door. He heard it ring on the inside. He waited. Finally, he knocked. He waited. He entered. He found it creepy the front door was unlocked. Maybe this house had a reverse policy for burglars. The ghouls wanted everyone to come in, and perhaps fall down some stairs and break a neck. He doubted ghouls would call an aid car, even though he knew they owned mobile phones with listed numbers. It was how he looked them up and contacted them. They probably also had Wi-Fi. What they needed was air fresheners plus the scented candles from the coven. The air was as thick with stench as it was dark. It was one hundred times worse than an all you can eat night at El Beano's Burrito Hut.

"Hello!"

Floyd yelped from fright, even though the greeting was pleasant and friendly. He watched as dust and bits of suburban detritus gathered in a whirl and became luminous. A smiling face beamed from atop the ghost. She wore a slightly dated business suit and held a spectral clipboard.

"Welcome to this home, offered by Spectra Real Estate," The ghost chirped. "Actually, that's my own company. I'm its sole agent. This used to be my house."

"Um—hah-what?"

"I'd love this place to have new owners. I can tell you would be a good owner."

"But," Floyd swallowed and wretched at the awful taste of the air. "I already have a home."

"This one is bigger!" the ghost chimed. "It's one of the largest in the area. There are plenty of rooms for you and the family."

"How can you know I have a family?"

"Oh, ghosts can learn new knowledge from a variety of places. It just depends on the type of spirit you want to present yourself as to the living. I want to find a new owner for this house. A living owner. Not a cursed, monster owner. And what better a person to show you the house than someone who lived and died here."

"Uh," Floyd took a step back to the door. "You, uh, you died here?"

"Yep. Murder. Shot dead in my own bedroom."

"I don't remember that in the news." Floyd scratched his temple. "Hell—um, excuse me. I mean, I know Les, the real estate guy here in town. We're both Chamber of Commerce."

"Well, you know, there are rules, and then there are people who follow the rules. Or don't." The ghost smiled and winked. "A fresh panel of dry wall and some paint, then presto! Who's to know? Except me."

"I suppose that true." Floyd said. "Unfortunately."

"The bullet is still in the wall." The ghost jerked her thumb to point down the hall. "Along with some of my skull and brain. Long dried, of course."

"Of course," Floyd said. "But, um, your murder—was it reported?"

"A small article in the paper a few decades ago. Major news sources don't report every killing in every town. Unless you lived here at the time, and you didn't. No one digs too deep into the past. Well, no one used to. That will change, now."

"I'm sure it will. Yeah." Floyd forgot his aversion to the moldered air and took a deep breath, and coughed.

"Other than that, obviously the house has never had termites or much of a rodent problem." The ghost slowly spun with arms out to present the house. "The plumbing was recently updated before the current, um, residents moved in."

"I guess that's a good thing." Floyd offered in sympathy.

"You have no idea." The ghost shook her head in disgust. "The toilet will certainly be haunted. The floor around it, too."

Floyd thought that was too much information. Obviously the ghost was not a very experienced salesperson.

"I'd really like you to live here." The ghost's eyes became sad and grew larger as she pleaded. "Please buy this house. I—"

A horrible shout ripped the air behind the ghost. It was a curse Floyd couldn't understand, but felt its violence across his skin as the ghost tore into glowing shreds and vanished.

What glared at him from the hall was more frightening than a spectral murder victim. It was a face that ate the dead. Grim, sunken eyes that burned yellow glared at him over gaping, skeletal nostrils and a sneer of flesh ripping teeth. Shreds of fabric swayed over the ghoul's blotched, blue body. They hung down as if sodden from a dark fluid. Perhaps they were tattered ribbons of skin worn as mementos of past victims. Floyd's heart raced at the fear of becoming this monster's neck tie. The ghoul pointed. Floyd saw another door. He knew where it went. Into the basement, of course.

Floyd took his life not in his hands, but by the soles of his shoes. He carefully stepped down the stairs. They creaked, naturally. Floyd descended without touching the two-by-four handrail or anything else to steady himself. The risk of doing so seemed greater than the danger of falling based on the dark, oily smudges left from massive, inhuman hands. The stench was so concentrated it rolled down the walls like slime. Floyd soldiered on. He imagined a past for this house with cheered football games, movies watched, and beer swilled and spilled in the once-typical basement. Those events were long gone just as his commonplace world, even in a suburban basement. The monster king sat in the main room at the bottom off the stairs. However, he didn't relax on an old sofa or recliner. The ghoul leader rested atop a throne of bowed ghouls that clutched each other to form a modular couch from Hell.

Two yellow eyes focused on Floyd through the dim light and heavy odor.

"You are brave to come here, mortal. Little, little mortal man." The ghoul on the bizarre throne said over a slight rustle of blue backs and shoulders.

"Yeah, hi." Floyd replied. "I'm Floyd Welker. I was hoping we could talk."

"Ah! You allow us your name. Spoken freely." The ghoul smiled and revealed many long and massive teeth.

"Um, yeah. I guess."

"I am Hermon." The ghouls said with pride. "I am king. I am lord. I am law."

"Herman?" Floyd asked with as an incredulous squeak.

"Her-mon!" The ghoul roared. "It is the name of the gathering place of the great ones. But you are puny, and mortal. I would not expect you to know anything of the truth. You are all far too weak of mind. It is why you are the promised herd. Strength to the dark harvesters!"

Floyd heard the last, shouted phrase repeated by many voices muffled by backs and other anatomy beneath Hermon. Floyd had hoped to reason with the ghouls' leader. Now he realized it might be like him hearing the pleas of a cheeseburger. He feared his negotiation was doomed, but he resolved to try, anyway. Good karma, he repeated in his mind.

"I'm hoping to reach an agreement. I own the cemetery, and you guys eat the dead. But—"

"Are you so sure, little Floyd?"

"Ah, yeah."

"Do you offer yourself, little Floyd?"

"Um, no."

"Then what do you offer as appeasement?" Hermon spat.

"I was hoping we could just talk business. Make an *agreement*." Floyd said.

"You risk much in ignorance, Floyd. Little Floyd!"

The phrase 'little Floyd' was again repeated in a skin muffled chant underneath Hermon.

"I don't think you guys kill the living." Floyd said and coughed. "I mean, you don't kill just for kicks. Right? I mean, I am here as a show of respect."

"Well, I guess." Hermon's tone and posture eased. He waved his fingers as he spoke as if to waft his words through the heavy stench. "You are right in that we enjoy, well, let's call what we eat as nicely aged."

"I'm still pretty fresh." Floyd attempted a smile as his eyes threatened to tear up from the horrid air.

238

"Yes." Hermon nodded, and then smiled widely. "But if you were to trip and fall hard enough—well, then."

"I'll watch where I step. But I'd like to ask that you stop eating my clients at the cemetery."

"Cemetery?"

"The place where the bodies are buried."

"Then you do have an offer of appeasement."

"Not quite. I know we mortals and other types can work together. I work with some magical people at my business. The Rock Folk. They make the headstones and plaques. At least now. Before, I got them from Karrsters Concrete & Masonry."

"Rock Folk. Rock Folk." Hermon repeated.

Floyd waited for the words to be chanted underneath Hermon, but there was only the slight sound of skin and calluses rubbing against each other.

"They are new to us." Hermon continued with a sneer. "And I don't like them."

Yellow eyes focused narrowly at Floyd. He wished he had worn his running shoes. They were at home in a box, in his basement.

"Bad blood?" Floyd asked.

"I would so imagine." Hermon mused. "And probably sinewy. Tough. Thick bones. I've never been much of a marrow man. A lot of work to break open bones. Although the crunch of a robust tendon—I like that. Cartilage. I do like cartilage."

"Uh, right." Floyd nodded. He tried and failed to block memories of Mrs. Channing's grave. "So, could you please stop eating the bodies in my—"

"That's enough!" A voice familiar to Floyd shouted from the top of the stairs.

Hermon and Floyd turned to see Ernest 'Larry' Tran come down the stairs, in a near charge.

"Tran?" Floyd blinked. "What in the h—what in the—what?"

"Yeah. Hi, Floyd." Tran shook Floyd's hand. "Good to see you. But right now I'm representing my clients."

"The ghouls!" Floyd yipped. "They need a lawyer?"

Floyd allowed himself a second to ponder how they paid for a lawyer.

"Everyone needs a lawyer, Floyd." Tran answered. "How many times have I told you that?"

"Uh, yeah." Floyd said. Tran's words triggered the merged memories of the frequent exchange of sale-pitches between them at Chamber of Commerce meetings. Nearly autonomous neurons switched on in Floyd's head. "How many times have I told you it's never too soon to prepare for death? Having a plot and memorial package already purchased will really ease the burden on your children. It's said the biggest reason for grieving—"

"Okay! Okay, Floyd!" Tran waved his hands and dropped his head for a moment. "Look, my client admits nothing. You can't come in and level accusations—"

"Larry! I'm trying to negotiate with, uh, with his highness." Floyd nodded to Hermon.

"Look, I get where you're coming from." Tran started. "Trouble is, they have rights to live here, and—"

"I'm not saying I don't want them living here." Floyd hoped his voice did not betray that lie. "Or, uh, being unliving and residing here."

Tran turned to Hermon. "Sir, I'd advise you to terminate—that is, simply stop talking to this man."

"Oh, c'mon!" Floyd protested.

"Hey, you want to talk, get a lawyer." Tran looked at Floyd and shrugged.

"Geezus, Larry!"

"Enough!" Hermon roared. "As if you're squabbling were not sickening enough, now you dare invoke names of oaths and mortal spells! Be gone!"

Hermon stood and clapped. His modular ghoul couch broke apart. The blue fiends swarmed over Floyd and Tran. The assault came too quickly to scream. Both men were carried aloft by cold hands and stabbing fingers. The ride came to an end as the ghouls hurled each man outside the house and onto the grassy easement in front of Hermon's duplex.

Floyd rubbed his neck. It was strained, but not bitten. He was glad to be alive, but now even this plan had failed. He sighed. He looked over at Tran who was just recovering himself. Tran brushed the tops of his expensive suit pants as he sat up, even though the seat and backs of his legs were an inch deep in the muddy ground. Floyd noted this was as still as he'd ever seen Tran. Floyd felt another slight vibration from the ground.

"Did you feel that?" Floyd asked.

"I feel my wet butt!" Tran answered. He then glanced down the street. "Is that your car? Could you give me a ride?"

"You need a ride?" Floyd asked as he pulled his own wet butt from the ground.

"Yeah. I took a cab, here."

"A cab?"

"Yeah! You think I'd park my car in this neighborhood?"

Floyd woke in the morning. He needed to take a shower. It would be his fifth shower since coming home from the ghoul's duplex. Dorene had stuffed the clothes we had worn in three layers of yard-waste bags. Floyd had to be at his most persuasive and pleading to convince Dorene against dumping a gallon of bleach on his naked self. Her searing glares at him last night for such a foolish act would likely be just as sterilizing. Floyd stretched and put his feet on his bedroom carpet. He felt a tremor. The tremor became violent shaking. It threw him off the bed, but the violence ended before Floyd could finish yelling:

"Earthquake!"

Floyd took his fifth shower and went into the work day in a fresh suit and heavy application of musk deodorant. He had one important stop before going to his office. There, he stood close to the edge of the massive subsidence that caused the earthquake and swallowed the section of duplexes occupied by the ghouls. Their clan was now completely missing. Sheriff Danridge granted Floyd this close access to the site. Danridge felt slightly guilty about his last meeting with Floyd.

"Local geologist just shrugged." Danridge sniffed. He leaned on a traffic barricade near the lip of the collapse. "Sinkhole is his best guess."

"But we don't get sinkholes around here." Floyd said still taking in the vista where a stretch of suburban housing was now a vast, deep pit.

Danridge cocked his head. "Yeah. And fairies don't exist, either."

"Good point," Floyd said as he marveled at the precision of the hole's circular edge and walls. It was a near perfect cylinder that descended into darkness.

Floyd entered his office in a daze. For the first time he didn't even glance at the trapdoor covering the Rock Folk's improvised entrance. His backside slapped into his desk chair. Something unusual sat in the center of his blotter. It was his daughter's stolen mobile phone. He looked at it and smiled. He was sure Glynis could safely walk in the park again. Another idea fell through his brain as Grady walked by his door.

"Deus ex terra." Floyd said.

"Huh?" Grady popped his head into the office and sipped from his coffee mug.

"Actually, it would be 'deum de terra' I think. I had Latin in High School. Tough elective." Floyd said.

"I still don't know what you mean." Grady said, and then slurped.

"No. But for once, I get it." Floyd smiled and picked up his daughter's phone. "And I like it. You know, I wonder if the Rock Folk ever thought of yard art."

"Huh," Grady shrugged. "You mean, like bird baths?"

"Yeah. You could sell those at a mall."

"Mall? Eesh. Weird place." Grady frowned at departed.

"Yep." Floyd nodded to himself as he looked over at the trapdoor. "But I'm beginning to like weird."

THE FEAST

She slipped through the window with silence and speed. Her feet touched the carpet. She paused for an instant to enjoy the gentle surface. She only had fleeting moments to enjoy most things. Speed was survival. An extra second lingered could mean capture. The people and things that chased her might use her for the same reason she came back to the old house. She was hungry.

She worried the sensation of the carpet alone might become too comfortable to leave again. Her home was her coat, more than a fixed place. Staying mobile was the best defense to avoid being eaten. Here, she had found a quiet place to stay for longer than a heartbeat. So long as no one or nothing else found her secret, it would be her daytime sanctuary. At night one needed thicker walls to sleep well. For now, the house and its contents were intact. She closed the window and crept into the home. Its occupants had left long ago. The house was a captured moment from before the world changed. Perhaps the occupants left early in the changes. With them gone, the house was never noticed by marauders or the things that came one night and stayed on Earth despite humanity's protest.

She had been born after the changes. She was very good at slipping and stealing from the roving bands. Some of them were human. Some not. But she was human. Or so she thought. Humans had built the city. She could use many things recovered in the ruins. However, she wondered if she was just a product of the new world adapted to aspects of the old. She shrugged to herself. She often did. And then, as always, she carried on. She walked from the bedroom down the hall. She could feel the impression of all the footsteps from the past, but the carpet was still so very soft.

To her, many things inside the house were strange relics. The missing people knew the purpose of a thin black slab hung on the wall, or a hand-sized version of it that also did nothing. Most curious was a small metal box with two levers and slots on its top. Like many other things, it connected to smaller slots on the wall with a tail. But it still did nothing. She wondered if a missing, big tail once connected to its top slots. Other dead weights sat in nooks behind small doors. She understood they were once tools. Now they might as well be art. The purpose of a picture or sculpture was clear, even if the image or form was vague. Abstract art from the lost age communicated with her much better than technology's husks. Some other things were clear. She didn't need to think about how to use beds or other furniture. The purpose of the fireplace was also obvious.

She crouched on the hearth and lit a fire. Although it was cold, the fire was not for heat. Her coat kept her warm. She had never cooked her food, but used fire to help her capture prey. She too was a hunter, and smart enough to find live things to eat without chasing them through streets or down dark places where other hunters lived. She knew how to bait things, such as the little munks that she dug from the riverside. There she also found fish that washed ashore. She took fish and placed it up inside the fireplace along with a leg of a sharp-scale she caught stalking her. The odor was a risk, and it didn't belong in this house. But the rotting flesh would attract flies. The flies would attract their hunters. She would eat them.

She knew how to build a hot, clean burning fire and one that smoldered. The thick smoke from this fire was also a risk. For now, no bands or solos came near here, and smoke in the air wasn't odd. This smoke caused her meal to appear. *As if by magic,* she recalled overhearing. She didn't know what magic was, or how it brought food. She never got to ask the people who said it. She risked revealing herself, but the people ran. Maybe they didn't like her coat.

She heard the rustle from inside the fireplace. She was happy there were many, and that they had grown fat. Their bulk caused the usually silent creatures to make noise when they moved as a mass. This was especially true when smoke and a little flame irritated them. She watched them follow a gust of smoke that blew back and up along the brick mantle. They, too, rolled down from the top of the fireplace and then flowed up along the mantle as an inverted, dark wave. Spiders were not typically communal creatures, but when the conditions were right they lived in large groups. Maybe it was another adaptation to the changed world. For her, it was a banquet in motion.

She moved her face close to them for a moment of camaraderie between hunters. Her stomach growled. She plucked the first, dazed spider from the brickwork. It flexed its legs as if sensing doom. She popped it in her mouth and chewed it slowly. They had a metallic taste. Their legs and fronts were crisp, but their

244

abdomens popped in her mouth like a little sack of goo. She would pluck more of them and eat those more quickly, but always savored the first. She saw them as the closest thing to friends. She wondered if the emotion of love was a sensation similar to hunger. She knew the spiders that noticed her hands regarded her with suspicion and fear, as well they should. She sighed, but kept eating.

Some spiders braved the heat below and dropped towards the mantle on strands. She snatched the strands and dangled them onto her tongue. She plucked another spider that ran quickly over the tops of it brothers and sisters. She knew things would become more chaotic if a second wave of arachnids crested over their first escaping mass. The increased spider collisions would excite them, and they would start eating each other. They did this when the fireplace was cool, and the flies and maggots were few. After a while, she would need to start the cycle over with fresh meat. She hoped this house would still be her sanctuary, then. The spiders helped her live. If she ever made art, she vowed it would be a silken tribute to spiders.

She pulled another spider from the bricks. It was a strong and fat one. She watched it try to bite her fingers, but its fangs couldn't break her tough skin. She tossed it in her mouth. And then another. She ate until she was full. The surviving spiders on the bricks seemed to stare and judge her. She created their little world, but then she ate them. She understood if they were confused. That was, if the plump and spiny things ever had thoughts. She plucked off another and ate it. The others stayed still. She knew she should never over indulge, unlike some of these larger spiders. She looked at the windows. It was getting darker outside. It was never bright as in pictures she'd seen. What passed for day, now, was ending. The surviving spiders could enjoy this quiet place. Unlike her, when she left they would not need to fear being eaten. Unless it was by one of their own kind. So, perhaps their respective fates were not much different.

She looked at the fire and watched the last curl of orange light die out. A twisting ribbon of gray smoke took its place. The fireplace would cool, and the spiders could return inside it. She smiled at them and revealed her sharp teeth with bits of spider legs. She moved her face close to her favorite, eight-legged prey. Several fled to the sides. They must be the smart ones, she thought. If they had thoughts at all, none of them they would be here when her hunger returned and she crept forth to sate it. She flexed her toes against the carpet, and stood to return to the streets and harder places. For tonight, the feast was over.

THE STREAM WITH DEEP, RUNNING WATER

Paul waited for Caroline to appear in the night. The forest was dark and cool. Wisps of fog drifted as ghostly veils where moonlight shone through the trees. All noise of owls and nocturnal life ceased. Paul knew Caroline was near. She stepped out from the shadow of a tree. She always came to him in the dark hours. Caroline had no choice. For so long now, she had been locked into an existence hidden from the Sun. Only moon glow and starlight ever lit her ashen face. For Paul, she was the image of true love.

Paul stroked her face as she smiled at him. Caroline always was as beautiful as their last encounter. Her appearance never felt the weight of time that his face endured. He remembered the past now with greater pleasure. All the days and nights, except for one. Paul and Caroline had moved into a small crofter's house near the woods before she was banished from daylight. Intense, urban professions both afforded and inspired their dream of a simpler and more natural lifestyle. The one artificial convenience that Paul missed the most surprised him. It was the laundry dryer. A load of wet clothes was as heavy as a large sack of potatoes, and more unwieldy. The amount of garden work in the warm months and perpetual maintenance of their home cost them more time than expected. They shared the chores and the sense of fulfillment and peace. One night, the peace was ripped apart.

The stranger was a young, handsome man, or so he first appeared. Paul had purposefully forgotten his name since they met. Whatever the stranger called himself was undoubtedly a lie. Paul first saw him on the road one evening, just outside of town. He had described himself as a traveling poet. Paul was attracted to the romantic ideals of personal experience becoming inspiration. He brought the stranger to meet Caroline, and they welcomed him into their home. The stranger was entertaining, charming, and enjoyed wine as much as they did. Paul went downstairs to get another, better bottle. Soon after he reached the cramped cellar, he heard Caroline scream.

Adrenaline entered Paul's veins, but they were still coursing with alcohol. Paul stumbled as he ran back up the narrow stairs. He heard Caroline's screams die out as he regained his footing and ran. In the parlor, a beast wore the same clothes as the young stranger. It worked its brutal jaws around Caroline's neck. Paul cried out and charged the monster biting his wife. A powerful arm swatted him back. The beast's eyes focused with hate at Paul on the ground while its jaws held fast to Caroline's neck. Her face shook and was white from and blood loss and total shock. Her eyes darted to the silver chain and crucifix on the floor. The beast had torn them from her neck. Paul grabbed them up and dug his hands into the monster's throbbing neck. It reached back to swipe at Paul with hands and fingers that were now talons. Paul tugged repeatedly and wrenched the creature back. It released Caroline. She fell to the floor. The creature broke free of Paul's savage grip. Its skin came away under his nails. Paul rolled and recovered himself as the beast howled. It grabbed at its own neck where Paul's frenzied attacked had imbedded the silver chain.

Paul snatched the fire poker from the hearth as the creature jerked itself to its knees and pawed its neck. The bloody chain fell to the floor. Paul thrust himself down at the beast and drove the poker through it chest. Their faces came so close that Paul smelled it's fetid, ferrous breath. Its eyes flashed wide with shock. It lurched back to grab the poker's handle. Paul pushed the monster down. On the floor it squealed like a hog dragged into an abattoir. Paul grabbed the cedar shafts he'd split and stacked beside the fireplace. For an instant, Caroline's complaint that the shafts were too big for kindling echoed in his mind. He glanced at Caroline on the floor. She was motionless on thin pool of her own blood. Paul screamed. The beast stopped its yanking of the poker handle and looked up at the cry of anguish. Paul stabbed it through the chest next to the impaled poker. The beast fell back to the floor as another rough shaft pierced its chest. Paul only stopped driving the wood shafts through the beast's torso when fatigue allowed the pain of the splinters that lanced his right hand to finally register. The beast was still. Its eyes were glassy and dim.

Paul cradled his hand and slid over to Caroline. She was faintly panting. Strangely, it was now only Paul who bled. Caroline pushed herself up and held her neck. They starred at each other in shock and perhaps relief that they were both still alive and together. Caroline finally moved her hands from her neck when she saw Paul cradling his splinter savaged hand. She took it and rocked it slowly. Paul saw her neck now bore no tears or scars. Caroline was pale. Still she had survived, but Paul knew she was not alive in the same way before the stranger's attack. In the hours after the horror, Caroline dressed Paul's wounded hand and they wondered what to do. This was not a normal emergency one could call the authorities for assistance. And if they did, they didn't know what each of their fates would be after tonight. At least there at that moment, they were still together. Paul said he would deal with the stranger's body. When he returned inside, they resolved to wait until morning.

After dawn, Paul could not wake Caroline. He kept the bedroom dark, perhaps on instinct. The following night, she woke. She was pale, and cold. She panicked, and pushed Paul away. She fled into the darkness of the woods. Paul chased after her, but she was too swift. Far too swift to still be governed by the natural laws they came there to respect. Paul collapsed by a deep stream with swift running water. After a time in the misty darkness, Caroline found him there. Paul would never see her in daylight again. Caroline said she understood what she must do to survive, but she would live within the balance of nature and never cause the same harm she had suffered. Paul understood his wife was now like the thing that had taken her blood. But she was still herself in spirit, and for him, that meant she would never become a monster.

The dark incident forced their love into the night, but not darkness. They refused to allow one incident of horror to push them from their dream, even if the parlor became the room entered least in subsequent years. The nearby farming community didn't ask many questions, and strongly respected privacy. No one asked why Caroline was only glimpsed from a distance on late hours when they both walked through the woods so close together. Strangely, it was Paul who took to avoiding the mirror. He read time's passing on calendars and the faces of clocks, but never wished to see it in his reflection. Caroline was always young, her body locked in a moment. Time had free reign of him. There were periods when Caroline was gone, sometimes for far too long for Paul. Her needs might take her far away. Caroline had to move through the country to avoid becoming noticed, or causing grave impact on the wildlife. Paul would read of people saved by a protector never seen, or of the acts of an avenger never known. Paul's faith was rewarded when Caroline finally came home. Typically, Paul knew the day was a time for work and longing. The night was a time for love, and the company of the person he loved. The nights became years. Paul saw the impact of them all in the almost sorrowful gaze of Caroline as she considered his face in the moon glow.

"I know. I've gotten old." Paul said and smiled as he dropped his head.

Caroline gently pushed it back up and spoke. "So have I, my love."

"No. You are as young as—" Paul stopped.

"As they day you met me?" Caroline smiled at him. "I've aged some years between that day and the one night we don't mention. And I still do. In my mind. My soul. I feel time as a weight. It grows heavier each night."

Now Caroline lowered her head.

"Paul, I want an end to this life."

When Caroline finished speaking, they both felt the world freeze. Caroline looked out through the dark between the trees. Paul stared at his wife, overwhelmed by his shock at Caroline's words. Even the fog seemed to stop. Existence became an eternity of complete stillness. Paul felt an icy cold from within. He could say or do nothing but stare. Caroline broke the spell.

"I want an end to the hunting," she said. "An end to the need of selecting prey, and the agony when I make a mistake. It is time these woods and the lands around them knew only nature's predators. It's a time to rest. My time. I want peace."

Caroline looked up at Paul.

"But death—" Paul halted his words. He was uncertain what to say. Caroline may well be dead in the eyes of nature, but he refused to see her as an abomination. She was alive and vital, especially to him. She was his life. Her end would also be his own.

"It's less about wishing to die, and more about ending this curse." Caroline smiled and caressed Paul's cheeks. "I've endured it for us. For me. I so wanted the life we dreamed of. And we've done as best we can for a lifetime, now. But death would be near, if my years were ruled by nature. And we came here for nature, my love."

"But for me. I can't—I just don't—!" Paul stopped trying to speak and shook his head.

"I want you to go on." Caroline drew close to Paul and took his hands. "Knowing you will live will be my afterlife. And, who knows? We may well see each other again. Somehow. Right now,

250

my only sorrow is leaving you, but I will bid this dark life a fond farewell."

Paul opened his mouth, but no words could escape his tightened throat. His whole chest felt as if it was collapsing from within. He turned from Caroline. This time, he was the one who fled into the night. He had never known sorrow so complete that it barred all other emotion and sensation. It was the mirror image of his love for her. He was certain of the reason she wanted to die. It was him. His own mortality. He was certain she could not bear to see him age further, until he could no longer make hikes through the woods or withstand the cold. Paul had already begun to imagine his final moment looking up at her face lit by starlight or a lamp at their side. It would be the last thing he saw. He could never imagine their roles becoming reversed.

As once long ago, Caroline found him. Paul had fallen to his knees while slumped next to a thick cedar tree. He knew she had never been far behind. Even if he could have run as fast as that long ago night when he chased after her, she could move faster than a sparrow though the air. Caroline cradled Paul's shoulders.

"I would spare you the sadness, if I could." Caroline said.

"I would not give it up, even if you could." Paul gathered his thoughts and straightened his back to look at his pale wife.

"But you would spare me pain, I know." Caroline said. "I need you to do that for me now."

Paul shook his head and looked away. Caroline rested her head on his shoulder.

"There are parts of my life you don't see." Caroline said softly. "The taking of blood, of life—I need that to be ended, for my sanity, if not my soul."

Paul slowly tilted his neck to rest his cheek across Caroline's head.

"I want my end to have the dignity of an old, beloved grandmother," Caroline continued. "Even if I could never know what it was to be a mother."

"You would've been a good one." Paul offered.

"Our life was fulfilling. I have never regretted our time together. But if things were different, normal, we would have to cross this bridge anyway. This way, it is by my choice and while I still am the woman you love."

"You will always be that." Paul said.

"Yes," Caroline took Paul's left hand and caressed his wedding ring with her finger tips. "Yes, I will."

Paul gave a long and deep sigh. He exhaled and his breath created a small cloud of fog. Both of them watched it drift from their cedar and among the other trees.

"The thing in the woodshed," Caroline began. "You must finally destroy it."

Paul turned to face Caroline. Concern and surprise folded his brow.

"How did you know?" Paul asked.

"My dear, you are my world, and I know every part of you. Even the places you try to hide in your mind."

"Is that from some power?" Paul asked.

"No." Caroline smiled and nearly laughed. "It's because we have spent a lifetime together."

Paul finally smiled. "So you know about the bank account in the Caymans."

"Of course," Caroline playfully rocked them both back and forth.

There was another moment of silence.

"Now, please do that for me." Caroline said, holding Paul tightly. "Burn it. It's best if you burn it."

"I will." Paul sighed deeply, again.

Dawn came and Caroline slept. For the first time, Paul dreaded her rising. It may well be her last. He didn't dread doing the thing she asked of him. Although it was one step in enacting her final wishes, he looked forward to once again killing the beast. Paul used sunlight as one more layer of safety. One more weapon, if needed. The wreaths of garlic were pungent and he felt ridiculous wearing them. However, he was a young man the last time he fought the monster. He might need more help than mortal strength and a silver chain and crucifix if the thing in the woodshed became animate. He doubted that was possible. But impossibility had become part of his life when his wife became a vampire.

Paul stayed in their home for more than romantic reasons. He had a duty to Caroline. Part of it was to protect her from further horror, as much as he could. Modern lore may explain vampire existence as a virus that makes monsters of humans. The bloodlust rose from microscopic demons. Paul didn't know if such plagues existed. He knew at least two vampires did exist. The consequences of one's actions cut across his life and Caroline's even more. Even as a vampire, Caroline couldn't separate all the aspects of her fate from fact, speculation, and legend. Not all the answer came with the transformation. The greatest certainties were the life in darkness and the curse of the hunger. To accomplish his awful task, Paul had to act with caution for himself and his wife.

Paul had never completely destroyed the beast's remains from fear of harming Caroline. In some variations of vampire lore, the original vampire is linked to those it spawns. If it were animate, it could control the ones it created. In other tales, the continued existence of a vampire's remains preserved the vampires it created. If it existed even as an immobile corpse, the progeny of its bite could not be destroyed. None of its spawn could die before the physical destruction of their—Paul stopped his thoughts. He refused to think of the beast as a master of anything. Paul had no way of knowing original vampire truth from the subsequent and extensive fiction. Still, on that night he gathered the remains of the beast from the parlor, and then secured and hid them. They were out of sight, but as Caroline revealed, never out of his mind. The hatred of the thing had never left him, either.

For years, Paul had kept the beast's remains in a concrete coffin. It was covered with religious and magical symbols, and any other markings he thought might keep it impaled and imprisoned, if not utterly dead. The doors of the woodshed opened with creaking protest. They were reinforced far more than normal shed doors. Bright, bleaching sunlight flooded the dusty, spider web shrouded interior. Paul was glad for it. Paul took up his axe. Its weight had somehow increased over the years, or Paul had become weaker than he wanted to admit. The axe became lighter as blood carried adrenaline through his body. Paul suppressed a shudder. He clenched his jaw hard enough to crack a dental crown. He inhaled, and then placed the axe head's cutting edge in the narrow slit between the massive coffin and its thick lid. Paul paused. He then pressed the axe to pry up the lid. It slid open only a few inches before he stopped to gasp for air. Stench hit his nose. He had expected that, but not what lay across the cement bottom revealed by the sunlight. Paul even anticipated hateful eyes glared back at him followed by snatching claws. Instead he considered the remains with a sneer of contempt. Any recognizable form of the body had rotted away and crumbled to black dust and fragments.

Paul thought that even a human corpse sealed for the same time would have visible bones. He dared to move his eyes closer to the gap between lid and coffin. His improvised cedar stakes were the only pieces familiar from that night. His memory of impaling the beast over and over would have to be enough to sate his lingering anger.

Paul thrust his full weight against the lid. It slid off far quicker than he expected. He fell forward as the lid slammed against the ground on the other side. He dropped his axe and caught himself on the edge of the coffin's rim. His heart beat rapidly from the exertion. He pushed himself away, not wanting his heavy breathing to disturb the black dust that he might then inhale. Paul stepped back. The thing might already be dead, forever. For Caroline, he would make sure. The sunlight seemed to slowly burn away the pathetic remains. Paul thought to help that process along, and far more rapidly. He had learned to make thermite in preparation for this very act. He opened the carefully placed canisters and pots he stored it in. The shed would start the blaze. The thermite would ensure everything inside and the shed itself would burn to less than ash.

Paul tossed a burning match on an oily rag inside the shed and left it to burn. After only a few minutes, the fire lit up the nearby woods brighter than the sunlight. The increasing heat warmed Paul's cheeks. Soon it would become intense. He stepped farther back. He no longer enjoyed watching fires. For years now he loved the touch of cold. It reminded him of Caroline's caress. He turned and left the fire. It was a rubbish fire, he thought. He refused to call it a pyre. This was not a funeral. This was the last act of long standing vengeance. And perhaps it was even justice. All philosophy aside, it was an end.

Paul knew Caroline could not be roused from her slumber in the day. She was in the house and shut up in the bedroom. He wished he could wake her, not to tell her he had honored her wish, but to spend a few more hours with her than they would normally have together. Soon those hours would also end.

In the full darkness of night, Paul and Caroline walked one final time through the woods. There was little to say, and nearly too much to feel in their final moments together. Caroline led him to a familiar place. It was the shore of the stream with deep running water. Paul knew this was the place of his wife's last moments.

"Now, you promise, Paul." Caroline clutched his checks. "No matter your sorrow, you will live on. You promise me."

"Yes, at least as long as I can." Paul' voice cracked. He blinked to clear the tears from his eyes and see Caroline smile at him in the starlight shining through the gap in the trees made by the wide stream.

Caroline squeezed his cheeks a little tighter.

"I promise," Paul said as a whisper. "But I will spend my time, long or short, longing to be with you again. I can't stop that."

"I know." Caroline smiled and kissed Paul. She glanced over at the stream. The knock of shifting rocks echoed from beneath its rushing waters.

"Perhaps we'll come back as two fish in a stream," Caroline said. "Or mayflies born on its shores."

"Maybe we'll be two giant redwoods." Paul glanced up at the trees reaching for the night sky. "We'll live forever with our boughs intertwined, in peace."

"I like that one." Caroline rubbed Paul's shoulders and hugged him. "Until then, my love. No sadness, now."

"You ask the impossible, there." Paul sniffed and rubbed his eyes.

"All right, but live on." Caroline smiled.

"As long as I can." Paul managed to utter.

Caroline drew her had across Paul's face in one last caress. She turned from him and slowly stepped into the stream.

Paul wiped his eyes to clear the tears. He watched Caroline slip deeper into the dark waters. She finally disappeared beneath a swirl of small waves. Paul slowly collapsed on the shore and stared where he last saw Caroline. If he could rise when the morning light came, he would get up and walk back home before the sunlight shone down to the bottom of the stream. If he could not, he would let the forest do with him as it pleased. At that moment, it didn't matter. Paul wiped his eyes again. He heard the sounds of the forest at night grow more audible just over the ripple of the stream and the rhythm of his heartbeat.

HARLOTS

The more things change, the worse they get. At least that's the new axiom for planet Earth. The sky is black. The air is toxic. The streets are ruled by the twisted beasts that have eaten all the muggers and gangs. For whatever reason, most people don't want to die. That wish to live creates my job: killing monsters. I've been called many things in different times. In this life the tag 'Killer' is as apt as the fearful slander whispered behind my back. In this perpetual nightmare the monsters never sleep. The shapes of the beasts are constantly shifting, yet certain monsters are classical. Some things remain the same.

"Hey! You're on time. Thought you'd keep me waiting. Y'know, play me like a tease." The voice from the dark said. The man who bought my services would not come out into the filthy alleyway for good reason. "Uh, did you see it?"

"No." I answered. "It's playing hard to get."

"You won't find that attitude in here. C'mon in. The thing'll get hungry soon enough."

I stepped down through shadows into his dank place of business. Only a burned-out and battered overhead lamp indicated the doorway. Inside was a cramped and oppressive hallway. The fat man, Queban, squeezed his way between two rows of plastic doors, the same kind on portable latrines. Only, these doors had the locking bolts on the outside. I followed sideways in Queban's oily trail of smoke curling over his slicked down hair. Once, organic leaves were rolled into cigars. Now, what smoldered in the brown stub on his lip was anyone's guess. However, his occupation was obvious. A few doors were opened. All the clientele were too busy with Queban's employees on the rickety cots to notice our passage.

"So your ad said your name is Joshua Grail." Queban raised his voice as music grew louder as we neared its source. "But the punks I heard talking about you called you Ice. Which is it?"

"I don't much care what you call me, as long as your payment clears."

"Okay, then." Queban stopped and turned to me. His round, oily cheeks arched in a flippant smile. "How about I call you—"

I looked down at him with a narrowed glare.

"Yeah, okay. Ice works, fine." Queban shrugged. "And so the thing outside is starting to eat my business. First it was just a couple of johns now and again. But then it took a couple of my girls, and a good business protects its capital, eh? Right now, nobody will even change the light bulb outside."

Queban squeezed by an opened door. A pair of wraith-like arms grabbed at him from inside the humid stall.

"Queban? Please just kill me. I can't do it anymore!" The girl pleaded. Her age was impossible to tell from her taught, wasting features.

Queban shoved her back inside. He then threw his weight against the door to slam it shut. "You can die when your contract expires!" He shouted and locked the bolt.

"When will that be?" I asked.

"Ha! Never. Anyway, if the thing shows up, kill it! You'll get paid when you perform, too."

Ahead, the hall opened into an aged club. At its center was a small circular stage built like a tiny, lurid amphitheater for the tiny, lurid people occupying half its seats. With me close at his back, Queban popped out of the cramped hallway like a bullet and bumped into his hired muscle.

"Geez! You guys should lay off the 'roids." Queban spat, and reassumed his head-forward gait.

"I don't use 'roids" I said.

Queban's bouncer replied with a sneering smile, and then followed his boss like a good dog. I looked across the skin yard. Another of Queban's girls danced on the stage. Above her a holographic sign read-out the competing bids for her private show.

"So you're the big Killer that Queban hired?" I heard behind me.

I turned and looked down to face the drab and haggard woman sizing me up. "And you're his official greeter?"

"I'm Silky," she said. "Show me some graft and I'll do more than smile hello."

"Sounds like you enjoy your work."

"I don't have a choice. None of us do. You think we like it here? Look at Gingy. She's just fourteen!" Silky motioned to the girl on the stage.

I noticed Queban's bouncer take an interest in my new conversation from across the club.

"But what do you care?" Silky asked like a challenge. "You're just another john. Except your date is in the alley."

"I am no john." I grated over the canned soundtrack. My professional and personal pride was not typically in play when I took a job. I kill monsters for money. It's a simple idea that's hard to pull off. So I'm usually regarded with fear, not arrogant scorn. Silky was getting annoying.

"Yeah? Then fix this." Silky tossed her head to the hallway. "You've got the license. Use it."

Silky was well informed. A clause in my license states that for the greater good I can do bad things in pursuit of killing a monster. It's based on the fact that people fear the hungry freaks more than mourning the loss of property, their neighbors, or their liberties. Or maybe it was just the government that decided to give my profession that power from their own fears of facing down the terrors at street level. Whatever the reason, I can do almost anything to anyone if it's justified. I'm a better shot than most, so I use my professional ammunition discount more than the legal loophole she pointed out.

"Sorry. I kill monsters." I said.

"Then kill Queban!" She hissed through clenched teeth, leaning aggressively towards me. "Someone has to. Why do you think I brought that thing here?"

"You brought it? How?" I didn't believe her. Only once had I seen a monster trained by a human. Usually they just regard us as food.

"Yeah. I found it when it was little. It grew." Silky seemed to wilt, dropping her shoulders. Maybe seeing some of her friends die from her supposed pet pulled heavy on her conscience. Maybe she was just changing her tactics with me. "I thought--"

Queban burst in between us. "I knew it! I knew you caused this! You filthy--!"

The bouncer hovered close in the background. Queban's fat, wet hand slapped Silky to the ground. I pulled him away from her on instinct.

"Zee-Zee!" Queban screamed.

The bouncer lunged at me with a serrated dagger in the air. I threw my forearm into his face. His nose snapped and exploded with blood. The rest of the struggle was rote. I twisted his right arm holding the knife out of its socket, and hurled him over my

258

shoulder. He hit the floor in pain, but not broken. Out come our handguns. Mine was much bigger and aimed first. My weapons are built to kill monsters hardened in the acidic pit the world fell into. The single blast shook the club. Zee-Zee's fragments showered Gingy and her audience in flecks of dark red and bone.

Now fear appeared. It gave Queban rare speed but stunted judgment. He bolted away from me down the hallway. I chased him, both trying to save his life and also wanting to snap his neck. He tripped on the short stairway and stumbled into the squalid alley. He cut his face on something tall like a spike-edged lamppost. Queban wasn't alone, and this time I was too slow. Through the doorway I saw him look up in terror. The lamppost moved in swift concert with seven others. Queban was snatched from the ground before he could scream. I leapt into the alley to see him dangle high above the ground. Queban's body seemed to spasm violently as the monster ate him.

At first, quick glance it looked like a towering spider. Instead it was some mutated arachnid cousin more closely related to the amblypygi, the tailless whip scorpion. It could have just been a new sequence of synthetic genes amping a nightmare to epic scale. Queban's cigar fell to the ground in a contrail, forced from his mouth by froth. For a fraction of a second the hideous thing loomed before me with the remains of its prize hung from sickle-like jaws and flexing pedipalp arms. I fired. The blasts rocked the walls of the alleyway.

I returned inside. Silky knelt on the floor cupping handfuls of her blood as if to keep it from mingling with Zee-Zee's spread across the floor.

"They're gone." I said. "I missed. Queban is dead."

Silky's hands became wet, red fists thrust above her head. Her bleeding face contorted in hacking laughter. The reasons were different than I imagined, but she was happy.

One day later, after a retouch at a medical kiosk, Silky took a new girl to a room in the darkened, oppressive hallway. Silky wore one of Queban's suits drastically recut for her own frame.

"You can leave when your contract expires." Silky told the girl, and steadily guided the reluctant victim into her cramped cell.

"You're going to keep them here, too?" I asked from the door to the alley. My own contract was unfulfilled.

"Queban was a lousy husband, but inheritance laws are wonderful to widows." Silky answered with her arrogant scorn also rejuvenated. "Besides, a good business needs its capital. Right?"

Silky smiled defiantly.

Most monsters kill for food. Hunger is a motivation I always understood. Queban severed life from people more slowly than but just as certainly as a monster's jaws. He fed off the cravings of the corrupt people that crept into this pit. Now Silky planned to do the same. That had always been her true goal. Better to be the spider than a victim bound to the web.

If I killed the monster, this business would bloom again. If I walk away the beast will still feed on its human prey, indiscriminant to innocent or oppressor. The problem was the predation of both monsters. One killed faster than the other. I needed to stop both horrors. I grabbed Silky by the arm.

"Hey! What are you doing?" She barked. "You want it rough, you pay first!"

"Yesterday you asked me to fix this problem." I said hauling her into the alleyway. "But then it was only a ruse to eliminate Queban. I need to kill the monster you brought, but it moves too fast. I need something to distract it."

I released Silky. She flailed and stumbled forward. It didn't take long. Silky screamed when reunited with her pet. She ran. The gigantic arachnid thing didn't seem to recognize her before it snapped her up and in half. The blasts from my gun lit the inside of the brothel hall in violent white flashes. The monster's blasted remains painted the alley walls with grotesque graffiti. I stood next to the monster's ravaged corpse. Some of its legs curled slowly towards its massive, overturned body. One severed leg twitched farther down the alley. The brutal symmetry was broken.

I walked over to the brothel's door. Some of the braver women were in the hall looking out. I reached up to the battered lamp over the doorway. The worn socket screeched but accepted the new bulb I put in. Stark light flashed over the women's faces.

"It's over." I told them, and walked away from the opened door. "All contracts are finished. All of you can leave. Now."

DARKER THAN SHADOWS OR THE NIGHT

The night was as cold as the absent moon. Unlike the unseen lunar wastes, life clung to sheltered spots in the desert now beneath the flare of stars. A figure looked down across a frigid valley from a rocky mesa. He stood without a horse or campfire, draped only in shades of black deeper than the space between the stars. If life in this part of the American West was ever wild, it was also hard. Some people in the distant towns made it harder for themselves and, worse yet, others. It was one such man sought by the figure in black. He was immune to the cold. Not so the man he sought. A small campfire burned in the valley below. It looked as a small spark of Hell from the mesa. It might well become just that.

The young man at the fire moaned. His wet, shaking palms made it difficult to re-grip his Colt .45 after he pulled his blankets up to his head again. Yet he was so close to the fire that the heat singed his wool blankets. He could not feel the heat. It was not the desert night chilling his bones. His cold grew within. Shakes rolled through his body with force enough to snap his head back like the crack of a whip. The tearing strain on the bullet wound in his gut finally made him cry out. Fear made for a sudden, powerful painkiller. His cry might have attracted wolves or worse, such as a killer like himself.

The horse was calm. The young man took that as a good sign. He knew his ride had never liked him. The horse had good reason. Right now it was content to stand next to the ironwood and not pull at the reins tied to the thin tree. The horse nuzzled the ends of the branches looking for an improbable bit of green. The orange glow of the fire captured the man's attention. He found some distraction to his pain and shaking from the gentle crackle and pops of the small burning logs. He knew the fire would need more—

The horse reared. It gave a violent neigh and pulled at the lashed reins. It tugged the branches taught as it recoiled from the small campsite. The muzzle of the Colt .45 pointed at the cause of the fear.

"Hello, Joe."

The greeting held a knowing tone aimed at the young man at the fire. He now struggled to hold the gun steady. His hand was numb and his arm week. The Colt felt as heavy as a railcar. He had no choice but to lower it while it was still in his hand. More so, he felt there was no point in lining up the sights, pulling back the hammer, and squeezing the trigger. Normally, he could do that as easy as twitch and always hit the mark. Yet, a notion just as sure struck his mind. It was an idea that he somehow understood was old and often shared. He couldn't kill the man in deep black. Shooting him would waste a cartridge.

"Wh-who are you?" the young man asked through a renewed bout of shakes.

"All in due time." The man in black's voice was clear over the campfire and the gusts of wind threatening the flames. "And time, well, it ends eventually. Even in the grand scheme. For you, the scheme is up."

"You just get out!" The young man shouted. "Leave!"

"Now, Joe, no need to be unneighborly. But, look who I'm saying that to. Joe "Kid" Kelly. Outlaw. Thief. Murderer. Not that I'm here to judge you."

"I got a rep! You h-here for a bounty? F-forget it!" Joe knew his defiance was a bluff. He then lamented that he was never good at cards.

"I'm here for truth, Joe. Or should I call you Larry?"

"Huh?"

"It's short for Lawrence, your true name. You were born Lawrence K. Lictenpoole."

The young, wounded man who now called himself Joe looked at the dark stranger. What the man in black said was true. Joe Kelly was the most recent name he took. A small-town reporter added the tag 'Kid' due to the outlaw's youthful face. Even so, drawings of his face on wanted bills were never true to his boyish but battered features, and he'd never sat in front of a camera. Changing his name kept him a step in front of lawmen and bounty hunters, if not always his conscience. Joe looked at the dark man whose own features were hard to guess in the flickering fire light. Joe could not quite see the man's eyes within folds of shadow. Yet, he had never felt a more purposeful, penetrating stare. Joe had seen many harsh glares from bank tellers, rowdy toughs, and lawmen. His own glare and reflexes had always proved sharper. Still he decided to look back at the fire and not the strange, dark face. Joe had not done that since first taking to the road, rail lines, and then the dusty trails. Looking away from a stranger nearly cost him his life on that first cold night on the run. Now, felt as though his life was doubling back on him. He shook off the thought this might not be a fight he could win.

"How do you think Mrs. Lichtenpoole, Laura, likes the idea of you changing the name she gave you? And so often." The black figure asked.

"Who?"

"You're mother, Lawrence."

"Oh, right. Everyone knew her as Lil."

"Not you. You insisted on calling her by her first name after the age of eleven."

"I was a r-rebel."

"No. You were a disrespectful nit. The fact that you precede her on the final trail won't come as a shock to her, I'm certain."

"Ya' said--ya' said ya' didn't judge. How the H-hell would you know, anyhow?"

"I know all there is about you, Joe. Mike. Lawrence. I speak truthfully. If that feels like judgment, then that is your own fault."

"Never been judged. Never been caught!" Joe spat.

"Until now."

"You ain't no lawman. I k-can tell. You smell like bounty." Joe writhed from his stomach muscles seizing and pulling at his wound that cut across his intestines and spleen.

"I am not a law man. Although, some say I am the final law that nothing can escape. It's a matter of philosophy."

"Never needed—oh, just, just shut up!"

"There is one peace officer I can bring here. You will recall Sheriff Lindsey Scott. A fine man he was. Respected. Now dead, thanks to you."

"He drew first!" Joe screamed, gripping his Colt tightly.

"No I didn't, boy!" The angry reply came from across the campfire.

Another bolt of fear acted better than thick, camp coffee to focus Joe beyond his shakes and pain. He knew Sheriff Scott well, even if he had only laid eyes on him for a minute or less. The face and manner of the man was forever fixed in Joe's mind. Such was always the case in the intense but brief encounters when people faced off to kill one another. Joe had escaped Scott's town, but not before putting a bullet through his chest. Yet, Scott was now staring back at him next to the dark stranger, and strong as ever.

"I gave you a chance to drop your gun, Kelly!" Sheriff Scott barked. "I'd seen too many young men as you drift through and die in the street, or worse places. Thought I'd give you a chance to die old. Last thing I ever did!"

"Y' did this t-ta me!" Joe pointed at the patch of blood that now oozed though his blankets. "It's your bullet in my gut!"

"I wish it was through your head!" Scott yelled. "Your bullet tore open my heart. The last thing I saw on this Earth was your grin, even as you doubled over! My last sight was your face, you bastard."

"You were still takin' breath when I climbed the saddle." Joe shrieked. "People were there!"

"Don't mistake a bleeding man for a living one, boy." Scott sneered. "There's a lot of blood inside the body. But now most of yours is spilled out across this valley. So, I'll see you again, soon. Real soon, boy. I'm counting the seconds."

Joe found enough strength to raise his well-used Colt and fire at Scott. Flame shot from the muzzle and from the sides of the cylinder where it met the barrel. The four loud booms echoed across valley. When they died out, Joe heard the sound of his horse at full gallop in the distance as it fled dragging an ironwood branch in it reins. The Sheriff was gone. The man in black still stood by the fire.

"Bullets have little effect on departed souls." The darkened man said with calm. "But they might remember spite. And sorrow."

Joe focused on the shadowed stranger. He knew the fire should light him up, clear as the noon Sun. He squinted trying to see him and guess what he meant as he felt the hot gun barrel against his side. His pale, sweaty face suddenly flashed to shock as he glimpsed the young woman now standing next to the man wrapped by night. She bowed her head slightly and held it turned aside. She obviously didn't want to look over at Joe. The firelight lit her brightly. Joe wished it were otherwise. His heart raced faster as the young woman's eyes slowly rolled beneath locks of her dangling hair and looked towards the campfire. She straightened her neck, and finally focused on Joe. The force of her sad eyes struck him, hard. He rose on his elbows and attempted to crawl backwards, but fell flat. Love was a powerful emotion. The most treacherous soul could understand the depth of its loss when it was forsaken, even if they couldn't feel the weight of such sorrow. That sorrow was clear in the expression of the young woman who once loved an outlaw. Despite his desire to reject what he was seeing this night, Joe knew that if she stood next to the man in shadows, then she was like Sheriff Scott. Dead.

"I see you remember Susanne," the shadowed stranger said. "Her love could have been your redemption."

"I gave her my love!" Now Joe averted his gaze at Susanne.

"If love is like a rattlesnake's kiss, then yes, you knew love." The man in shadow said. "But whatever you felt for Susanne was not as strong as your fear. You left her because you felt that to stay in one place, or with any one person, would bring your capture. Her fear was of losing you. That became reality. You avoided your fear at the expense of her heart."

Wood cracked in the fire. Cinders erupted from the coals and disappeared over the torn ironwood tree.

"How did she die?" Joe asked.

"Ask her, yourself."

Joe said nothing. He kept his gaze on a burning branch. It collapsed into the fire. More cinders swirled over the flames and vanished as a low howl rolled through the camp on a rush of wind. The cold air had cooled Joe's empty gun. He released it from his grip. A rare sense of guilt weakened Joe further. He felt pushed flatter against his blankets on the hard ground.

"You have no bullets left," The shadowed man observed. "And no words, either?"

Joe growled.

"Well, at least there will be no chance of a reckless stranger shooting themselves with that Colt after they find your belongings and bones scattered by coyotes. Who would guess your last use of that gun would be a benefit to others."

Joe dared to look over at the man in black. Susanne was gone, although the weight she left on Joe's heart remained. Joe figured this dark figure was no bounty hunter. Joe took solace in thinking he was just another ghost. Yet, he knew the truth was far worse. His shaking returned.

"I've never believed in—in anything I couldn't see, or couldn't feel." Joe took a deep breath and winced.

"I assume you mean with your fingers. Your mind has been callused to emotion since you were young. Not that you are all that old now."

Joe tried to summon an expletive, but couldn't muster the energy to shout it.

"You can see me." The shadowed man continued. "More so, you feel my presence under your skin. As the sepsis grows, life ebbs. It's one type of life, very small life, that now overwhelms your own. Like me, they are always with you. A part of the order of things. Predatory in a way. Perhaps that's a balanced destiny, for you. A swift bullet would not do. Don't you find this cold and lonely end fitting?"

"Sounds l-like judgment." Joe said and rocked his head against his bedding.

"It's a question. I ask them a lot. It entertains me. I am the ultimate answer. Yet I find the more vague aspects of existence intriguing. Nevertheless, I hope I'm not overwhelming you."

"You're just pi-pissing me off. I'll-luh, I'll find a way to beat eh-even you!"

"Sorry, no. You won't. Even if you were to heal, you will see me in the end. And you can guess that I wouldn't be here if you were healing."

"I ain't dead, yet."

"Nor has the sun risen. Nevertheless, you can be sure it will. There is constancy to things from a mortal point of view. That view will be gone for you, soon."

"We'll see. I k-can still see the stars. They're still cut-cutting trails, in, un, the black."

"The one thing of beauty you enjoyed in your brief life was watching the stars travel the night sky. You even understood their motion as a time piece."

"They tur—turn. Stars spin 'round the North Star just like points on clock arms move 'round the middle of—of the clock's face."

Joe's hand brushed his empty gun. Its presence, once so important, brought him no solace.

"Yes, they do." The shadowed face glanced up at the night sky and all its stars before focusing back on Joe. "Oh, the things you might have learned. No matter. You enter my arms now. Young man of many names, time for you is at an end."

266

Joe saw the dark man's face as he stepped forward. Although, it wasn't a single face at all. It was more a portal for many faces looking out from the past. People flickered by like shuffled cards. Although death might not judge who it takes, the last images Joe saw felt like a trial. The final sentence was to look into a dark mirror. In a reflection, a person's own eyes see the truth even if that truth is hidden in a deep, dark place colder and farther down than the deepest well. Joe's last sight was his own face. He tried to turn away and run, but failed. The stars rolled on and the fire died. By daybreak, hunger rose in the sky and crept across the dust toward the camp. The vultures and wolves were out.

The fleeing horse still kept his path to the North under the rising sun. He sought to return to the woman who called him Keeper. He was the family horse until one morning the woman found Keeper gone from the barn, as were most hand tools and anything else the thief could carry. Keeper had witnessed scavengers gather many times now. It was always after the young man who rode him hard had done his worst to others. Now, Keeper saw vultures make a circle for the man's own corpse. No doubt the coyotes would also do their worst. Keeper trod well away from the ring of vultures. He stayed clear of the scent of coyotes, wolves, and slower creatures that summoned gloom darker than shadows or the night.

ABOUT THE AUTHOR

Bruce S. Larson is typically found in his native environment of the Pacific Northwest. Most sightings of this elusive writer occur nearby and occasionally in Seattle. When Bruce is not dodging enormous spiders on mountain trails, he weaves Horror stories and species of other fiction. On his rare ventures into civilization, people glimpse him in art galleries, as well as darkened back rooms. It is rumored that Bruce acts as a roadie for local Rock bands in his seasonal coat of black leather. He has been called diabolical, but also a dear, dear soul. As yet, no one is quite certain which is true. A certainty is his gratitude to you for reading his work.

Bruce's website is **www.thewritebruce.com**. There, readers can find more fiction, an irregular blog, and articles on Earth's alternate histories.

This print edition collects the two e-book volumes of Nightmares and Other Vices. Bruce S. Larson's other works include the SF/Fantasy collection Within and Beyond: The Realms of the Sun available in both e-book and print. The next SF/Fantasy volume Within and Beyond: The Storm will be available in both forms in late 2014.

www.ingramcontent.com/pod-product-compliance
Lightning Source LLC
Chambersburg PA
CBHW071124170626
46809CB00002B/486